REDEMPTION

*xx
Rebecca
Sharp*

BESTSELLING AUTHOR
DR. REBECCA SHARP

Redemption
Published by Dr. Rebecca Sharp
Copyright © 2019 Dr. Rebecca Sharp

All rights reserved. No part of this book may be reproduced, distributed, or transmitted in any form or by any electronic or mechanical means, including information storage and retrieval systems, photocopying, or recording, without permission in writing from the publisher, except by reviewers, who may quote brief passages in a review and certain other noncommercial uses permitted by copyright law.

This is a work of fiction. Resemblance to actual persons, things, living or dead, locales or events is entirely coincidental.

Cover Design:
Najla Qamber, Qamber Designs and Media
www.najlaqamberdesigns.com

Formatting:
Stacey Blake, Champagne Book Design
champagnebookdesign.com

Editing:
Ellie McLove, My Brother's Editor
mybrotherseditor.net

Printed in the United States of America.
Visit www.drrebeccasharp.com

First, To all of us who have made mistakes.
To all of us…
It's not our faults that make us failures.
Only an inability to forgive.

Next, To Pap. This will never be enough.

Last, To all those struggling.
I see you.

;

Keep fighting.

PROLOGUE

ASH

Five months ago
Denver, Colorado

"W-Who the f-fuck called you?"

When you're marginally drunk, you hear how you're slurring your words. When you're fucking shitfaced (an extreme sport for me, given how much and how frequently I indulged), slurred words registered as perfectly enunciated.

And I was perfectly fucking enunciated.

My vision, on the other hand, was a different story.

Taylor Hastings swayed slowly in my vision, like an angel descending to Earth. *No.* I shook my head even though it made my double-vision worse. She was too good—too pure—and I was too fucked up; if Taylor were descending anywhere for *my* sake, it was straight to hell.

Her lopsided short brown hair framed her angelic face—one I'd watched transform from the young girl who'd been my sister's best friend to the breathtaking woman before me. It was a transformation I'd had to pretend not to notice, though it claimed all the attention of my dick.

No wonder I was so good at pretending by now.

Her full arched lips pinched tight with concern over what

I knew was a fucking sky-falling brilliant smile. And those bright green eyes that normally looked like the clearest emeralds, now burned at me like Wildfire from *Game of Thrones*.

And if that shit could take down all of King's Landing, it could certainly take down me.

I ripped my gaze away, my head swimming as I searched for something else to focus on. Too bad everything else—the dark dive-bar, the fuzzy TVs, the shitty people—blurred into a piece of abstract art that, if I could capture it, would probably make me a fucking fortune.

It could hang in the Met and people would pass by it, astonished by the shock-and-awe it evoked, the intense anger and betrayal that flowed through each red, vengeful line.

I laughed bitterly. *Wrong.* It was just splatter on paper, and I was just fucking drunk. *And there was no talent in either.*

"The bartender did." It took a second to remember what I'd asked as I watched her mouth mold around the words. "Let's get you back to the hotel."

I pictured that mouth molding around my dick, my jeans tightening unbearably at the thought. Not that it mattered what the hell I imagined. Taylor Hastings was goes-to-church-every-Sunday prim and fucking proper.

"I told him to call the band." *Didn't I?*

"Yes, well, he called the hotel, and they called me asking to put your sister on the phone."

Fuck. I pinched the bridge of my nose. The last person I ever wanted to see me like this was Blake. She was too good, too. *Just like Taylor.* But my famous little sister would blame herself for the hole I'd dug around me in order to make her star sit higher.

"Well, I d-don't need a fucking babysitter," I drawled with a sneer. "Just another drink and a good fuck."

I gripped the edge of the bar for support as I swayed

dangerously trying to turn away from her. Fuck me if the disappointment in her eyes was more incapacitating than the alcohol could ever be.

"I have to disagree, Ash. You're falling apart." Her voice didn't waver, that was only one more misperception from the alcohol. "This whole tour… You've gotten worse and worse after each show. It's like every time I turn around, you're trying to go out for drinks and party with the band."

My head fell for a moment, concealing a self-deprecating laugh. *If only she really knew…*

Thank fuck she didn't see the flask always tucked in my pocket at all times, or the bottle of water that was never filled with water as a back-up, or the tiny stash of Listerine bottles I kept on hand as cover-up.

The trick was to follow each drink with a shot-sized bottle of mouthwash—*and swallow;* it kept the buzz going with a minty-fresh kick to throw everyone else off my habit.

"I'm fine," I ground out.

I couldn't stand all her good-intentions wrapped up in a perfectly pitiful bow. *And I couldn't explain myself to her.* It would be like trying to describe how the moon felt to the sun. She'd never understand what it was like to never be the one to shine. *She'd never understand what it was like to never be enough.*

"Do you… Do you realize how much you've been drinking on this tour? I know it's a big opportunity for Zach and the guys, but it's getting out of hand."

Anger burned through me. Of course, I knew. But I kept it together so it wasn't a problem. I managed the band. I coordinated PR. I got shit done and the band was thriving. Therefore, I wasn't a fucking deadbeat alcoholic.

Therefore, I wasn't an alcoholic because the alcohol wasn't a problem.

I glared at my empty glass, wishing it had one more sip left inside. I didn't give a fuck that the bartender told me he was cutting me off. *Prick.*

My eye caught on a double of clear liquid sitting in a glass within reach.

Fuck it.

I reached over in front of the tatted-up guy next to me and took his glass of straight vodka, held it up in silent 'cheers' as its owner stared at me with wide eyes, and downed it. Because fuck it.

Fuck Blake.

Fuck Zach.

Fuck friendship.

And fuck the angels who came to save us sinners.

"What the fuck do you think you are doing?" The angry rasp from the victim of my alcoholic theft growled into my face.

Damn. When did he get that close?

My one eye squinted up at the much-larger-than-drunk-me-anticipated biker who stood and gripped my collar, yanking me against him. I winced at his stench.

"I-I'm so sorry, sir," Taylor gushed, wedging her petite form between us.

I snorted as Taylor called the gigantic mural of tattoos 'Sir.'

"I'm taking him home right now," she continued as she dug into her perfectly coordinated purse. "Please. Here's fifty dollars for the drink he took and another round on me."

I should be the one giving this guy money for the drink but fuck if I even still had my wallet on me.

He looked between the two of us until his pity for Taylor superseded his desire to kick my ass.

I knew I was pitifully drunk when Sir Tats-A-Lot dropped my shirt with a snarl instead of punching my face in.

"You didn't have to do that," I grumbled.

"You're right. I could've just let him smash your face in," she mumbled as she turned and hooked one of my arms over her shoulder, linked her hand with mine, and snaked her other arm around my waist.

I stumbled against her as she led us from the bar.

Just her hand in mine made my dick want to fucking explode, it was the most I'd ever touched her. *Hell, probably the most anyone had ever touched her...*

Her hand was so warm. *Warm and soft.* Just like her heart... and like the rest of her was. Not that you could ever see enough to even imagine. Even now, she had on dark jeans and a loose sweater over a white button-down shirt. She always looked like she was on her goddamn way to church.

"You can't keep doing this, Ash. You can't keep partying and drinking like this—it's how you end up with an addiction."

The pity in her voice felt like acid rain over my skin. She was right. It *was* how you ended up with an addiction. *Or how you continued to fuel one.* Taylor had only been on tour with us for a few months; she'd missed the years I'd spent *ending up* where I was.

I tried to pull away from her, but her small but firm grip tightened to stop me.

"Please, let me help you," she pleaded.

Hell fucking no. The last thing I needed was her constant reminder of just how far I'd fallen.

"I'll be just fine in the morning. Always am," I bit out forcefully.

"Being able to act fine on the outside isn't the same as being fine on the inside, Ash!" I swayed into her again, this time because I wanted to feel her softness against me, and the way my touch made her uncomfortable. "And you're not fine on the inside... This is the third time in two weeks someone has gotten the two A.M. call that you're too drunk and need a ride home."

Her desperate frustration rang like a siren in her words. And I remembered how fucking cruel it was for her to be so beautiful even when mad.

I was going to have a word with the other members of the Zach Parker Project on how to keep their fucking mouths shut when off-stage. Especially if they were going to talk about me. Their fucking friend and manager.

"That's my own goddamn business." Her fingers on mine tightened.

Taylor never cursed. Not now. Not in high school. Not ever. Never drank. Never partied. And yet, she was still one of the most popular girls in school, because when someone has that much heart, it's damn hard to criticize her uncommon preferences.

"It's not when it affects the people around you," she said with a low voice.

I gritted my teeth.

Well, who the fuck would be thrilled to watch their superstar little sister fake a relationship with their best friend?

Yeah, it was to save Blake's floundering reputation. And yeah, it was great for his band—*the band I managed*—to open for pop princess, Blake Tyler; it would open doors on streets that hadn't even been listed on our previous map.

Keyword: faking.

Correction: former best friend.

It felt like we kept walking and the car kept getting further and fucking further away—just like what remained of any good opinion she could have held for me.

"Just take me home, Pixie." Resignation coated over the nickname I'd given her small, cheerful and spritely self years ago.

Taylor was a lighthouse—a towering pillar of strength and a beacon of hope. And I was nothing more than a shoddy ship in stormy seas, drifting farther from her light, drinking myself until I drowned.

Truth was she was too good for me even at my best, which is why I let her see me at my worst. *Because only then would she come to me.* And even though it was out of pure pity, she'd try to save me and, in the process, let down her guard enough for me to see her truth: that she cared about me more than she would ever admit to when I was sober.

"The car is here."

I blinked twice, registering how we'd stopped and how her warmth began to drift away.

We stood by one of the tour's rental cars. Taylor had the door open and held onto it like it was a lifesaver and I was the storm trying to drown her. *And the extent of my sins probably would.* Still, her tiny, perfectly compact frame held her ground, rigid with righteousness.

"Careful getting in," she chided firmly. "Let's get you back to the hotel."

Grumbling, I fell into the passenger seat and struggled to remember how I'd gotten here. I remembered Sir Tats-A-Lot, but not why he was angry. I remembered the sense of betrayal and anger I'd felt seeing my sister and Zach together, realizing their 'fake' relationship was now very, very real. But I couldn't remember how many drinks it led me to have.

And I remembered knowing the second I saw Taylor at the bar that tonight would change everything… *But I wouldn't remember how for a very long time.*

"Let'ss see whaat kind of s-selection we have here." My announcement made me aware of my surroundings again.

I'd reached the next level—the triple-platinum-awards-level-drunk, complete with a second serving of lucidity, a mini-bar of regrets, and the one-hundred-percent money-back guarantee that I wouldn't recall any of this in the morning.

Good.

The nauseating beiges and blues of our five-star accommodations slurred through my vision. I was on the floor, my back propped against... something... as my hand rifled through the mini bar.

"Ash, stop! You're too drunk already. You need to get in bed."

Fuck.

My eyes yo-yoed over to the bedroom where Taylor was pulling down the comforter and fluffing my fucking pillow like she was about to tuck me in.

But maybe she was right.

But as I pinched the bridge of my nose, the image flashed in my mind again: Zach and my baby sister sucking face like it was a goddamn Olympic sport. And rage fed the beast inside me.

I didn't know why I was angry.

But alcohol justified it.

Alcohol turned hurt into unrestrained anger. Alcohol turned an unexpected surprise into an unforgivable betrayal; it turned friend and family into foes. Alcohol didn't just make me see the world through shadowed lenses, it ripped my fucking eyes out, made me blind, and rewired my brain to think I was seeing twenty-twenty.

Betrayal. Betrayal. Betrayal.

"You're not my mom-ager," I snarled, grabbing the tiny bottle of vodka and uncapping it. "You've done your job. You got me back. Thank you. Now, you can leave."

Her hand wrapped around mine, preventing that tiny glass

opening from reaching my mouth and providing me with the only legal amnesiac I had access to.

"I'm not leaving. And I'm not here because this is a job," she said firmly, her eyes piercing right through the rotted walls around my heart. "I'm here because I," her eyes dipped, "care about you. And you need help."

"Give it to me," she demanded, her perfect Cupid's-bow lips parting when I released the bottle so quickly. "You have a problem, Ash. You need to stop drinking and go to bed."

Anger poured through my veins like rain on top of an already raging river.

"If you wanted a drink, all you had to do was ask," I sneered, nodding to the bottle she now held.

"I'm dumping this down the sink."

"Leave and I'll just drink o-one of these other treats while you're gone." The minibar was freshly stocked and waiting for me. "Unless you want to drink it."

I couldn't remember ever seeing her drink. *Something else she was too good for.* It was wrong to feel a thrill when she looked down at the bottle in her hand. But then her shoulders gave a small slump before she extended her arm and put it on top of the dresser and out of my reach.

"Why are you doing this to yourself, Ash?" she asked quietly.

My throat bobbed. "Did you know?"

She gulped but didn't run. *Miss Goody-Two-Shoes had a backbone of steel.*

"Know what?"

"That they weren't faking it," I growled.

The anger inside me was like a black hole; it came from nowhere and latched onto any slight and turned it into a bottomless pit where no vengeance would ever be enough.

"Does it matter if they love each other?"

Yes.

No.

Fuck. I grunted as my hands crashed onto my face and yanked back my hair as my gaze snapped to hers.

"Why does no one see me?" I demanded in a voice I didn't recognize. "Why does no one see me as I drown?"

I was at the peak of my inebriation where things became so clear. Like the eye of the storm, I'd survived the destruction of drunkenness swirling inside me to make it to these moments of calm lucidity. *Even though they'd be lost come morning.*

Small hands with pale blue nails reached out and cupped my face.

"I see you, Ash," she murmured, the green in her eyes so damn clear. "I see you, and you are a good man."

Through it all. The drinks and anger. The self-destruction and shame… I knew she wasn't lying. I knew she saw the better man who'd gotten lost somewhere along his way.

My mouth parted, warmth pulsing from her fingertips onto my skin. It was the smallest touch, given in compassion, but still it made me want her more than I'd ever wanted one more drink.

It made me want her more than I'd ever wanted one more breath.

I told myself I had to be imagining it—the way her head dipped toward mine. I breathed her in—lemon and honey, so crisp and pure. *So hopeful.* And the need to taste her was stronger than any addiction burning through my blood—the need to cling to her and never let go.

"Taylor…" I rasped her name, and it might've been the first prayer I ever prayed.

But I was too far gone for forgiveness.

She pulled back with a start, her hands jumping to my arms and her face a safe several inches away.

"Bedtime," she informed me as she tugged me up.

I stumbled slightly over my own feet. *Just because my mind was clear didn't mean I was magically coordinated again.* She didn't tighten her hold, instead her arms came around me and she reacted by pressing her entire body against me, like she thought David could hold up Goliath.

Maybe it was in slow-motion or maybe my clarity fucking faltered, but I felt her chin against my chest as she slowly tipped her head up to mine, feeling how we fit together.

I groaned. We were both completely clothed and yet, I'd never been so fucking hard.

All those moments, all the times I tried to get close to this woman and she'd pushed me away collected in the heavy breaths between us. But it was when she licked those perfect fucking lips, I knew she hadn't been immune all this time. I heard her unsteady breaths. I felt the ragged tumbling of her heart. I saw the pink stain on her cheeks.

She wanted me.

She saw me at my lowest and still wanted the man underneath.

And with her arms wrapped around me, there was nothing else left but to hope.

Hope it would stop the suffocating sense of inadequacy which chauffeured me right to the door of my favorite bottle— *which was Belvidere, by the way.*

For most, inadequacy is handcuffed to the green god of jealousy; I wasn't most. I wasn't jealous of the success around me. I'd done everything to help my sister reach the mind-numbing level of stardom where she sat, and I was doing everything to help my friend's band do the same. I followed along in their shadows and made their stars shine brighter all the while letting my own flicker out.

I gave them everything and left nothing for myself.

And it was the little things, day after day, which built the insurmountable wall of inadequacy around me until I drank to forget that I was drowning.

I wasn't good enough for my own success.

I wasn't good enough for my own story.

And I certainly wasn't good enough for Taylor Hastings—a deeply-rooted fact I'd tried to ignore for a long, long time.

But the alcohol blacked out those notions... it also managed to black out everything else along with it.

"Come with me," I pleaded, slowly dropping my forehead to hers as my arms pulled her tighter. "Stay with me..."

Just once, I wanted to feel like I was enough... enough for her.

"I can't," she whispered softly even though she didn't move.

"Can't or won't?" I pressed. "Don't lie to me now."

I felt her nervous breath against my cheek.

"Both."

What the fuck was I doing?

She was never going to stay with me, let alone give in to what lay dormant between us all these years.

I'd already been betrayed today, no reason to beg for more misery.

I dropped my arms to my sides, their weight heavier from all the things I wasn't good enough to hold.

"Then go," I advised, accepting the inevitability. Until more of my own words invaded the space between us.

"I want to be better, Tay," I confessed like the bruised and broken man I was. "I want to be fucking better so I can be good enough for you. I don't care about the world. I don't care if I never hear a crowd chant my name or if I'm never more than Blake's brother. I just want to hear my name from your lips. Just once. Just once to know I wasn't alone in this... all this time... all this aching... Just once..."

Thank fuck I wouldn't remember this in the morning. Desperation made even my good looks turn sour.

She didn't let go, but I expected it any moment. The loneliness, the door shutting behind her, the cold bed... I was ready for it all because it was always the same.

Until it wasn't.

The warmest, softest lips pressed to mine. *I'd gone from clarity, skipped over blackout, went straight through hallucinations, and onto pure insanity.*

A raw groan broke in my chest as the tip of her velvet tongue pressed against the seam of my lips. I wasn't insane. I was kissing Taylor-fucking-Hastings. And, so help me God, if I could remember the lemon-honey taste of her innocent intoxication, I knew I'd never drink again.

Slanting my mouth over hers, I teased it open and gave her what she was searching for.

I worshipped her body like I was the sinner and she was the Samaritan.

I was a drunk. I was an asshole—bitter and self-destructive. But tonight, I was shown mercy—whether by God or by her.

I didn't deserve her. I didn't deserve what she was giving me. But I took it.

Because who wouldn't take grace? Who wouldn't take mercy? Especially when it was so beautifully given...

In the morning, I wouldn't remember any of this. Not her touch. Not her kiss.

In the morning, I'd go back to my life... my job... back to the high-functioning alcoholic no one realized I was.

But I wouldn't be the same.

Something had changed inside me tonight. She'd broken through the angry, shattered, scarred, and stitched together pieces of my soul and saw the wounded heart underneath.

I see you, and you're a good man.

I groaned against her lips, giving in to the baptism of her kiss.

The water of my sins had swallowed me whole, but it was her touch that pulled me gasping from the depths. And even though I was still drenched in the consequences of my past choices, I could breathe again. I could break free from my watery grave.

I could redeem myself.

Taylor

Five months ago
Denver, Colorado

Ashton Tyler was a Pandora's box.

Beautiful on the outside, begging to be opened, *begging to be known*. But inside, there were troves of troubles itching to be released. And the only thing he fought harder for than to keep himself locked up tight, was to help everyone around him follow their dreams.

In high school, he encouraged the dreams of his friends on the football team. Even though she'd been the one to ask for it, he convinced his parents to get Blake a guitar for her birthday; he was the one who gave her the charm bracelet she always wore and told her to never stop reaching for her star.

And look at her now… the biggest popstar in the world.

He was the one who got his best friend, Zach, and his band to play at every possible gig in town during high school even though Zach tried to pretend he was all about the football life. And it was Ash who encouraged and supported Zach when he left Alabama's Crimson Tide after sophomore year to focus on the Zach Parker Project—now one of the most popular country bands in the country.

If Zach Parker was George Washington—the leader everyone knew—then Ash Tyler would be Alexander Hamilton, the man responsible for so much behind-the-scenes that there wouldn't have been a country to lead, or a career to be had, if it weren't for him.

But Ash's dreams? They were a little harder to find.

He was like an unmarried wedding planner—too happy, too eager to help everyone else find their happily ever after, he had no time to find his own.

And everyone assumed because he was happy to help, it must mean it *was* his dream.

No one saw how he put aside his dreams to focus on those of his sister and his best friend. He never mentioned it. He never spoke about what he would do with his life if it wasn't for them.

No one but me.

It wasn't their fault; Ash was good at hiding the demons that plagued him. But I'd known the boy whose ambitions would let him conquer the world, the boy who believed every dream was within reach, and I'd watched him become the man who gave up his identity to be Blake Tyler's brother, and gave up everything else to be Zach Parker's manager.

He'd done everything for them because he was loyal to a fault—and that fault, that loyalty, meant sacrificing a future he could have created for himself.

But how do you regret giving up pieces of your life for someone you love?

You don't.

But the toll it takes on your life comes with a hidden interest collected from your soul, until the price becomes too much. *Until you have nothing left to give.*

Over the past few weeks, while on tour, I saw his edges begin to fray. Worried about his sister, his emotions began to destabilize like a kite in the sky, sailing smoothly one minute and the next, whipped and torn asunder by the wind. Normally, the carefree go-getter, I watched Ash's distorted anger claw away at the edges of his life.

He reminded me of a Jenga tower—but one near the end of the game. With so many holes, so many teetering layers, it wouldn't take much to send him crashing down.

Because that's what happens when who you need to be to support the ones you love means sacrificing who you'd hoped to become… the real you becomes locked inside.

In Ash's case, drowning in his party lifestyle.

In mine, buried under so many rules and regulations that all the lawyers in Tennessee couldn't argue to set my soul free.

I'd always *wanted* him in the ways which made my gaze linger and my body warm when he was near. But, I'd been raised a certain way.

Catholic. Composed. Chaste.

High necklines, low hems. Church on Sundays. Choir. Missions. Charity. Santa Claus had nothing on the religious requirements to keep you on the nice list.

Don't harm. Don't covet. Don't touch. *Don't sin.* The list of do's and don'ts was longer than the Bible itself. Especially in my parent's house.

And everything about Ash was definitely a *don't*. I knew the second I let him touch even the smallest part of me, I wouldn't be able to say no—not to him, but to myself and the way I'd always been drawn to him.

I'd lived my teenage years buried under the guilt that my body wanted something sinful, something against the rules—something that would turn me into a '*whore,*' as my mother would caution.

I thought the guilt would go away when they moved to Florida. I knew they were disappointed when I began to run PR for Blake—*'The entertainment industry is too depraved for even the Devil himself.'*

Unsuitable for a good, Catholic girl.

Maybe that was why I strived even harder to maintain the proper, unimpeachable appearance I'd been raised with.

And Ash…

Ash was the apple from the tree of temptation.

And I was Eve, finally too tempted to taste, to sin, to care how one bite… one touch… would make me fall.

But it was his heart-wrenching plea that stripped away the last reservations from my chaste self—the confession torn from his chest which I couldn't turn down because I didn't want to.

I kissed him even though I knew it wouldn't fix him.

I kissed him even though I knew he may not remember it in the morning.

I kissed him because, for just once, I didn't want to feel alone in this either.

And what I was told would be a sin, instead felt sacred.

His lips were soft where hurt had made him hard and his touch freed the parts of me buried under shame… the parts that always desired him.

And that desire quashed the guilt I should have felt when I wrapped my arms around his neck silently urging him on. It stifled the guilt I should have felt when I whispered for him to hurry as he first removed my clothes and then stripped of his own. It obliterated every shame I'd been taught to feel when I moaned and writhed as his mouth claimed every square inch of my skin before I begged him for more.

And finally, when I was breathless and panting, I reached for his hot arousal and positioned him against my slick and swollen core. And when the tip of his hard length pushed inside my entrance, stretching my unused muscles, the pain I felt only made the pleasure burn that much brighter.

I felt the moment he took the piece of me I'd been told to save, and I knew I'd been saving it for him. *All this time, I'd been his.*

And as he moved inside me, I became lost in so many sensations I never knew existed. I savored the fullness. I savored the pleasure-drunk words he murmured against my lips about how good I felt, how this must be heaven. I savored it all.

He tried to go slow like I tried to be good. *Unsuccessfully.* He took me savagely like the apple took Eve. It ripped her from pure and chaste Eden. But the knowledge of being one with someone who held as much turmoil inside as I did was worth the fall.

And when my body exploded with a pleasure that felt so unearthly it either had to be completely divine or completely devilish, I screamed his name like it was a Halleluiah as he jerked inside me, filling me with his hot release.

And my desire smothered my rationality because it was only one time…

Maybe I wasn't made for a guilt-free life. Maybe, for one night, I wanted to be a sinner just like everyone else… for one night, I wanted to be human so that I wouldn't be alone.

But one night is where my story's similarity to any fairytale would end.

The truth was that guilt had been built into my genes and the more minutes that passed, the more I knew I needed to go and pretend like this had never happened.

And not just for my sake.

Ash wasn't okay. He was battling things I didn't understand, things I didn't know the full scope of. But most of all, he was struggling with loyalty. His to others. Theirs to him. *And his to himself.*

I didn't want tonight to add more weight to his chains—not now when it seemed like one more burden might break him. He wasn't obligated to me. We were both adults. We'd both made a willing choice. And my choice was to walk away without the expectation of more.

So, I waited until I was sure he wasn't going to be sick... and until I was strong enough to let him go.

Pulling on my clothes, I wished the growing sunlight could wipe my memories along with his. Instead, I stepped into the hallway and walked away from the apple in a worse predicament than Adam and Eve.

I'd tasted the knowledge of good and evil—the knowledge of relativity. It taught me good because it let me taste bad; it taught me light because it showed me darkness. *And it taught me pain by having me shun such pleasure.*

I'd tasted the emotions which allowed you to live fully.

And now, I had to pretend I knew nothing.

CHAPTER ONE

ASH

Present
Carmel Cove, California

"Hello. My name is Ash. I'm an alcoholic and it's been one-hundred and forty-nine days since my last drink."

"Hello, Ash," the rest of the Tuesday afternoon Alcoholics Anonymous group responded in unharmonized chorus from the circle where we sat inside Our Lady of Mount Carmel Church.

This was my Tuesday lunch—and it had been for the past four or so months. I sent a tight smile over to Larry, my sponsor. *My savior.* He sat in front of the small table which served coffee from his coffee shop, Ocean Roasters. And next to him stood the proud banner that symbolized the battle cry of our congregation.

Recovery is the gift you give yourself.

There wasn't a week that went by where I didn't need the reminder. It was the first gift—*the first thing*—I'd given myself in a very, very long time.

Larry Ocean was the unofficial king of Carmel Cove, a small town about two hours south of San Francisco, famous for its breathtaking cliffs, world-renown golfing, and, of course, Roaster's rich and addicting coffee.

But he wasn't King like Caesar; he was King like

Cincinnatus—the dictator who ruled Rome to save it from defeat and when the war ended, instead of keeping power for himself, went back to his farm and his normal life.

Willing to stand up when needed. Knowing to step down when necessary.

I kept speaking, choosing to tell my tale as though it were a weekly confessional.

"I know a lot of you have heard my story, but I thought about having a drink last night, so I hope you don't mind if I share again."

Here, I felt safe in my failures and my weakness. Here, I wasn't alone because the rest of the people in the room saw me for more than my mistakes, just like I did for them.

"Last night, my sister called to tell me she's engaged. For those who don't know, my alcoholism almost cost my sister her career and the love of her life."

My hands folded in my lap. It never got easier to speak about what I'd done. I hoped it never did.

"Five months ago, I found out she and my best friend were in a relationship and had kept it from me. I drank so much... I got so drunk—which is saying a lot for an alcoholic." There was a small rumble of laughter through the group. "Because of my addiction, it felt like the ultimate betrayal. Because of my addiction, my hurt became hate. And I drank so much that what should've been fixed with a conversation, instead awoke a monster of rage who lied and threatened to hurt them like they'd hurt me."

I paused and let my gaze scan the room, making sure I looked each and every person in the eyes because there was no hiding from this; there was no hiding from the truth.

"I threatened to ruin my sister's reputation—a reputation I'd given so much of my life to help her build—if my best friend didn't break her heart."

Bile still rose in my throat every time I said those words because I didn't recognize the man who'd done that and yet, that man was me.

I felt like a real-life Jekyll and Hyde—only it was either the Alcoholic or Ash.

"Five months ago, I realized my alcohol addiction turned me into a man I still don't recognize, and that man did things I never would have imagined."

Guilt was a drug. One I took every day to mitigate the cancerous mistakes I'd made. But while it might be saving me, the fine print on the bottle said the side effect of regret might kill me in the process.

And the longer I stayed sober, the more I realized how alcohol had affected me even when I wasn't drinking—*which wasn't often.*

It shorted my fuse and grew the bomb. It made me distrust those around me. It made nothing I did good enough. And it made me unforgivably vengeful toward two people I loved. It made a situation that didn't involve me become a personal attack, a breach of loyalty. Regardless of what I told Blake about my feelings—about why I did what I did—there was no true excuse for the asshole I'd become. There would never be.

A man is no better than the pain he's caused his loved ones.

And I'd caused a lot of pain.

Larry's old, not-so-wrinkled eyes stared hard at me. I knew there was a cup of espresso to be had at his shop when this was over.

Pushing eighty, Larry owned Ocean Roasters, the town's only coffee shop. It had been in his family for four generations, and the legacy his family built for this town was the reason why he was its grumpy, stringent king. Beneath the rugged, no-nonsense exterior was a heart of gold; it was just heavily buried under strong cups of coffee, four glazed donuts, and a face which had weathered war, and far too many losses to tell.

"I'm happy for her," I went on. "But I almost cost her that happiness. And when she asked when I was coming home, that was when I thought about having a drink. It was just for a split second, because she doesn't know; she doesn't know just how much of a failure I was," I confessed, my fingers thumbing over the rubbed-worn five-month chip I'd transformed into a bracelet. The thought had been fleeting—a shadow of the crutch I'd once relied on. But leaving it to the shadows is what would allow it to fester. "But, I didn't. So, today, I'm grateful to have made it to one-forty-nine."

Everyone clapped for me. Everyone but Larry—the worsening arthritis in his hands made it hard, especially on rainy days like this. The group's support filled the hole of inadequacy where I used to dump oceans of alcohol even though it never made a difference.

After the hour was over, I waited outside the small community church until I felt a hand on my shoulder.

"You going back?" Larry asked as he came up behind me, letting me steady him as we walked down the front steps and began the few-block trek down Ocean Avenue, the main drag in Carmel Cove, toward Roasters.

My jaw ticked and then released with a sigh. "For the wedding, of course. But now?" I shook my head. "I don't think so. I'm not ready."

Translation: I'm not good enough yet.

Two weeks after the tour ended… two weeks after everything had worked out for Blake and Zach, I told everyone—family and friends—that I was heading out west for a change in scenery and a new job for a little while.

Only there was no job. There was barely a destination. *And there definitely wasn't a choice.*

I didn't tell anyone about my addiction because it wasn't their problem to fix; it was mine. So, I left them with the impression I needed a change and some space after what happened on tour—that I needed a break, though the truth was that I was already broken.

It was one more lie, but it was the only one I didn't regret.

Something happened to me the night I found out about the two of them. Something that I couldn't explain—though 'the beginning of the end' had a poignant ring to it.

I'd continued to fall after that night, only harder and faster. Reprehensible choices. Disgusting lies. But it was when I stood at Blake's hotel door after my sister had ripped me a new one that my eyes met Taylor's and the expectation held in those green spheres was both familiar and a slap to the face; she looked at me like she needed me to remember how to be a better man.

Like she could still see that better man.

I shuddered. The memory of it still unnerving for reasons I couldn't explain.

Funny how some people forget that rock bottom and the moment things begin to look up are one and the same.

I didn't stop drinking cold-turkey. Guilt wasn't a magic pill for sobriety. But the more I tried not to touch any liquor over the next few weeks, the more I realized the life I lived and the industry I was involved in would make what was necessary, impossible. I didn't know what I needed in order to get better, but I knew I wasn't going to be able to find it there.

"Your usual?" Larry asked over the steam of his still-manual espresso machine which had survived through every generation of Ocean since they opened.

I nodded, waving to a few friendly faces already inside.

"Hey, Larry," Josie, the owner of the Carmel Bakery down the street, sing-songed as she strolled in for her afternoon coffee. Kind eyes and a round frame said she enjoyed sampling her pastries just as much as she enjoyed baking them—*a fact she would cheerfully admit to.*

Ocean Roasters was a daily stop for most of the locals—and not just for coffee. Everyone knew Larry, and Larry knew everything. I hadn't been here long, but it was long enough to learn coffee meant community in this town—and Larry was the heart of it.

"Mornin', Josie," Larry greeted her with a weathered smile, shuffling about to make her usual large, half-decaf coffee. "You want to look at photos?"

Larry had served in the war with Josie's dad, only her father hadn't come home. They'd been good friends, so Larry had looked out for Josie ever since. And one of their frequent pastimes when she stopped in for coffee was Larry would pull out an older-than-the-Bible photo album and they'd look at pictures of Josie's dad from before and during the war while Larry recounted old tales. I was sure she'd heard the same stories hundreds of times by now.

But a good memory of a loved one never grows old.

"I can't today." She gave an apologetic smile. "I have to get back to Cam."

"How's Cambria doing?" Larry immediately asked.

Cambria was Josie's daughter who'd just moved back home after finishing her massage program. I hadn't met her yet, but I'd chalked it up to being too busy with my restaurant to do much else.

"Good," she replied, and a look passed between them that said there was more to discuss about her daughter later.

"Ash." Josie turned her attention to me and smiled. "How's the restaurant coming?"

"It's coming," I replied with a chuckle. "Homestretch now."

"Oh, wonderful." She reached out and pulled me in for a

hug. "I'm so proud of you. I can't *wait* to taste your first official meal."

"Who says you get the first one?" Larry teased, handing Josie her coffee.

She gasped and waved him away with a laugh, murmuring to me conspiratorially, "I'm willing to bribe you with extra apple fritters."

"Coffee is more important than fritters," came Larry's response.

He had a point.

"We'll see about that." Josie winked at me. "Alright, boys. I have to run. I'll be by in the morning with fresh muffins."

The bell dinged signaling her departure.

Roasters was small and looking a little more rundown even in the five months that I'd been here. An L-shaped counter held a glass partition behind which sat various plates of food and pastries, some that were made here, and some made by Josie which she brought over at the beginning of each day.

And sitting front and center behind that counter was the original La Pavoni espresso machine that Larry's great-grandparents had brought over from Italy; it had been here so long, it was nicknamed Pavi. And it still shone and purred just as smoothly as probably the day it was installed.

Nothing made an espresso like this machine.

Not Starbucks. Not Nespresso. *Not even God.*

The rest of the space which appeared not to have been updated since the eighties was filled sporadically with small cafe tables. On the left, just inside the entry, was a wall-length bench, the navy and white stripes of the fabric so worn they looked light blue at first glance until you went to sit.

Above it was a mass of framed photos, going all the way back to when the first generation of Oceans opened the place in nineteen-oh-six. Photos with the roads still unpaved in that dusty sepia-tone that made the place seem like the Wild West instead of the West Coast.

But it was the photos of the people, the generations of the Ocean family, spreading down the wall like a branch of the family tree that made Roasters feel like it was the roots of this town, like everything that grew in Carmel Cove, came from here.

New people. New businesses. *New futures.*

Maybe that was why it had been easy to stay here—because the fact I wasn't family never seemed to make a difference in how I was treated as though I were.

"Hey, Eve," I greeted the cheerful, local girl who popped out from the back carrying armfuls of travel mugs.

She brightened when she saw me. "Hey, Ash." Her small smile was as brief as a breeze as she deposited her haul, grabbed new plates filled with food and was off to serve them to waiting customers, tossing over her shoulder, "Any chance you miss this and want to come back?"

I chuckled.

My first job out here had been behind this bar, serving a different kind of addiction.

Eve had been here part-time, so we'd worked together for two-and-a-half months until I finally purchased the house and land for my restaurant. Since then, she'd been bumped up to head barista while I took more and more time off for my own business.

"Tempting," I threw back.

The head barista position at Ocean Roasters seemed to be a revolving door for broken souls. It made sense... *If there was one thing coffee could teach you, it was that being in hot water only made you turn out stronger.*

Ever since Larry's granddaughter, Laurel, left for school

and hadn't come back, filling the position had also helped soothe the piece of him that missed her.

Her picture hung on the wall, too. Laurel, her father and Larry's son, Mark, and Larry—it was taken shortly before the boating accident which killed both Mark and his wife, Fiona, leaving Laurel in her grandfather's care. He never talked about it—or Laurel. And I didn't ask...

I knew the look of someone who'd failed a loved one all too well; it was one that greeted me in the mirror every morning.

"When is Eli coming back?" I wondered, realizing it had been a few days and I couldn't remember what he'd told me.

Eli Downing was broken barista number one, AKA my predecessor. He'd gone up to Monterey a few days ago for a job; he was the best and the most trustworthy contractor in the area—and not just because Larry said so; but he'd started off here, in Roasters, just like I had.

And if Larry and I were close, well, Eli was like a son to him even though they weren't related.

"Next week sometime," came Larry's gruff response.

Just like I did, Eli had stepped back from Roasters to grow his construction business, and recently partnered with Madison Construction, run by two brothers—*twins*—Mick and Miles Madison. They were new to Carmel, having moved up from Texas.

But more and more, Eli was being pulled back to the coffee shop because Larry was getting old and worse, far too stubborn to be left to his own devices.

"You think I should go back?" I asked with a low voice, returning to our earlier conversation about my sister's engagement.

Eyes peered at me from underneath loose lids that made them always look partially closed and as though he was constantly scrutinizing you—*which he probably was.*

"I still… I still have thoughts. I'm still struggling," I admitted, taking the Americano from his hand. "I don't think I'm ready. Still feels like I'm missing something."

And I didn't want to go back until I was whole—until I was whole enough to tell Blake and my family the truth of why I'd come out here.

I didn't want them to worry.

I didn't deserve their worry.

"Gonna be waitin' a long time if that's what you're holdin' out for," he groused, pulling off the lid to the hopper. "You'll always be missin' somethin', boy. You're human."

I cleared my throat. My gaze catching on the carved wood plaque mounted above the machine.

Start where you are. Use what you have. Do what you can.

The phrase almost as well-known as Larry Ocean—the man it came from.

It gave me déjà vu to the day I arrived in Carmel Cove with no plan, wandered into Ocean Roasters and couldn't stop staring at the words, wondering where I was, what I had, and what the hell I was going to do with myself.

And then Larry handed me my coffee in a to-go cup with the name of the church and a date and time written on the coffee collar.

I didn't need to ask… hell, I didn't even need to show up to know that it was an invitation to an AA meeting. But I'd gone the following day, intrigued by the man who knew more than I'd told him, and I'd been going to the same one every week since.

"Was that a compliment?" I chuckled, trying to lighten the profound truth of his words.

Larry was notorious for guarding full-blown compliments—worse than Gollum guarded the ring. Not the chatty type, Larry only spoke when necessary and with a purpose, which meant when he spoke, everyone listened.

And when he complimented, it was more confirmation than seeing your name on Santa's nice list that you'd done the right thing.

"You tell anyone, they'll never find your body," he straight-faced retorted as he wiped down the steamer on the machine.

I laughed, taking a long drink of the dark, unsweetened liquid.

It wasn't just with that coffee collar that Larry changed my life. He gave me a place to stay even though I had enough money to afford a hotel, threatening me bodily harm if I left before I was stable enough in my sobriety to get a place on my own.

Leaving Nashville, the band, and the entertainment industry was a huge step in getting alcohol out of my life, but it also meant leaving friends and family who cared about me. Maybe I was dumb to walk away from their support, but I didn't deserve it. I'd fucked up my life—demolished it like the explosion at Chernobyl. And they'd survived the blast; I wouldn't ask them to linger in the toxic environment to help me clean up the pieces.

Larry didn't ask questions. He saw the void and he filled it with his donut cravings, trips to the gym at six in the morning to leg press weights that would have good old Mayor Arnold Schwarzenegger balking, and his famous Sunday spaghetti and meatballs topped with magic marinara was open to anyone who needed to be anywhere but where they were, and with anyone who would listen; he filled it without asking and without asking for anything in return.

"So, you were spackling?" he asked as we made our way out the back.

Tuesdays were shipment days so I knew there would be a truckload of boxes with to-go cups, napkins, utensils, filters, and, of course, paper straws. With Eli away, I wasn't going to let Larry try to carry it all inside like his stubborn mule of a self would attempt to do.

"Yeah." I grunted as I hoisted the box marked 'Heavy' over my shoulder. "Mick and Miles are working a job over at the Rock Beach Resort, so I figured how hard could it be?"

I'd never been one for manual labor before. But here, there was something to be said for building up something from scratch with your own two hands, my business and myself.

After two months of recovering, of living with Larry and earning my keep working at Ocean Roasters, I finally felt like I had a footing—not completely stable, but with enough support to help me weather the challenges ahead. So, I used my considerable savings which, thankfully, hadn't been wasted on anything but alcohol, and bought a property along the Big Sur coastline.

I paid cash for the expensive but rundown house which probably would've been cheaper to tear down and rebuild, but maybe that was what drew me to it.

At one point, I thought it would have been easier for life to just tear me down instead of fixing me up. And here I was. *Being fucking fixed.*

After the purchase, I reached out to Eli who brought Mick and Miles into the project and the rest is history.

"How long?" Larry asked as we carried the last of the boxes inside.

"Four weeks," I said, my heart pumping faster at the thought. It had taken three months, a new foundation, almost a new everything, but the original framework was preserved. And now I was four weeks of hard-ass hustling to finish everything in order to open in six.

Six weeks until I opened my own restaurant. Until I was responsible for my own success instead of someone else's.

And I was fucking proud.

It didn't matter if it wasn't open yet, and that I had essentially nothing but an empty space with a bomb-ass view. I'd climbed out of the worst possible version of myself. I'd scratched, clawed, and beat back demons I'd invited into my soul years ago and was doing something good.

"On track then," he mumbled. "Good."

"For now." And for the duration, if I had anything to say about it.

"You pick a name?"

"Larry's Lounge," I joked.

His glare made me laugh harder. "Don't you tease me, boy, I'll push you right off that cliff if you go and do something foolish like that," he said with a tone that was ornery rather than threatening before changing topics, "You coming for dinner tonight?"

Most days that I saw Larry came with his invitation to dinner. And it wasn't just to me. His door was always open to anyone in town who needed a friend, a conversation, and a good meal to remind them the little things are just that… *little*.

"Nah, I'm good but thank you." I glanced down at my watch. I had a few hours before I had to meet Danielle at *Ciao!*, the Italian restaurant in town.

"You seein' that girl again?"

Couldn't put anything past him… not in Carmel Cove. "You know Danielle. You know everyone here. You should stop calling her 'that girl.'" The air quotes came complete with an eye-roll.

Danielle was a master vintner at Cliffside, one of the many wineries sprinkled along these parts. But that's definitely not where I met her; we'd met at Roasters. She came in for her hazelnut latte every morning since before I'd moved here.

I knew Larry was concerned because of her profession… and my problem… but Danny was great; she never even ordered wine when we went out to dinner, playing it off as it was her job to drink all day, and no one liked to work after hours.

But the best part was that things were casual between us—and that's what I needed. We'd only gone out a handful of times, and neither of us was looking for anything more right now. I needed a foundation for my life before I could think about housing someone else on it with me.

"She's not the one for you. That means I call her 'that girl.'"

Even he recoiled at the hard edge in his voice. This was happening more frequently, the sharp contrasts between good and bad moods… good and bad days. I'd have to give Eli a call; he would know what was going on.

"Larry—"

"Have a good night," he ordered, and then turned and walked to his old Nissan pick-up to head home.

That was another thing on the list.

As soon as we were done with my restaurant, I needed to wrangle Eli and the crew over to Larry's house which was almost in as bad a shape as mine had been, only he didn't do anything about it. It was a shame, too, since his house had to be worth tens of millions for the property it sat on, peaked along the jagged coastline with a view even God, looking down from the heavens, would be jealous of.

I sighed and made for my own beater. An '82 Ford truck. Donation courtesy of Elijah Downing.

Yeah, I'd found more than just my future here. I'd found the friends to support it.

Chapter Two

ASH

The best thing about my work-in-progress restaurant was the view. Hands-down. Without a doubt. I swore I'd stumbled into a corner of heaven when I'd first stepped on the property.

The building sat on a secluded bluff along the Big Sur cliff-covered coast. Set several hundred feet down a gravel driveway off the main road, the views of the ocean and the cliffs, no matter the time of day, were an ever-changing canvas of the most vibrant colors.

The second-best thing about this property: it came with a guest house. Although guest house was a generous term. The rundown, two-room-plus-bathroom shack sat just off the top of the drive with trees and foliage partially obstructing the ocean view. Having it meant I'd been able to move off Larry's couch the day the papers were signed.

Quietly, I slipped out of bed, not wanting to wake Danny after last night. Glancing over, I saw her naked form sprawled in my sheets, sleeping soundly. We'd had a good night... *satisfying night*... and part of me wished she didn't turn the bed into a midnight mash pit while she slept. I'd always imagined ending up with a woman who'd wake up in my arms. *Then again, she'd never been the woman in those fantasies.*

Instead, images of uneven short hair, brilliant green eyes, and a body so compact I could cage it with mine—and never let it go—came to mind.

Tugging on my sweats, I tucked my morning wood up against my stomach and padded down the small drop step into the kitchen-slash-living-room-slash-dining room. Basically, the place where coffee and food came from, complete with a small sofa that Larry had given me, TV, and a foldout table and chairs.

I'd used the word 'cozy' to describe it to Danny which was guy speak for a room with a bed and a coffeepot.

It was only seven, but I couldn't stay in bed any longer. Something felt off this morning. Glancing out the window, I noticed the candy red sky along the horizon.

Red sky in the morning is a sailor's warning.

And that was how I felt—a sugar-coated sense of foreboding.

Figuring it was just the amount of shit I had to get done, I brushed it off and flipped on the coffee grinder.

Larry's Life Lesson Number One: Always use fresh-ground beans.

My attention snapped to the small kitchen window, thinking for a second I'd heard something outside on the gravel driveway.

Note to self, check on when the drive was supposed to be paved.

Probably just the grinder, I figured.

The rich aroma easily filled the small space as I poured two mugs full of Roaster's Morning Brew; it was enough to wake you up without a single sip. I'd barely taken two steps back toward the bedroom, mugs in hand, when there was a soft knock at the door.

I had heard something.

My brow furrowed. *But who the hell was showing up at my hovel at seven in the morning?*

My brain quickly sped through the list of possibilities. Larry would be at Roasters. Miles and Mick were working in Monterey. Eli was out of town. And Danny was in the other room.

My heart jumped into my throat, immediately worried it was some local official coming to tell me I hadn't signed, dotted, danced and licked all the right lines of the numerous permits and licenses I'd needed; this was California, after all.

God, if something happened to push back my timeline, I had no idea what the fuck I was going to do.

Forgetting the coffee, forgetting my houseguest, and forgetting I was shirtless, I stalked over to the door, heart pounding, and yanked open the latch handle with the mugs in one hand expecting anything. Or everything.

Everything but emerald.

"Taylor?"

I gaped and stared at the angel from my past, her jewel-cut eyes crystallizing around my gaze.

Taylor.

Here.

I would've been less surprised to see the Pope, dressed as Santa, here to wish me Happy Hanukkah than to find Taylor Hastings at my door.

Like everyone else from my past life, I hadn't seen her in five months. But unlike everyone else, Taylor was the only one with the perspicacity to see my demons and know they'd driven me here.

My heart continued to race for a whole slew of reasons I couldn't give name to, and my body felt like it was waking up for the first time in months. *All because of her.*

I couldn't believe she was here… and it looked like neither could she.

"Ash... Hi..." Her brilliant smile flashed for a split-second.

She stammered like she'd expected someone else to answer the door to a rundown shack on the other side of the country.

She licked her lips and I felt a shock of desire straight to my groin. The alcohol might have elevated—and exacerbated—most of my other emotions, but the desire drunk-Ash had felt for Taylor was nothing compared to the Earth-shaking need sober-Ash suffered right now.

Months, miles, and sobriety hadn't dulled the way I wanted her.

But I'd wanted her for decades... I doubted even death could stop it now.

I shook my head. "Sorry. I just can't believe you're on my doorstep. What... what are you doing here? Is everything okay? Is my sister okay?"

She nodded frantically. "Yes, I'm sorry. Blake is fine. Everyone is fine. Well, everyone but me." At that moment, her eyes ducked down and, for better or for worse, my gaze roamed down the length of the small frame that managed to create a Goliath-sized amount of lust in me.

As always, the gentle slope of her neck was cut off by a collared shirt, layered over with a royal-purple sweater. NorCal was chilly this time of year, so I couldn't hold that against her, but it only hinted at the slopes of her tits, and that I would always protest. But there, instead of the fabric falling back in over her stomach, it pushed out.

Jesus Christ.

Was I... Was I seeing this right?

My mouth went dry and my heart ran like the fucking cops were chasing it.

Was Taylor pregnant?

My gaze whipped to hers. "Taylor..."

Where the hell did I even begin?

'*Are you pregnant?*'

No, definitely not. I knew better than to ask that to any woman. *Fuck.*

There were a million questions, so many things I needed to know, and every second that went by felt like my body and my brain were stretched farther on the rack—tortured with wondering.

"Can we talk?" My eyes jerked back up to her face hearing her soft, strained voice. "Can… Can I come in?"

Yes. Talk. Explain.

What. The. Fuck. Was. Happening.

I was unable to process that the most innocent and chaste girl I'd ever met—the girl who'd never had a boyfriend to my knowledge—was standing at my door with a bump in her sweater that was never there before. *And I would know because I was always fucking looking at her.*

"Shit. Sorry." I nodded, biting my cheek. "Of course, you can. I wasn't expecting… you," I finished dumbly. "You surprised me."

I wasn't an idiot. At least, for the past four-ish months I hadn't been an idiot. But five seconds in her presence turned me into a goddamn fool—forgetting every fucking thing around me.

"Ash," Danny's voice coming up behind me was like a bucket of ice water over my head. "Who is it…" She trailed off in surprise like any normal woman would, walking up behind the guy she was casually seeing to find him standing at his door, talking to a woman who was obviously knocked up.

I knew what Danny was thinking, but she was wrong.

Alcohol may have damaged many of my brain cells, but I still knew the difference between fantasies and fucking—and fantasies, no matter how realistic or how frequently I'd had them about Taylor, couldn't get her pregnant.

So, there was no way in hell that I was the father.

Chapter Three

Taylor

Lord, give me strength.

The silent, succinct prayer seemed like a single drop in a sea of insecurities.

"Can we talk?" I choked out. "Can... Can I come in?"

For weeks... months... I'd imagined this moment, gone through it in my mind, trying to prepare myself. But it had been like practicing to skydive.

I could strap on a backpack and jump from my couch onto the floor all I wanted, but it would never prepare me to leap from a plane, thousands of feet off the ground.

Nothing could prepare me for the weightless freefall of my heart crashing back down to Earth at the sight of the man I'd always wanted—the man who was the father of my child.

Ash.

"Shit. Sorry." His eyes fell as he stepped to the side. "Of course, you can. I wasn't expecting you," he offered in explanation. "You surprised me."

My heart beat wildly in my chest with the kind of exuberance and anxiousness you feel coming home after a long time, happy to be there but afraid of what has changed.

My eyes drank him in. Greedily. *Desperately.* They traced over the image of the man that had begun to fade from my mind for how many times I'd closed my eyes and sought his face.

That was the bittersweet reality of memories: the more you visited them, the foggier they became.

The unruly waves of Ash's hair fell like spun gold over his forehead. And his eyes… so blue they looked like miniature oceans caged by his lashes. They were so clear and vibrant now, not the stormy gray I'd last seen in Tennessee before he left.

Was it possible he looked even more gorgeous? Or maybe more golden? *This was California, after all.* Or maybe it was that he looked more… like himself.

Or maybe this was all just because of my hormones.

Yes. Hormones. That was a good reason.

If my mouth hadn't already dried out of anxiety, it did at the sight of his naked chest, cut sharply into various lean muscles I'd dreamt about frequently since that night in Denver. The way they vibrated under my touch and tensed with each ragged breath he took. Their heat and hardness against my own breasts as we…

I cleared my throat and dipped my chin for a moment, unused to the crush of feelings inside my chest. *Unused to being around him.*

In my parents' house, there was an eleventh commandment—and it was one that through sheer determination, and the threat of eternal damnation, I'd tried to train myself to stop looking. *To stop feeling.*

But it never worked for Ash.

My eyes always made their way back to him like the sun returns to the horizon. No matter how far away I got, how high I climbed, I always fell back down to him.

"Thank yo—" I began with such a quiet, strained voice it took no effort for it to be drowned out by another.

"Ash, who is… it?" I watched in abject horror as an almost equally naked woman appeared beside him.

Wait.

What... Oh, no.
I swayed as blood rushed to my head.
Don't faint.
Don't fall.
Don't puke.

"Hey, I'm Danny." My attention fractured as the beautiful brunette introduced herself with a curious but kind smile.

Morning sickness had nothing on this moment, and embarrassment didn't even begin to cover the range of vomit-inducing emotions that washed over me.

What had I been thinking? It was a Wednesday morning, why wouldn't I find him alone? *No. Wrong.*
So. Very. Wrong.

Of all the ways I'd imagined this scenario going over, him answering the door with his girlfriend still in bed wasn't even on the radar.

Like the iceberg that destroyed the Titanic, I hadn't seen the warning sign: the two mugs he held in his hand. So, my eyes sunk with watery miscalculation and anchored on the steam rising from *both* mugs and wishing it could make me disappear.

"Sorry. Danny, this is Taylor," his calm, smooth-as-silk voice introduced me, extending a mug filled hand as I stepped to the side to include her in the conversation. "Taylor is my sister's best friend and PR manager."

Yes. Of course. That's me. The family friend.
I never should've come.

But the second my hand rose to my stomach to steady my breathing I remembered that I'd had to.

"Hi. I'm so sorry for interrupting..." A blush rose to my cheeks, feeling like the biggest intruder on the planet. "I wasn't thinking. I just got off the plane and came right here and... It's very nice to meet you, Danny."

I released the sweaty death-grip on my beige, let's-just-blend-in suitcase, extended it to Ash's girlfriend who was, I just noticed, wearing one of his t-shirts. It was a fact almost as distressing as Ash's face, flashing with shock as he, apparently, just noticed the suitcase sitting behind me.

His knuckles turned white around the handles of the mugs as he met my gaze.

"Is everything okay?" Ash cut in to ask again. "Is everyone—"

"Yes. Everything and everyone is fine. I'm here... Well, it's not an emergency why I'm here," I reassured him lamely. In my defense, I had tried to call once I landed, but it had gone straight to voicemail—consistent with the absence of cell service once I stepped onto his driveway.

"This was a mistake. I can come back." My tongue felt like it was coated in peanut butter. Embarrassment was just as sticky but harder to dissolve. "I'm so sorry. I wasn't thinking."

I wasn't thinking, and I was now wishing that I was anywhere else but here.

"You're not going anywhere." Demanding, firm words pulled goosebumps over my body like a blanket. "Not until you tell me why you're here. And... well... yeah. That."

I heard what he meant. *And... well... why you are pregnant.*

It was his house, I knew,—*at least according to the old man at the coffee shop*—still, I looked to Danny like I needed her permission.

"Yeah." Danny nodded nonchalantly, her expression concealing her concern about the knocked-up woman on her boyfriend's doorstep. "I need to get going anyway. We've got a bunch of big tours coming through so I should head out."

As she turned, I caught her 'we-need-to-talk' look she sent Ash as she took her cup of coffee from him and walked back where she came from—*and where I hoped she'd find her pants.*

"Come in," Ash instructed, his eyes never having left me even while Danny was there.

I stepped over the threshold, the subconscious barrier in the doorframe said there was no going back now. My suitcase caught on the uneven lip and, swearing under his breath, Ash pulled the handle from my grasp.

"Let me get that," he said gruffly while I tried to recover from the split second where an inch of his hand touched an inch of mine.

If possible, the… cabin… was even smaller inside than it looked on the outside.

Was this one of those tiny homes Blake was always going on about? I knew I should've paid attention when she was telling me about that show.

"Sit. Give me a minute," he ordered, stalking from the room before I could even turn around.

Not like I had anywhere else to go at the moment.

I reached for my water bottle, my throat still parched, and gulped down what was left.

The couch I sat on was a worn, light blue denim. It sat on the same wall as the front door and faced the entry to the bedroom where Ash and Danny had disappeared to.

On the wall in front of me was a small cabinet with a modest TV sitting on top, and to say the décor was sparse aside from those things was generous. There were no pictures, no art, no nothing that made the space personal to Ash. There was only a stand lamp to my left and a deep green ottoman in front of me which clashed with the couch.

How long had he lived here?

And *none* of the furniture matched the faded floral wallpaper that I could see bubbling in some spots near the old, worn molding.

Was this his house?

To my right was the kitchen and dining room. The appliances plastic and pastel, suggesting their old age. And the dining table looked like something you'd find at Ikea. Long and skinny, it was shoved up against the wall almost like a counter with two chairs in front of it; I could see the layers of wood stacked together where it could unfold into something a little larger if necessary.

I glanced down at my stomach. *It was going to be necessary.*

Who was I kidding? I groaned to myself. There was hardly enough room for two people in the shack, let alone a baby.

I tried to lick my lips, but my mouth still felt dry. Hesitantly, I stood and walked the few steps to the kitchen sink to refill my water bottle.

"I'm not that kind of girl, Ash, and I don't want to be—you know, the ones that are crazy and demanding and jealous. I know we started this with zero expectations, but I don't want to be involved with someone who is involved with someone else. I just want your honesty... please... Were you in a relationship with her? Is she... is that... your baby?"

My heart stopped and so did my breathing, realizing I could hear every word through the old, thin walls.

"Danny, Taylor is my sister's best friend from childhood. That's all she's ever been, I promise. I have no idea why she's here, but I've known her for most of my life, and if she came to me because she needs help, I'm won't turn her away. I can't. Not after everything. But I can promise you that is not my baby. I've never touched her. Not like that."

Clutching the counter, I repeated to myself over and over that he wasn't lying.

How could he be lying if he didn't know the truth?

Still, my breaths labored as my heart cramped listening to his promises.

I shouldn't have come.

Turning on the sink, I let the running water drown out whatever came next; I'd heard enough.

I knew he didn't remember that night but learning the truth could ruin the life he'd made for himself here. *Oh God. I should leave.*

My heart beat back its response defiantly; *he has a right to know. He has a right to know what happened...*

Again, my hand went to my belly.

I was lost. Like a sheep that had wandered away from the flock. I'd been lost for months—since the moment I'd tested myself because my period was a day late, and I'd never been late for anything in my entire life.

I squeezed my eyes shut.

This wasn't how any of this was supposed to happen. It was only one night—*only one time...*

Tears collected in the corners of my eyes and I quickly wiped them away when Ash and his girlfriend reappeared, the tension I'd caused between them much less. I pretended not to see when they kissed goodbye, but there was no use pretending I didn't feel the sting.

"Taylor."

My name rang out in the silence, like a call for truth—*a truth I was not willing to part with right now.* He stared me down as I walked back to the old, well-worn couch and sank onto it as though my legs had just run a marathon.

"What the hell is going on?"

My mouth opened and shut like a fish searching for food, only I was searching for words where there was suddenly none to be found.

"I'm sorry," I choked, shaking my head.

"Shit. I'm sorry, Tay," he apologized, dragging a hand through his hair. "I just didn't expect..." I heard his long exhale as he sunk onto the ottoman in front of me, elbows resting on his knees, and his hands clasped between his legs. "Let's start with the most important. Are you hurt? Are you in some sort of danger?"

Only my heart. And only from you.

"No—No, I'm fine." I took another sip of water, but words still felt like they were trying to slide down a partially-wet water slide, sticking and pulling to the sides of my throat as gravity ripped them past. "I'm sorry, it's just been a long night of travel and I didn't sleep well on the plane, plus the time difference."

"And the fact that you're pregnant," he deadpanned, but neither of us laughed.

It was the first time the obvious fact had been spoken.

I was pregnant.

"I can see that nothing gets by you," I returned with a tight smile, scooting to the edge of the couch.

"You're pregnant," he repeated, staring at my stomach like it would deflate any second.

"Yes." I nodded again, seeing the shock begin to consume him.

"Pregnant…"

"Yes, pregnant," I huffed. "As in with child, knocked-up, expecting, going-to-have-a-baby-in-a-few-months pregnant." I pulled the sides of my sweater tight so it molded over me and made the small bump clear.

Hormones.

I blamed the hormones.

His attention snapped to my face and I drew a steadying breath, I began where I felt safest, "I'm pregnant, Ash, and I'm here because my parents are moving back to Nashville."

It was half of the reason why I'd ended up on his doorstep.

There were many decisions I'd had to make since I read

those two little lines. *Is this real? Who do I tell? What do I do? Do I tell Ash? Do I wait until the baby is born? Do I tell him before? Do I tell him right now? Do I wait until the chance of miscarriage has passed?*

And then…

What if he wants me to have an abortion? What if knowing this prevents him from coming back home? What if he thinks I did this to trap him?

What if he doesn't believe me?

Some were more logical than others. Some more important. All equally unnerving.

It wasn't the sheer volume of questions which bothered me as much as how none of the answers, even the ones I chose, seemed right. Everything I picked looked right in one light and wrong in another.

Because hearts were like funhouse mirrors; they distorted everything.

Was he okay? Why did he leave? Was he ever planning on coming home? What was he doing with his life?

But *Who was he now?* and *What if he didn't want our baby?* were the ones which reigned supreme.

And that was why I'd come to the decision to wait until after the baby was born to tell him; there were just too many unknowns.

I wanted to have this baby regardless of whether Ash wanted it or didn't want to be a part of our lives. And when I told him, it would be with the confidence and security that I could do this on my own if walking away was his decision.

I'd lived a lifetime walking through a minefield, avoiding imperceptible bombs of guilt and judgment—one wrong step liable to set off a chain of explosions; I refused to put that kind of guilt on someone else, and have it affect my child in the process.

My child.

I wondered if the phrase would ever seem less earth-shattering.

"So, if your parents are coming back and you left... I'm assuming you haven't told them."

My chin dipped.

Barely three months into this unexpected journey, my mother called to tell me she and my father, who'd retired to Florida several years prior, missed their church and social circle in Nashville and decided they'd split the year between Tennessee and Florida.

As much as I disagreed with my parents on many things, as much as I worried them by working with Blake in an industry 'littered with lust and hate and falseness,' they were still my parents. I loved them and they loved me, but in their own, regulated way.

And unwed and pregnant with the father currently M.I.A... I swallowed over the bitter lump in my throat.

Twenty-six years with Miriam and Isaiah Hastings had given me enough first-hand evidence to know I wouldn't have their support, even though it broke my heart to admit it.

"No, they don't."

I was going to have this baby, but I wouldn't do it in Nashville with the storm-cloud of their judgment drenching me in shame with each step I took.

"I couldn't stay. I mean... because of the baby. You know how they are. I think—I think it would kill them to know..." I trailed off in a whisper, loving God but hating religion for the way its rules destroyed the love founded in faith.

Without experiencing it firsthand, I knew many saw Catholic guilt as something inconsequential to be shrugged off. But if you lived it, *you knew...*

It was like shrugging off a three-hundred-pound cross off

your shoulders only to have religion pick it up and nail you to it.

My confirmation wasn't met with any surprise. Ash had known my parents for many years while we were growing up. He knew the extent of their kindness and charity just as much as he knew the severity of their stringent adherence to what they believed.

Of course, there would be a time and place to challenge their beliefs and test their love, but it wasn't right now. *Not like this.*

And that was how my choice to wait until the baby was born before telling Ash went out the window.

"So… you came here?" he choked in disbelief, wincing when I couldn't hide the hurt from my face. "You know what I mean, Tay. Why did you come to me?"

"Because!" I cried in frustration. "You're the only other person left. Blake, your family, the rest of my small group of friends, they're all in Nashville, and I can't stay there. I'm pregnant, Ash. I'm pregnant and scared and most importantly, I'm doing this alone. I don't want to be alone, and you're the only person I have left who isn't there."

None of that was a lie.

It wasn't the whole truth, but it definitely wasn't a lie.

"You were the only one I knew enough… felt safe enough… to come to," I continued thickly, noticing his surprise. I had a feeling 'brave' wouldn't be one of the first words that came to mind if Ash were to describe himself. "I need to be brave now and I didn't think I could do it completely alone. I need some time to figure out a new plan for my life. For our lives…"

I meant mine and the baby, but the way he looked at me, a flicker of possessiveness I'd only seen one other time flashed in his beautiful blue eyes as though I meant him and me.

He rubbed a hand over his bare chest.

Why hadn't he put a shirt on yet? I licked my lips, really wanting to lick along his chest muscles that stretched with his deep breaths. He looked like Rodin's 'Thinker,' poised in contemplation, each harsh plane carved with concern.

This was not the right time to feel this—to want him.

"Who's the father?"

My heart stopped. The question I dreaded most. The question I knew would be inevitable. I was too close to him… to his sister and family… for him to feel too uncomfortable to ask.

I swore I was going to tell him before he got the chance to ask. I swore I was going to look him in the eye when he opened the door and tell him I was pregnant with a child he didn't know he had because of a night he didn't remember.

But then reality opened his front door instead (And reality was rarely what you expected it to be) with Ash's girlfriend by his side. And I just… *I just couldn't tell him right now.*

I needed to know who the man in front of me was… I needed to know who the father of my child had become.

I needed to process before I could progress.

"Please don't ask me that right now," I pleaded firmly, averting my eyes from his. Maybe it was one more wrong choice, but there was too much at stake. "What matters is that I'm here… why I'm here…"

"Because you couldn't stay in Tennessee," he reiterated slowly.

"Because I came to see if I could stay with you."

Chapter Four

ASH

'I came to see if I could stay with you.'
Each word echoed screamed that there were more secrets behind every answer she gave me. But I was in no position to demand she share them. I knew, because I'd been in her position.

Okay, not fucking pregnant. But I'd been the one to show up here not that long ago, lost and looking for a safe place to collect myself and craft a new beginning.

I knew what it was like to combat an army of questions inside your own head; the last thing needed was an influx of outside support.

No. My help wasn't contingent on her full-disclosure. If she needed me, I would be there. *Just like she had done for me.*

"Okay." I stared down at my locked fingers as I answered her question. *As though there were any other answer.*

I knew her parents and the circles they kept. They were the embodiment of my perception of the Catholic church. So much good layered on top of a foundation which could be so unforgiving. And Tay was too lenient in how she framed their assured response; I knew the unique brand of hell she'd have to live in if she stayed home.

There was this girl in high school, Melanie. She'd been much less interested and less concerned about the church-life her parents, friends of the Hastings and prominent church members tried to impose on her. She'd gotten pregnant my junior year with one of the varsity football players.

Two months after finding out and telling her parents, Melanie committed suicide. I didn't know what was done or said—my family didn't really go to church. But I heard the rumors. I heard they were going to force her to give the child up for adoption. I heard they were going to send her to a nunnery after graduation.

Maybe they were exaggerated—*like rumors usually are*. But then again, she had fucking killed herself.

I didn't care what the hell religion it was, when the punishment for one sin was so severe it drove you to commit another, it seemed to me someone, somewhere had gotten the real message completely wrong.

Taylor was too strong to be shaken like that. She was always strong. Unwavering in her beliefs.

Even in high school, she'd never been teased for being a prude, never mocked for not going to parties or drinking. She was universally liked and unsurpassably popular because people recognize strength, even when they don't understand or agree with where it comes from.

Still, it didn't make me any less relieved that she'd come to me rather than face her parents.

I didn't have much to offer, but what I did, sure-as-hell was judgment free.

"Look," I said, dragging a hand through my hair. "You've had a long night, Tay. Why don't you lay down and rest for a little bit while I take care of some work I have to get done, and then… we can talk again later."

Her head shook side to side, almost frantically. "I can't sleep. Not right now," she confessed. "My mind is just… too much… at the moment." She licked her lips—still the perfect pink arches like I remembered. "I mean, you don't have to stay with me, but I think I just need to go for a walk or something to clear my head."

My mouth thinned. No way in hell I was going to let her go wandering around by herself. Not in her condition. Not after hours of travel. *Not on my watch.*

"Alright, then you're coming with me." It wasn't a question.

And I didn't leave her time to disagree before I went into the bedroom to change.

Aside from Larry and the guys, I hadn't taken anyone out to my restaurant yet. Not even Danny.

But she'd shared her secret, and now it looked like I was going to share mine.

Or one of them.

Taylor trailed behind me out to the construction site which would soon turn into my restaurant. She might have come asking for a place to stay—a sanctuary—but the look in her eyes said she was here for much, much more.

Not just a sanctuary, but salvation.

I'd be lying if I didn't need a walk *'or something,'* too. She'd just dropped a *fuckton* of information on me—too much for my tiny shack to handle—and ocean air always seemed to help with processing.

Maybe some manual fucking labor would make understanding this easier.

...And give my body something to do besides think about how much it still wanted her.

"Where are we going?" she asked quietly.

I was surprised she'd made it this long without asking; I knew how not-knowing ate away at Taylor's need-to-know mind. The Taylor I knew carried around a planner for her planner, and still had every event or engagement for my sister on her computer and phone. On the tour, if anyone had a question, they went to Taylor. Costumes, staging, lighting, sound, songs, timing… she was the know-it-all.

"To my restaurant." That familiar pride bloomed in my chest; *this was mine.*

I turned to check on her as I heard her trip behind me. "Y-You have a restaurant?"

"Almost. It's still being finished," I grinned, enjoying my chance to surprise her.

We emerged from the end of the path down into the clearing, and she didn't ask any more questions.

Sitting out on a jutting piece of rock and earth stood my future. And as if on cue, the first full rays of sunlight streamed over our backs and onto the building. This moment—the beginning of a new day—was never lost on me; the moment when instead of giving in at the darkest hour, you can still choose to rise again.

We'd expanded the house's frame into the modern, single-story structure that sat here now. On the east side, the side that we'd approached from, the exterior still resembled a house with stucco and smaller windows.

"Wow…"

I shouldn't have, but I turned to glance at her. Even though I could still see her exhaustion from traveling, she was still the most beautiful girl… woman… I'd ever seen. My eyes locked on her stomach again.

Pregnant.

Taylor was pregnant.

I knew I wasn't good with processing change—especially change I didn't see coming. And this… I huffed. In my mind, Taylor Hastings had always been this mythical creature. Good and enchanting, but not real. Timeless. *Untouchable.*

But now she stood beside me with undeniable proof that she was real—*and that she had been touched.*

My fist tightened with the inappropriate reaction that someone had touched what belonged to me.

There were so many things wrong with that thought, it was pointless to delve into each of them. But I still had it. I still felt it.

I'd looked at Taylor for so long that at some point, it was a natural assumption that no one would ever touch her. And if someone did, that lucky sinner would be me.

"I bought the house here two-and-a-half months ago. Actually, nine weeks and three days," I began, the memory etched into my mind as I cleared my throat and I unlocked the door. "So, yeah… it's come a long way."

As soon as the door opened, the magic of the location came to life.

The coastline and ocean was visible from the left and front sides of the building, so I turned those walls into windows. Huge fucking windows. The right side, more obscured with trees, was an ideal spot for the kitchen.

I watched as she passed me, wandering right up to the large, thick glass that had been a sonofabitch to install and a downright expensive motherfucker to purchase. And her expression alone was worth all the trouble.

I would've paid ten times what I had if it meant I got to see the way her eyes widened ever so slightly.

"This is… incredible," she breathed. "You did all this?"

"No." I chuckled. Sober or not, I'd never be *that* handy. "I hired people who know what they're doing. But now that most of the big renovations—floor, roof, walls—are almost done, I'm helping where I can. Actually, I don't mind it." I nodded down at the containers of spackle that were here waiting for me, "I'm currently in the middle of spackling this wall. That's my goal for today."

She gaped at me. "I can't picture you spackling." Biting her lip adorably as she laughed.

"Well, I'm not the man who left Nashville five months ago, that's for sure," I drawled somewhat cryptically.

I'd meant it as a good thing, yet the worry that flashed over her face had me rethinking both the words and my tone.

Before I could say anything, she turned back to the window and asked, "And there's a deck?"

I'd almost forgotten about the patio. Two tiers of decking led out even closer to the cliffs above the ocean. There would be a pergola over the first level and then open on the second.

"Yeah," I answered, walking toward her. "We still need to lay the rest of the trek there"—I pointed to the one corner that wasn't finished—"and then, there will be a pergola over this first part."

"You could cover it with twinkle lights," she offered with a half-smile. "Like a little cluster of stars on the coast."

I blinked because I could envision it exactly as she said. She'd been here all of two minutes and suggested something that hinted she could see this place like I did, like a light in the darkness.

"Yeah... maybe," I replied gruffly. "I haven't gotten that far yet."

"It's beautiful," she whispered, bright green glancing up at me. "It's going to be so beautiful, Ash."

I began to reach for her before I realized what I was doing. Thankfully, I did realize—and I realized in time to stop myself.

In that moment, nothing had felt more natural to me than to want to pull her into my arms and rest my chin on her head while we looked out over our future. *Nothing.* Only she wasn't mine to touch and the future I was looking at didn't involve her.

At least in the long run.

"I should go," she continued quietly.

"I left the house open, so you can go back if you want—"

"No." Her soft laugh was like a sad lullaby. "I mean that I should *go*. Like I shouldn't have come to you. I shouldn't have imposed like this—"

"Tay," I cut her off as I grabbed her small hand, stunned by its softness and shocked by the heat it sent raging through me. I'd pictured these hands a lot over the years. Holding them. Touching them. *Them touching me.* "You're not leaving. You're my sister's best friend, practically part of my family. If you came to me because you need me, Pixie, I'm not going to let you go."

I'd forgotten about the nickname I gave her until the moment it slipped from my lips, needing her to know how serious I was.

I didn't know why that last promise sounded a little more permanent than the situation it should have been referring to, but the way her pert lips parted suggested she heard it, too.

"No, Ash, you don't have to." Her voice wavered because even she didn't believe the words she spoke. "I don't have to stay with you. I can get a hotel. I can do something. I'm sorry. It was a moment of weakness. I just never planned on all this." Her voice caught, and I knew she was instantly on the verge of tears. "I don't need to impose on your life; you obviously have a lot going on. I didn't realize… You didn't tell anyone…"

She drew an unsteady breath, and I wanted nothing more than to pull her against my chest like I could squeeze the guilt out of her.

"You don't need to let me just because I'm Blake's friend or because of what happened with her and Zach…"

"*That's not why I'm doing this*," I growled, releasing her hand to tip her face up to mine; there was going to be no mistake about my life here or my actions. "That's not how this town works. That's not how *I* work," I broke off, my jaw tensing as I stepped toward her, eliminating almost all of the dead space between us.

"When I came here, I needed a new, safe place, too. And if that ornery old man you met at the coffee shop who directed you here had turned me away, well, I... I don't know what would have happened. So, no, this isn't out of guilt. This is because at some point, we all need something... someone to lean on. And if you need to lean on me, Tay, I can do that. I will be strong with you... for you. Not for anyone else or because of anyone else. *For you.*"

My head drifted closer to hers. Unstoppable like clouds that followed the breeze.

The way her mouth parted didn't just look like it was made for mine, her lips looked like they were incomplete without me.

But the small hitch in her breath stopped me short.

What the hell was I doing?

I jerked back and, releasing her chin, walked back over to where the spackle was waiting for me. *Nice, simple spackle.*

"Thank you." Her voice was almost as quiet as the steps she took toward me.

I grunted in response, about to suggest again that she could go back and take a nap on the couch while I figured out just how the hell this situation was going to work.

But I didn't get a chance when she asked, "Do you want some help?"

My body tightened feeling her close to me again. Being in her vicinity lit the fuse to a bomb which would inevitably go off if I didn't find some way to diffuse it.

"I'll be okay. I'm a master spackler by now." I picked up some plaster on the spatula and layered it on the drywall with a splat. "You should get some rest." I glanced back, my eyes instinctively settling on her stomach.

Way to be obvious, Ash-hole.

"I'm pregnant, not dying," she teased. "You might as well let me help, now that I'm here."

"Now that you're staying, you mean?"

She gulped. "Now that I'm staying, the least I can do is help you." She reached down for the other spatula. "Plus, it'll get done faster."

I brought the spatula to my nose and sniffed, searching for any scent of chemicals. *Was it safe for a pregnant woman to be around spackling?*

Fuck if I knew.

Cursing, I yanked my hand away when a spot of it brushed on the tip of my nose, causing Taylor to start shaking with laughter.

"It's fine, Ash," she reassured me and began to layer the thick white material onto the drywall.

"You sure you know how to work that thing?" I grunted, wiping off my nose as she spread the goop around.

The eye-roll she sent me, the one made to make me feel ridiculous for asking, that was the Taylor I knew. I mean, mostly everything about her was still the Taylor I knew—from the way she dressed to her eagerness to help to her attention to the small details and the way she always found a way to make an idea better—*like the twinkle lights.*

It didn't end with the eye-roll, though.

"We… my family and I and people from our church… would go on mission trips every summer for as long as I can remember," she spoke as we worked side-by-side, gently layering along the seams and nail holes in the new walls.

I recalled how we saw less of her during the summer. Blake even tried to invite her to the beach with our family a few times, but with no success. No wonder my sister was always trying to hang out with Zach and me over summer breaks… because her best friend was off saving the world.

"Various countries. Sometimes in the states, too. Our church had a volunteer program similar to Habitat for Humanity, and my parents always signed us up. So, moral of the story, is I've got spackle skills."

I chuckled. "Did you like it?"

"Oh, yes." I loved the way her short hair bobbed every time she nodded, like it was trying to make sure the small gesture from such a tiny person was acknowledged. "To see how little some people live with… to see how happy and grateful they are… And to help give them something considered so basic here… There are no words for it."

Her enjoyment was clear as day, but it didn't hide there was still a cloud that drifted over her face.

But before I could ask, she turned the conversation to me. "Was this what you came out here to do?"

I thought for a moment, knowing I needed to tread carefully with my response.

"I came out here to do something for myself," I began with a very vague but very true statement. "And this is where it led me."

She nodded, absorbing the fact. Like the rest of my family, Tay only had a vague idea that I was out here working a new job and doing alright. I knew that was the case because that was all I told Blake or my parents when I checked in with them.

"Was building a restaurant always your dream?" She went right for the sucker-punch.

"I don't know about always, but it is now."

It was hard to remember my dreams before. They felt like needles in a haystack, buried under everyone else's goals and blurred together with alcohol. And, in the process of trying to make those I cared about stand out from the crowd, I'd gone blind to the sight of my own aspirations.

She paused and her attention on the wall turned to me. "Why was your address that coffee shop?"

I laughed. "I helped out at Roasters when I was new in town and didn't have a very… permanent… living situation. And when I bought this place, it was just easier to let what little mail I got continue to go there."

We worked for a while in focused silence, settling into the situation—into our new reality. Concentrating on a simple, repetitive task was like pushing your thoughts through a filter system. With each smaller grade of mesh, the bigger, distracting irrationalities were filtered out until it was only small, simple truths which were left.

That's what I'd found Carmel Cove to be—the finest filter, leaving nothing but love, loyalty, and support behind.

We'd almost finished the largest expanse of the wall when I admitted that her spackle skills far surpassed mine; I wasn't the least bit surprised.

About to comment on it as she bent down to reload, I saw her gaze fog and her head sway as she rose back up. A second later, her body followed suit and she stumbled to the side with a soft groan.

Dropping my spatula onto the floor I lunged for her and gripped her arms, holding her upright before she could topple over.

"Shit," I swore. "I'm an idiot."

She yelped when I hoisted her up into my arms and made for the door.

"Ash! What are you—"

"You're done helping for today," I bit out, kicking the door shut behind us as I carried her back down the path to my shack.

"Wait, no—" she cried. "I'm fine. It was just a head rush!"

"You just got here, Taylor. You just traveled all night and all morning to show up practically crying at my front door. I shouldn't have let you out here when you're exhausted and *pregnant;* you need to rest."

"Pregnant but not handicapped," she shot back, fierceness lighting up her green eyes.

"Well, then consider me too dumb to have remembered that fact when I saw you about to *pass out*," I retorted.

She huffed, her small, soft form sinking deeper against my chest. "I'm fine now. I can walk."

I snorted as I ducked under a tree branch.

"Yeah. And you walked yourself onto my property, into my house, and asked for my help. And that means if I feel like walking is a danger to you, *you're not walking*," I shot back, knowing I was going a little overboard.

Her agreement was muffled into my shirt, reminding me just how too-good it felt to hold her against me like this.

"Fine..." she admitted. "I just wanted to help."

I chuckled as I carried her into the house, setting her feet slowly down to the floor. "And you can still help me. *After you rest.*"

A minute of defiant silence later and she sighed. "Fine, I'll take a nap. But not a long one. Otherwise, I'll never get my sleeping pattern straight."

"Bathroom is in through the bedroom. Only one." I didn't know why I clarified. There was obviously only one bathroom. The shack was hardly big enough for one person.

Taylor froze as I turned back to her, the vulnerability in her face crashing over me like a tsunami and pulling me under this insane need to protect her... care for her... and her baby.

"What are you—Will you—"

"I'll be just down the path for the next few hours if you wake up and need me, alright?" Her shoulders dropped with relief—like she'd been afraid I was going to leave her here... like I had anywhere fucking else to go.

Like there was anywhere else I wanted to go.

"You're safe here, Tay," I said. The simple statement held very serious promises.

"Thank you." She folded her arms over her chest as though hugging me was something she had to hold herself back from.

It was for the best.

Nodding, I shut the door behind me and headed back toward the restaurant and my solitude. I needed to get as far away from this reality which had only ever happened in my dreams.

Taylor Hastings was in my bed.

Taylor

What was I thinking?

He didn't need my help.

He'd come here for help months ago and now was building a restaurant and had a girlfriend.

Did he love her?

My heart felt like a punching bag for life. I wasn't sure how many more hits it could take.

Jetlag and growing a baby made a million thoughts swirl in my head as I bee-lined for the bathroom. Being carried over the threshold made me realize how badly I had to pee.

One thing was for certain, the Ash who opened the door this morning wasn't the one who left Nashville after the tour ended. He still looked the same. He still smelled the same—a kind of spice that made your toes tingle and lingered in your nose, like the scent of cinnamon, long after the smell itself was gone.

And his sense of loyalty was still the same.

'If you need to lean on me… I will be strong for you…'

I pressed a hand over my mouth with the urge to cry. Again.

I didn't cry. *I didn't feel.* It was how I'd stayed calm and rational and *content* for so long—by keeping my emotions locked inside a fence, invisible to everyone else but shocking to me whenever my feelings tried to cross it.

He didn't even know the half of it. He didn't even know how much I needed him for, I thought as my hand sat on my stomach again.

Would he have still said the same if he knew the truth? Would he have still been as calm? As caring?

Or would he have freaked out... turned me away... shut me out... like he did to Blake and Zach?

Ash had always been a wildcard while I'd been raised to value only stability and safety. And this would've been a whole lot easier if I wasn't so hopelessly attracted to the father of my child. But how I felt—how I wanted him—didn't matter anymore. What mattered was the life inside me.

I needed to know what happened to Ash. What changed him. *Who he was.*

Right or wrong, even though I knew this baby was his, I needed to know just *who* the father of my child had become, because it wasn't the same man who'd left Tennessee several months ago.

I thought he'd come out here for a change, but now that I was here—now that I saw the life he was building, I realized how wrong I was.

Now he lived in a shack. He had a restaurant.

He spackled.

There was more to Ash's story. More to his reasons for coming here. And I had no idea what they were.

But I did know there was no indication he had any plans to move back to Nashville—one more thing that added weight to my confession.

I never thought coming out here would be a permanent

thing. It was just until I told him. Just until I settled things between us and could face my family at least with that part of the situation clear.

But this was permanent for him. The way he looked around his restaurant, the way he spoke about it... *This was his dream.*

And telling him he had a child meant the choice he had to make was far more heart-breaking: *to be a part of his child's life, or to pursue the dream he'd finally been given a shot at.*

I splashed some cold water on my face, knowing it probably washed some tears away with it.

Just get some rest.

I turned to the bed and sucked in a breath as my heart zinged. The sheets were still in disarray, painful evidence of what I'd interrupted earlier.

Somewhere between walking out of this cabin and coming back to it, I'd forgotten that he had a girlfriend.

I covered my mouth as nausea rolled through me.

Guess my nap was happening on the couch.

The last thing I did before my head hit the worn threads of the worn denim pillows was to reach for my phone, holding it up to catch one bar of service so that I could text Blake; I knew she'd be worried. She'd been worried before I left.

TAYLOR
I'm here. I found him.

She immediately replied.

BLAKE
Thank God.
Are you okay? Is he okay? Let me know how it goes. Let me know if there is anything I can do. Love you, Tay.

I loved my best friend. I loved how much she supported me with the pregnancy, finding out it was Ash's baby. I loved that she offered to stand up to my parents for me, and I loved that when I refused her offer, saying not only did I need to get away, but that I needed to tell Ash, she bought my flight to California without even asking.

She was a light shining in the dark. But like every other star, just because she could tell me where to go, didn't mean she had any insight on how I was supposed to get there.

Unfortunately, navigating my and Ash's unexpected situation and admitting to him what happened that night was something I needed to figure out how on my own.

With a sigh weighed down by pure exhaustion, I closed my phone, hardly noticing the uncomfortable lumps in the couch as they pushed into my side and let my eyes drift shut; I'd figure out how to answer her when I woke up.

CHAPTER FIVE

ASH

"Larry!" I yelled through the stockroom in the back of the Ocean Roasters Coffee Shop. "Where the hell are you?"

A growl brewed in my chest. I didn't have time to hunt down the stubborn old man who was probably lifting boxes that I—*and his doctor*—told him he shouldn't.

I didn't have time for this.

I'd come back to the shack feeling like a fucking asshole when I saw Taylor curled up on the couch.

Motherfucking Ash-hole.

Of course, she wouldn't want to sleep in the bed where I'd just slept with another woman last night—*another woman that she'd met*. Christ, only a few hours in Tay's presence and I'd completely forgotten about Danny. Or that she'd been there. Or that I probably owed her more of an explanation now that I'd actually talked to Taylor.

I pinched the bridge of my nose as I pushed out the back door.

I hadn't wanted to wake her; she'd looked like a sleeping pixie, exactly like I always called her, with her hair falling over her face, swaying softly with her breath. One hand rested on the slight swell in her stomach, which was hard to even see at this angle, and it made my hand itch to touch her.

I'd seen it before. I knew it was a thing—people wanting

to touch a pregnant woman's stomach. *It hadn't been my thing, though.* Until now. Maybe because I'd known her my whole life, I reasoned; that's why I felt this fucking magnetic draw to the baby she was growing. *That had to be it.*

After stripping the bed and tossing the sheets in the stacked washer and dryer in the closet, I'd woken up Tay since her nap was knocking on the three-hour mark. She looked like she could use a few more, but she was right, it would screw with adjusting to the time change.

I only had mac n' cheese to offer her for lunch. With all the work I'd been doing on the restaurant, I was barely in the shack to sleep, let alone eat.

Making sure she was eating and relaxed, I left to run some errands in town and pick up something at the store for dinner.

"Larry," I shouted with a huff, seeing the suspender-wearing grouch attempting to lift two bags of garbage into the dumpster. I jogged up and took them from him, doing the job myself. "I told you I would handle it."

"I'm not an invalid, Ashton. I can take out the damn trash," he grumbled, turning back to the building. "Did your girl find you?"

I froze in shock. "Danny was looking for me?" *Shit.*

"Not that girl," he said, staring me down with eyes that were old enough to be wiser and more perceptive than myself... and also a helluva lot more irritating. "Taylor."

My head jerked back in shock. "She's not my girl," I corrected him firmly, like I needed to be sternly convinced as well. "She's my sister's best friend, and she's going through some stuff. Needed a friend... and a place to stay."

"I see." He nodded knowingly, having been that safe place himself more times than I knew of and probably more times than he could count.

"What did you tell her?" My eyes narrowed.

He'd called Taylor 'my girl.' Now my guard was up.

"Only the important things."

"Like..."

"Like where to find you," he snapped in frustration before waving me off with a huff and heading for the dumpster.

My eyes narrowed on the back of his skull, wishing I could see into his thoughts. The way he said it made it sound less like he'd given directions and more like I was lost and he'd sent Taylor to find me—to bring me home.

"What does that mean?" I asked cautiously.

He hoisted the bag over the side of the dumpster with a grunt.

"Her baby yours?"

"No." I crossed my arms.

He walked up to me and demanded, "Does anyone know what you're doing out here, Ashton? Because your girl thought Roasters was your home address."

"She's not my—"

"*Does anyone know?*"

"Does it matter?" I countered and immediately regretted it.

Anger waved over his wrinkles. "You know damn well it does. Step eight. Be willing to make amends," he quoted me from the program, though I knew each step by heart.

"I am willing," I shot back and speared a hand through my hair, not prepared for *this* conversation. "But it's not just about apologizing and being forgiven, Larry." I was angry, so angry it made my voice low and tight. "It's about repairing the damage."

He pointed a knobby finger at my chest. "Let me tell you somethin'. Not drinkin' is the easy part. Facing the feelings, that's the hard stuff." His finger tapped against my muscle. "All those good deeds you're doin' won't fix you. You can't repair the damage until you have a foundation of forgiveness."

My chest rose and fell like I was in the middle of a fight, though the only battle really going on here was inside me; I wasn't arguing with Larry. I was fighting against the truth he just happened to give voice to.

"And that first means forgiving yourself."

I spun away from him and gripped the side of the dumpster, hearing the crunch of his footsteps over the gravel as he walked back to his shop.

"And, for the record, I can take out the damn trash, Ashton. Been taking out the garbage in this town for more years than you've been alive," he said it as though used coffee cups and pastry napkins were the least of the garbage he'd had to get rid of. "You should be busy taking care of yourself and your girl."

"She's not my—" I broke off and bit into my tongue. There was no point arguing with him.

"Looks like that'll be the second biggest lie you tell yourself, then," he groused.

I already knew what the first was: *that I didn't deserve anyone's forgiveness, which was why I hadn't asked for it.*

"Now, if you're done hollerin', I've got an appointment with Shelly, unless you want to go talk to the woman 'bout your feelings… might be more productive." He shuffled over to his truck and climbed inside, the faded purple Nissan grumbling to life.

Shelly was really Dr. Shelly Goldner, psychiatrist and friend of Larry's. I'd never met her, but this was the first time he'd indicated that he was seeing her on a professional level and not a personal one.

We all had our demons. But, as Larry pulled away from the building, I realized that he might be even better than I'd been when it came to hiding them.

Shaking my head, I headed for the stack of delivery boxes sitting just outside the door. At least, he hadn't been foolish enough to try and lift these.

Taylor

"Taylor!"

I jumped when I heard him yelling for me, turning my back on the watery horizon that was slowly staining with the vibrant, warm colors of sunset. It looked like there was another good hour or so before the sun was completely down, which is why I decided to go for a walk before Ash got back, hoping the cool air would help clear the fog in my head.

"I'm here," I shouted back, hearing him approaching on the path.

Ice blue eyes pinned me as he appeared in the clearing by the restaurant. "Christ, did you think to leave a note?" he asked with hard desperation. "Scared the shit out of me."

"I-I'm sorry." I shook my head. I hadn't thought to because... "What time is it?"

"A little past six."

Oh, dear.

"Oh my," I gasped, covering my mouth. "I didn't realize I'd been out here for that long. I'm sorry. It was so nice out. I just thought I'd come out here and read for a little." I held up my small, pink Bible I'd brought with me, stickies of all colors turning the edge into a rainbow of marked verses. "I thought I'd be back before... but I was distracted by the sunset."

"It's fine," he interjected, running a hand through his wavy blond hair.

My fingers still remembered how soft it was that night, how they sunk into the silken threads like sand, searching for something to hold on to that would mean I wouldn't have to let go.

"Just... just next time text me or something."

I only nodded. No point in telling him that I left my phone back at the cabin, too.

"The sound of the water, it's so soothing… like I could stand here and listen to it forever," I said quietly as I walked back to him.

"It is… and you can," he agreed. "And in six weeks, hopefully, you can be enjoying a good meal while doing it, too."

I smiled, and we made our way back to the house in silence.

"I got stuff to make fish tacos. Hope that's cool with you."

"Yeah," I said, bobbing my head in thanks as he held the door open for me. I stopped abruptly to turn to him, and he crashed into me, his strong, hot grip closing around my shoulders.

"Woah—what's wrong?"

I just wanted to ask him about dinner. A stupid question about the fish and all of a sudden, I found myself with barely a breath between the two of us, my heart swimming like desire was a great white shark chasing after it.

"I-I just wanted to know what kind of fish…" I said hoarsely.

"Mahi Mahi." His eyes searched mine for explanation.

"Okay, good. I just… I can't have certain kinds of seafood because of the baby." I gave him the reason, but I couldn't hold his gaze as I did it.

"Shit." He dropped his hands and looked down between us. "I didn't even think."

The look on his face assured me he'd have the list of forbidden foods during pregnancy memorized by tomorrow.

"It's fine, really," I said with a shaky laugh, putting my hand on his chest in an attempt to persuade him that it was no big deal. *And it wasn't.*

But my hand on him was.

Right hand. Of course, it was my right hand that chose to rest on the hot muscle pulsing over his heart. I sucked in a breath as desire flared low in my belly, moisture pooling between my thighs as my traitorous memory—that couldn't bother to remember he had a girlfriend—had no problem remembering the way he'd touched me that night.

Girlfriend.

I yanked my hand away and walked backward into the room.

"Taylor…"

I froze—like a kid caught sneaking downstairs in the middle of the night on Christmas Eve, trying to get a glimpse of Santa.

Biting my lip, I turned guiltily around to him, my eyes catching on each of the neatly organized stacks of papers and plans, receipts and invoices that I'd sorted through and organized this afternoon.

He gaped, dragging his eyes along the magic transformation of his clutter.

"What did you…"

"I organized it. Just a little," I admitted.

"Just a little?" I didn't know if it was possible for a guy to squeak, but Ash certainly came close as he walked up to the nearest stack—a pile of invoices that I'd separated based on vendor and date and then color-coded to designate whether, as far as I could tell, it had been paid or not.

"Well, you were gone all afternoon, and you know I need to organize when I'm anxious," I mumbled. "Don't you remember the night before the SATs—"

"When you reorganized my mom's entire spice cabinet?" he drawled. "Yeah, I remember."

I'd grouped the spice jars based on region of origin, then alphabetized, and then stickered with expiration dates.

"You did all this… in the last few hours?"

I whimpered and rushed forward, placing my hand firmly on the pile of receipts he'd been about to thumb through.

"You have to be careful with these," I advised. "They blow over so easily; I lost the pile twice before I finally sorted it all."

I turned to him and realized my heart was even less stable, the look in his gaze blowing over the feeble thing and taking down my breath along with it.

"I see," he said hoarsely. "So, what exactly did you do?"

Gearing up with a long breath, I took the next several minutes to explain how I'd sorted all the papers he'd left in hodgepodge disarray over every surface of the room.

"You know I knew where everything was, right?" Ash asked as he began to unpack the groceries he'd clearly dumped just inside the door, realizing I wasn't in the house.

"I'm sorry, but I can't believe that," I said with a quiet smile. "Not in that mess."

He grunted.

"You didn't have to do that."

"I know, but you should figure out a system early, before things get up and running," I told him. "I can help you, if you want. It's the least I can do…"

He turned the stove on and refocused on me. "You don't owe me, Taylor. Not for staying."

I opened my mouth and clamped it shut as he stepped closer to me. There was only the small corner of the narrow kitchen island that separated it from the cramped dining room.

"My house. My rules."

My pulse thudded and the silence between us became deafening. He was so serious—so insistent—as though he were making up for something… but what that something was, I had no idea.

It certainly wasn't for getting your sister's best friend pregnant while too drunk to remember it.

I pulled my lower lip between my teeth and ducked my head. The oil spitting in the pan broke the tension. "Is there anything you want me to do? Anything I can do to help?" His glare intensified. "For dinner, I mean."

"I think I'm good." He spun away from me and flipped on the sink to wash his hands. Then, in a lighter tone, added, "Have to keep myself primed and ready for when we open."

He winked at me and my lower parts lost their cool. *I didn't know if Ash had ever winked at me.*

Bee-lining for the couch, I sank into its uneven lumps where nothing embarrassing could touch me as it practically swallowed me whole. It was safer to watch him cook from a distance.

Chapter Six

Taylor

I never thought something like cooking could be sexy. And maybe it wasn't. Maybe I was weird, or this baby was doing even more things to my body that I wasn't prepared for. But, *oh my*, did watching Ash make us dinner in his worn jeans and tight tee do things to my body that only in California would be legalized.

Yes, this desire is for medicinal purposes, heart, I swear.

"Do you have a chef?" I squeaked out, trying to distract myself with something.

"You're looking at him." He shot me a devious grin over his shoulder as he flipped the fish in his frypan without even looking.

Wrapping my sweater tighter around me, I tugged the collar up to my mouth as I stared at him in astonishment, finally blurting, "You know how to cook?"

"They didn't call me 'Chef' down in 'Bama for nothing." He chuckled.

I didn't know much about his college life. He wasn't my friend; his sister was. I knew him for a long time, but we hadn't kept in touch; I wasn't even around on holidays because my parents always had a whole host of church and country-club functions that we'd had to attend. Anything I learned was only through Blake… And she'd never mentioned 'Chef.'

"They called you 'Chef'?" I asked as he plated our dinner.

"Our frat house did, yeah. I mean, I'm no Anthony Bourdain, but I would watch cooking shows while I studied and then I figured, why not give it a shot?"

"So, you move out to Carmel Cove, California, buy a building to *renovate* it into your own restaurant and now, you're telling me that you are going to be head chef in that restaurant," I clarified as I met him over at the tiny dining table which had unfolded into something marginally larger. "Who are you, Ash? What happened to you?"

I meant to ask lightly, but the truth was I was desperate to know. The questions burned on my tongue and came out more like an interrogation.

The plates froze just an inch above the table as my questions slipped out. I needed to know, I'd decided.

I needed to know what happened to the father of my child before I gave him this piece of me.

I knew high school Ash who flirted with me either as payback to his sister for crushing on Zach or because collecting my virginal blushes was a far more glorious achievement than sleeping with the string of girls waiting in the wings. And I knew the Zach Parker Project's Ash, manager and professional partier; the man who went out and did whatever it took to make connections and make someone else's dreams come true.

But the man in front of me was neither of those versions.

"Says the girl who used to put nuns to shame and yet showed up at my door pregnant and needing a place to stay. I could ask you the same thing," he returned quietly.

I winced even before the plates clattered on the faux-wood top. He could ask. And right now, I didn't think he'd like the answer.

"Eat up. Hopefully, this makes up for my poorly prepared lunch."

My stomach grumbled.

If there was one thing that could dull the white-hot desire flowing through my veins, it was a delicious meal. *And delicious was a poor description of how good these fish tacos were.*

"Oh my goodness, Ash, these are incredible," I gushed with a hand over my mouth so that I could compliment him *and* continue eating at the same time.

His lips quirked up and moisture rushed between my legs. *Guess it couldn't dull my desire for long.*

"Thanks. They're definitely going on the menu."

I could only nod in agreement because I was too busy stuffing my face.

Blake and I were both tiny but being able to put down ridiculous amounts of food was at the top of the list of all the things that we had in common.

I shifted in my seat when I noticed him staring at me. *Oh no, did I really look like that much of a pig...* My mouth slowed.

Wiping my face, I mumbled, "Sorry, I was really hungry. And I'm eating for two..."

"Well, at least you have that excuse for it now," he said with a laugh.

"Hey!" I swatted him with the back of my hand but couldn't stop myself from laughing, too, before I dug into the second taco on my plate. *They tasted like heaven; I wasn't going to be ashamed.*

"Tell me something," he requested a few minutes later, the serious look in his eye forcing me to pause and my adrenaline to pick up. "Why did you sound sad earlier?"

Slowly, I chewed and swallowed my last bite.

"When you talked about the volunteer work," he continued. "You had this sad look in your eyes even though you sounded like you really loved it."

My gaze dropped to my empty plate, wishing there was something to eat so I didn't have to answer.

Instead, I opted for, "Why do I have to answer your question when you didn't answer mine?"

It didn't matter that I took my chin up a notch; he pulled it right back down.

"My house. My rules."

I sighed, feeling the chill of sadness creep back into my chest. "It just... reminds me of my parents. Hard to believe that people who can care so much and do so much for others can also care so little... How they can be so stuck on rules that they forget the principles behind them... like love... and forgiveness."

A few seconds of silence passed, as we both mourned how people could make choices with the best intentions but lacking love.

"I'm sorry, Tay." He grabbed my hand and his warmth fought back against the cold pain. "You're sure—"

"Yes," I said tightly, cutting him off. "I'm pregnant and not married. I'm sure they won't be okay with it. I wish I wasn't but I am."

I squeezed his fingers, not for comfort, but I needed him to stop pushing. I'd lived with Miriam and Isaiah Hastings for twenty-six years. There were certain things... certain commandments, I'd say if I were feeling poetic, that they'd carved in stone.

Having a baby out of wedlock was one of them.

They were Catholic and old-fashioned and *yes*, there were still people like that in this world.

"And what about the father? I know you don't want to tell me who he is, but what does he have to say? Are... are neither of you interested in marriage? I mean—" he broke off with a harsh breath, "I mean, does he not want to be a part of the baby's life?"

Don't cry. Don't cry.
Do. Not. Cry.

I leveled him with a calm stare, taking a breath so deep that not even sonar could see the bottom of it, and asked, "Would you?"

He was taken aback by my question, his brow furrowing harshly. I thought maybe he wondered if, somehow, my baby could be his; but the rapidity with which it disappeared indicated he was confident it wasn't.

"Honestly, can't say I've ever thought about it, Tay," he admitted, pulling his hand from mine to wipe the back of it over his mouth. "But right now, I can't think of a reason in Heaven or on Earth why I wouldn't. I mean, it's my kid. Of course, I'd want to be a part of his life."

My throat clogged even as I managed a smile.

Even if it meant having to give up your peace, your girlfriend, and your dreams?

The man in front of me was both the same and different from the Ash I'd known, and that knowledge made me even more uncertain and afraid of what his answer would be.

"But he doesn't?" he asked, bringing me back to the moment. "The dad… he doesn't feel that way?"

This time, my gaze plummeted to where my hands were clasped in my lap. Of all the poor timing I'd had since arriving on the 'best' coast, my prayers for mercy—or at least for time— were answered.

Saved by the house phone ringing, Ash groaned and pushed back from the table, he picked up the cordless receiver, about to decline the call when he looked at the caller ID and saw who it was.

"I have to…" He trailed off as he stood, pulling open the front door to take the call outside.

"Hey, Danny. Sorry, babe. Busy day…"

The chair squeaked against the wood as I pushed it back; I couldn't bear to listen anymore. Washing both plates and realizing that there were no dishtowels to dry them, I began to notice just how minimalist Ash's cabin was. *And how it needed a good cleaning.* Thankfully, there wasn't much in it so there wasn't much to keep organized.

Something to do tomorrow—after I found a new OBGYN and made a doctor's appointment.

I didn't want to be here when he came back in. I didn't want to answer any more questions, when there were so many left unanswered to myself.

At least there were clean bath towels in the small linen closet in the hall. Grabbing one, I locked the bathroom door behind me and cranked the shower on hot.

How would his girlfriend feel if she knew?

Shampooing my hair, I chastised myself for thoughts that were borne a little too much out of jealousy and not enough reality.

Danny seemed decent and I hadn't been raised to dislike someone just because she had something that I wanted. And I'd wanted Ash for a long time—a long time filled with strings of other women who'd 'had' him.

But Danny was really pretty. Like a model, with her long brown hair and matching brown eyes, she and Ash looked perfect together.

I glanced down as the water washed the suds off my body. I, on the other hand, was short. Bordering on midget territory. It was okay before… I'd always thought everything about me was at least proportional, though small. But now… the skin of my stomach was stretched with its slight bump, my breasts were much larger—maybe not in the grand scheme of all boobs, but for me, they definitely stuck out more.

And around Ash, they tingled.

Especially because everything he said, about wanting to be in his supposed-child's life, was all the right things. But this wasn't the Ash I knew. And while this version certainly seemed better, it wasn't my life... or my heart at stake... It was my child's.

It wasn't my life or my heart at stake... did you hear that, Heart?

Maybe one night's good sleep in bed would reset my whole body—including all the parts that seemed to wake up only around him.

Groaning, I remembered that there was no bed, only a small couch that, while made for my size, was definitely *not* made for sleeping.

They say sleeping while you're pregnant is incredibly uncomfortable at the end... guess this will be some good practice, huh, Baby?

"Oh, no..." I groaned as I dried off.

My brain seemed to be failing me more and more. In my attempt to avoid further questions, I'd forgotten to bring my suitcase full of clean clothes into the bedroom.

Wrapping the towel around me, I unlocked and peered out the door.

No sign of Ash.

Maybe he was still on the phone...

I cringed as the floor squeaked beneath my bare toes.

"Taylor."

I jumped with a squeal, frantically clasping the towel that was about to drop and reveal behind door number two.

Ash stood in the kitchen, partially hidden by the refrigerator. He looked over at the commotion I created and froze. His blue eyes stormed as he took me in.

In an instant, I was back in Denver. That same look accompanied with so many words of adoration, and even more touches that defied description.

"You… scared… the crap out of me," I said, gasping for breath between each word, my heart beating like a bass drum.

"Sorry. Thought you saw me." And then the look was gone.

My thighs squeezed together as he fully faced me, resting the side of his hip against the counter as his muscles flexed until his shirt pulled tighter over them. All that manual work on his restaurant was paying off in ways that football never seemed to accomplish.

My thighs were wet.

They were dry when I left the bathroom a minute ago.

Maybe I hadn't thought this through.

I'd always been attracted to him. Wanted him. But now I was putting myself in a one-thousand-square-foot proximity to him. All day. Every day.

And with all my hormones.

I gripped the towel tighter, knowing my nakedness wasn't the only thing it was hiding from him now.

My attention snapped to the mason jar he was holding filled with clear liquid, and it reminded me of how much he drank on tour.

"Water," he said as though he knew what I'd been thinking. "For you."

"Oh… thank you. I just… I just came for my suitcase." I rambled, my eyes searching everywhere for something to hang onto before they fell back onto him. "I'll change in the bathroom and then you can have your room—"

"Taylor," he cut me off with a small laugh, strolling toward me. "I'm not letting you sleep on the couch."

"But—"

"No buts," he cut in as my breath got cut off.

When he got close to me, it was as though he were a vacuum, sucking all the oxygen from my air.

"I said you could stay here, and I'm not going to make a

guest sleep on the couch. No fucking way, Pixie. *And I'm certainly not going to make my pregnant guest sleep on the couch."*

I swallowed hard, the steel edge in his eyes threatening me if I continued to argue.

"Okay..." I agreed, reaching for the handle to my suitcase while my other hand tried to keep the towel from dropping.

He just shrugged with another laugh as he took my suitcase from me, the movement brushing his chest against my towel-covered one, my nipples hardening instantly against the coarse fabric.

"I... ahh... washed the sheets, but if you need anything else..." His words trailed off just like my breathing had. He picked up my case with one arm and hauled it into the bedroom without a backward glance.

I rushed over to the couch to fluff the pillow and open up the blanket that was folded on top for him, even more guilt rushing over me and my eyelids fluttered to try to keep the tears at bay.

Anyone would have given me the bed, Heart. What did we just talk about?

"Thank you, Ash," I said from the doorway into the bedroom. "Really, thank you."

Even though it was my decision to come here, I hadn't expected all of this and those two words didn't seem like enough.

He half turned and gave me a lopsided grin that made my need to get to a pair of panties all the more critical.

"You're welcome." He held my gaze for an extra second.

So many times, people brushed off 'thank yous' with 'not a problem' or 'don't worry about it.' But, in the last twelve-plus hours, I'd imposed on Ash's life, relationship, dreams, and home. And he gave without asking for anything in return— *without hardly asking anything.* So when he said, 'you're welcome,' I knew he'd acknowledged how much I'd asked of him and my gratitude for it. And for some reason, that made me feel just a little bit better—as though we both understood just how much it was.

Goosebumps rushed over me in a forceful wave as he walked by me.

"Goodnight," I said quietly.

He paused when we were shoulder-to-shoulder. "I... ahh... have breakfast plans in the morning." *'With Danny' went unsaid but not unfelt.* "I bought eggs and cereal and waffles so make yourself at home and feel free to sleep in, just don't freak out if I'm not here when you get up."

My head jerked in a manner that sort of resembled acknowledgment.

"And don't—" he growled "—disappear without at least a note before I come back," he said with a low, hoarse voice.

His mumbled 'goodnight' reached me just before the bedroom door shut.

And then I was alone. Again.

Although, I was never really alone anymore. I tugged my flannel sleep shirt over my stomach which was much more pronounced after how much I'd eaten.

Still, it felt like there was a piece of me missing when he was gone.

Go to bed, Heart. You're delirious.

Chapter Seven

ASH

I woke up to the most horrible sound. One that still haunted my nightmares and brought me right back to the past. To college. To frat parties. To football parties. To concerts. To after-parties.

To all the morning afters.

I shot up from the couch that I regretted accepting from Larry now having had to sleep on it. The cushions had so many lumps and bumps in them not even a whole fucking season of *Nip/Tuck* would be able to save them.

For a second, I was actually afraid the vomiting noises were coming from me. There were countless times where I'd heard the sounds and didn't think anything of them—until I woke up the following morning covered in my own vomit. But it took even less time to realize they weren't—and that meant there was only one other person who could be throwing up violently in my bathroom.

Throwing the blanket off me, I didn't even think about putting pants on over my boxers. I didn't even think about my morning wood from dreaming about my unexpected houseguest. I didn't think about anything except that she was deathly-fucking-ill.

My hand jerked on the handle.

"Taylor! Unlock the door!"

"No…" She trailed off with a whimper as I heard her begin to heave again.

"Taylor, open the goddamn door right fucking now," I yelled.

I didn't—*couldn't*—care how harsh I sounded. My heart was pounding like a bull trying to escape into the ring. She sounded terrible. *Fuck, what if it was the fish? What if I'd fed her bad fish? What if it hurt the baby?*

Fuck. Fuck. Fuck.

Click.

I threw the door open. Taylor was sitting on the floor in flannel pajamas, her hair in messy, stuck-together strands as one of her hands tried to hold it back. And her face looked greener than the Wicked Witch of the West.

"*Christ, Taylor.*" I fell to my knees beside her, cupping her cheeks, my fingers sliding back to thread into her hair and force her gaze up to mine. "What happened? What hurts?"

"Ash…" She trailed off into a strangled groan and, even though it couldn't physically be hurting me to see her suffering, *it did.*

And it hurt so fucking bad.

She tore her face from mine just in time to dry heave once more into the toilet.

"Shit, Tay, I'm sorry. I'm such a fucking idiot. *Such a fucking idiot,*" I swore, on the verge of strangling myself for doing this to her. "I'm calling an ambulance and taking you to the hospital. It must have been the fish. *Fuck.*"

Her head began to shake an angry 'no' until the sudden movement worsened her nausea and she heaved over the bowl again.

"See, even your body says not to argue with me, Pixie," I grunted.

My hands were on the floor about to push me up when a tiny grip around my wrist stopped me.

"It's not food poisoning," she rasped, her voice sounding painfully ripped apart and raw. After the last round, it looked like the vomiting had vacuumed out every trace of color from her cheeks. "It's because of the baby. It's just morning sickness."

Understanding crashed over me like a hangover after a blackout.

I was an idiot.

I didn't know shit about babies or pregnancy, but who hadn't heard of morning sickness?

Like the explanation cost her the last of her energy, Tay's eyes drifted shut and with a muffled curse, I caught her as she began to tip to the side.

"Are you sure?" I asked against her hair. "Can I get you out of here?"

All I needed was the slight nod against my chest before I carefully lifted her so as to not disturb the beast.

Instead of putting her back in bed, I carried her out to the couch. Yeah, that shit was uncomfortable, but there weren't windows in the back and for some reason, I felt like she needed some fresh ocean air.

Throwing open the windows and the front door, I grabbed a cup and filled it with water. Kneeling in front of her, I held the glass up to her lips, her small hands rising to tip it. After a few hesitant sips, relief spread through me as some color crept back into her face.

"Any better?" I asked, taking the cup back from her and pushing the hair away from her face.

To see her so sick… I couldn't even remember any of my drunk friends—and definitely not myself—ever looking so terrible.

"I'm okay," she said, softly. "Sorry. Hasn't happened that bad for a little while."

Probably from the flying and stress of yesterday, if I had

to bet. Still, I offered, "I'm still willing to let my fish tacos take the blame."

That brought a weak smile to her face.

"Well… maybe you should put a disclaimer on them for pregnant women…"

"Ouch." I laughed. "Alright, guess I'll have to do something a little more low-key tonight. You're really testing my chef-ing limits, Miss Hastings."

The hardly a quarter of an inch that her smile grew made my chest swell farther.

"*Damn*," I swore, finally letting out the breath that had been wedged with pure panic inside my chest.

Returning briefly to the kitchen, I wet a paper towel with cold water and brought it over to her. Brushing a strand of hair back from her face, I gently laid the cool compress on her forehead before my hand drifted down to her cheek, my thumb brushing over the soft skin that had just a touch of pink back in it. "You scared the shit out of me, Pixie. You really did."

I lost myself in her eyes, their murky green clogged with the emotions she fought so hard not to crumble under. Eyes that were always strong, eyes that always had a plan and knew everything; they were still strong but also wary. There was no plan for this—for the turn her life had taken. She saw only a few steps in front of her, but the rest was an unknown. I knew that life; *I saw only a few steps because I was too drunk to see any further.* But she didn't. No plans. A different future. I knew what that meant to a mind like Taylor's—and I knew how hard she was trying to hold it all together in front of me.

"Sorry…" she croaked, her eyes falling from mine. "Thank you… I-I'm really okay now. You can go… I know you have plans."

Shit.

I'd forgotten about Danny.

I looked up at the clock on the microwave; it was quarter

'til eight. Even if I was going to meet her for breakfast, there was no way I was making it on time. Unfortunately, late or on time didn't matter because I wasn't going.

"Not anymore," I said firmly, reaching for one of her hands and pulling it between mine, beginning to rub the muscles in the webs between her fingers.

Her eyes widened and her lips parted into that tiny 'oh' that made my dick hard in an instant. *Rock solid.* For the pregnant woman who still may or may not still have a trace of green on her face from being sick.

"Ash, please," she pleaded, guilt sickening her features. "I'm really fine. This has happened before, it's just a little morning sickness. I'll be back to normal in just another minute... Please, don't cancel your date. Not after yesterday..."

As much as I mostly believed her, I wasn't going to take the chance in case she really was sick and needed me.

She exhaled a soft moan as I rubbed the muscles harder, the movement slowly taking more green from her face.

My body tightened at her lie... *and her moan...* and the way her eyes squeezed shut as she beat herself up for intruding in my life. This needed to end right here. She'd come to me and asked for my help.

No one had ever asked for my help like this before.

No one came to me for shit like this because I was just Ash. Ash, the asshole. Ash, the partier. Ash, Blake's brother. Ash, Zach's manager. I'd always been a means to an end. Then Taylor showed up and for the first time, I was the answer, not the fucking question.

My decision was made. It was final and it was done. Whatever effect it was going to have on my life, I'd accepted it when I told her to stay. I wouldn't have her continue to guilt herself over something I'd freely decided.

And in this case, there was no way she would be back to

normal that quickly which meant there was no fucking way I was letting her out of my sight.

"Taylor, look at me," I demanded, reaching up to cup her face, and waited until her gaze finally found mine. "I'm not leaving you—not after what I just saw. I don't care how normal you tell me it is. I don't care how much you insist you'll be better in a hot fucking second. *I. Don't. Care.* I'm not leaving."

All the while I spoke, my thumb brushed over her cheek, creeping lower and lower as protectiveness pumped through my veins until it touched the plump pink flesh of her lower lip.

"But—" Her lip quivered under my thumb.

"No buts. My house. My life. My decision," I said tightly, adding, "Danny will understand."

At least I hoped she would. Although, it probably would be best to leave out how Taylor had needed to remind me about her and our date.

"I disagree, but I feel too gross to argue," she replied begrudgingly, pulling a laugh from my chest as I rubbed my hands on top of my thighs.

"Good. Now, what do you need? I don't know about morning sickness—or any of this, obviously… but it does sure look a helluva lot like a hangover and I do happen to know a bit about those, and eat, even though it feels like it could make it worse, actually helps," I assured here and offered, "I also happen to have a magic breakfast meal for just these situations."

"Mmm, it does help, actually," she murmured. "Food… and then maybe more of that hand massage."

I winced. The feel of her small fingers in mine, soft and strong. *Capable.* I rubbed them while I thought about them wrapped around my dick that was as hard as a goddamn pole.

"Let's start with food," I grunted. I needed to recover before I touched her—however platonically—again.

As I stood, she tacked on with that adorable

embarrassed-to-be-asking tone of hers, "Also… if it's something spicy, for some reason I've found that help—"

My attention, which had been focused on ticking off in my head the ingredients for my hangover waffles, dropped down when her voice strangled to a halt.

Fucking great.

With the emergency of the moment passed, I—*and she*—both realized my lack of clothing.

Forget an outline of my dick, I'd been staring at those lips of hers too long for me to not have a full-fucking erection right now that was right at eye-level for her.

I expected a million things. Turning away. Full-blown fainting. Hell, I wouldn't have been surprised if she burst out some Hail-fucking-Marys to cleanse her soul. I wouldn't have been surprised because that was how it had always been with her. Never affected. Never interested. No matter what I did. *No matter how it made me burn up inside.*

I didn't expect hooded eyes and heavy breaths.

I didn't expect her to lick her lips like it was all she could do not to lick my cock.

I didn't expect to want someone, so entirely untouchable, so unbelievably badly.

"Ash…" she said, a little too breathless and a little too dangerously.

What the hell was wrong with me?

Here I was, standing in front of her with my dick waving a goddamn white flag, eager to surrender my sanity. Meanwhile, she was physically ill. *And pregnant.*

Both things one might think would make me want her less. They didn't. They made me want to make her feel good. *Better than good.* They made me want to make her feel safe and protected and beautiful. They made me want to mark her as mine. To offer her more than my help.

It wasn't the familiar spark of desire. I knew because desire was what I felt for Danny.

This... this was so much more. It was consuming. Demanding.

I knew exactly what it was; it was everything I'd come to escape.

It was the beginnings of an addiction.

"Let's get you some food," I rasped, sounding like my voice had just been dragged over a cheese grater as I turned and walked away, pretending that last moment had never happened between us.

The only thing worse than an addiction was an addiction to something you couldn't have.

"Hey, Isla," I said with a half-smile as the tall, pale blonde's head appeared above a vase of flowers.

"Hey, Ash." She peeled her gloves off and came over to the end of the counter where I was standing. "What can I do for you?"

Isla was the owner of Fleurtations, the local flower shop in Carmel Cove. And there was only one reason why a guy like me was walking into a shop like this: *I needed to apologize.*

"I need a bouquet. Don't care what or how much it costs. Nothing too flashy, just nice."

Her nod said that she knew exactly what (and probably who) it was for.

Pushing a small card at me, she instructed, "Just write down the name and address where I should deliver it. I can probably get it there tonight if you want. I have two weddings tomorrow over at Rock Beach, so my day will be shot."

The Rock Beach Resort and Spa was one of the major golf resorts in the area, owned by Larry's daughter, Jackie, and her husband, Rich Vandelsen; actually, it was *the* major golf resort in the area—world-renowned and all the hoity-toity bullshit that came along with it. I'd never met Jackie, but my impression was that she'd cut all ties from her *commoner* family when she'd married into old money.

"That works perfect. Thanks so much." While she charged my credit card, I quickly scribbled down Danny's name and address on the card, writing a brief note on the back that I was sorry. *Again.*

Danny said it was fine on the phone. That 'she understood.'

And that's how I fucking knew it was not fine and that there was no excuse. I was a recovering alcoholic, not an idiot. I still had a few working brain cells left.

Thanking her, I barely heard the door ding on my way out.

As soon as I was on the sidewalk, all thoughts of Danny vanished as I trekked eagerly back to the Carmel Market, a few blocks down from the flower shop, where I'd left Taylor.

After breakfast, I'd instructed her to make a list of everything that she needed. Crackers. Vomit bags. Whatever the hell it was, she needed to write it down and we were going to go out and get it. Relying on her love of absolute preparedness, I hadn't had to ask twice.

I was almost to the grocery store, passing right in front of Ocean Roasters, when I heard shouting coming from out back. And part of that shouting was definitely coming from old lungs that, just because they could project the volume, didn't mean they should.

"Now, you listen here. I told you I wasn't sellin'. I don't care how much you offer me. This is a family business and it's gonna stay that way. Now get the hell off my property before I call the cops."

My feet picked up the pace as I heard a new voice respond to Larry.

"You can refuse all you want, old man. But, from the looks of it, you won't be around much longer, and I don't see any of the rest of your family lining up to take over. Fact, looks like they've all moved on from this... from you," the other voice snarled.

I rounded the back, seeing the two men standing behind the building next to a giant blacked-out truck with the emblem 'Blackman Brews' in written in gray flames on the side.

"You're done, Ocean. No one gives a shit about your stupid coffee shop and your family doesn't give a shit about you. Do them a favor... leave them with something worth something. They're not here for you now, you think they're gonna want your piece of shit business?"

"Hey!" I yelled, my chest vibrating with rage. "Who the fuck are you?"

The tall, built man in a dark, expensive suit and tie whipped around, his bald head like a goddamn reflector screen as it caught the sun.

"Could be asking you the same thing." He eyed me up and down, the only purpose to assure himself he could take me down if necessary.

"Leave him alone, Ashton," Larry said, his voice shaking with an emotion I'd never heard before. "And you," he addressed the asshole. "Get the hell off my property. *Now.*"

The cocksucker had the nerve to just smirk, like he knew he'd won something.

"You'll be calling me, old man," he said with the slippery confidence of the snake who convinced Eve to taste the apple. "You'll be calling me when you realize that this town and your family are over you. When you got nothing left, you'll come crawling back."

His truck roared to life like he'd trapped the hounds of hell inside the engine, and he drove off.

My gaze whipped to Larry whose shoulders collapsed the second the truck was out of sight.

"What the hell is going on, Larry?"

Wild eyes met mine. "None of your business, Mr. Tyler."

I drew back.

I was always 'boy' or 'Ash' or 'Ashton.' Never 'Mr. Tyler.'

"What the fuck do you mean none of my business? I just happen to walk by and hear some nut-job yelling at you, threatening you..." I trailed off, my arms waving, as Larry just walked by me, his face having gone from red to white.

Too white.

"Goddammit." I grabbed his arm, forcing him to stop. "Do I need to ask Eli? Do I need to call the Covingtons?"

The Covington brothers—Dex and Ace—were former military who'd come home to Carmel after their service and opened up a private security firm just outside of town. Their family had been close friends with Larry for a long time.

With surprising strength, he yanked it from my grasp, the unquiet in his eyes really beginning to worry me.

"Just trying to bully me into selling the shop, happy now? Been dealing with scumbags like that for longer than you been alive, boy, and I expect to continue to have to for the foreseeable future. Happy now?"

"No," I ground out.

"Too bad. Now leave me alone." And then he was gone.

I'd never seen him like this before. And I'd never heard of Blackman Brews.

But this was the goddamn problem with people who lived their lives answering everyone else's call for help: after so long, you only know how to respond... you forget how to ask.

What happened to Taylor pushed her to ask. What happened to me pushed me—*forced me*—to ask.

I had a feeling that there was no force strong enough on

this earth—aside from maybe his granddaughters or Eli—that could push Larry Ocean to reach out to the *many* whose lives he changed for some help of his own.

My jaw tensing, I pulled out my phone and called the only person I knew who knew Larry better than me.

"*Hello, you've reached Eli Downing. Sorry I missed your call...*"

I stalked toward the grocery store, seeing Taylor waiting outside for me, amusing herself by looking in the window of the art gallery next door.

"Hey man," I spoke into his voicemail. "Know you're on a job so I'll keep this brief. Not sure if you've talked to Larry lately or know anything about Blackman Brews, but some guy was just harassing and threatening Larry about Roasters. Something's not right—and something's not right with Larry." I paused. "Also, did you know he was seeing Dr. Shelly? As a patient? I wouldn't call if I wasn't fucking worried. Call me back."

Chapter Eight

Taylor

"Mick, Miles, this is Taylor," Ash introduced me to his two, hunky construction-worker buddies as they stepped down from the giant white truck that had Madison Construction emblazoned on the side.

Aside from the old man at the coffee shop and Danny, these were the first two people I'd met from Carmel.

I hadn't realized how much of a toll that travel and stress combined with growing a human would have on me. Morning sickness had wiped me out for most of the morning the last two days, leaving Ash to go about some semblance of his prior life until about lunchtime.

Eager to feel like I was doing something besides eating his food and stealing his bed, he gave me all of the information and papers and internet access I needed to organize the business end of the restaurant. Though I think he really caved because my other offer was to help him with the manual labor inside the restaurant—sanding, spackling; I also knew how to cut and install molding.

Needless to say, he gave me as much information about what still needed to be done as he could find.

"Mick Madison, ma'am." The much larger one on the right stepped forward first with a teddy-bear smile and deep Southern accent as he pulled off his hat to reveal buzzed, sandy-blond hair.

"Nice to meet you." It felt like I was shaking the hand of a bear as he gently clasped my fingers in greeting.

"Miles," the other twin grunted, his smile much shorter and briefer than his brother's before his attention picked up the small bump in my loose tee and swung up to Ash with an arched brow, clearly believing there was more to the story.

"Taylor's a family friend," Ash answered the unasked question with a steady stare. "She needed a place to stay, so she's going to be my guest for a little while."

I caught Miles' chuckle and dancing eyes, suggesting he obviously thought there was more to our situation, but my attention reverted back to Mick when he spoke.

"Are you enjoying it here?" he asked pleasantly as we began to walk out to the restaurant. "My brother and I moved up from Texas a few months ago. Best decision we made." He paused. "Well, except for the paper straws and the strict carry laws. But, you can't win 'em all."

I chuckled.

"I am enjoying it. It's so beautiful. And this…" I trailed off as we walked through the clearing, the view off the cliffs stealing my breath once more. "This is incredible."

Mick nodded. "Ash has definitely got a success story in the making right here with this property, with his ideas. No doubt about it."

"I got lucky," Ash grunted behind us, listening to our conversation.

"You know luck had nothin' to do with it, my friend," Mick smirked.

The four of us paused at the front door. "You puttin' her to work, Ash?" Miles demanded jokingly. "That doesn't seem very gentlemanly of you."

His hands rose up in innocence.

"Actually, I asked to help," I interjected and proudly

presented the stack of papers I'd held underneath my arm. "So, I spent the last two days organizing what's left of the construction schedule, made a timeline for when inspections need to be complete if Ash wants to open on time, and have spreadsheets of what needs to be ordered—broken down by equipment, technology, supplies, and disposables."

When I finished, I had to look down and make sure I still had all my clothes on because I wasn't sure I'd ever had *three* sets of male eyes trained on me so intently before.

Miles nodded to Ash, pleasantly surprised by my answer.

"Damn," Mick muttered and then asked, "Can we hire her?"

"Well, unfortunately, Miss Taylor," Mick informed with an apologetic smile. "We're workin' on the kitchen drywall for the next few days, so I don't think you'll be able to stick around with the dust and chemicals and all... in your condition..."

My stomach dropped. "Oh, okay." I nodded. "That's fine."

It wasn't fine.

I'd organized everything. Everything that I could. And cleaned. I needed something to do.

"Have you been into town yet?" Miles asked, earning a sharp glare from Ash.

"No, I haven't."

"Let her take your truck, man," he continued.

Ash's expression tightened as he put a hand on my shoulder and when my eyes met his, I realized he wasn't upset that I was going into town; he was concerned that he wouldn't be with me.

"Keys are on the counter," he said, staring at me as though we were the only two people on the planet. "Just be careful."

"It's Carmel, Ash," Miles snickered. "She'll be fine."

I gave him a reassuring smile. "Thanks."

"Make sure you grab a blueberry muffin at the bakery and coffee at Roasters," Mick suggested. "Cove classics right there."

"Decaf coffee," Ash said, crowding toward me. My brow furrowed. Maybe it was common knowledge that pregnant women needed to avoid caffeine… "Call me if you need me."

His fingers tightened for a split-second on my shoulder, pulsing warm, protective heat to every corner of my body before he released me.

I nodded and swallowed over the lump in my throat. I needed to stop reading into every concerned touch and caring gesture. I needed to, or my heart was going to end up with a confession of its own.

"Nice to meet you," Mick grinned.

"See you around, short-stack," Miles tacked on, leveling me with his own nickname.

Ash let out a low growl and Miles' intrigued smile only grew.

What I wouldn't do to be a fly on that new drywall over the next few hours…

"Good morning!"

The friendly exclamation came barely a second after the welcome bell signaled my entrance into Ocean Roasters.

"Hi." I flashed a shy smile at the brunette standing behind the counter.

Her cheerful eyes were framed by large glasses and her long brown hair was plaited down the back of her skull in a French braid to rival Rapunzel.

As I walked up to her, I glanced around the coffee shop which, as the sign outside indicated, had been around for over a century. It felt familiar—and not just because I'd been in here a few days ago looking for Ash. There was a sense of communal nostalgia which seemed to bleed from the dated furnishings, worn fabrics, and numerous photos.

It felt comforting. Warm. Even to an outsider.

"I'm Eve," the barista introduced herself with a sunny smile. "You must be Taylor!"

My step shuffled ever so slightly. "I am... How did you know?"

"Oh, crap!" she exclaimed. "Sorry, I'm not a stalker. Larry told me Ash had a guest, and then when Ash stopped in the other day, I asked him about it, you know, because we used to work together, so I figured I'd get the scoop—" She broke off with a small shake of her head. "Sorry."

I laughed and relaxed against the counter. "It's fine. I am Taylor, Ash's guest. It's nice to meet you."

"So nice to meet you," she beamed back. "And I love your hair, by the way," she gushed and my fingers instinctively went to my short, wavy locks. "I wish I could pull off short hair. I do a *ton* of yoga, which makes this old thing"—she pulled her braid over her shoulder—"a huge pain in the butt, but I've just never looked good with short hair."

I chuckled as she shook her head.

"Contacts and short hair... Both just not made for me." She sighed with exaggerated resignation before her eyes popped wide and back to me. "I'm so sorry. I'm totally rambling." She adjusted her glasses again. "What can I get you?"

I glanced to my stomach. "Decaf. Something decaf, please."

"Not a problem." She winked and set to work on my drink. "So, you're a friend of his from Tennessee?"

"His sister's."

She nodded. "So, what are you up to today?"

I sighed and glanced outside. "Not too much," I confessed. "I wanted to help Ash with his restaurant, but I've been barred from the premises because of the baby."

"Oh, no."

"Yeah... I was told to get some coffee and a fritter." I shrugged. "I guess I'll take a look around town. I'm going to be staying... for a little while, at least... and I'm nowhere near maternity leave, so I'm going to see if there is anywhere looking for part-time help."

"We are." Her smile bloomed as she set my mug of steaming, dark liquid in front of me.

My mouth parted. "Really?"

I hadn't had a chance to talk to Ash about it, figuring I would help him with his business until I couldn't and then look for something else. I just hadn't expected that day to come so soon.

"Absolutely!" She clapped her hands together. "It's just Larry and me now. Although, my sister, Addison, runs a recovery house for women, Blooms, so I may have a few girls from there willing to help out, but we could totally use you!"

Excitement bloomed in my chest. I wanted to do something—to give back—somewhere. And if there was any place Ash wouldn't take issue with me working at, it was here, where he'd worked, too.

"Use her for what, Eve?" an age-worn voice rasped from the back room a second before Larry, the old man and owner who'd I'd met the other day, appeared.

Unlike most men his age—I assumed seventies though I had a feeling it was more like eighties and he just looked really good—Larry had a full head of perfectly combed gray hair, tan skin, a strong jaw, and a full smile of straight teeth (when he chose to reveal them.)

Eve patted a hand on his shoulder. "Taylor is looking for

some part-time work, so I offered if she wanted to help out here."

His gaze focused on me from behind narrow frames.

"I'd think you have your hands full over there, Taylor," he drawled slowly.

I took another fortifying sip and replied, "I was just telling Eve how I can't help Ash with the restaurant right now because it's not safe for the baby."

"I wasn't talking about the restaurant," he informed me without missing a beat.

Oh. He meant Ash.

I caught Eve's small smile in my periphery.

Well, I did have my hands full with Ash.

My hands... and a lot of other parts of me...

"Do you want to work here?" he asked bluntly, moving on from his loaded statement.

I couldn't say that working in a coffee shop had been the first thing that came to mind. Honestly, and ironically, my first thought was to head to the church and see if they needed help with any of their charity programs.

But instead, I surprised myself by saying, "I do."

I felt comfortable here, even though I had no clue what to do. I felt welcomed. And, selfishly, the thought lingered in the back of my mind that Ash had worked here, with these people, so maybe they could give me more insight into the good man who was guarding his own secret.

"Well then, you're hired." Larry went on with matter-of-fact gruffness. "Eve can show you the ropes."

"Thank you."

Well, if that wasn't the easiest job interview I'd ever had.

"Oh, this will be so great. It's just been me for like two months now and, before that, it was only Ash, so it'll be awesome to have another girl here."

"I should warn you, I have no idea how to work that thing." I stared at the espresso machine behind her.

"Pavi?" *The machine had a name?* "Oh, I can teach you that." She chuckled. "Come on, let me give you the official tour before I send you on your way for one of Josie's muffins. Whoever suggested them was absolutely right; they are little bits of heaven in every bite."

Chapter Nine

Taylor

"Hi, Taylor. It's your mother..."
I looked down at my stomach, my mother's voicemail fading against the voices in my head.

I loved this baby, each day more than the last, but it would be a lie to say there wasn't at least one moment out of the day where the vestiges of my upbringing made me feel ashamed of my situation.

It had nothing to do with being strong—even strong people felt guilt.

And it had nothing to do with being Catholic.

You should be skinnier, reality TV said.

You should have more curves, tabloids of the Kardashian's whispered.

You should be able to have a job, raise your kids, keep a perfectly clean house, full social life, exercise, and have a healthy relationship with your husband, social media insisted.

You should be married before having sex or having a baby, religion reminded me.

Whether it was Facebook or the Holy Book, guilt was universal.

It stared back at us when we looked in the mirror and reminded us of all the areas we fell short and all the ways we were *less*.... Less than perfect. Less than acceptable. *Less than loved.*

Guilt was like intoxication. It didn't matter what kind of drug or which kind of alcohol was used, they all distorted reality until you no longer saw who you really were.

A fat teardrop landed on the face of my phone as I stared at my reflection in it.

My mother's voicemail had been short. *Guilt doesn't mince words.*

I wondered how long it would be until I heard from my parents. I hadn't told them I was coming out here, afraid of the conversation it would spark.

"Why are we just finding out, arriving to an empty house, that you've gone out west on vacation? Don't you think you should have mentioned it? I had so many events planned with women from the church. I thought it would be good to cleanse you of the sins I'm sure you were exposed to while on that... tour."

She said tour as though it had been a VIP exclusive journey through Hell itself.

"Hey."

I yelped as my phone clattered to the floor and I jumped up from the bed.

Ash stood in the bathroom doorway, wearing nothing but a white towel wrapped around his waist. I'd thought he was still outside working, but I must just not have heard him over the washer and dryer running in the closet right in front of me.

"Sorry. Hi." I grunted as I bent forward and retrieved my phone. "I didn't hear you in there."

I could foresee the single bathroom situation becoming a problem. Well, any situation that involved Ash in a towel felt like an act of terrorism on my nerves. An unexpected attack that completely destroyed me.

Towel terrorism.

It wasn't like I hadn't seen him in a towel before. There

were plenty of times I'd seen Ash in various states of undress when I used to stay over with Blake. But the crush of a girl was a whole different ballgame than the desire of a woman—and this woman had wanted her best friend's brother for far too long.

"Shaving," he muttered as he took a few steps toward me. "What's wrong?"

I set my phone to the side like the voicemail made its judgment infectious. "Nothing." My fingers knotted in my lap.

He just stood there. Waiting.

I sighed. "My mom just called and left me a voicemail. It's not a big deal."

"What did she say?"

I pursed my lips and looked up at him, noticing a spot just underneath his bottom lip where a drop of blood pooled where he must have cut himself.

Without thinking, I pushed off the bed, grabbing a tissue from the nightstand along the way, and reached up and wiped the drop off his skin.

Without thinking how close it brought me.

Without thinking how intimate a gesture it was.

His nostrils flared and I saw the domino of the way his jaw tensing tipped down over the muscles in his neck and onto his chest.

I jerked my hand back, relieved when no more blood appeared. "Sorry, you were bleeding."

"I see that," he replied with a low rumble, wiping his hand over his chin. "What'd she say?"

I shrugged. "The usual."

"And California of all places... Taylor, they are loose with their morals out there. I'm just so shocked and disappointed. I sincerely hope you are going to church at least twice a week, and that you call or just come home soon. I have a list of good,

Catholic men for you to meet. You've waited far too long to settle down."

His eyebrows rose like golden arches.

"I didn't tell them I was coming, so of course she's upset to come home and not find me there."

"You mean upset that she doesn't get to parade you around as the Bible's poster child?" he retorted.

I managed a brief smile. "And the fact that I came out to California…"

He sucked in a mocking breath. "Seventh Circle of Hell right here."

That managed to draw a laugh—but the laugh loosened the tear that had been trying to hang on from the corner of my eye.

"Don't worry about her, okay?" He grabbed a tissue and brought it to my face, gently capturing the tear. "Don't call her back. Don't deal with her until *you* are ready."

My lips parted when the warm pad of his thumb brushed against my skin, dispersing a warm spray of sparks along my cheek.

"I'll try…" My voice was frail and flickering.

Drawing back with a forceful clearing of his throat, Ash let his hand fall away from me, as though he realized he'd gotten too close.

"I'm heading into town to meet Danny," he informed me, walking over to the chest of drawers and pulling out clothes.

"Oh."

Do not covet.

Do not covet.

"Okay."

Do not cry.

"You okay here?" He looked over his shoulder. "I don't have to—"

"I'll be fine." I refused to meet his gaze. "I'm *not* a baby... I'm just having one."

He chuckled. "Yeah, until you see a mouse in here."

"What!" With a squeal, I scrambled onto the bed. "There are mice in here?"

By now Ash was snort-laughing at me. I didn't know what it was, but mice were just the one critter I couldn't handle.

"No," he said between laughs. "Remember that one time—"

"Yes," I snapped.

Blake and I had been having a sleepover spa night when we first started high school. We bought face masks from the grocery store, complete with freshly sliced cucumbers, and whatever else we thought happened at the spa.

We'd had our robes on and were relaxing on their couch downstairs when Ash and Zach snuck into the room and planted a dozen tiny rubber mice all over our stuff and then, announced their presence by throwing one at us and yelling, '*There's a mouse!*'

I didn't know it was possible for my heart to stop and then beat so fast before.

"You guys screamed *so* loud, I think you woke all of Franklin up."

I groaned even though I was chuckling too. "Not cool."

My laughter died when, instead of going into the other room to change, Ash walked back into the bathroom and only partially shut the door.

I couldn't see anything—but that wasn't the point. I could if I walked over there and pushed it open... I could see him if I wanted to.

"Anyway, how was your afternoon? Did you get a muffin?"

"Good." I kept my eyes down and resumed my spot on the bed, folding my legs underneath me. "I did get a muffin—with Eve, actually, who I met at Roasters. And I talked to Larry again."

"Oh, yeah?" He opened a drawer and pulled out some of his clothes. "How did that go?"

"Well…" I began slowly, hesitantly allowing my gaze to slide back to him. "I might have ended up with a job at Roasters."

"*What*?" The door flung open wide.

At least he had a shirt and jeans on now—even if those jeans were only partially buttoned.

I cringed as he stalked a few steps toward me.

"Why would you do that?" He huffed. "I'm going to have to talk to Larry—"

"No! I asked for it—if I could help."

"What is it with you and wanting to help?" he demanded.

"Because I just can't sit around and do nothing, Ash," I argued. "I won't."

He crossed his arms. "I don't think growing a baby is doing nothing."

I rolled my eyes. "You know what I mean," I told him. "I need to be productive. Otherwise, my mind will start making all kinds of other lists"—*like all the ways I'd fallen short*—"that I'd rather not think about."

He didn't look convinced.

"It's just in the afternoon. And it's not like you can stop me," I challenged. "That is outside of your house and therefore, outside of your rules."

"It is outside my house, but without my truck, how are you going to get there?"

Crap.

I hadn't thought that all the way through.

"I can walk."

"*Christ*," he swore and wiped a hand over his mouth with a heavy sigh. "I'm not trying to stop you, Tay. Just want to make sure you aren't adding too much weight to your shoulders."

"It's just going to be a few afternoons, that's all."

"Well, you're welcome to take my truck, if you need it," he offered. "I just have a meeting… community thing… on Tuesdays, so probably better if it's not then."

It took me a second to respond because the way he mentioned this meeting seemed strange. I wouldn't have thought anything of it except that he said it with almost too much information made me feel like there was something he was hiding.

Was it Danny? But why wouldn't he say that?

My pulse deadened to a heavy thud. Or was it something to do with why he'd come all the way out here?

"Thank you," I replied before my thoughts got carried away. "I just want to have something to do while I'm here."

"How long do you think you'll stay?"

I froze.

Until I know what's changed about you, Ash Tyler. Until I feel safe enough to tell you about your child.

"I'm not—"

"Tay," he cut me off. "That's not how I meant it. I was just… wondering… you're welcome to stay as long as you need."

I nodded silently.

"You sure you're going to be okay?" When I looked up at him this time, he was dressed and ready to leave.

He looked so good. Jeans molded along his legs. Gray long-sleeve tee tight against his muscles, the three little buttons in the front opened to reveal a tempting triangle of skin.

For a second, I let myself wonder what it would feel like if the way he took care of me was because he felt something more for me than obligation to his sister's friend.

For a second, as I sat cross-legged in my old flannel

pajamas, the front of them starting to strain against my stomach, I let in jealousy.

"Taylor?"

"Yeah." I nodded frantically. "I'll be fine."

"Seriously, don't worry about your mother. Not now."

I smiled at him, wishing my mother was who I was thinking about. "Thanks."

He stared at me for another long second and I could see the debate in his eyes whether or not he should leave me right now.

"Go," I insisted. "I'm sure I've already made you late. I'm fine, really."

With a tight nod, he murmured goodnight and left the room and, a few seconds later, the house altogether.

Falling back onto the bed, it was only when I heard his truck climb the gravel drive that I let silent hot tears begin to fall.

I shouldn't want him. *I couldn't want him.* It would only make what I had to do that much harder.

Because wanting him would require climbing over a mountain of obstacles I hadn't come prepared for.

And after a full day ending with that familiar *less than* feeling, my tears quickly drew my out onto a deep sea of sleep.

So deep, I missed the messages Ash sent to check on me that made it through the black hole of cell service.

So deep, I only vaguely recalled him returning, peeking in through the bedroom door to make sure I was okay.

So deep, I didn't notice he'd come back less than an hour after he'd left.

And that was for the best.

Otherwise, that mountain of obstacles would've gotten ever so slightly smaller—*and ever so slightly within my reach.*

Chapter Ten

TAYLOR

Two weeks later

I stared at my phone, clearing my second alarm so I wouldn't miss my doctor's appointment this morning. I'd never needed alarms, though I always set them. And I definitely never needed two. Until a few days ago when Ash told me to take his truck and meet him and the Madison brothers for lunch in town—*and I'd slept right through it.*

I didn't know who was more freaked out—Ash, rushing home, freaking out that he thought I'd fallen off a cliff. Or me—panicked that I'd never slept through—never missed anything in my entire life.

It had taken some time for me to do my research to find the OBGYN I wanted to see out here. But after listing all the options, reading all the reviews, looking up every past job and office she'd worked at, I'd decided Dr. Lee was the one. I'd become a borderline doctor stalker, but I was willing to accept the title if it meant I felt a smidge more comfortable heading into this appointment.

Blake had gone with me, back home in Nashville; she'd come with me to every doctor's appointment after the first—after I went and confirmed the news the pregnancy test had broken.

But now I was alone.

I thought about telling Ash—asking if he could take me. But I worried it was asking too much without giving him the truth. And I still wasn't ready to do that. He said all the right things. He did all the right things. He didn't push me. He cared for me... protected me... if not a little too much... *But he hid something.* And sometimes, a lot of good somethings hide a really bad something. Each day that passed left no doubt that he held onto a secret just like I did, and I needed to know just how good or bad it was.

After that first night, every meal was curated around what I wanted, what I craved, and what I was allowed. He claimed it was good for him, after spending so much time out working on the restaurant, to have a reason to come home and cook and keep his skills fresh.

After that first morning, he didn't make breakfast plans again. I knew because he was always waiting with seltzer water in hand, followed by some sort of egg concoction with a healthy dose of hot sauce.

I insisted again on finding a hotel room, seeing the toll his lumpy couch was taking on him. Or an apartment. Something so that he could have his bed back. The problem was, every time I tried to suggest something that he didn't like, he got close to me; he got in my face. And it made my hormones—pregnancy and otherwise—run faster than Secretariat winning the Triple Crown.

But my heart wasn't extra-large. My heart couldn't handle the impossible pace without faltering. My heart couldn't handle being in a race it couldn't win.

I couldn't want him.

Even though I was having his baby.

I tried to help... to make up for my imposition in other ways but he always refused.

So, I began to spend a majority of my afternoons helping out at Roasters. Except those Tuesdays. Tuesdays were still a part of the mystery I hadn't been able to solve. But what I did realize was that he was seeing Danny less and less.

He'd gone out with her one time—that he'd told me about—since that night. And every time he stepped outside to take her call, all I heard was how he made excuses about not being able to see her with so much going on.

Most of the time, he said it was because of the restaurant—which wasn't a lie. He was out there from dawn until dusk almost every day. But it was also hard to completely believe when he treated me as though I was his only concern.

I was pregnant and far from home. *I knew that.* But it always felt as though it was just a little more than that.

I knew I should've been torn up with guilt—an emotion I should have a Ph.D. in by now. Instead, my heart jumped when he fought to keep me living with him. My heart jumped at the lingering looks and brief touches, as though our bodies were passing secret notes behind our backs. Soon, I'd have to see how high the darn thing had gone so I knew just how far I should expect it to fall.

Because it was going to have to fall.

Hearts don't have wings.

I jumped as the screen door shut.

"Ash, hey," I stammered, shying back behind the kitchen counter. "I-I didn't expect you…"

He looked at me strangely because I was being strange. "You didn't expect me… in my own home?"

Yup, I was being stupid and strange.

"I mean. That's not what I meant. I just… you said you were working out at the restaurant all morning. I was just about to come out and ask if I could borrow your truck this afternoon."

"Oh yeah? I told you, you don't need to ask to borrow it."

"I know, but I don't want to take it if you need to run for something for the building. I just… it's just better if I ask first." That's how I was raised. There were certain rules that I, clearly, could be tempted to break—asking before taking wasn't one of them. "I won't be long. I should be back before one."

"Shit," he swore under his breath. "Forgot what day it was. I actually need it this afternoon. It's Tuesday," he told me like that was explanation enough. "Let me see if Mick can just drop me off."

Tuesdays at one.

At first, I thought this sacred time was for the dates he'd managed to squeeze in with Danny. Of course, I'd asked, but he just brushed it off as some community meeting. *But why wouldn't he be able to tell me about a community meeting?*

I had a feeling this was the bad something—the thing that held me back every time I wanted to blurt out that I was carrying our baby.

Whatever he'd been doing out there had him in a sweat. His shirt clung to every lean rise and fall of his chest. If he just moved his arm, I'd be able to see the outline of his nipple and—

"What are you heading in for?"

I froze and my eyes widened as he looked at me. Remembering what day it was made him recall that I didn't work at Roasters on Tuesdays for exactly this reason.

"Taylor?"

Fire blazed into my cheeks. Maybe the wanting him had gotten worse recently. The staring at him when he wasn't looking. The only pretending to sleep so that I could catch a glimpse of his chest and the sharp V that led below his towel when he came out of the shower at night.

Goodness, Taylor. Keep it together. Keep it in your pants.

"S-sorry. Pregnancy brain fart." *I still felt guilty for blaming everything on my—our—poor child.* "Just errands… you know…"

I shuffled around him, my hands just making the keys jingle when strong male fingers wrapped around my wrist.

"Taylor."

Oh no.

I felt the oxygen begin to respectfully depart from the room as he stepped closer to me.

"Why are you going into town?" he demanded.

With the way he was dressed—and the way I was already fantasizing—I confessed the truth before I did something even worse, *like kiss him.*

"I have a doctor's appointment. For the baby."

His eyes narrowed. "Why didn't you want to tell me?"

I wetted my lips. "I didn't want you to feel like you had to—"

"I'm coming with you," he interrupted me, plucking the keys from my hand and stalking toward the bedroom.

"No!" I blurted out like I was afraid that the nurse would take one look at the ultrasound and announce to Ash that he was the father. "Ash, this was exactly why I didn't tell you!"

His sense of loyalty and duty was beyond compare.

"Just gonna rinse off and then we'll leave."

"Ash, wait. Please," I begged, startled and almost crashing into him when he spun and actually listened to me.

"Taylor," he said with that gravelly voice that melted everything below my baby bump. "I understand that this is your baby. I respect that. *I respect you.* But I also respect that you came to me, you asked me to help you, to help… you get through this. And here, that doesn't mean you just crash on my couch and I try to live my life as close to what it was before you. *Here… with me…* when you ask for help, you get my commitment to see this through. You get my promise that I'm going to be there every fucking minute whether you need to lean on me or not, *I'll be there.*"

Panties. Heart. Resolve. They were all dropping like flies.

It was a wonder that Secretariat managed to live with his giant heart because mine felt like it was about to tear at the seams any second; it was already leaking tears down from my eyes. Tears that he carefully, because his hands were dirty, wiped away one after another as my shoulders silently shook.

"I know I don't have a right to be there. But the only way I'm not going is if you can stand here right now and tell me it's because you don't want me there. Not because you feel bad or guilty or embarrassed. *But because you don't want me,*" he uttered, holding the keys out to me.

I looked to the keys, tempted to take them. Tempted to run from a scenario that *should* be happening. He *did* have a right to be there. And I *did* want him there. *That was the problem—it was too close to everything I wanted. And too close is always too far.*

Dragging my gaze back to his, I whispered thickly, "I… I think I'd like it if y-you came."

"Well, Miss Hastings, your baby is perfectly healthy and the size of a bell pepper," Dr. Lee said as the wand slid around in the cool gel on my stomach.

Dr. Lee was a petite Philippino woman with short black hair that flared out at her shoulders as though it caught the wave of the nineties and never looked back. She had kind, wheat-colored eyes, a stout frame, and enjoyed talking about her four cats as though they were real children.

I hadn't realized how anxious I'd been until I heard Dr. Lee's words. I'd worried about the flight… the travel… I don't know what I thought, but I'd worried about the worry.

"Thank you so much." I sighed with relief.

"And it's okay that she got really sick two weeks ago?" Ash blurted out from his post the corner of the room.

My gaze swung slowly over to him. He'd been standing there, entranced since the first image appeared on the screen. The black and white moving blob moving as the ultrasound tracked the life inside me.

I didn't know how to describe the look on his face, though I knew it was one I'd never forget. Part awe. Part fascination. And a little bit of something that made my heart beat harder and my body heat up.

It had been awkward; there was no doubt. We got here and I assumed he would wait in the waiting room. I even thought about mentioning it to confirm. But I didn't. Selfishly, the unfamiliar environment made me desperate for his warm, familiar presence by my side, even though I wouldn't ask it of him. *Selfishly, I wanted the father of my baby with me whether he knew it or not.*

Spoiler alert: he followed me.

He didn't correct them when they called him Mr. Hastings—which made me giggle at how ridiculous *that* was. And he didn't even have to step out of the room because I hadn't needed to undress. Though, I felt like nothing short of a stripper when the nurse asked me to lift my sweater over my stomach.

"You were sick?" Dr. Lee asked, looking to me with concerned eyes like I'd forgotten to discuss this with her.

"Just some morning sickness," I insisted. *Not a big deal.*

"But you said that you hadn't been sick for a few weeks," Ash again interjected with a huff. "Sorry, Dr. Lee. I don't know much about this process, except from what I've read."

I gaped at him. *Read? What did he mean 'read?'*

"All I know is she woke up looking like death, vomiting worse than a frat brother after homecoming, and said that she hadn't been sick like that in weeks."

Busted.

Glaring at him, I explained, "I also flew across the country the day before and had little to eat and even less sleep."

Dr. Lee seemed to relax at that. "It's not uncommon to have a few latent spurts of morning sickness even after the first trimester. It may continue for the rest of your pregnancy or it may subside altogether." She pulled the wand off my stomach. "But everything looks healthy on the ultrasound, and we'll have your bloodwork back in a few days to confirm."

"Thank you."

"Of course," she said with a calm smile. "And… Mr. Hastings?"

"Just Ash. Please."

"Ash." She nodded as she cleaned off my stomach. "It never hurts to ask. I'm glad Taylor has someone like you here for her. It's unfortunate how increasingly rare that is becoming."

My heart squeezed. *I was lucky.* Ash didn't even know he was the father and he was still here, making sure everything was okay, looking out for me… looking after me.

His hair was still damp, the blonde strands slightly darker in some spots as he walked up to the bed. Instinctively, my hand went to my stomach, worried that he could see right through the skin to the baby holding the 'I'm yours' sign up in my womb.

When I looked up, Dr. Lee was gone.

"Just making sure you're okay, Pixie," he rasped unapologetically, brushing that one strand of hair that always seemed to fall right in front of my face like it was waiting for his caress.

"I know, I'm sorry," I said like it was enough. *It wasn't.* "Thank you for coming. You didn't have to, and you didn't have to come back with me."

"I did," came his firm reply.

My gaze dropped to his other hand that hung right next to him. I wanted him to know I was grateful; *I was more than grateful.* And this was the only way I knew how to show him.

Grabbing his wrist, I met his look of surprise and clung to it as I pulled his hand up, praying I wasn't pushing this a step too far.

He saw my intent and didn't pull away. His eyes darkened to deep-sea blue as I placed his palm on my stomach.

Instantly, his attention snapped to the firm softness underneath his fingers. While he stared at his hand, which seemed to dwarf the expanse of my stomach, I couldn't stop staring at him.

The gradual tightening along his hard jawline, the way his eyes flooded with an almost animalistic possessiveness laced with need the second the tips of his fingers touched onto my bare skin.

"Thank you," I uttered with a breath just as strangled as my heart was.

It was all I could do to not burst out into tears and admit right then that it was okay for him to check and worry, that he wasn't an outsider, that he belonged here if he wanted it…

And in equal measure, it was all I could do to not push his hand lower down to where my thighs squeezed together.

I swallowed a moan as his fingers either rubbed or twitched against me, setting off trails of fireworks all along my nerve endings. I hated how I was both desperate for his gentle care and possessiveness but also starving for more of him… his body… his desire.

"Ash…"

I'd forgotten what it was like to be touched. I'd forgotten what it was like to be touched by him.

That's how things that are too much for us to process work—like childbirth, or so I'd read; at some point, the body forgets the stress and pain it endured to protect itself.

That was me.

I'd forgotten what it was like to have his hands on me

because I knew it could never happen again, and living with knowing what did happen could never happen again was more than my body felt prudent for me to suffer.

"I should get you home," he said, each syllable clogged with honor and protectiveness, along with a thousand other things that couldn't be said. "I'll be outside."

The heavy moment between us ended. *Even though the brand from those fingertips still lingered on my bump.* And without another word, he turned and left the room.

I'd been raised to have a very long fuse when it came to desire—one that was only set to go off once there was a ring on my finger. But around Ash… and especially in my current condition… it felt like that fuse was barely perceptible, and the bomb it was attached to was the size of California.

And there was a good chance that when it went off, it would send the state sinking into the ocean.

Chapter Eleven

TAYLOR

"What did you mean when you said you'd read?" I asked once we were back in the truck.

I caught the faintest trace of a blush rising to his cheeks.

"I read stuff." He shrugged.

"What stuff?"

He huffed. "I borrowed a book from the library, alright?" he confessed. "After the whole morning sickness incident, I freaked out. I don't know shit about pregnancy, so—"

"You borrowed a book?" I gasped. I couldn't believe what I was hearing.

"Yeah." He tried to brush it off like it was no big deal. "I borrowed that *What to Expect When You're Expecting* book. Apparently, it's like the baby bible or some shit like that."

"When have you been reading it?" I was surprised my mouth could form words with how dry it was.

I had my own copy of the book downloaded onto my phone. I'd already read it three times, took notes, and made several cheat sheets.

"After you go to bed," he told me. "Don't want to wake you by watching more of *Vikings*, so I read."

After a full day of working on his restaurant, checking in on Larry at Roasters, and making me dinner, instead of sleeping, he was taking the time to learn…

To be there for me.

"Ash—" I broke off with a hand in front of my mouth, instantly on the verge of tears.

Gosh darnit, Hormones. I couldn't get one day? One day in peace?

"I'm about halfway through." He held up a finger, and I knew his manly clarification for the exquisitely sweet gesture was coming. "I was only getting a couple of pages in a night because I'm a slow-ass reader, and it's pretty boring. Obviously, not for you. But I think my nose is permanently damaged from the few times that damn book has fallen on my face because I nod off."

I covered my mouth as I laughed and felt like I wanted to cry. Pretending to squint and examine the perfectly straight and sculpted ridge of his nose, I told him, "I think you just managed to make it away unscathed."

He smirked at me. "Yeah, well, that's because I realized it was on audiobook. So, I've been listening to it while you're at Roasters and the guys and I are workin' on the restaurant."

My mouth dropped. "Seriously?"

With Mick and Miles?

"Yup." He met my eyes. "And yeah, Miles is *exactly* how you would expect him to be about it."

I bit my lip and laughed, imagining just what kind of response Ash was met with when he told two grown men to turn down their blaring country music that I could normally hear from the cabin if I was home, to listen to a book about pregnancy.

"So, shouldn't you know if it's a boy or girl by now?" Ash asked as we turned out of town, once again alluding to the store of knowledge he'd accumulated under my nose.

I wanted to say more about the book—about him reading it—but I could see how desperately he didn't want me to turn it into the big deal I felt like it was.

"Yes, technically. But I don't know if I want to find out." I'd indicated on my forms that I didn't want to know the sex of the baby, though as time went on, my decision could still change. My head jerked to him hearing his snicker. "What?"

"What do you mean 'if?'" He laughed harder. "If planning was an Olympic sport, you'd take home the gold, silver, and bronze."

"Actually, the only thing I'm taking home is baby," I retorted, watching as that quickly quieted him. "You're right. I probably will. I guess, I'm just kind of getting used to not knowing everything about the future. It's uncomfortable, but I think it's good for me."

"Well, if it's a boy, I think you should name him Ragnar."

"Oh my—No, we cannot name the baby after your favorite Viking," I said, shaking my head and laughing.

I'd walked out of the bedroom the third or fourth night after my arrival to find him engrossed in a show on Netflix. I'd just finished up an online sermon from Life Church; I'd found them while on tour with Blake and watched their services weekly when I couldn't make it to church. And now that I was out here, I found myself back on their website, seeking comfort in my faith and God's love, trying to drown out the shame my parents' version of religion had instilled in me.

I hadn't planned on staying, but the way he was watching, I couldn't help but stop to see what the fuss was about. Thirty minutes later, I'd watched the rest of the show and Ash looked up at me with expectant eyes, wondering if I was down to watch another. Usually by the second episode of the night, I was half-asleep with Ash rubbing my feet.

My laugh cut short when I realized he wasn't laughing. Weighted eyes sunk into mine and I realized that I'd said 'we'... when I'd implied that he was a part of the naming committee that should have solely included me.

The loud grumble from my stomach interrupted and sent his eyes to the clock.

"Shit."

"What's wrong?"

There was a beat of silence as he tried to figure out how to tell me something without actually telling me.

"I'm gonna drop you off at the coffee shop, if that's okay," he said, turning off toward the center of town instead of continuing back to the house. "Otherwise, I'm not going to make my meeting in time."

It was almost five to one. I'd completely forgotten he'd said he had something to do at one.

"Of course, that's fine. I told Eve and Jules we needed to re-organize the stock room to work with the inventory system I created, so I can get started on that," I rambled slightly.

"You met Jules?"

I nodded.

Jules was Larry's youngest granddaughter by his daughter, Jackie. I hadn't met Jackie or Jules' father, Rich, but I gathered from Eve they thought they were too good to associate with the Ocean family or the town Jackie had grown up in.

"She's only stopped in a few times—the first, just to talk to Larry; I didn't even know who she was until Eve told me," I went on as Ash pulled the truck up outside. "But she'd been sticking around and helping me. She seems really nice."

And it was easy for me to empathize with someone who, too, felt like she wasn't living up to her parents' unrealistic expectations.

"I haven't met her," he told me. "Honestly, I wasn't sure she was even let off the resort."

I hummed. *Interesting.* "Well, she mentioned wanting to go back to school, so maybe we'll see more of her."

Being incredibly organized, I found my niche, spending

the afternoons creating spreadsheets and systems to get things back in order. Still banned from the restaurant, and having cleaned the cabin to the point where surgery could have been performed there without concern, I'd made a lot of headway with the storage and inventory system at Roasters along with Jules' help.

"Thanks."

This was the first time I'd be there on a Tuesday. Usually, Ash had the car for his weekly 'meeting'… maybe Larry knew what they were all about.

"I think we could maybe order some shelves online for the back here so that everything isn't just stacked in boxes everywhere. This way it's easy to see what we have and what we don't," I strategized with Eve as we stood in the back room, looking at the mess of boxes that disappeared and was replenished almost every week.

Roasters was still doing well, but it was easy to see—especially from the photos on the wall—it wasn't what it used to be. *That Larry wasn't what he used to be.*

I'd only met him a few weeks ago, but even over that time, I noticed a change.

We both jumped at the loud banging from the roof.

"Are they up there *now?*" I shook my head, pushing out the back door to look up on the roof.

Eli returned to town yesterday from a job in Monterey. Tall, dark, and handsome, the contractor stopped by the restaurant in the morning, greeting me with equal parts of Mick's kindness and Miles' intrigue before he shared a few amusing stories of what the building had looked like when Ash first purchased it.

They'd both gotten a good laugh when I made the mistake

of thinking that Eli was Larry's grandson, but seeing them together today made me feel justified in my mistake.

He'd driven me to Roasters on his way out and he'd mentioned he'd be stopping by today to fix something on the roof.

"Eli!" I yelled.

"He's on the other end, Miss Taylor." Mick's jovial gaze greeted me over the edge of the roof.

For a second, I wondered if the old roof was sturdy enough to support that large of a man.

"Would you tell him to keep it down? The lunch rush is here!" I shouted back, hoping Eli would at least catch a few words.

With a mock salute, the grinning giant disappeared again.

It was easy to live in Carmel—*it was easy to feel like you belonged*. Strangely enough for California, the Cove seemed to be a small pocket where no one pretended to be perfect. Not that Nashville wasn't overall kind and welcoming, but there, there were too many people—too many friends of my parents or part of the giant congregation of my old church that judgment felt like it was infused into the air and disappointment laced into the leaves and the fields and the trees.

Here, everyone came together and looked out for one another, all knowing that life will throw things at you that you least expect—*knowing that sometimes, you just couldn't do it alone*.

Walking back inside, I saw Eve talking to Larry and my heart began to pump faster. He hadn't been here when Ash dropped me off about forty minutes ago but now was my chance to find out something about this mysterious meeting.

"Didn't expect you here this morning, Miss," he said with that gruff warmth that made me smile and press up to kiss his cheek. "They better not be making you work any more than you already badgered me into letting you."

"I'm pretty sure I asked, not badgered," I said with a grin. "Ash… had a meeting… so he had to drop me off here."

The glimmer in his eyes answered my first question—he knew exactly what, or who, Ash had a standing reservation with every Tuesday.

"How are you feeling?" He glanced down to my stomach.

"Good. Better." My hand rested on my bump. "I think the ocean agrees with this baby."

He winked at me—a sight that had become less and less frequent over the past few weeks. "Or maybe it's just Ash that agrees with baby."

I flushed, knowing he thought there was something between us no matter how I (and I presumed Ash) insisted that there wasn't.

"Larry," I chided. "I told you. It's not like that. It can't be like that."

"Can't?" He chuckled as his hand on my back pulled me toward the front of the shop. "Life's too short for can't, Miss Hastings."

"He has a girlfriend." *I didn't even know why I was bothering to argue. Maybe I hoped he'd be able to convince me otherwise.*

"Irrelevant." He waved me off. "He's not right for Danny and she's not right for him."

"I doubt she thinks that," I grumbled. "And even if you're right, there are still too many things… between us."

"So, share them." *Like it was that easy.* He began to run the decaf espresso machine, making me a special baby-approved blend with a splash of coconut milk.

I stared down at my stomach. "Sometimes sharing comes with a lot of responsibility."

When I looked up, he was watching me again and anxiety hit me like a brick. *Had I just given it away?*

Please, Lord. No…

"I mean, he won't even tell me where he goes on Tuesdays, let alone what happened to him... what made him... move across the country," I said nervously, trying to pass it off like I didn't have bigger secrets of my own.

"Maybe it's better that way," I rationalized quietly. "I've already got so much to process, maybe I'm not strong enough to handle whatever it is."

He stared at me for a long second before returning his attention to the machine, until it was finished. Part of me wanted to keep talking—to change the subject. The other part won out and kept silent, waiting for whatever was brewing in Larry's mind to pour out along with my cup of coffee.

"People," he began as he added milk into my cup, "are like coffee beans, Taylor. We all got different flavors, come from different places, different climates. Some are blonde. Some are dark. Some Italian or French. But none of that matters when you put that bean in some hot water, whatever's inside will always come out stronger in the end."

Was he talking about me?

I really hoped that a normal person would be on the verge of crying like I was. *Goodness, this pregnancy was going to cost me a fortune in tissues.* I sniffed and reached for a napkin just in case.

"Larry," Eve sighed lovingly as she walked by. "Are you giving the coffee bean speech again?"

She shot me a wink as she kept working and let the old man get back to what must be one of his classic pearls of wisdom.

"Sometimes," –he put the toasty to-go cup in my hands, ignoring Eve—"hot water happens, and people don't like to admit they're stronger for it, because admittin' something like that comes with the responsibility of bein' stronger, you understand?"

I nodded.

"But it also means admittin' to the time before... a time when you were less strong. Sometimes, that comes easy to people... and sometimes, people are stubborn and need a little push."

I dabbed the corners of my eyes, catching the hopeful, hinting glint in his stare.

"You look a little overwhelmed, Taylor. Maybe you should enjoy your coffee while walking up three blocks and then making a left once you reach the Isla's shop, Fleurtations; you'll probably finish about two blocks after that on the right."

And then he was gone—leaving me with coffee, a roadmap, and a whole lot of wisdom.

Although I couldn't be sure if it was Ash or me who needed the little push.

My mind lost in thought, my feet followed his instructions. I waved at Isla, who was in the window of her floral shop redoing the gorgeous displays. I followed my feet two blocks down on the right, taking the last sip of my latte as I looked up at the Carmel Catholic Church.

Why would he send me here?

Did Larry know about my parents? My past?

I looked up and down the street, searching for another explanation, until the doors opening captured my attention.

No, he didn't. He'd sent me here to find Ash.

Sure, there was that chance that in Ash's transformation, he'd turned into a church-going person.

However, there was no mass on Tuesdays. *There was only one reason to go to church on a Tuesday afternoon...*

Chapter Twelve

ASH

I should have just skipped the AA meeting today and taken Taylor home. I just… I hadn't missed a meeting since Larry brought me to my first one. It wasn't a crutch, it was a commitment—the one I'd made to myself. And after what just happened in the hospital, I needed something familiar to calm the swell of feelings I didn't recognize.

"Hi, my name is Ash, and I'm an alcoholic." My introduction came after several in the group had already spoken.

The words weren't repetitive as much as they were a reset, reminding me each week where I started; because the first step in going anywhere is to know where you are.

Start where you are.

I looked around the room. Larry wasn't here today. He didn't make it to every meeting the last few weeks, claiming he had some things to handle at Roasters. I knew they were short-handed since I left, so it didn't bother me so much that he wasn't here, but I was still concerned where his head was.

"I've been thinking a lot lately about labels." Seven pairs of eyes watched me intently as I spoke. Two of them—Drew and Mindy—were new today. "I've had a lot of them. Brother. Son. Football player. Manager. Friend. That's not the full list, though the ones I left out were for the sake of avoiding profanity."

I paused as a small chuckle rippled through the group.

"But alcoholic…" I sighed. "That's a tough one to shoulder…. Alcoholic."

There was a murmur of agreement.

"But today, I touched a pregnant woman's stomach—Wait, that came out wrong." My groan was swallowed up by the laughter that overtook the room. "Alright, alright. I'm not a creep. My friend is pregnant, and I took her to her doctor's appointment today…" I trailed off, waving my hand as the rest of the explanation was obvious.

"So, my friend… she came to me for help," I continued as the room grew silent. "Nothing crazy, just came and asked for a place to stay—a place to get things together."

The group nodded, understanding the premise of the situation.

"If you don't know, I live in a shack," I informed them with an ironic laugh. "And I'm talking accommodations might be better if you committed a crime and were sentenced to a cell rather than the tiny, decrepit cabin I live in." I held up a finger. "Though I promise you, the food wouldn't be nearly as good."

I shook my head until their amusement softened.

Use what you have.

"So, I don't have much, but I offered it to her—whatever she needed." I bent forward, linking my hands in front of me. "And I gave her my support. Every day. I'm still giving her my support."

Do what you can.

"And, it made me think about that label. Alcoholic." I dragged a hand through my hair. "Because of that label, I'm here. Just like all of you." My eyes linked with each of the other's in the circle. "Because of that label, I'm judged. Maybe just like some of you. Because of that label, I wake up each day feeling like I have to do more than the rest of the world to make up for the mistakes I've made. Maybe just like some of you."

I drew an unsteady breath.

"But because of that label, I was able to be here for her. I was able to take care of her. To feel her baby," I said, the awe I'd felt when my hand rested on Tay's stomach and the life moving inside it permeating my voice and making my throat thicken.

Because of that label, she was here, and I was able to feel a whole lot more for her than I should—than I had any right to. *But this wasn't the time or place to share that…*

"Because of that label, I was able to help someone, just like you can."

A strange laugh slipped from my lips and I brushed a hand over my cheek, stunned by the wetness I found there.

"I regret the things I did while alcohol ruled my life, nothing will change that. But today, I was less ashamed of that label than I was grateful for where it led me."

My eyes drifted shut and all I could see was Taylor lying there with my hand on her stomach. There was so much emotion to that moment it felt like it exploded inside of me, blowing through everything I thought I knew, everything I felt.

"It was only a split second, but if I'm being honest, it was the first time I felt nothing but gratitude for everything that happened to bring me here. It was the first time, I thought to myself, '*I wouldn't change a thing.*'"

The silence drew out and I wondered if anything I said even made sense.

It probably didn't.

How the hell could I regret what I did but not where it brought me? The whole idea of it seemed wrong, and yet, it was how I felt.

"Thank you, Ash," the leader of our group in Larry's absence, Dan, said softly.

There was soft commotion as everyone stood and he closed out the meeting. As I gathered my few things, I was stopped by every single person in attendance to privately thank me for sharing. In all the times I'd shared my story, this had never happened before.

"I wish Larry had been here to hear that," Dan said as he walked with me to the door.

"Well, I'm sure somehow... someway... it will get back to him," I replied dryly with a crack at a smile as I stepped through the door.

Glancing at the clock on the way out, I saw we'd finished a little early. Wondering how I was going to explain this to Taylor, I stepped out behind a few others from the group onto the steps of the church and realized there was nothing to figure out.

She was here.

My body lit up with tension, first at seeing her, and then noticing the cup in her hand—realizing who was responsible.

Dammit Larry.

This wasn't his goddamn secret to spill.

My discussion with my sponsor on how to mind his own damn business was going to have to wait though, judging from the look in her eyes.

"Ash..."

I growled, "I know I owe you an explanation, but not here."

I *could* say the things I wanted to publicly, but I wanted to tell her privately

Taking her free hand, I led Tay to where I'd parked my truck half-a-block down the street. She trailed after me, jogging slightly to keep up.

I yanked the door open. "In."

I hadn't felt this on-edge in a long time. From the second

I touched her at the doctor's office—it wasn't just the connection I felt to the life growing inside her, the feeling of responsibility for her and for the baby, the feeling that all my fuck-ups had led me to this moment. It was the need I felt for her. It thrummed through my body like electricity with no limiter.

My phone buzzed on the console about a second after I began to pull away. Without thinking and desperate for a reprieve before the questions—and confessions—began, I answered.

"Ash, hey," Danny's voice echoed on the other end of the line. Taylor's face flicked toward mine, hearing the other woman on the phone.

Murphy's Law... Ashton's Law... Same difference.

"Hey, what's up?"

"Ash, we need to talk."

My fingers tightened on the steering wheel; I'd been around the block enough to know what was coming next. I knew this was coming. I bailed on her so many times because of Taylor, she had every right to break up with me; she deserved better.

Still, I wasn't too thrilled about the idea of being dumped with Taylor next seat. Just one more thing for her to add to her already inflated sense of guilt.

"Can I actually, ahh, call you later?"

The strained, regret-filled laugh on the other end of the line was my answer.

"No, Ash, I think it's better if we just did this now. I want you to know that I admire what you're doing for your family friend, and I do believe you that there is nothing between you, but regardless of whether we hold the same position in your life or not, there isn't room for the both of us. At least right now."

I bit back a curse. The flowers I sent her would have made a much bigger impact had I not gone and broken four of the five subsequent dates that we'd tried to have since Taylor got here.

I tried. *I swear I fucking tried.*

"Shit. Danny, I'm sorry. Really, I didn't mean to—"

"I know," she cut me off. "I'll be fine. You're a good man, Ash Tyler. We were friends when this started, and I hope that's where we'll get back to."

"I'm sorry." I let out a long exhale that was filled with more relief than I was ready to admit.

"*Goodbye, Ash.*"

The click of the line was the bullet from a gun. My chest ached as the burning from the wound spread, radiating once more through my body what a disappointment I was—not treating Danny right, letting Taylor down.

The last time I felt this sense of self-loathing was the day Blake slammed the door in my face, hoping I would be happy with the knowledge that I'd broken her heart and her chance at happiness with my best friend.

Taylor had to know what that phone call was about, and I almost wished the next question out of her mouth had to do with it. But my Pixie always kept her focus on what was most important.

"You're an alcoholic?" she rasped weakly as I turned off Ocean Avenue.

"Recovering." My fingers tightened on the steering wheel.

"For how long?"

"Larry took me to my first meeting the day after I got here. Been sober five months," I told her bluntly.

She stared in shock out the front window. Color was gone from her face, those eyes not seeing the road ahead only the road behind that led me to this point.

I'd never felt sicker.

I'd always wanted her, and I'd never felt good enough.

Back then, the alcohol made me forget. Now, I had nothing to erase the sight from my eyes. Soon, that disbelief would change into abhorrence for my sins. I knew her family. I knew it would.

Drunks, liars, and cheats. They were to be scorned, left for only Jack or Jesus to save.

Chapter Thirteen

Taylor

Ash was an alcoholic. *A recovering alcoholic.*

It made no sense and every sense all at the same time.

It fit easily with all the partying and the drinking, the easy to set-off mood swings, and the inexplicable choices he'd made. It fit with why he'd left Nashville and the band. It fit with why I hadn't seen him drink anything but water and coffee even after the added stress my unexpected presence put on his life. And it fit in the space where I'd felt him hiding something from me.

But it didn't make sense why he'd come here to heal. It didn't make sense why he'd shut out his family and friends. *It didn't make sense why he just hadn't said something the first day that I asked him what had changed.*

Here I was, running to him with my life, my fears, my guilt, practically an open book, and he couldn't even tell me that he struggled, too? *Was I not worth it? Was I not worth the truth?*

Anger and hurt mingled in me like a hurricane—wind and rain spiraling and forming something dark and destructive.

"Does anyone know? Does Blake know? Does Zach?" I asked, my voice elevated to hurricane-level hysteria.

Silence burned through all the oxygen in the air, leaving me desperate to hear anything—anything that would keep me alive.

"Why?" I demanded. "Why didn't you just tell me, Ash? This whole time... why couldn't you just tell me?"

No answer as we pulled down the drive and he threw the truck into park, his face harder and sharper than the jagged cliffs that dropped into the ocean.

How could *this* happen after this morning? After he swore to be there for me whether I needed him or not—never saying that he was only giving half himself?

Some people are too stubborn to be proud of the progress they've made because it means acknowledging where they came from. The gist of my talk with Larry hit me full-force.

His door slamming shut brought me back to reality. I hopped out and met Ash around the back of the truck, pointing an accusing finger at his stupidly-sculpted chest.

"How. Dare. You."

"Excuse me?"

"How could you not tell me? *Why would you keep this from—*"

"Why?" he cut me off with a laugh so cold and so hard I swore it could bring snow to the shore. "You want to know why? Why the hell do you think, Taylor?" he demanded as he got in my face, my finger now definitely pushing against his chest. "You think it's easy to admit I was so fucked up for a really long time? You think it's easy for me to admit I had no good reason for *having* a problem, for having an addiction? Good family. Good friends. Good grades. Why was I any different than any other frat football player in college? I wasn't— and still, I ended up this way."

My heart raced as the pain seeped from his words like a sink overflowing.

"It's not easy to think about how I didn't have my shit together. How, *at my own choosing*, I buried my dreams—shutting them out to help Blake and Zach with their careers because I thought it was the right thing to do? When the truth is it made me resent both myself and them though they had nothing to do with it."

His breath was hot with anger on my cheek. It vibrated with the same intensity I'd seen that night, only now, without the shroud of alcohol, its vengeance was trained inward.

"But you wouldn't understand that. You always have it all together. You've always had a plan from the start. I didn't. And I don't need to hear how it's no wonder I got so fucking lost."

My head began to shake because he was wrong. I didn't have a plan. *Not anymore.*

"I'm trying damn hard to fix myself. It's hard enough to live with the knowledge of what I did. I know I messed up. I repent every goddamn week in that church. I don't need to be reminded of how much of an asshole and a failure I was… when I live with what I did to Blake."

His laugh was like a chisel against my heart, hammering it into little pieces with the self-loathing in his voice. And my heart complied easily, breaking so many times for the man who wouldn't stop punishing himself.

"Actually, you want to hear how I don't even remember? How the last thing I truly remember was seeing the two of them in the car in Denver? How between then and the moment she confronted me I drank so much I can't recall anything clearly?" Revulsion coated every word like the smoothest wax.

No, I didn't want to hear. My hand went to my bump. *I already knew.*

"These are my demons. My mistakes. You don't need to be tainted with them," he rasped so hoarsely I thought he might lose his voice. "Haven't even been able to get through step—the part where I make amends to those I've hurt. How could I tell you, Taylor, when you've always been the one person who is too fucking good? Without even trying, it's just who you are…

always too fucking good. You've literally lived the law when all I ever did was fall short. The last thing I needed was for you to look at me with *alcoholic* added to my already extensive list of sins…"

"How dare you," I charged as tears leaked down my cheeks. I hated how my lip quivered with sadness even as I spoke with anger.

"What?" He gasped.

"You still think I have it all together? Me? Do I need to remind you of this?" I motioned toward my stomach. "Do I need to remind you how I showed up on your doorstep and basically overthrew your life because *I* was scared? Because *I* was the one who needed to get away from the disapproval of my family? Because I'd been raised to be ashamed of the position I'm in?"

I was yelling and crying, and I no longer cared. Everything hurt because of him and even though I knew he was hurting, knowing he'd kept this from me because he thought I would judge him… it was too much.

It hurt too much.

And my heart felt like it was going to explode.

"You told me all that stuff about how things were different here, how you were there to lean on if I needed it, but I'm not good enough to return the favor? *You think I'm here to judge you? After everything?*"

Calloused hands cupped my cheeks to calm me, but I pushed them away.

"I'm not here to judge you," I forged on, desperate to make this one point clear as my breath choked and tripped trying to get into my lungs. "I'm not here to judge you, Ash," I wept. *"I'm not my parents."*

"*Jesus,* Taylor…" This time, when his hands framed my face and began to fend off my tears, I welcomed their warmth. "You're too good." His lips pressed to my forehead first. "You've always been too good for me." Then they drifted lower and began to kiss up my tears as he murmured against my cheek, his mouth so close to mine. "And I think you're here as my cosmic punishment… to see how long I can survive around something I can never have."

Now, it was my turn to laugh bitterly. *Never have.*

"You don't want me," I murmured regretfully as my eyes locked on his deep blue ones, his mouth poised just in front of mine. "How could you want—"

His lips on mine silenced me.

Warm, firm, and everything I wanted. *Everything I needed.*

This had only happened one time—but that one time emblazoned every detail into my brain like a secret code only his lips could unlock.

So, when his tongue pressed against the seam of my lips, they parted and let him inside.

Silken and strong, he savored every inch of my mouth like it was the most exceptional meal he'd ever tasted. My hands wound up fisted in his shirt and then slid up around his neck when he lifted me, setting my butt on the back bumper of the truck, his hips wedging between my thighs.

He kissed me like he was starving, eating at my mouth and tongue in ways that need and pregnancy hormones made my body drip with desire.

I arched up against him, the back latch of the truck digging into my back as I craved more. More friction. More fire. *More Ash.*

From firm and demanding—punishing me for ever thinking he didn't want me, to deep and heavy, his tongue stroking along mine, every pass leaving a trail of burning hot embers down the length of my body right to my core, to soft and sweet, nipping and tugging on my lips, he kissed me, *claimed me,* in every way.

And I wanted more.

So much more.

Rolling my hips, I felt him long and hard between my thighs and I moaned against his mouth. My body needed this almost as much as my heart did. Instantly, I was reminded it wasn't wrong to want this—to want him.

I never should have been ashamed of this. I never should've been ashamed to show feeling in ways where words fell short.

We were both broken, and when we kissed, those jagged pieces fit together and became whole.

Lean on me.

Seconds later, big fat raindrops began to fall in a slow-clap around us. It wouldn't be long before the thunderstorm's full applause came pouring down.

With a strangled groan, he tore his mouth from mine and stepped back.

"I'm sorry," he rasped.

Our heavy breaths appeared like flickering fog in the space between us. The rain feeling as though it sizzled right off me for how hot my body was.

The line had been crossed.

The one between redemption and resolve.

The one separating him and me.

"Let's go inside before it opens up," he said with a low voice. "I'm thinking I should get busy making you some real food for dinner. I'm sure you only ate sweets at Roasters."

He *might* not have been wrong.

I wanted to tell him that food was the last thing on my mind, but I didn't have the courage; I was too overwhelmed by so many emotions to act on that one.

Taking the hand he offered, I tried not to be too obvious in the way that my thighs rubbed together, feeling the way my damp panties slid around between them as we jogged inside.

ASH

I shouldn't have kissed her.

She was pregnant and emotional and just because she kissed me back didn't mean she really wanted me.

And she definitely didn't want to be fucked in the bed of my pick-up. In the rain.

But fuck, I wished she did...

She tasted new and familiar at the same time; it made no sense. It was like I could remember her taste but not tasting her. It was the most fucked-up kind of déjà-vu I'd ever had. Maybe because I'd thought about—dreamt about—kissing her so many times, it was as though I already had.

But I hadn't.

I sucked in a breath as pain seared through my head, feeling the soft touch of her lips against mine... but the recollection wasn't from tonight. A hesitant kiss. Pleading words. Frantic touches.

I looked over at Tay and shook my head.

I was delusional. I'd wanted her for so long that one kiss and I was going crazy.

We'd come inside, both of us needing to collect ourselves—and our thoughts—from where they'd burst through every boundary outside. The kiss... was something to talk about, but there was a bigger conversation to be had first, and an unspoken agreement passed between us that the conversation shouldn't happen without some food first.

So, I cooked while Tay pretended to read though I knew her mile-a-minute brain was trying to process it all.

"I'm sorry about Danny... if I ruined the start of something," she said softly from where she sat on the couch with her legs crossed and the book she'd been pretending to read open between them.

Shit. I'd completely forgotten about that.

I felt her eyes on me as I stood at the stove, the sizzle of my lemon-rosemary marinated chicken fell into beat with the rain splattering on the shack, its scent infused the heavy air.

"Not your fault," I insisted.

Her head dropped like a silent gong of guilt told me she disagreed.

"It wasn't serious, Tay," I admitted, flipping the chicken thighs one more time and sending another burst of rosemary into the air. "With her job and the restaurant… it just wasn't the right time or place. She was nice, but she wasn't—" I broke off with a start.

"What?"

Shit.

"She wasn't the right one." I cleared my throat. *Dammit, Larry.*

"I see," came her soft reply, and I pretended I didn't hear the faintest hint of hope threaded through her voice.

There was another prolonged silence as I finished up the chicken and vegetables, but I knew what was coming.

"How, Ash…" she started quietly.

The rain landed in hail-like splatters on the windows. This was the first time I was having the conversation about my addiction with someone outside of my AA group. It wasn't lost on me that the heavens opened up at the same time I did.

"No good answer, Tay. Wish I had one. College. Football. Parties. Drinking was just part of the game. Then I was drinking more and more, but why wouldn't I think it was normal when I was still acing school? When I wasn't—*most days*—slurring and incoherent?"

That was my problem. It made me a dick, but it hadn't made me a failure. *Until it did.*

I continued, "And then I began working to help the band,

and with a band, you know… it's all about the after-party and the Tennessee whiskey."

"What did it do to you?"

If it had been anyone else asking, I would have tensed in insult, like I was too fucking dumb to know I had a problem and see how it was affecting me.

"Aside from making me a short-tempered asshole?" A short laugh escaped me. "I mean, I think that was enough." I let out a sigh. "You know there was always a justification—either celebrating some new milestone or to relax from the stress. And it wasn't like we didn't go out enough for it all to be masked by the social life of the job. So what if I got piss drunk? Everyone else was right there with me. Except they weren't. Not in the way that I was."

I felt my teeth clench as I tried to really describe what it felt like. I'd never tried to explain it to someone else before. Everyone in my meeting, they knew—they lived it; they didn't need an explanation for what happened to us.

"It's like you go to the beach for the day and you sit in the sun, soak up the rays. You don't see the sunburn as it's happening. Only later, after a shower, does everything turn redder than Santa's pants."

I caught her grin out of the corner of my eyes as I flipped the chicken one last time before serving it onto our plates next to the roasted red pepper and asparagus.

"I didn't see it happening. And by the time I did, it was too late, and alcohol kept me too busy looking for monsters in the madness of the world—people, things, that would try to ruin me or those I cared about."

I sighed heavily, walking over to the table and setting her plate in front of her.

She waited patiently, cutting into her chicken but waiting to eat so she could give me her full attention.

"After what I did to Blake... forcing Zach to break her heart... I looked in the mirror and finally saw what I'd become. I saw the man who could function but not feel. I saw the man who could perform but whose perception was completely broken."

I set my utensils down and reached up to pinch the bridge of my nose. *Hard*. Before my hand fell to the table with a remorseful thud.

"I always thought that monsters were the things that lived beneath the bed or in the dark and shadows. That day I saw the real monsters were the ones that lived inside me."

"Ash... you're not a monster," she said softly, grabbing my wrist before I could pull away.

"Not anymore... I hope."

Her green eyes brimmed with emotion, making them glow with compassion. And her small hand squeezed my arm once more before releasing me. "So that's why you left?"

"You can't recover from addiction in the same environment that created it or fueled it," I told her. "I needed to get away from the reminders of what I'd done."

"I understand," she said softly.

I waited to say anything more until she took a bite. She needed to eat and I needed a minute to think about something else than the weight resting on my chest.

The slight warming of her cheeks and the way her eyes squeezed shut were enough to tell me that she enjoyed it. But then she went and let loose one of those soft little moans and the erection I'd just barely managed to forget came roaring to the forefront of my mind.

Great.

"Ash..." Forget the restaurant. Right now, I'd be happy just to cook for her for the rest of my life if it meant that she'd always say my name like that. "This is delicious."

"Probably just your hormones," I said gruffly, shoving a large bite into my mouth.

Taylor shook her head. "Only I'm allowed to give that excuse," she informed me teasingly as she popped another mouthful in, eliciting the same breathless moan.

I cleared my throat, refocusing on my confession before it got to the point where I had to excuse myself so I could yank a quick one off in the bathroom in order to maintain a coherent conversation.

"I had no idea what I was going to do when I got here. And then I walked into Roasters and met Larry." A smile spread up my face at the memory. "He took me to my first meeting, brought me into the program, became my sponsor... he helped me get clean." I looked down at where my most recent sobriety chip stayed wrapped around my wrist. "He gave me a place to stay... Hell, that doesn't even begin to describe it. He kept me from liquor. He cleaned me up when I looked like you did the other morning. Worse probably, from the detox."

Taylor was almost finished with her dinner, meanwhile, I'd only had a few bites. I guess needing to eat wasn't as critical as getting this out.

"Damn man hid my wallet in case I had a thought to buy booze. Took care of everything so I didn't have to do anything except claw my way back up to where rock bottom looked like a vacation postcard." A shadow of a smile tugged at one corner of my lip. "He taught me what it meant to be a part of this town—to look out for one another. And to look out for myself."

I saw the way her breath caught.

Realizing it was okay for her to say something, she told me quietly, "I wondered how... I mean, it makes sense. Larry certainly seems to hold everything together around here."

Even in just the few weeks she'd known him, I heard the emotion in her voice; it was hard to meet Larry and not feel like he'd do anything for you—including making you face the hard truths about yourself. He'd do it and he'd stand by your side the whole damn time.

"Yeah, don't know what I'd do—what I would've done—without him," I said with a low voice. "Just hope he's saving enough to hold himself together, too."

"Are you… Are you ever going to tell them? Are you ever going to go home?" she asked, standing beside me at the sink, taking the wet plates from my hands and drying them with a towel she must have bought because I'd never seen it before.

"Step nine," I replied, picking up our empty plates. "Just figured that the least I could do is give them something to show for who I am now. For who I want to be."

"The restaurant…"

Again, I nodded.

"They wouldn't judge you, you know," she said softly, her hand on my arm stopping me from walking past her. "They love you. They've forgiven you."

"You saying I'll be like the prodigal brother?" I tried to joke, to play off that I felt like a failure leaving, the last thing I wanted was to go back home and have them think that I needed something… anything… from them aside from forgiveness.

She shook her head. I should have known better than to make a scripture reference to the girls whose family didn't *live* in the Bible belt, they *wore* it like a damn pageant sash: *"Miss Bible Universe."*

"The greatest gift you can give the people you love is your recovery. And I know they will love you no matter how you come to them, ashamed of who you were or proud of who you've become—but I think you should be proud," she replied, sadness seeping into her eyes like red into fall-crisped leaves.

"And it doesn't matter if you deserve it… none of us do; that's the definition of grace. *Forgiveness without fault.* It's the whole point of the Bible. Trust me, I know what it's like to lean on those who profess their love of God yet prefer judgment over Jesus; I know what it's like to lean on them, searching for support, only to find myself falling."

No matter how many people I met, no matter what I managed to accomplish with my own recovery, I didn't think I'd ever look at someone—in the mirror or otherwise—who was as strong as the tiny woman standing in front of me.

I cupped her face, tilting it to mine.

"I'm sorry you went through this alone," she murmured.

She was like those Greek statues, the ones that looked soft and were covered in curves yet made of the strongest stone.

"I was never alone, Pixie," I promised her. "I might not have been home. I might not have been with family. But I was never alone."

A flicker of a smile tugged at her pink lips and it was just enough to make me swear one taste of them would rip away the guilt that hung like an albatross around my heart.

"I'm sorry for what I said earlier," I murmured. "I'm sorry that I said you would judge me. I'm a moron."

"It's okay." She smiled. "I forgive you."

Her lips barely moved to speak the words. They were so close to mine and I just wanted to taste them again. I wanted to finish what we started—what I felt like was started years ago.

"I'm sorry about your parents," I offered sadly, wanting to call them and ream them a new asshole the way Tay's face turned into my palm like she needed it to hold back her tears.

"Don't be. I love them and I pray for them," she uttered, her breath warming my skin. "I pray that when I tell them about the baby, they'll choose to see it as the blessing he or she is."

Her voice gave away what a long shot she thought that to be. But her smile said she would never stop hoping.

"Sweetheart, Blake and I and all the people who care about

you, we will celebrate this. We will lift you up, not drag you down."

"Thank you," she whispered as my head drifted down to hers.

It seemed natural, like God using Adam's rib to create Eve, for me to kiss her—for me to give this to her.

My lips locked back on hers—drinking in everything warm and succulent in her mouth. Just like outside, she tasted like a favorite memory—a strange thought to have about a first kiss. Then again, kissing her was something I'd just as eagerly revisit.

Long and slow, I savored every inch of her. I licked away the sadness that lingered on her tongue because of her words.

"I should let you go to bed," I rasped against the warm sweetness of her mouth.

I should step back. I should let her go. I should *not* throw something else into her life that was already fraying her well-kept edges.

I should do a lot of things.

Instead, I waited for her to tell me to go because I wanted this too badly to do it on my own. I wanted her warmth, her goodness. I wanted her faith in forgiveness.

And I wanted her.

Her kiss. Her hesitantly desperate touch and her needy mouth on mine.

I wanted to unwrap every inch of her sacred body and worship it like she deserved. I wanted to make her feel things that she never felt before.

It registered in my mind that someone had put a baby in her stomach, but I refused to believe she knew what true pleasure felt like—not when she kissed me like I was the only man who could give it to her.

I refused to believe she knew just how good and perfect

someone could make her body feel. I refused because the thought of anyone else besides me giving her that made me burn with a raging possessiveness I'd only ever felt when I was drunk, and my emotions ran on extremes.

And at that notion, I let her go, making sure she was steady before I released her.

"Get some sleep, Pixie," I said gruffly, turning back toward the fridge to search for something that didn't exist. *Forgiveness.*

Her muffled 'goodnight' was a bittersweet chaser to my shot of chivalry.

She might taste like a memory, but I refused to let her become one.

They always said that heaven was some indefinable place filled with bright lights, clouded comforts, and golden gates. It was none of that, really. It was a petite brunette with eyes that glinted like molten emeralds and a heart of gold.

How was I sure that she was Heaven?

Because when I thought about dying, the only place I imagined wanting to go was wherever she was.

Chapter Fourteen

Taylor

"What is going on here?" Larry's disgruntled voice made both Eve and me jump.

We spun away from the espresso machine where she'd been showing me how to work the hopper and pack the right amount of grounds in order to get the perfect infusion.

"Goodness you are so quiet!" Both of us caught our breath with a laugh as Eve adjusted her glasses on her nose and explained cheerfully, "I was helping Taylor practice how to make espresso so she can start serving."

Larry walked right up to me and stared hard into my eyes for a second. "Think you're ready for that, do you?"

My breath whooshed from my lungs.

"I guess we'll find out," I teased with a small laugh.

After our encounter last night, I'd barely caught Ash this morning as he was about to run out of the house, citing errands to run and approaching inspection deadlines.

It had taken a long time for me to fall asleep—my thoughts vacillating between processing Ash's addiction and deciphering those two kisses. And I wasn't going to spend an entire day lost in the same turbulence.

So, even though it wasn't my usual day at Roasters, I asked Ash if he could drop me off on his way out wherever he was going.

"Alright," Larry said hesitantly, nodding back to the machine. "Then how about you make me an Americano and we'll see what you've got."

With Eve's instructions, I navigated the completely manual espresso machine, topped off the shot with some hot water, and made my way to the end of the bar to see whether or not I passed the test.

"I knew you were the right one," he said with a self-assured nod after he took the first sip.

"If you think that's good, you should let me bake some pastries for you. I make a mean apple fritter—though the competition is pretty stiff with Josie's," I said with a chuckle.

My laugh faded as I watched sadness creep into his face. The kind of sadness that's like cancer in the marrow of your bones—virtually impossible to eliminate.

"My granddaughter, Laurel, loves apple fritters." I knew he wasn't even seeing me anymore.

"Where is she?" I almost didn't ask. I'd been raised not to pry into personal matters, but with that look on his face, I couldn't stop myself.

His silence was painful, and when he just shook his head and shook off my question along with it, my heart broke.

"You can come bake anytime. You're Ashton's girl. This is your home," he stated like it was the soup of the day instead of soup for my soul.

My cheeks heated like they'd been steamed. "I'm not—We're not—"

"Don't argue with me, Taylor," he grumbled, walking past me. "I'm too old to deal with denial."

"It's not denial, it's just—"

"Is that boy being stubborn?" He rounded on me. "Did he do something stupid?" He huffed. "And he was doing so well. Look, Taylor, Ashton is a good man. He had a rough go, to be sure. Made mistakes. But nobody makes it through life without those—and if you do, frankly, you shouldn't be trusted. He needs to realize sooner than later that the more he tries to punish himself, the more things he's gonna have to regret. Like losin' you."

My eyes flew wide, completely unprepared for his emotional outburst.

And as though Larry controlled everything in this town, the moment he finished, the door jingled as Ash walked inside like he'd been summoned by the conversation.

His hair was blown off to one side, shirtsleeves rolled up to where they stretched above his elbow, and his pants had a little more dust on them than when he'd dropped me off, but still, he was the most gorgeous man I'd ever seen.

He looked between the two of us like he knew exactly what was going on.

"Larry..." he drawled.

"Don't gimme that look. Just makin' sure you're taking care of your girl and baby," he scolded, missing no beat in attributing the baby to Ash.

And then he turned and made for the back, calling for Eve as he went. And with the respect you would show a grandparent when they spoke to you, even if it was with something arguably controversial, Ash's mouth just thinned until he was gone, holding a retort inside.

"I have to stop one other place on the other side of town. I'll come back for you, just wanted to make sure you didn't need anything from the truck."

"Can I come with you?"

His mouth opened and shut. And then, like he knew what Ash was about to do, Larry reappeared with a box of travel mugs and said, "Take her to meet Addison."

"You're going over to Blooms?" Eve asked immediately, following Larry back out front.

Eve mentioned her siblings before, but I hadn't met them yet.

Ash nodded which sent Eve jogging to the back for a second before returning with a huge box of wrapped muffins.

"Can you drop these off with Addy while you're over there? They're muffins for Blooms Donor Breakfast tomorrow morning." She pushed the box into his chest, not giving him the opportunity to say no, even though I knew he wouldn't.

A few minutes later we were back in the truck and weaving through town.

The tension in the silence built, especially the way he postured himself in the seat.

With one elbow resting on the edge of the window, the other arm one-handing the steering wheel, he looked like a blonde James Dean and the sight made me squirm.

"Did Eve tell you what her siblings do?"

I nodded. "She said they run a recovery house for women."

"Well, it's a little more than that," he continued as though searching for anything else but our kisses to talk about. "They provide them a safe place to live, food, counseling, and resources to get back on their feet."

"Oh, wow." I guess I hadn't realized the full scope of what she'd meant.

We pulled into a parking spot in front of an enormous, three-story old Victorian home.

I hopped down from the truck, following behind Ash as he walked inside.

"Hey, Addy," he said, and I could hear the smile in his voice. "I have some goods for you."

I was taken aback when the woman who turned to greet us looked almost exactly like Eve but slightly older.

"Taylor, this is Addison, Eve's sister," Ash introduced me.

Wearing all black, contrasting her sister's colorful

wardrobe, Addison was a bit taller than Eve with the same face skin and same eyes. The most noticeable difference though—*the most noticeable thing period*—was Addison's long bright blue hair.

"Hey, call me Addy," she greeted me warmly and wrapped me in a hug.

"Nice to meet you," I squeaked. "You look so much like your sister."

Addy smirked. "Hard to believe my twin is actually our brother, Zeke, huh?" she joked. "So, Eve told me Ash had someone staying with him. I asked if it was someone or a saint."

"*Christ*," Ash grumbled.

The blue-haired woman laughed and patted him on the back. "And I think I have my answer."

"I don't know about that, I mean I did make him sleep on the couch." I laughed. "It's nice to meet you, too."

I stood for a few minutes while the serious deal of muffins exchanging hands was transacted. While Eve was bright and bubbly, Addy had a humorous sarcastic edge to what seemed like an intense personality. (If the blue hair hadn't given that away.) I watched their conversation, waiting for the moment when I'd find out just what Ash had come here for.

"Zeke is in the back."

When she turned, her jacket dipped, and I saw her back was completely covered in tattoos. I was curious as to what they were—and then I realized what they were meant to hide.

Scars.

My sharp inhale was barely audible. Scars crisscrossed her back from wounds that must have been painfully deep judging from the way they healed, puckered and shiny.

"Tay." Ash's voice jolted me back to reality and I quickly tore my gaze away before she realized I was staring. "This is Zeke, the brother. Zeke, this is Taylor."

"Nice to meet you," the third good-looking sibling greeted me with less enthusiasm than his sister. I barely returned the pleasantry before his attention was back on Ash.

"Don't mind Groucho," Addy's muted voice drew my attention. "We had a small disagreement earlier. He's still not over it. *Men.*" She huffed.

I laughed, feeling guilty because I really wanted to hear what Ash and her brother were talking about.

"So, you and Ash..."

I shook my head. "No! I mean... we're just friends. He's just... helping me out right now." I glanced down at my stomach.

Like her scars, the distinct bump was something that didn't go unnoticed.

She nodded but her expression said that I wasn't convincing enough. "When are you due?"

"The end of January." *My winter baby.*

"Congratulations."

I murmured my thanks, glancing back as Zeke handed Ash a stack of papers.

"He's great," she continued, looking at Ash. "I was just giving him a hard time earlier, but he's done a lot for this place since he's moved here."

"He has?" I tried not to sound as desperate as I was.

She nodded. "He met Cam and me at Roasters not long after he got here; we stopped in to see Evie and grab a cup of Joe. He made shit coffee back then, by the way." I laughed with her. "A week later, he showed up here with a woman from his... ahh... church group who needed more support, I guess you could say."

I didn't bother to interrupt and tell her that I knew about his AA meetings; I wanted her to keep talking.

"A few weeks after that, he shows back up again wondering

why we don't have a kitchen. We just moved into this place at the middle of last year; it used to be our grandmother's house. By the time we renovated and brought everything up to code, we didn't have the funds yet to update the kitchen." She sighed as she crossed her arms over her chest. "Next thing I know, we've got Madison Construction rolling through here with appliances and all sorts of goods, turning the back room into a full-fledged kitchen for us and the girls to use."

"Wow."

"Honestly, that's not even the most impressive part. At least to me. Ash came several times a week for the next month and taught my girls how to cook healthy meals for themselves," she revealed with a tone that told me not only how grateful she was to Ash, but just how much she cared about each of the women in her charge.

"And that was after working at Roasters," she went on to inform me "And when he was done here, he'd leave to go work on his own place. I swear, I don't think he's slept since he bought that property," she said wryly while I listened in shock.

"I… I didn't know." My hands went to my stomach. I hated that I didn't know. I could see why he didn't want to tell me about being an alcoholic, but why try to hide this?

"Fear."

"Excuse me?" My head jerked to hers.

"That's why you didn't know," she began with a sad smile and, with a stare that drove right into my soul.

"I see people living in fear every day—hell, I used to be one of them; that's why I opened Blooms," she admitted honestly. "And it's not just fear of acknowledging the bad; that fear is easy to spot. But more often than not, it's fear of accepting the good that holds us back. That's the fear that hides in plain sight. The only thing scarier than what you've been through is that the good you've found won't last."

I stood mute, acknowledging that very fear inside myself.

"Sorry." Her face broke into a gentle smile. "I do most of our counseling here, so I tend to get too deep and personal with people in normal situations. I just… I know what I see. And I don't like to see fear."

The Lord has not given me the spirit of fear but of peace, love, and a sound mind.

Out of nowhere, the scripture from Isaiah hit me. I was afraid. In varying quantities, there was a lot in my future that worried me. But with Ash… first I was afraid that I didn't know him, really, or what he was doing here.

That wasn't wrong.

But now that I knew the truth, I was afraid of losing the good. It kept me paralyzed and my secret locked behind my lips.

Loyalty—misguided or otherwise—had always been Ash's forte. I didn't want to be one more responsibility he felt he had to take. I didn't want to be one more, however admirable or honorable, chip in the collection he'd been growing to buy his forgiveness or barter for his redemption.

I wanted desperately what we had now. Well, more than what we had now—more of what I saw coming, what I could almost reach out and touch.

I wanted him to want me. Just me. Not because of the baby.

And I wanted him to want it, too.

ASH

"Thanks for letting me come along," Taylor said, turning to face me as I held the passenger door open. My body tightened as I smelled sweet muffins, fresh coffee, and pure woman. She was so close—too close. Desire ripped through me.

I felt a twinge of guilt for making her feel like I didn't want her with me. *I did.* I just didn't want to be that fucking guy who carted her all over town just to show her all the *great* stuff I was doing—the 'hey, look at me, look at how I've changed and how I'm now God's gift to Carmel.'

I did what I did because I needed to, not because I needed to show it to everyone else.

"Yeah, sorry. Just told Zeke I'd pick these up before the weekend."

"Why didn't you tell me about Blooms? Or what you did for them?" she asked with a soft voice.

I cleared my throat to hide a groan.

"Did for them? I mean it's not like they aren't going to be helping me at the restaurant…"

"W-what do you mean, helping at the restaurant?"

My eyes darted to her for a minute. *Shit.* Addy must not have told her everything. But now I had to.

"I'm hiring them. That's what I stopped today to pick up—resumes from some of the women. Or lists of skills that they have."

Some of them held similar jobs in the past. Some had resumes. And then there were some that ended up in bad situations early in life. It didn't matter to me whether they knew it all or knew nothing;

"Like as waitresses?"

"And hostesses. Some might help in the kitchen, too." I sighed heavily. "Many of them don't have college degrees. On top of that, with histories of drug and physical abuse, most of the resorts and wineries around here won't hire them and even the ones that will, a lot of the girls are still hesitant and anxious around strangers."

Out of the corner of my eye, I watched understanding dawn on Taylor's face.

"They want to contribute. They want jobs. But Roasters can only take so many, so when I decided to open the restaurant, I told them I was going to hire my staff exclusively from there and the church's AA group," I explained steadily as I turned onto the drive down to the house.

"Because the restaurant is about a new beginning..." she offered quietly.

I nodded. "But not just mine," I clarified. "I want to do for others what Larry did for me; I want the restaurant to be a safe place to start again." When I saw her try to quickly wipe a tear from her cheek without me seeing, I warned roughly, "Don't, Pixie. It's not that big of a deal. I'm not doing the heavy lifting like they do over at Blooms. I'm not helping them rebuild from scratch. It's just a job."

"Don't tell me *don't*," she demanded, staring at her hands in her lap. "You won't make this less than what it is, Ash. Don't try to make yourself less than who you are."

I grunted, turning off the car. "I'm not. I'm human—just like everybody else. I do both good and bad things and there's no use crying over either."

As soon as the shower turned off, my body vibrated with awareness that it was only a matter of time before Taylor was within touching range again. Of all the things I'd tried to keep to myself since she got here, my hands were the hardest.

I stared at my phone, waiting for Eli to get back to me and hoping Tay would come out to say goodnight and head back to bed. Hoping our usual routine of dinner, an episode of *Vikings*, a second if she decided to shower in the morning, and then bed, wouldn't be broken.

I shouldn't have kissed her. Never should have crossed that fucking line.

She came here for a safe space and I couldn't control my dick long enough to not take advantage of her. I didn't even know how long she planned on staying—not that I would ever ask and risk her thinking that she wasn't welcome, but the truth was I didn't think I'd survive until the baby came.

Maybe I could stay in the restaurant once it opened. Or back with Larry.

It was only a few weeks out. The deck needed to be finished. Everything needed to be painted. I was planning on ordering the furniture this weekend. Inspections. And then open.

At least Addy and Zeke had been a huge help training the girls from Blooms so they'd be ready to go for opening day.

My phone buzzed with a message from Eli.

ELI
Couldn't find much on Blackman Brews. Just opened not that long ago. A few stands in the resorts around here. Having Dex look into it.

ASH
Who owns it?

ELI
Xander Blackman. Looks like a tool.

ASH
Something is going on. If you saw the guy... Talks like he's in charge but acts like he's still answering to someone else. And the way he talked, whoever it is wants Roasters for more than fucking coffee.

ELI
Dex will figure it out. He's with Ace on a case in Frisco; he'll

be back next week. But I already told him about the situation. Let me know if you see Blackman again.

Dex Covington was the tech end of Covington Security. Background checks. A/V surveillance. Wiretaps. Phone taps. Internet records. There was nothing he couldn't dig up. His older brother, Ace, was the boots-on-the-ground muscle of the firm. They'd both been in the military. Ace was a navy SEAL and Dex worked in a position he couldn't really talk about, which we naturally all assumed meant he'd been some sort of spy.

They'd opened up their private investigation and security firm just outside of Carmel when they'd left the service.

If you were a local with a problem, you didn't go to the police—you went to Covington. Being right on Big Sur and on the coast, the police were too busy dealing with tourists and their issues to have time to deal with the actual residents of Carmel Cove.

There was one more Covington brother—the youngest—Bennett. He was probably the one I had the most in common with, since he'd gone to school to be a chef. Unfortunately, he'd just purchased the Carmel Pub, so in addition to being busy with my own restaurant, I didn't get in there to see him for obvious reasons.

Their father, George Covington, had been the plumber for Carmel since, well… since plumbing was probably installed in the town as far as I could tell. He was as close of a fixture in Carmel as you could get before becoming Larry.

Regardless, we had no proof of anything unlawful except that motherfucker who berated and seemed to have no reservations about assaulting an old man to get what he wanted. My fist tightened around the phone. I had a bad feeling about Blackman and Dex was the only man I knew and trusted to get to the bottom of it.

"Everything okay?"

My eyes darted up to see Taylor standing there wrapped in only her towel.

I groaned. *God, couldn't she at least have put the flannel back on? The towel was too fucking easy.*

I clicked off my phone, setting it on the counter. "Yeah, you okay?"

She nodded, stepping even closer toward me. *Barefoot and pregnant*—the thought wasn't lost on me. Although this was never how I imagined it happening for me—not in a million fucking years. Then again, now that it was, I wouldn't imagine it with anyone else. *I couldn't.*

"Sorry for crying earlier. I feel like I'm always crying," she said with an adorable laugh.

Groaning, I pushed back from the counter, trying to gain a little more space between us.

"Don't apologize, Taylor. It's fine," I said gruffly.

"I just want you to know." Her breath shook and I didn't miss the brief quiver of her lower lip as she spoke again. "That I've been around people... lots of them... who only help people for how it makes them look to their fellow churchgoers."

I let out a hiss when somehow, she made it close enough to reach out and put her hand on my chest, and I was powerless to stop her.

Who knew that the strongest force in the whole damn world was the softness of a woman's touch?

I was hard and aching and just wanting to hold her and love her and fuck her so fucking badly, I was going to lose my mind.

"I know exactly what that kind of person looks like—they look like my parents; they look like the people I grew up with and was told to admire; they look like the community I left behind—a community that would not only turn a blessing into a mistake. But just like that's not God, and that's not love, you, Ash, are not that person." Her eyes looked into mine like green lanterns of truth. "You are doing something that will do the exact opposite, something that will turn mistakes into blessings. You should be proud of something like that… of what you are doing… of who you are."

My jaw tightened. I shouldn't be proud of something that ultimately resulted from the mistakes I made. But then Taylor showed up, chased here by the same judgment she'd been raised on, and yet didn't judge me at all.

If I were ever to believe that God was giving me a sign—was showing me the true meaning of grace, this… *she*… would be it.

"I don't want to be proud of it if it's going to make you cry again," I rasped softly, my face drifting closer to her like I was the sea and she was my shore.

At least that got a small laugh from her. "That's not what's going to make me cry."

"Oh?" I grinned, but just for a second until I realized there was *something* that would. I dragged in an unsteady breath, my thumb brushing across her cheek, as I asked, "Then what's going to make you cry?"

I watched it happen—the pink that rose into her cheeks, the way her mouth parted slightly but didn't take in any air, and her eyes… green, gilded cages well-fortified to hold back her desire, now let it free to burn in the brightest, *wildfire* flame.

Her lips brushed over my thumb as she spoke. "If you don't kiss me again."

Fuck.

It wasn't her words that rang in my ear, it was the sound of the gauntlet being thrown.

And my restraint being broken.

I tried to find reasons—any reason—to convince myself that this was a mistake, that I was taking advantage. But as my lips drifted down to hers, I realized nothing about this could ever be wrong.

"Taylor..."

And I could punish myself later as long as it meant I could have her now.

Chapter Fifteen

Taylor

I wanted him to kiss me.

The thought had been chained to my mind like the most dangerous kind of felon, cinched and shackled tight, bound by locks with no keys. Yet, like a heavenly Houdini, it escaped from my mouth as though its chains were nothing more than costume jewelry.

And maybe my restraint against him had always just been for show.

But when his cool blue eyes looked at me like I was the key to his salvation, my fear evaporated and the only thing left to my body was its desire for him.

Goosebumps invaded my skin as his strong, solid hands cupped my face. And the way he held me... well, I just knew I was safe to ask for anything in that moment; I felt it in every fiber of his being, every deep and steady breath, that he would do anything for me.

But the only thing I wanted was him and that started with a kiss.

"Taylor..."

Soft and warm his lips brushed over mine, gently touching and teasing them. It was with a sweetness that almost bordered on cruel as I felt my nipples tighten painfully against my towel. I darted my tongue out to push on the seam of his lips, wordlessly begging entry inside.

With a groan, his mouth opened with mine and the kiss from yesterday—the one ruled by need rather than the one that needed rules—returned. His hands slid back into my hair and pulled me tighter against him as his mouth devoured mine.

On his tongue, I tasted both desire and possessiveness. That who I was and whatever I felt was safe with him—*belonged to him*. And my mouth tilted underneath his, begging for more.

I came to tell Ash the truth. But as he pulled me closer, I felt my darker, self-serving desperation bubble to the surface...

I wanted him to want me.

I wanted to know if he could feel something for me without that something being obligation to our child. And so, I kissed him harder—because I wanted to know that truth more than I needed to tell him mine.

Dragging my tongue along the velvet length of his, I felt his growl against my chest and the way his arousal thickened against my stomach. Power bloomed inside my chest, bright and freeing, knowing it was because of me. In that moment, our kiss was my world, Ash its inhabitant, and I was its god. Every stroke and lick, every small moan and gasp, they were my cosmic forces that created his desire and destroyed his restraint.

I moaned as he sucked my lower lip into his mouth, tugging the flesh between his teeth. My body drifted closer to him, knowing that he was the end to everything it was searching for. Warmth rushed between my legs, feeling his hard length against my bump.

His hands left my hair and reached around my back. Skimming down over my back, his fingers searched out the fleshy part of my butt. My back bowed slightly, needing the bend because of our difference in height and I wrapped my arms around his neck.

And then he yanked me hard against him, my gasp fueling the fire. Feeling his thickening erection against the swell of my stomach between us drove my need for him even higher.

It seemed as though pure fire was pumping through my veins as I arched against him, the ache between my thighs dropping off the cliff of needy into the abyss of unbearable.

"Ash, please," I begged him.

Not for a single second in all of this did it feel like a sin. Instead, the fire in my body was cleansing, rather than damning. There was no guilt for the way he touched and kissed me—or for the way I wanted him to.

"*Taylor.*" The way he said my name sounded like he'd dragged it down from heaven to his desperate, imperfect earth.

My breath hitched and I choked out. "D-did I do something wrong?"

"Wrong?" This time his groan was mingled with a hint of a laugh. "No, Pixie," he rasped. "Just I want you so fucking bad and if I don't stop now, I'm not sure I'll be able to."

"I want you," I blurted out, my mind in a fog of need. I definitely didn't want him to stop. At this point, I didn't think my body would be able to come back down "I mean… I don't want you to stop."

His mouth claimed mine as I felt my back up against the cold hard plastic of the old refrigerator. My gasp sent his tongue back into my mouth, licking and running along the edges of my mine as his hands on my butt lifted me.

I let out a small yelp, my legs instinctively wrapping around his waist as he picked me up.

"Where are we going?" I asked breathlessly.

Dumb question, Taylor.

He chuckled again. "Are you sure you're pregnant?"

I gasped as his tongue trailed a line of pure fire from the corner of my mouth back to my ear where he tugged on my earlobe. "You have to have some experience with what happens here."

"I-It only takes once." I let out a shaky laugh, but it caught in my throat as his head jerked back.

"Only once? You only had sex once?" Blue eyes pierced mine, searching for the truth.

My face flushed. I didn't realize what I was saying—what I was admitting to while trying to excuse my ignorance. I lost sense of everything when he touched me—everything except him. *And how much I wanted him.*

My mouth parted but I couldn't answer. I wondered if he thought me completely unbelievable. *Though I remembered feeling that same sense of incredulity.*

My feet touching the floor again made me realize that we'd made it to the bedroom. His eyes bored into mine, a new intent in their depths—one that was inescapable.

"How many times have you had sex, Taylor?"

I swallowed hard, my embarrassment growing. "Once." The word rushed out like the fall of a guillotine. "Just once. What difference does it make? Do you not want to do this? B-Because I don't know anything—"

His mouth on mine cut me off.

"Taylor," he growled against my lips as he dug his hard length into my stomach. "If you can't feel how much I want this, then maybe you don't know anything. But it matters because... one fucking time. *Christ.* You've basically never done this before, and I bet the asshole didn't even know what he was doing."

My cheeks flushed deeper.

I love the hint of jealousy in his voice—*even if the man he was jealous of was himself.*

Licking my lips, I kept silent rather than contradict him with the truth: that the *asshole* did know what he was doing; he just didn't know he was doing it.

"You deserve better than that, sweetheart. You deserve to be worshipped. And the things I want to do to you—" He broke off on a groan and I felt the way his erection pulsed. "Well, let's just say I want to do something completely different now. I want to treasure every inch of your body before I fucking possess it."

I shivered.

I'd always been taught not to swear. But those words weren't a curse when they came from his mouth—they were a promise.

I felt the heat from his gaze as it traveled south, lingering on the way my breasts swelled slightly over the edge of the towel. My pulse spiked when the tip of his finger hooked underneath it and paused, as though daring me to stop him.

His eyes fixed on mine as he slowly pulled the one corner securing it. I let out a breath and lifted my arms slightly from my sides, letting the heavy fabric fall to the floor, landing with a soft thud along with the rest of my reservations, as my whole body was bared to him.

Goosebumps marched a celebratory path down my body like an army returning to celebrate their victory.

I pulled my gaze up from where it had settled squarely in the center of his chest, all the way up to his tumultuous blue eyes.

He looked like he'd just revealed the eighth wonder of the world—and it belonged to him. It made me feel sexy and powerful and beautiful. And it made me all those things to the point I thought they might burst from my chest having never been free to be felt before.

Ash's harsh intake of breath went straight to my core, and my nipples tightened even further, a harsh shade of red against my pale skin as the need pumping through my veins made them vibrantly aroused.

My knees shook as one palm came up to test the weight in his hands.

"Perfect," he rasped as his thumb rolled over my nipple and I almost crumbled to the floor right alongside my towel.

Maybe a small part of me had thought that he'd remember something from that night if he saw me... if he touched me. It was a foolish assumption; there was a reason it was called a black-out. Still, I hoped for the unreasonable as his hand kneaded my swollen flesh.

His other hand cupped the side of my face as he bent and took my mouth with a growl. This kiss was harder—more desperate—as his hand pinched and rolled my nipple, sending my desire drenching between my thighs.

He pushed against me until the back of my knees hit the bed.

With a gasp and an awkward plop, I landed on the bed, looking up to Ash's lusty gaze that held mine as he knelt between my legs, putting him eye-level with my breasts. Propped back on my hands, I felt like I was dessert—and someone hadn't eaten dinner.

"You know how many times I've dreamt of your tits, Pixie?" he asked as both hands now teased my flesh. "Probably since before you even had them."

"They're... bigger," I managed to breathe out amid his torturous touch. "I mean, they're... not normally this big." I moaned as he pinched both nipples and pulled them out toward him. His mouth was so close. I just wanted to feel that sharply sweet suction again.

"Wrong. They're perfect, sweetheart," he said, watching as his fingers rubbed and pinched me until I was arching my back painfully to get them closer to his mouth. *"Perfect."*

The word disappeared into a growl as his mouth closed over one tight peak. White-hot lightning zigzagged through my body and had me jolting against him. I'd had months of remembering… dreaming… engraving this sensation in my mind, and strangely, it was nothing like I could have remembered. It ripped through me, burning a trail straight down to where I felt my sex clench frantically for him.

Staccato gasps echoed in the room as he bit and sucked on me. Licking and teasing the sensitive bud until I was just about in tears.

Minutes or hours later—I couldn't be sure—he pulled back, my nipple popping from his mouth redder than a candied apple. Air dragged into my lungs, feeling like it weighed more than a freight train.

His gaze met mine, thunderclouds of desire booming inside of it as his lips tugged up on one side. I whimpered, not knowing, yet knowing at the same time that this moment was all the reprieve I was going to get.

I vibrated as I watched his hand pull my other breast closer to him. Just within his reach, his eyes never left mine as his tongue darted out and flicked over my nipple.

"Ash!" His name turned into a whimper as he captured the other peak, torturing it the same, if not more than the first.

My body felt like it was on fire, every cell unraveling underneath his touch. My skin felt as though it were knit out of nettles, so sensitive and desperate for release.

I searched for it… that distant memory of pure ecstasy from months ago that in so many ways was responsible for this moment right now.

One hand made it into his hair, unable to decide whether it wanted to pull him closer, desperate for more, or push him away, overwhelmed because it was too much.

"A-Ash... *please*..." I moaned with a voice that played to the tune of *wanton* but didn't feel wrong.

Growling, his teeth pulled on my nipple, making my hips roll and writhe against the bed.

"I want to taste you," he said with a rough voice, his hand sliding down to the waist of my pants.

Wasn't that what he was doing?

The question never made it from my mouth as his lips began trailing over my belly bump and all thought was lost. I didn't know what I was feeling, watching the way his lips caressed my skin with a kind of reverence that, if I did such things, I would swear to God that some way, somehow, he knew my baby was his.

And then I imagined what he would do if I told him... And the thought took the air from my lungs with the way I imagined he'd treasure me.

The cool air against my naked sex shocked me; I'd only been vaguely aware of what his hands were doing while his mouth played on my stomach and tugged at my heart.

"Ash!" I gasped, my knees trying to jerk closed but broad shoulders got in the way.

We'd had sex. *Obviously*. But he'd been drunk, and the hotel room had been dark and shadowed. And that night, both of us had been desperate for something that we never thought we'd have.

I always thought I'd savor it—my first time. That it would be slow and sweet. It wasn't—and I was glad. Until that night, it felt like I'd been living with my head shoved underwater, holding my breath and waiting for someone to finally bring me to the surface.

When you're drowning, you don't *savor* the first breath of air that you're given. You take it. You gasp it in like you'd kill anyone who would try to rip it from you. *That* is how my first time was. Kissing him, touching him—being touched by him… it was the first breath in lungs that had been filled with water for far too long. I'd wanted it all—and more—and fast wasn't fast enough.

And that meant he hadn't stopped and looked at me like this.

If there was a mirror, I was pretty positive that I looked like a cherry—both in color and shape. I squirmed under his stare that felt

"Ash…" I choked out his name.

Immediately, his head jerked to mine as he rasped, "What's wrong? Are you okay?"

My head rolled around in a circle, unable to decide if the answer to that was yes or no. "What are you…"

It could have been the blatant uncertainty in my voice or the deep red of my cheeks, but I saw the second he understood.

"Has anyone ever tasted you, Pixie?" The gravelly texture of his voice was now a caress in and of itself.

I had a hard time shaking my head no, the way his thumbs brushed back and forth along the insides of my thighs.

Wetness ran down toward my butt the way his groan seemed to crack open his chest.

"The last time I felt this desperate for a drink of something, I ended up with an addiction that stole my life." Crystal blue eyes took me prisoner. "But you… one taste of you would start the addiction that saves it."

I gasped in eager shock as his head sank toward my aching sex.

"Wait," I choked out and instantly he pulled back, concern marring the beautiful way desire turned his face into a masterpiece.

"What's wrong?"

I gulped. "You can't… You can't blow in it."

Like a hot air balloon with only half its tethers cut, his head tipped, off-balance, to one side. "What?" he rasped.

Oh, goodness.

"I don't—I mean, the book says—"

His eyebrows rose. "The book? What does the book say, Pixie?" he rasped, pressing a gentle kiss to the tingling skin of my inner thigh, a small smile creeping over his lips that promised ecstasy.

"The pregnancy book says not to blow on it," I blurted out. "Or in it. In me." I groaned. I was botching this. I was ruining the moment.

I felt his smile grow against my leg. "Explain," he demanded.

I closed my eyes, trying to focus on the passage I'd recalled while my body raged against the delay of its satisfaction. "During oral sex, if you blow into the vagina, you could cause an air embolism by blocking a blood vessel," I said in a rush. "It's dangerous."

I pried one eye open when I felt his shoulders begin to shake against my thighs and the rapid releases of his breath against my sensitive core.

He was laughing.

But his eyes weren't when they lifted to mine.

"Did the book say anything dangerous about licking?"

I swallowed over the massive lump in my throat. "No," I said steadily.

My mouth parted. A silent gasp lodged in my chest as his thumbs spread my glistening sex open wide and I watched as he drank in the sight of my obvious desire for him. Tipping his head back up to look at me, I watched a devilish half-smile spread over his lips.

"Good."

Before the word even fully registered in my mind, the sound was obliterated by the broad, firm velvet of his tongue as he licked me from the base of my slit all the way up to the swollen bud that felt like the center of it all.

"Ash!" I cried his name as my body tensed and fractured in cells and synapses I never knew existed.

"How about sucking?" he demanded hoarsely. "Any danger in sucking?"

Unable to take my eyes off of him—unable to do anything but exactly what he wanted me to—my head jerked in a short but unquestionable *no*.

The heavens exploded in my eyes as the heat of his mouth vacuumed over my clit and he sucked. Long and hard, he pulled against me until my head was arched back into the mattress and my fingers curled viciously into the sheets.

I let out a loud gasp as he pulled away again.

"And how about stroking, Pixie?" The strain in his voice almost fooled me into thinking he was as tortured as me.

Almost.

My head turned side to side, feeling as though my pulse was thrumming directly from the center of my thighs in angry, demanding beats.

"*Was stroking dangerous?*" His ragged question was accompanied by an electric shock to my thigh as his teeth nipped into it.

"No!" I exclaimed breathlessly.

I arched off the bed as his tongue pushed inside me, stretching my sex and stroking along the muscles that vibrated with desperate and needy tension.

"And how about making you come, Pixie?" he growled, hardly lifting his lips from against my core that dripped with desire, pleading him to drink his fill. "Is it dangerous to make you come all over my tongue? To drown me with the sweet honey from your pussy?"

I moaned, his delicious and dirty words a new kind of torture on my inexperienced body.

"Is it?"

Only to me, I wanted to reply but lacked all capacity to do so.

"No." I looked to him. *"Please, Ash..."*

My need for more overcame the paralysis of pleasure, and I was rewarded with the warmth of his breath against my wet sex.

Heaven.
Hell.
Hot.

And then his mouth closed over all of me, covering me with heat that was only the beginning of my destruction.

Licking, swirling, sucking, stroking... I watched the way his head rocked until I couldn't watch any longer. Squeezing my eyes shut, all I could do was feel. Every lap. Every flick. All I could do was hear the wet noises come from him—or maybe from me—as they mingled with moans I didn't realize I was capable of making.

All the way down to the tips of my fingers I felt it, the spiraling tingle—the warning that my body was hurtling toward something I still wasn't sure I could have remembered correctly. His fingers tightened on my thighs and his tongue moved faster, darting just inside my entrance before running up to my clit.

Panting... unraveling... I inhaled his name over and over until it no longer sounded like a word. Maybe it was his feral growl against me. Or maybe it was the way his lips suctioned around the swollen, dripping bud of my sex and pulled it hard into his mouth, drinking from it as though it were an antidote rather than an addiction. But it was definitely the way one hand drifted back up to my stomach, almost able to completely palm the slight swell, with a possessive grip that sent my body soaring.

I screamed in a way that I could repent for later as my body came apart once more underneath his touch.

I stayed frozen and trembling, unsure if my heart was ever going to return back to normal. Meanwhile, Ash drank down every drop of my release. His lips were gentle now, no longer demanding my pleasure, but basking in it as he carefully licked up the moisture that flooded from my body.

"Was that dangerous, Pixie?" he drawled, self-satisfaction and self-denial warred in his tone.

"I don't know about dangerous," I said, drawing a shuddering breath. "But it definitely felt too good to be safe…"

His tortured chuckle vibrated against me and I shook as he placed one more tender kiss on my sex. Then, his lips dragged higher, placing another on my stomach as he murmured, "Perfect."

My eyes drifted shut and for a moment, I basked in it all. The pleasure. The release. The adoration.

When I opened them again, his face was above me and then, those lips that had just devoured every part of my sex, pressed to mine. I could taste myself on him and the thrill stoked the embers of desire I didn't think would ever die.

"Let's get you ready for bed," he decided with a low, gravelly voice.

"What?" I blinked, sure I hadn't heard him correctly. "What about…" I trailed off, glancing down to where the thickness of his erection was painfully outlined against his jeans, so hard I could practically see the imprint of the veins pulsing against the fabric.

His hand cupped my face and he tethered me to the ocean in his eyes. "I need to earn you."

I wondered if it was even possible to convince him how wrong he was. Wanting him the way I did was like freedom. Not earned. Not given. It just was. *And it was essential.*

"I'll be fine, Pixie," he insisted firmly, flashing me a tight grin.

I wasn't completely naïve. I knew how *that* extremity worked—and I knew what happened when it wasn't allowed to. "But you…"

"Have learned to recognize when what I want might get in the way of what I need," he finished for me.

My heart stopped on a dime.

Need.

Did he need… me?

Before I could even think to say… anything… Ash rose up from the bed and pulled out one of his t-shirts from the drawer and handed it to me.

How many times had I watched as Blake stole a t-shirt of Zach's to keep? To sleep in?

I finally felt like that girl—the girl who wanted to be covered with *him* in any and every way that I could.

And after I was all cleaned and brushed and tucked beneath the sheets, unsure of how any dreams could beat my reality tonight, Ash came out of the bathroom and my stomach coiled into a tight knot.

I didn't want him to sleep on the couch. Not tonight. *Not again.*

I wanted him to hold me.

I wanted him to stay with me.

But knowing the state I'd left him in, I couldn't ask that. So, I turned away before I did something I shouldn't.

A small gasp escaped me when the bed next to me sagged under his weight.

"Ash." I turned over, my eyes wide.

"Taylor," he growled, one arm coming possessively over my stomach and tugging me back against him. "I just had my tongue buried inside your sweetness. I'll be damned if I'm sleeping on the couch for one more fucking night."

Well, then.

I bit my lower lip, but it couldn't stop my smile as I settled in against him.

I wanted everything about this moment to last forever.

And I hoped that he might want the same thing *before* I told him about our baby.

And after...

CHAPTER SIXTEEN

ASH

Hi. My name is Ash, and I have a new addiction.

I couldn't stop looking at her, walking around on the far deck as she talked to my sister on the phone. The wind blew strands of hair across as she smiled and I felt its warmth from where I stood.

With each day that passed, the cloak of guilt she'd arrived in began to disappear. It was a process—*removing guilt always was*. First, the edges began to fray from her decision to come here. Then threads began to unravel as she found a place for herself in this community—and in my life. And after the other night, the seams were barely holding it together and she was finally moving with a freedom that had always been restrained.

It was a universal truth.

Loving yourself is the hardest love to give.

Especially when the world hands you power tools and an instruction manual on all the ways to cut yourself down.

She had on jeans and one of my t-shirts; I'd insisted because we were painting today, and I didn't want her to get anything on her stuff.

I'd insisted because I liked her in my clothes.

My dick twitched, thinking about that night... thinking about how insatiably I'd wanted her since.

I wanted to fuck her, sometimes more than I wanted to fucking breathe, but I needed her to stay with me. So, I'd kept my hands to myself for a few days—but just barely.

I kept waiting for the moment she'd realize it was a mistake to want me and tell me that it couldn't happen again. There were so many things changing for her, the last thing I ever wanted to do was let her decide something in the heat of the moment that she would rationalize later as a mistake.

It wasn't.

I knew it wasn't, and I'd move Heaven and Earth to prove it to her if she didn't know it herself.

But her regret never came.

Instead, I saw more frequently—more desperately—the looks, the not-so-mistaken touches, the tension that kept building between us. I just… I'd never fucking forgive myself if I took things too far, too quickly for her. Especially now. Especially because of the baby.

The thought of 'too far' had my cock throbbing again, angry that my mouth had feasted on the most perfect pussy I could ever imagine, and it hadn't been let in on the fun.

But Taylor wasn't experienced. A smile pulled at my lips, remembering the innocent panic in her eyes when she thought I was going to blow her up like a damn balloon.

God, she was so damn adorable.

I didn't want to sleep with her and have her regret it. *I didn't want her to regret me.* Because it was more than just the desire to fuck her. It was the mountain of moments in between, working on my restaurant and watching her boss all us guys around, hanging out at Roasters and ignoring all the 'I-told-you-so looks Larry sent me, dinners together, and TV shows put on pause every time she felt the baby move.

So, even though I *wanted* to fuck her, I *needed* her for all those other things.

Waking up with her curled in my arms put everything in perspective, one that had a future centered around her.

"How is she?" I asked when Tay came back inside.

"Good." She smiled. "Excited. Happy. They were looking at venues."

I turned back to the wall in front of me. My sister's happiness would always be tainted with my remorse, knowing that my selfishness almost ruined it. "You could have talked to her. She misses you."

My chest ached. I missed my sister, too.

But she'd forgiven me too easily for how I'd hurt her. So, I kept my distance and would continue to until that forgiveness was earned—until I had some proof that the man no longer existed. And that was what the restaurant would be—both hope for the future and forgiveness for the past.

It was tangible evidence I was a changed man.

"How are you?" I asked instead of responding, watching as she sat on one of the folding chairs Mick had brought over the other week.

"I feel fine." I loved the way her hand went to her stomach when I asked.

Fuck, I loved kissing her bump—the way the skin was like hard velvet; I loved seeing the way her body was creating new life, feeling it under my lips and tongue. Even if the baby wasn't technically mine, *she was.*

"That's not what I meant." I chuckled. "I know baby Ragnar is doing just fine the way you devoured my chicken parm last night."

Her face scrunched. "Ash, the baby's name is not—"

I interrupted her with a smile. "I want to know about you up here," I said, tapping on my head with the end of my spatula, "not down here," I said, tapping then on my stomach.

"Oh." She always licked her lips when she was thinking.

First the bottom, tugging it into her mouth, and then along the top. "I'm okay..."

"Liar."

She bristled—an expression that only made her look adorable for being so tiny.

"You don't always have to be strong." I cleared my throat. "It's okay to lean a little when you are struggling. Not that you are..."

"I feel better... better than I did when I first got here." She stared out the large windows as she spoke. "Sometimes, I worry that I don't feel guiltier," she said ruefully. "Don't get me wrong, I know I would've been broken by my parents' reaction to this. And sometimes, I do feel it—ashamed of not telling them, ashamed for disappointing them. But I thought I'd feel it more, if that makes any sense."

I dropped my paintbrush and crouched in front of her. "You have nothing to be ashamed of."

Her eyes widened a fraction, and then, in true Taylor fashion, she replied selflessly, "Neither do you."

My lips thinned and I reached out and put my hand on her stomach, smudging my own shirt with light blue paint with a possessive grip.

"What was your first thought? When you found out?"

I wanted to know it all.

Her limelight eyes sparkled with surprise. "I know you think I probably freaked out, and I can't say I didn't. But it wasn't my first thought."

Warmth suffused through her face. "Okay, maybe it was the *very* first thought. But only in an instinctual way, not in a meaningful one," she clarified. "It's going to sound strange but before all of this, I'd felt lost. The tour was done. I was home. I was working on other projects. Everything was ordered and organized, Blake's image and popularity was soaring, and there was nothing to worry about; I should've been in heaven, right?"

I nodded in acknowledgment.

"I wasn't." Her stomach quivered under my hand. "I was lost. Surrounded by structure and plans and time to make sure it all went off perfectly, but… It was like I took a boat into the ocean with all the maps and charts and tools I could ever need for my journey, only to realize I had no idea where my destination was anymore. Somewhere in all that planning and preparedness, I lost sight of where I'd intended to go."

She stood as she spoke. My strong girl. She'd planned her whole life. Hell, I remembered when she'd had her college picked out before she'd been in high school a full year.

"Like you followed all the directions, step after step, only to finally look up and take stock of how far you've come and realize you've no idea where you are."

"Yeah." Her agreement was more a breath than anything else. I lost myself in her eyes, like for a second I was a part of this amazing woman who'd come to me in her moment of weakness. "So, the first thing I thought when the test came back positive was 'Thank you, Lord.'"

For Taylor, that wasn't like most people's 'Thank God.' It wasn't casual relief or a nonchalant exclamation. No, she was truly grateful for what she'd been given.

Her chest shook with an almost silent laugh.

"I'd been praying for direction. For… something. And then… I found out about the baby, and I knew it had to be my answer. They say God works in mysterious ways and that's true—I never thought the answer to my prayers would come like this; they also say He never gives you more than you can handle; that one was a little harder for me to swallow, I will admit." A small sheepish smile crossed her face. "After that is when I freaked out a little bit."

"I think it's okay you freaked out a little," I reassured her.

"I think so, too." She licked her lips. "I know that a blessing is never the answer to a problem; it's a gift to help you grow through whatever you're facing—a blessing is who you become by accepting it."

I swallowed hard. Her words filtered down into the finest cracks still left in my soul, healing them just a little bit more.

Sobriety wasn't a gift. Recovery was. Who I was without alcohol wasn't the same thing as the man I became through my recovery.

I searched her eyes. "And did He bring you here?"

Her breath hitched. "Something like that."

I pulled my hand away as she stood, gently rubbing her lower back once she was upright.

I rose, watching as she paced along the wall we'd finished painting yesterday. "Are you afraid?"

"Not really." She stopped and turned back to me. "Not when I'm with you."

"*Taylor...*"

"Sorry." She shook her head. "I rambled. No one... has asked how I felt in a long time."

"What's still worrying you?" I asked with a low voice, closing the space between us. My hands burned to hold her. "What can I do for you, Tay?"

Her nose scrunched as she thought for a second and it took everything in me not to lean down and kiss the tip.

"You don't—"

"No, I do. *And I want to.*"

"The truth?" she replied hesitantly, and I nodded. "I'm worried about making a mistake. I'm worried about doing something so utterly and completely wrong I'll mess the poor child up forever. But I think that's normal, too." She laughed and tried to play it off casually, but I knew it was anything but.

I listened to what she said, but I heard what she meant.

I heard her fear that she'd been programmed to raise her baby like she'd been raised.

I tipped her chin up, not caring that I smudged some paint on her skin.

"Taylor, you are going to love your baby more than anything in the world. Hell, you're going to love your baby more than the world. And I'm sure even you are going to make mistakes, but there's nothing you can do to mess up something—or someone—you love so much," I promised her. "And the fact you came here should prove to you that you're nothing like your parents—that your love isn't contingent on loyalty to certain rules."

"Ash..." Her lip shook violently.

I refused to let her eyes go. Not now.

"You're here because your love is unconditional, sweetheart," I rasped. "Now, don't let the number of times I've said the words 'God,' 'Christ,' or 'hell' fool you into thinking I know a whole helluva lot about religion, but I have heard that unconditional love is what it's all about."

I thought it was the right thing to say. It sure as fuck sounded like it when it came out of my mouth. But the way she immediately burst into tears had me second-guessing every word.

"Hey, hey..." Trying to wipe each one away was like playing pong except only there was more than one ball that I was trying not to lose. "What's wrong? I'm sorry, sweetheart. What did I say?"

She shook her head, pulling out of my reach, tugged the edge of my shirt up to wipe away the wetness.

"Nothing," she said with a watery laugh. "Nothing is wrong. I just... I don't understand how you always say the right things."

Jesus. I wiped a hand over my mouth.

"Maybe because I've had so much practice saying the wrong things," I teased, hoarsely.

Taylor laughed and I knew then and there that right or wrong, I'd say anything to hear her laugh, see her smile, wipe her tears, and soothe her worries every day for the rest of my life.

"Ash." Her hand on my arm make me freeze. "I'm not the only one who will… or who has… made mistakes. I know you think you have, but there's nothing that would make Blake—or Zach—love you less. Even not knowing everything, they know your heart is in the right place, even if they don't know your mind might not have been."

My jaw clenched, not expecting my own advice to be used against me. "Maybe I don't deserve it, Tay." I sighed, brushing her hair back behind her ear. "Maybe I don't deserve their understanding."

"Too bad." She shrugged. "Did I deserve all this?" Her arms opened. "You don't just say the right things to make me feel better, you do them, Ash. We weren't that close and yet, I showed up here with no notice—an interruption—and you dropped everything for me."

I shifted my weight, finding it more uncomfortable to talk about my good deeds than my bad ones.

"You let me stay—you let me stay in your bed while you took the couch. You've cooked for me, introduced me to your… family… out here, taken me to doctor appointments, held me when my body felt like it was trying to kill me, held me when I cried…" Her breath faltered. "It's not about accepting their forgiveness, is it?" Her eyes widened as she realized my battle. "Ash… why won't you forgive yourself?"

I felt my throat clog as, in just a few words, she dug down into the deepest, most raw and wounded part of me, and demanded why I couldn't stop punishing myself. "Forgiveness is the greatest form of strength, Tay… and I just don't know if I'm that strong yet."

Her face glossed over again and I knew more tears were coming. So, I cut her off with a hard kiss. It was a cheap shot. But I knew if I heard everything I'd done from her eyes, I'd see the one truth that I was still more comfortable passing off under the guise of 'the right thing to do.'

But while that kiss might have saved her more tears, it sunk both of us under lust that begged to fuck her right here against the wet-paint wall—to finish what I'd started last night. And what should have ended after a few seconds became a beast of its own.

"Fuck, I want you," I growled against her sweet mouth.

Her hips rolled against my cock and I saw stars. Before I could think better of it, I had her up against the half-painted wall, my tongue angling down her silken throat. Swallowing her whimper, I ground my dick against her pussy, feeling its heat even through the layers of clothing.

Here I was, thinking I was Mr. High-And-Mighty, restraining myself from her when the next second it felt like I might actually go blind if I didn't bury myself inside her tight little cunt.

My teeth sank into her lower lip, lust jolting through me at her shocked whimper, as my hands cupped her tits. I wanted to fuck them too—their swollen, soft weight. I wanted to come all over them, cover them with my desire and then trail it down right over the hot as fuck bump of her stomach.

At one point I wondered if it was normal to find a pregnant woman so fucking hot. But then I realized I didn't give a shit if I was normal—not when it came to her. I wanted her. I wanted to own every inch of her tiny body to the point where it didn't matter what fucker gave her that baby, the only thing her body knew was that each and every inch of it, inside and out, belonged to me.

"*Ash,*" She moaned as I pinched her nipple, my other hand cursing my own shirt for being too long on her that I had to go searching for the waist of her shorts.

Panting, my mouth nipped down to her neck, latching on to the smooth joint between her neck and shoulder and sucking.

"I know, sweetheart, I got you," I grunted as my fingers pushed under the edge of her panties.

I just reached the slippery edge of her pussy when I heard it—the gravel of the road crunching under the weight of a car.

"Ash?" Her eyes were panicked when I pulled back. With only adrenaline to smother my desire, I righted her shorts and shirt. Slowly peeling her off of the wall to find a streak of pale blue paint along the back of my shirt along with a light smudge on her cheek where I held her.

I didn't even need to hear the voices outside to know that it was Mick and Miles pulling down the drive—the roar of their truck was unmistakable. What I was surprised to see was Eli come through the door first, his brow furrowing as he looked back and forth between Taylor and me.

God, she was so adorable when she turned cherry-red.

With a murmured greeting, she sidestepped the three men who looked like giants compared to her and bee-lined for the house.

"Did we interrupt something?" Eli raised a brow, now seeing the smudged paint on the wall.

"No shit," Miles laughed. "We just cockblocked A-man from christening the new place."

I grunted. "Shut up, Miles."

"Looks like you did a number on the wall. Seriously. Hope we didn't interrupt too soon."

"Miles, give it a rest," Mick chided, walking past his brother toward the deck that was going to be finished today.

Eli just shook his head and followed the level-headed brother outside.

I stood stock-still, my eyes still trained on the door where Taylor had disappeared through as my body still buzzing with adrenaline and desire. I'm sure it was clear from the look on my face that it had definitely been too soon.

"Hey." Miles walked up to me until we were almost shoulder to shoulder, clapped a hand on my back and leaned in. "We're gonna be out back for a little cuttin' some boards. It's gonna be loud. You probably shouldn't help with your chef-hands and all." He shifted just a hair closer. "You probably *should* put those hands to better use finishing what you started with your baby mama."

And with another pat of his hand, he was gone.

My heart thudded the way he referred to Taylor.

Mine.

Pregnant. Not pregnant. Deserving or not.

She was mine.

Chapter Seventeen

Ash

Taylor jumped as the door shut behind me.

"W-what are you doing?" she stammered, backing up until she ran into the couch.

"Finishing what I started." My growl echoed as I came for her. Her cheeks were still flushed from outside. If I were a betting man, I'd swear that five more minutes and I would have walked in to find her with her hand down her own pants *where mine was about to be.*

"Ash… But… They're right outside. What if—"

I swallowed her objection. It was potent and sweet, and I found that I thoroughly fucking enjoyed making her want me more than she wanted to act properly.

"What if they see me making sure I didn't leave my girl aching?" I cupped her ass and yanked her hard against my front. "What if they know that I'm in here making sure my girl is taken care of?" Biting along her jawline, I searched for her ear. When I licked along the rim, her legs buckled and she collapsed against me.

"Yeah…" she murmured. "That…"

I grinned as I kissed down her neck.

"Good. They should know. They should know that you are my priority. Every fucking second. Not them. Not the restaurant. Only you."

Her clothes were off within a minute—not because I needed to rush to get back to work, but because I couldn't take another fucking second where I couldn't see her.

My fingers sunk into the soft flesh of her waist and spun her, pulling that delicious little ass right up against my dick. With her head tipped back on my shoulder, my lips ate at her neck, swallowing down her moans that vibrated the skin underneath.

Fuck, she was so perfect.

Both hands filled with her breasts, squeezing and needing until she was grinding back against me begging for more.

I thought I'd feel guilty for leaving the guys out there, working on my business—my dream—without me. But as soon as I saw her... touched her... I knew that dream wasn't going to mean shit without her in it.

One hand drifted to her stomach.

Without them in it.

My teeth dug into her shoulder as my fingers slipped into her dripping pussy. My body fucking screamed to know how wet I made her—how wet she was wanting me.

Every moan, every rock of her hips reminded me that this was all mine—that no one but me had given her this and it made me possessive and hard as fuck.

"Bend," I growled against her shoulder.

Shuddering, she tipped forward, presenting me with that sweet little ass of hers—something I'd have to work her up to claiming—and her glistening pussy, all puffy and pink, shining with need.

I took half a step back, not trusting myself to be so close. Vibrating, I trusted one finger to her body, pushing inside her entrance. She whimpered in time with the way her body squeezed around mine, driving me insane with lust.

My palm slid up the soft skin of her back and tangled

in her short hair, tugging on it so that she was forced to arch back.

"So fucking tiny, Tay," I growled, pushing a second finger inside against her whimper. "Christ, I don't know how you're going to get a baby—" I broke off with a silent curse. Probably not the best time to tell how that I think her cunt was too small to pop a baby through it.

She rocked back against me, her desire running down onto the back of my hands as I pushed my fingers in and out of her. Moving slightly to the side allowed one cheek of her ass to bump against my angry cock with each sway.

"Ash... more... I need..." I loved when she wanted me so bad she couldn't fucking speak. When all that propriety that had been ingrained in her from the womb melted like snow under the California sun.

"What, baby? Tell me what you need."

I released her hair so that I could grab one of her swollen tits that hung in front of her. *Fuck,* I wanted to suck on it, but not now.

"You need this?" I taunted, my voice deepening to that place where desire ruled, as my two fingers curled inside her, searching and finding her G-spot.

She let out a yelp as her knees buckled. A tight smile tugged at the tense muscles of my face, feeling the way her pussy tightened and gushed around me.

"Ash?" Her head tilted to me, the most maddening mix of concern and desire mingled on it.

"They can't hear you, sweetheart," I roughly assured her, pushing my fingers back into her and pressing on that sweet spot again.

"*Oh, God,*" she moaned, and it was like fucking music to my ears.

There was no restraint left in her. She arched into my palm

as I pulled at her nipple while her hips savagely ground back against my hand, demanding more.

So, I gave it to her.

Three fingers suctioned inside of her, stretching those torturously tight muscles.

"That's it, baby. Fuck my fingers." Her skin prickled with my words. God, she was so responsive. Every touch. Every taste. Every word… her body ate it up and gave it back to me ten-fold.

She was so wet, I couldn't stop myself from shoving a fourth finger into her, not when her cum drenched my hand and ran down the inside of her thigh.

"You feel me inside you, Tay?" I growled, my hand slapping against her skin as I moved faster. "Your tiny little pussy has four of my fingers in her and fuck do I want to feel you come."

And then I twisted them right against her front wall and sent her soaring.

"*Oh God, Ash!*" she screamed as her orgasm destroyed her.

"*Christ,*" I swore as my free arm wrapped underneath her torso to hold her weight as her legs gave out.

Meanwhile, I saw red as her pussy savagely strangled my fingers that were buried inside it, riding out the waves.

I held her, kissing all up and down her back, reminding my dick with every movement that this was *not* about us.

When her shaking subsided into deep, heavy breaths, I slowly slid my fingers out of her, watching as her tight little hole closed up behind me before I took my discarded tee and gently cleaned her.

"Holy shit," I murmured as I pulled her up and turned her so that she could sit on the armrest of the couch.

"What's wrong?" she asked with a voice that still trembled weakly from her climax.

Softly pressing my lips to hers, I uttered, "Not a fucking thing, sweetheart. Just don't think I'll ever get over the experience of making you come. It's like the fucking heavens open up every time."

"I think... you're blaspheming," she murmured lightly.

"I think... as long as I make you feel like that, you don't care." I gave her one more hard kiss, my grin still in place before I stood. "*Fuck*," I swore, my jeans digging murderously into my hard cock.

My eyes clamped shut as I tried to rein in both the pain and the goddamn crippling need.

Outside.

Get outside.

"I'm gonna head back out—" I broke off with a hiss as she reached out and put her hand over the bulge in the front of my pants. "Tay..."

"I want you," she whispered and whether she intentionally licked her lips or not, my nuts seized up aching to be tasted.

"Taylor." I groaned her name again as I felt her undo the waist of my work jeans, the pull and release of the fabric almost enough to send me over the edge.

"Do you not want me to?" she demanded, indignation flared in her eyes as she tugged, forcing me to step closer to her, putting my dick right at mouth-level.

I bent down, gripping her chin between my fingers.

"You have no idea how bad I want to fuck your mouth, beautiful," I growled. "Every time you lick your damn lips all I think about is them wrapped around my cock and that tongue tasting my cum. Are you sure you want that?"

Her response was to tug my pants down, letting them drop to my ankles as one small fist gripped my dick. I watched the almost imperceptible flicker in her eyes when she realized that her hand couldn't close all the way around my width.

Meanwhile, my teeth clenched so hard I thought my jaw might break as her fingers firmly felt along my length.

When her thumb brushed over the tip, I hissed and reared back, my gaze locking around her small hand fisting my erection. I pressed my palm to her cheek before running it back into her hair, the soft waves burying my fingers.

"You sure?" I rasped, seeing stars from my restraint.

A string of expletives escaped me as she leaned forward and licked over my tip.

Guess that was a yes.

Once Taylor Hastings set her mind to something, that was the end of it. And right now, she set her mind on sucking my dick. Hell if I was going to waste any more time debating.

Her mouth tortured me. Not in the experienced way, in fact, the complete opposite. From the second her mouth closed hesitantly over the purpled tip of my cock, I knew she'd never done this before—the thought making me swell even larger.

I didn't want to rush her. Maybe another day when I wasn't so fucking insane with the need to come I'd let her tongue spend quality time with the very end of my dick, but today wasn't that day. Gently pushing on the back of her head, I groaned in encouragement as she took more of me into her mouth.

"That's it, sweetheart. All of it," I growled, watching the way her eyes widened up at me as I kept feeding her my length. My body seized when I bumped the back of her throat. "Fuck, you feel so good, Tay."

She moaned around me and I knew I wasn't going to last long. I fought the urge to close my eyes because I'd fucking dreamed of this sight so many goddamn times, I wasn't going to waste it.

I was frozen—glued to her perfect pert mouth—I watched my cock slide back out all wet and red from her lips. Yeah, she'd never done this before, but she wanted it—she wanted me to lose control—and fuck if that didn't make up for her inexperience and then some.

The sucking and slurping noises from her mouth, feeling them against my dick made it impossible for me to hold on any longer. My grip tightened as soon as she took me all the way back in, my cock rubbing against her throat.

"Swallow," I demanded harshly, my voice losing the last thread of stability.

Her eyes told me she had no idea how she was supposed to swallow with me stuffed in her mouth, but she tried. And the trying was what I needed.

A shout ripped from my chest and even though my eyes were open, my vision went black as I came, the hot jets of my release shooting down the back of her throat. I tried to pull back a little, for her sake, but her hands locked into my thighs forcing me still.

My whole body shook with the force of my release, now held back for too many fucking days. She didn't have to do this. She could have let me pull out. Instead, her mouth became a vise around my pulsing cock until every last drop was drained. I felt my pulse skip every time she swallowed, reminders that I could easily want more of this. *And more right now.*

Finally, as my fingers gently rubbed against the back of her head, did she loosen her hold. I groaned because it was fucking torture to slide my dick out from inside her warm mouth.

"Wow... That was... wow," she whispered, and I couldn't hold back a moan, seeing her lips so red and swollen. Glistening with her spit and my cum. Fuck if I wasn't ready to go again at the sight.

"Yeah, you can say that again, sweetheart." I chuckled roughly.

My eyes flicked to her as she stood, ready to reach for her

if she was still unsteady. I squeezed my dick a little harder as I wiped it off—a warning for it to calm the hell down—seeing her standing there like a petite, pregnant nymph.

God, I was going insane.

"You okay?" I asked, my hand reaching out to her stomach before I could stop myself.

I didn't even think if this was okay for the baby. I mean, I'd never heard of giving head as being a problem, but I hadn't really hung around pregnant women too much before now, especially given my old favorite pastime. *Head might be okay, but alcohol definitely wasn't.*

"Yeah." I heard the small smile in her voice, but I couldn't look away from her stomach. Even in just a few weeks, I could see how it grew—especially on someone as small as she was. Still, underneath my hand, it looked small.

I didn't know why I couldn't pull away. It wasn't like the baby was moving. It wasn't like I could feel anything underneath the firm softness of her stomach. And still, I felt *something*—something that wouldn't let me let go.

It was only when goosebumps covered her skin and I realized she'd gotten a chill, that I pulled back with a mumbled apology and looked up at her.

Another mistake.

Her eyes were swollen with desire—and not just the plain 'I'm horny' kind, but the kind that said whatever I'd just felt, she'd felt it, too. It was desire that ran deeper, that spread into every cell and every emotion and claimed a piece for itself; it was desire that demanded more than joining two bodies—it wanted both souls, too.

"Stop looking at me like that," I instructed gruffly as I took a half-step back.

She stood there watching me—staring at my cock like she was hungry for it again.

She flinched, her eyes flicking to the floor and then to her clothes, bending down to clasp them to her chest. "Sorry."

When she stood, I was in front of her again, my lips diving down for hers. She immediately sighed into me and I knew that stare was just the beginning.

"Don't apologize." I tipped her chin up to meet my gaze. "Just I'll never make it back out there if you keep looking at me like that."

"Oh." She sighed. "And you have to make it back out there?"

A mythical sound escaped me—half laugh, half groan—as I rested my forehead on hers. "Yeah, Pixie, I do."

"Okay," she said, her voice dragging with disappointment until it ended with a small laugh of disbelief. "I'm sorry. I don't know what's going on. I feel so..." Her blush deepened. "I think... I think my hormones are a little out of whack."

"Tay, trust me. I want nothing more than to stay here and keep you naked until all your hormones are satisfied... until it would be legal for me to tattoo 'USDA Organic, No hormones' on your perfect ass, but I gotta get out there; it's my business, my dream."

That brought a smile to her face and she nodded. As much as I could see how her body, betrayed by her hard nipples, disagreed, Taylor knew how important this was. *And I hoped she knew how much I would make it up to her later.*

"I think maybe I'll go to Roasters early then. I promised Eve I'd teach her and Jules how to make my apple fritters."

With a nod, I pulled my keys from my pocket and handed them to her. "I'll catch a ride into town with Eli and meet you there so we can ride home together." She nodded and I added, "See you later."

Waiting until she was back in the bedroom before I opened the front door, I mentally kicked myself for giving in to her. Not that I didn't want to, but there was damn sure going to be a conversation *before* I fucked her. Because from there, there was no turning back. Not out of obligation or responsibility. No, after what just happened, having her would be like signing up for an incurable addiction. No therapy, no drugs, no woman would ever make me right again after being with her. Which meant she needed to be damn sure she wanted me without those hormone-colored lenses on.

I ignored their smirks (mostly Miles') when I made it back out to the deck almost an hour after he'd told me to go inside.

It didn't do shit.

"Restaurant isn't even open and A-man's already got a bun in the oven. Now that's commitment," Miles joked.

I threw one of the scrap towels at him, helping Eli lift the pile of sized and cut trek to be laid on the last corner of the deck.

He had no idea.

Hell, I still only had a vague idea.

Taylor was right—what she said earlier about how I didn't need to let her stay. I didn't need to take the couch or cook for her or take her to the doctors or stop seeing Danny. But that was the thing—I *did* need to. It was like when she showed up at my door, once the shock subsided, the only feeling left was that she was exactly where she should be—*and that she'd always been mine.*

"What are you thinking about?" Eli asked quietly as we laid down board after board.

"Forever."

For the first time.

Chapter Eighteen

Taylor

"Taylor?"

I jumped as Eve said my name, her tall form reaching in front of me to open the oven and letting a wave of sweet heat plume out. The candied-fruit aroma of the fresh apple fritters stuck to the inside of my nostrils.

"Sorry." I groaned, hitting the button on the timer that beeped obnoxiously before helping her unload the pastries I'd almost ruined.

Thankfully, apple fritters were very forgiving.

They'd been one of my favorite things to make and bring to Bible study on Sundays. Maybe that should have been the first sign... apples... of my fall from grace.

"You okay?" she asked, turning to me and wiping her brow. "You've been spacey all week." Her eyes narrowed. "Did something happen with Ash?"

It had been easy, I thought, for this place to feel like home.

There had been no effort to fit in. And somewhere, between helping with the restaurant alongside Miles and Mick, my stomach hurting so much from laughter I thought I might puke, to spending my afternoons at Roasters with Eve, Larry, and sometimes, Jules, I realized that I'd wound up with a new type of family around me—the kind they always talked about in my church but never seemed to be able to accomplish.

"Did he say something?" I asked, knowing that the question would give away my answer.

Eve's lips quirked up into a grin—she and her sister both smiled the exact same way. "You know he didn't," she replied, picking up one of the pastries, she held it out to me. "Fritter for your thoughts?"

I laughed. Even though I'd eaten far too many sweet treats since coming out here than I'd like to admit, Dr. Lee said the baby was still perfectly healthy and to keep doing what I'm doing.

And what I was doing was indulging in my desire—for pastries and Ash.

It was almost too hot to take a bite. *Almost.*

"You don't have to tell me," she added quietly.

But I wanted to.

I wanted to because as much as I loved Blake, this was her brother we were talking about. I didn't know how to explain what was happening between us. I also didn't know how to justify why I hadn't told him yet.

Part of me felt like there was no good reason. That it was so simple to just sit him down and say 'hey, this baby, it's yours. Remember the nights you don't remember? I was one of them.'

It felt like being explained how to fly a plane. It could make a world of sense. I could know every intricate detail about everything. Yet all of that goes out the window the moment those wheels leave the ground and you know that there is a chance you could lose everything.

"Sorry," I gushed as my hand reached for her. "I do… want to talk to you… to someone. I just don't know what to say."

It didn't feel right telling her Ash was the baby's father. I couldn't bring myself to tell anyone else before I told Ash.

"My sister would say to say what you feel because feelings come first. Gotta know what you're up against before you decide how to handle them."

"I feel overwhelmed. Like I feel too much of everything all at once." I sighed as I rested my hip against the counter. "Things... happened between Ash and me," I confessed. "Things I've never done before. It was only one time that made this... I'm not... I don't..." I huffed and patted my stomach. "Anyway, now, I feel like I want more but I'm afraid of wanting more and I'm afraid that he doesn't want more. I'm afraid because more with me comes with a lot more than just me..."

She wiped down the counter in silence, thinking before she spoke again. When she turned, I could see that my confession was about to spark one of her own.

"I'll be honest with you, Tay," she spoke softly. "I've never been with a guy. After what happened to my sister and meeting the women who they help... I just... I'm holding out for Prince Charming."

My eyes widened. My decision had always been religious. My path determined by the *rules*, not leaving any room to question whether the rules were always right.

Meanwhile, Eve was always friendly, effortlessly flowing between flirting and friendship with a bunch of the good-looking guys that came through here. Not that I'd seen her do anything more, I just assumed...

I don't know what I assumed.

I just didn't think she was a virgin.

I also didn't know Addison's story, but if it was anything like the ones of the women at Blooms, I could easily understand Eve's decision not to jump into bed with just anyone.

"Anyway, this isn't about me," she quickly rushed to clarify. "But I just wanted you to know I really do understand at least part of how you feel—the part that knew nothing. The other thing that I know is that the way Ash looks at you… takes care of you… I know that is the something I'm waiting for—that is the something I'd give up my ignorance for."

I shuddered, warming at the memory of how he did take care of me so well—like it was all he was made to do.

"But what if he doesn't know something, Eve?" I whispered so softly, I'm surprised I could even hear my words. "What if he doesn't know something about me that could change everything?"

"Taylor." She gripped my hands in hers, warm and caring. "If I take this fritter outside right now and drop it, what happens?"

"You go to Hell," I said without missing a beat.

We both broke into laughter—pastries were sacred.

"Okay, okay. Seriously though," she pressed. "What happens if I let go?"

"It falls…" I half-questioned, trying to see where she was going with this.

"It's kind of cloudy out today, but what if I did the same thing tomorrow when it's supposed to be sunny?"

"Um… it still falls."

"And how about in the rain? Or in the snow?" She pushed and didn't wait to hear the same answer. "How about up in the mountains? Or on the east coast? The North Pole?"

"It always falls, Eve," I cut in.

"Exactly. That's the point. Whatever you tell Ash could change everything about your world—it could turn it into a place you might not even recognize—but it will never change gravity; it will never change how that man feels about you."

Oh my.

Before I could thank her, the door rang; the lunch rush was starting.

"Hey, Evie!" I heard Eli's voice yell as we walked toward the front. "Is Larry in?"

We walked into the cafe area where some of the girls from Bloom were taking orders and making drinks. Eli and Ash stood, waiting, at the counter, and heat flooded my body seeing him.

"He was in earlier," I offered, "but he said he was going home for a little—Oh!" she exclaimed and spun around, searching for something under the counter. "Are you going to see him? Dr. Shelly popped in right after he left and dropped this off; she said he forgot it."

Eve handed over a plain white bag. I couldn't see inside it, but the soft rumble of its contents indicated it contained pill bottles.

"I'll take it." Eli's face tightened as he took it from her.

I knew Ash and Eli were going back and forth about Larry; he wouldn't tell me about what though. Aside from the obvious reasons that Larry wasn't a young man anymore but still held a stubbornness that didn't fade with age, they spoke... sometimes argued... like there was more to it than that.

For all the people who Larry had surrounding him—who viewed him like family—I still always caught a glimpse of loneliness so devastating in his eyes it made my heart hurt.

"Alright, thanks," Eli said with a hint of frustration before turning to Ash. "Let's go talk to Dex. I'll head over to see him later."

When Eli turned to Eve to grab a coffee, Ash stepped closer to me, his hand reaching on top of mine that sat on the counter, fiery sparks shooting right up my arm and then right down deep to the achy parts of me.

Definitely more.

"Hey," he greeted me with a voice that was coarse like coffee grounds and just as strong. "How's your day?"

"Good." I licked my lips because I really wanted to kiss him, always forgetting until it was too late the look it produced in his eyes. I always got snared by his feral stare. Equal parts hungry and possessive. No matter how many times he'd pleasured me, I needed him just as badly again, if not more. "When Larry was in, he invited us over for dinner on Friday. I mean," I stammered, "I told him I would talk to you."

"He did?" He looked taken aback.

I nodded. "And then he just laughed and said he'd see us on Friday for spaghetti and meatballs like he knew you'd say yes."

"Yeah, we'll go."

I looked down the counter before asking, "Is everything okay?"

"Yeah." He sighed heavily. "Just have a feeling that there are some people harassing him to buy Roasters and, not that I really think anyone could, but I don't want them to take advantage of him. Or worse…"

A shiver ran up my spine. It sounded like he was more concerned about the 'or worse' part.

Ash

"It's getting serious, huh?" Eli asked as we got back into his truck.

I said nothing for a moment, figuring out the simplest way to explain the truth.

"For me… with her… there was never any other option." I looked at Taylor and saw forever. Always had. Maybe it was because I knew her family—knew what they expected. Or maybe that was just the easier explanation of how I felt about her back when making it through the next day was task enough.

"Because of the baby?"

We pulled out of town and headed toward Monterey Bay; Covington Security sat about halfway between the two.

"No," I admitted. "I mean, of course I'm going to be there for the baby; I get that she's a package deal now. But even before that, there was always just something about her. Baby or not, I've always known that at some point, I'd fucking risk it all just for the chance to make this work."

I sighed, running a hand through my hair as we turned into the parking lot. Every moment I spent with her, especially the ones with her panting underneath my touch, the need to make her mine with my body and my name strangled me.

But I wouldn't rush it. No matter how the fuck it might kill me, she needed to be sure this was what she wanted.

She might be a package deal, but I was a fucking lifetime guarantee.

"That's good, man." He gave me a slap on the back as we headed for the entrance. "I think love looks real good on your ugly mug."

I stumbled through the door.

Who said anything about love?

Was that what this was?

"But you didn't hear him threaten Larry?" the man on the other side of the table asked.

Dex Covington.

Bond-like was the best way to describe him, not just in his perfectly groomed black hair, fitted suit, and quiet demeanor, but also in his tactics. Dex was the one who found the information—*however it needed to be found*. Ace was the one who decided how to use it; that made sense, too, if you saw him. Ace was big. Like SEAL team, fuck-you-up big. And the way they worked together had made their firm well-known and successful in a very short amount of time.

"I heard him say Larry wasn't going to be around for long," I repeated, letting the thread of frustration show.

"Yeah, but I can't fucking go off on some jackass just because he called Larry old."

"You could and you would if you fucking heard the way—" My voice rose angrily.

Eli broke in with his typical calm. "Hey, chill, Ash. Look, Dex, we know it's not much, but it's Larry. He won't tell me anything and he hasn't been himself lately. We have to do something."

I clenched my teeth as Eli tapped his fist on the table.

"Did you even look into Blackman? I couldn't find much. Doesn't seem like they've been around for long. And I get that anything on the main strip there is going to be valuable property wise but why now? And why so fucking desperately?"

Dex stared at us both for a moment, the silence like nails on a goddamn chalkboard as he decided whether or not he wanted to tell us what he knew—*and I could see that he fucking knew something.*

"Fuck," he swore, leaning over the table as he pinched the bridge of his nose before meeting our gaze again. "Look, of course I'm going to look into this for Larry. Christ, I've known the man practically my whole goddamn life; he's been like a grandfather to me, to this whole town. Of course, I'm going to do something."

"What do you know?" I demanded. I believed him but it didn't make me feel any better about what was coming next.

He unlocked one of the drawers in his desk and pulled out a folder, hesitating a second before opening it.

"Blackman Brews was only created at the beginning of this year." He pushed a few papers toward us with addresses and images on them. "Along with a few empty buildings that are nothing more than dots on the map. The best I can tell, the only thing they own with Blackman Brews stamped on it is the truck you saw him get out of."

"Shell corporation?" Eli asked.

"Maybe. Or maybe just a brand new fucking business. I don't have enough information to know."

"But there's more you do know…"

Dark brown eyes peered at me through slits as he flipped to another sheet. "Couldn't find much on Xander Blackman, but in addition to visiting Larry, a man matching his description was seen at Rock Beach meeting with Vandelsen."

"Shit," Eli cursed and threw his head back.

I'd only met Larry's son-in-law one time, but there was a cosmic reason his name was Richard; while Rich was one possible nickname to describe him, the more appropriate one was Dick. I didn't know much about the Ocean family drama except that Larry didn't speak to his daughter or her husband; Larry never wasted time on ungrateful people. The only person he cared about from that side of his family was Jules.

We'd all heard the rumors.

Rumors that whispered that Rich Vandelsen, and his resort, were expanding in ways they couldn't afford—and that they were involved with illegal business to do it.

"You think he's working for Rich? Or trying to buy the resort?" I asked.

Dex's face was carved out of stone. Hard and impassive. "Not sure. Unlikely a coffee company—even a fake one—is trying to buy a resort. More likely they are working together but it's hard to say whether Blackman is working for Rich or if it's the other way around."

"Larry is going to be pissed if he finds out we're looking into Vandelsen," Eli muttered.

My exhale was forced. This was a fucking shit situation and the look on Eli's face told me that it was *more* than likely there was something shady at best—illegal at worst—going on here.

"Why? If Blackman threatened him—is working with him—"

"Larry doesn't bother the Vandelsens and they don't bother him. That's what's best for Jules, and that's all Larry cares about," Eli advised.

"They wouldn't do anything to harm their own daughter..." I trailed off because Eli's expression contradicted me.

"Some people will do anything for money and power—even destroy family," he said hoarsely.

"Look," Dex began. "I'm going to look into it. But I'm going to be fucking sure before we tell Larry, *and* before I confront Vandelsen. I don't need to tell you that he owns people in this town—and those he doesn't, he certainly has enough money to sway."

A fair number of the Carmel police force were on Vandelsen's payroll. *Unofficially, of course.*

"I'll be in touch." Dex stood as he spoke.

The three of us parted with tense handshakes, knowing a storm was coming.

"What are we going to do?" I said when we got back in the truck.

After a beat of silence with the car not moving, Eli replied, "The same thing he's always done for us. We're going to look out for him."

Chapter Nineteen

ASH

"Thank you, Larry. This was delicious," Taylor gushed as she cleaned the last of the spaghetti and meatballs off of her plate. She had no idea what her tongue running along the edge of her fork did to me. *Or maybe she did.*

We sat around Larry's small round dining table—a fixture that always seemed too small for the number of people who'd gladly sit at it with him. I'd watched him all through dinner, talking to Taylor, asking her how she was liking California, how she was feeling. Spaghetti and meatballs was Sunday dinner for Larry—and today wasn't Sunday.

"There's still chocolate." His gruffness only softened slightly when he looked at her.

I tried to look for a change in him. He'd been more absent from Roasters since the confrontation with Blackman, and I worried he'd taken matters into his own hands... *taking out the garbage,* or so to speak.

The atmosphere at the coffee shop had suffered for it. I would swear half the people came in there just to see him and check in, tell him about what's new in their life, or ask advice. Taylor said a few people had wondered where he was, almost demanding to know if he was okay. Even Eli, who normally held his cool composure like fucking Atlas held the world, who was still calm after meeting with Dex, had finally begun to crack.

Eli stopped by the restaurant yesterday and his eyes held the bleakness of burned wood—an ashen frustration rolling around in them that didn't bode well. But he didn't say anything, even when I asked what was going on. I wasn't going to be the one to point out that though he and Larry weren't related, they both sure-as-shit had the same gene that didn't know how to reach out for help when they needed it—or even when they didn't.

That was the thing about people who spend their lives looking out for others, they don't know how to let the rest of us return the favor.

Meanwhile, we still knew no more about Blackman Brews or its connection to the Rock Beach Resort and Larry's estranged family. I had a feeling that Eli probably asked Larry about it and Larry pushed him away. And if he wouldn't tell Eli, he definitely wouldn't say anything to me.

"Of course." She grinned.

My girl loved chocolate. I think even more now that she was pregnant than before. Everyone always thought the dark chocolate bars requested backstage at every show were for Blake; I was one of the handful that knew they were Taylor's secret stress indulgence.

"You sure it's good for you to have a whole bar of chocolate every night after dinner, Larry?"

It was no secret that four donuts in the morning and chocolate at night were Larry's secret to a long life. As I asked, I gave him an eye, not that it mattered.

Larry harrumphed and replied, "My doctor said it's good for you. Something about antioxidants or some mumbo-jumbo. More importantly, he hasn't told me to stop yet."

"Larry," I said incredulously. "Of course, he didn't tell you to stop; Eli told me your doc died more than ten years ago."

In my defense, I tried to say it with a serious face, but it was impossible. A smile broke out on my face as he waved me off like that was only a minor detail. Meanwhile, Taylor burst out laughing.

"How's the restaurant?" The gravelly voice of the King of Stubbornness broke through my thoughts. Perceptive eyes locked on mine, like he knew I was thinking about his stubborn ass. "You pick a name for it yet?"

I wore a guilty face as I shook my head.

We were getting close now. All the furniture was set to arrive next week, along with the inspections. And then it was only another one or two tops after that point assuming everything passed final inspections before my dream would be living and breathing. And even with that deadline looming, I still couldn't settle on a name.

"Taylor, please tell this young man he can't open a restaurant with no name."

"Larry, it's going to have a name," I assured him. "I'll come up with one eventually. It's not that important. Trust me—having walls and a roof and a kitchen… slightly more important than the name right now."

"Ashton Tyler." Both our eyes widened at his hard tone. "A name is everything. A name is what turns a dream into a goal. A name defines. It gives meaning. A name means you take possession of it—whatever the hell it is. A restaurant. An addiction…"

My muscles tensed at the reminder.

And just like that, the harshness disappeared. "A name means you've made it a part of you—whether it's a part that you need to grow out of or grow into."

Christ.

It felt like the man had just reached out and grabbed me by the throat with those words.

"Larry, I'll pick a name," I said with a choked voice,

leaning forward to grip his shoulder reassuringly. "I'll pick a name."

He seemed to visibly relax with that.

"Here, why don't I clean these plates off for you and you boys can move into the living room?" Taylor murmured, reaching across the table to collect our dishes before anyone could stop her.

As soon as she disappeared into the kitchen, Larry pushed back his chair with a grunt and stood, walking over to the windows that faced out the back.

His house had even better views of the ocean than my restaurant. Rumors from Eli were that he'd been offered at least twenty million to sell the house, always refusing because it had been built by his great-grandfather. Honestly, parts of it still looked like it might not have been updated since then even though when Eli lived with him, he'd made some improvements.

"Larry, what's going on?" I asked, standing next to him, unable to see much of anything except the way the moon reflected off the ocean.

"She needs a name."

Christ. "I just told you, I'll name the damn—"

"Not that." I just caught his eyes as they looked to me from underneath his heavy eyelids. There was a tiredness. Maybe even pain, hidden in them.

"Taylor has a name," I said with a low voice. "You know that. Seems to be the only name you can remember when it comes to any girl I've ever been with."

"Because it's the only one worth remembering to me for you." *I couldn't disagree.* "But I want to know who she is to you."

"Larry, it's not that simple."

"Yes, it goddamn is, son. It *is* that simple," he accused. "Just like when I took you to that first meeting. All your anger... all your mistakes... all your mess that you trailed here with... You stood up and said, 'Hi, my name is Ash and I'm an alcoholic,' and all of it became simple. It had a name and that name let you face it. That name gave you something to conquer."

I didn't know what the hell to say, mostly because I had no idea where this was coming from. It was all true though.

It was all so fucking true.

"There may be a million things between you and her, but they only need one damn name. *One.* To tell you if you're fighting for more or fighting to let go."

My mouth thinned as I stared him down.

I didn't want to admit it because it was the same thought I struggled with earlier—that I wasn't enough for Tay. That she deserved better and until I was *better,* I couldn't have her. Even though I could acknowledge my shortcomings, I couldn't stop punishing myself for them. But it was no longer my place to judge or to punish.

"I can't stop feeling guilty," I admitted quietly, for a second needing him not as a mentor or as my sponsor but as my friend. "I can't stop feeling guilty that who I am still isn't enough."

It was that kind of thinking that pushed my drinking over the edge in the first place. It was that kind of thinking I'd tried to drown out. Now, I admitted it. *Step Ten. Continuing to take inventory of my shortcomings and admit to them.*

"I know," he said with a haggard voice, reaching into his pocket. "Dan told me about what you said the other week." He held out his hand and I jerked back, realizing he held the six-month blue sobriety chip between his fingers for me to take. "We all fall short, boy. Mistakes don't mean we aren't enough; mistakes just mean there's an opportunity for us to be more. You either take that opportunity or you don't."

I hadn't for a long time but now I did. I took every opportunity to be so much more than the self-loathing asshole that I was.

Swallowing over the boulder in my throat, I took the warm metal from his fingers and stared at it.

I knew it was time.

I'd confessed to Taylor. It was finally time to confess to my sister and the rest of my family the mistakes I'd made, and the opportunity I'd taken to become more.

"Now. *Who. Is. She?*" he demanded.

He could wait for the name of my restaurant; he couldn't wait for this.

With a harsh exhale, I turned toward the window. Just like the ocean reflected the moon's light, there was no hiding the truth. There was no more running from it.

"She is mine." But it was more than that. "*She is my redemption.*"

Taylor

I chewed on my lower lip. Ash had been basically silent since we left. Even after I rejoined him and Larry for that promised chocolate, he didn't say much. Although, I caught him staring at me with a new kind of intensity that drove straight through my heart before traveling further south.

"Is everything okay?" I couldn't stop myself. "Is Larry okay?

He just nodded, making my anxiety worse.

What if Larry had chastised him for getting involved with me? Because of the baby? What if he was upset for Danny?

My mind rattled through all of the possible options while my heart shrunk farther back into its cell.

"How's baby Ragnar?"

I blinked twice before I had the wherewithal to frown.

"That is not *her* name." My arms crossed over my stomach,

as though I could save him or her from hearing what their father insisted on calling them.

Even his smile didn't reach too far as we pulled into the drive. There was a heaviness between us. I could say it was a lot of things, but I knew it was mostly desire—the kind so intense that it was like trying to use a pail of water to put out a forest fire. No matter what we did to put out the edges, at the core, everything inside us was consumed by it.

Ash shut the front door behind us. There was the sound of the ocean surrounding us as it broke over the shore and echoed up the side of the cliff. A cool dampness in the air lingered from the rain earlier, and the pale blue moonlight streamed so brightly into the cabin, bathing it in an ethereal glow, that I could see every shadow and hard plane of his face, the rise and fall of his sculpted lips, without any trouble even though there were no lights on.

The silence between us was the noiseless moment before a sonic boom—and we were about to go from frozen still to faster than the speed of sound in barely a second.

"Ash..." I turned and whispered his name, sighing as his warm hands cupped my face. His thumb brushed over my lower lip like it was knocking, begging for confirmation from them.

"Taylor" –my eyes fluttered open—"I want you. I want you so damn bad sometimes I think my body might give out if I don't have you. I want to mark every inch of your body, watch it go from pale to red from my teeth. I want to feel your tight little pussy around me... strangling me as you come."

I gasped and his eyes pinned mine.

"But I need to know it's what you want. Because, fuck, Tay, I know things are complicated for you. Being here. Your family. The baby. I know it can't be easy for the girl who always has a plan to not have one right now. But I don't want this to turn into a regret. I won't let that happen. You're too important." His voice broke on those words and set off fireworks in my chest. "I'll be here, sweetheart. I'll be here for you no matter what happens or what you decide."

Licking my lips, I leaned in closer to him, needing to feel his warmth and protection. Tears pricked in the corners of my eyes—again. Every time he swore to take care of me, to not let anything stop him from doing that... I couldn't even describe how it made me feel. More than just safe and secure. More than cared for.

He made me feel cherished.

No one ever made me feel like this before. And especially not since I became pregnant. I'd been treading murky waters filled with guilt and shame, trying to keep my head above water before I came to find him. In his presence, I couldn't remember how I'd ever let myself feel like that about something so beautiful.

"I just want you, Ash," I whispered, trailing my eyes up the pulse in his neck until they finally dropped off into his blues. "I've always wanted you."

Demanding lips captured mine as I felt his groan against my chest. He tasted like red wine and chocolate. Dark and decadent and everything that had invaded my dreams long before he'd ever kissed me.

His mouth always took my breath away. *Every single time.* At least now I was prepared for the theft.

Strong fingers threaded through my hair, pulling it back and cupping my face at the same time. Tilting my head, his tongue dove deeper inside my mouth, marking every inch with a new possessiveness.

The room spun, twisting me away from reality into a world built solely around him. The ground made of his body. The air made from his breath. The sun made from his mouth—bright and burning, warming my body from the inside out.

Just one time, I promised myself. *Just one night.*

And then tomorrow, I would tell him. Even if it only changed the world and not how he felt, I wanted one night under the sun before I weathered the storm.

Chapter Twenty

Taylor

I shivered as he pulled my light sweater up over my head, the soft fabrics leaving a trail of embarrassment over my skin.

There was no reason for it.

We'd been naked and fooling around every day and sleeping in the same bed every night since that first time, but tonight was going to be *more* and for some reason, that made me feel like less.

My bump had popped out further in the past week and a half, making me feel well on my way to a beach ball with legs. My mind knew he'd seen this. My mind knew he'd seen all of me—if not when his mouth was on me, then when he was rubbing my back or my feet because they ached. Still, *knowing* did nothing to calm my nerves.

I shivered as he unbuttoned each ivory attachment down the center of my shirt, his touch whispering over my body until the whole thing was undone and he gently pushed it off my shoulders, leaving me in nothing but my bra.

He pulled back, desire flaring in his eyes as they drank in the way my breasts spilled just a little higher out of my bra that stretched to its limit over them.

My knees went weak when he felt down my back for the clasp. The tension released with a soft pop and I whimpered as the support fell away.

It was shameful and sacred how my body responded to his gaze. My breasts tingled, my nipples hardening into eager peaks, reaching toward his touch. Heat pooled between my legs, preparing—*knowing*—what was finally happening. My body ached to be filled by him once more.

"Ash…" I moaned his name as his lips trailed along my jaw to my ear. Goosebumps laid heavy tracks all over my skin, easy trails to follow to the very source of my desire.

His strong hands pushed down the elastic waist of my jeans.

"Off," he growled at me, moving back only enough so I could comply and peel the jeggings down off my legs.

I shuddered. Not that there were people around to see but standing in the middle of the living room in nothing but my white lace-edged panties with all the windows open was probably something I shouldn't feel comfortable with—*but I did*.

I waited for the embarrassment. I waited for the guilt of *less than* to remind me I was bigger and bloated, to remind me my boobs were too big for my small frame, to whisper how I was a million shades of not-sexy… until I caught his gaze.

I waited for the guilt to remind me how bare my left hand was.

But it only lingered in the distance. Like water behind a dam—one that Ash had built and continued to reinforce every single day.

In his eyes, any lingering embarrassment disappeared. *Melted.* Evaporated under the heat of his feral desire, his lip twitching as though he were about to devour me on the spot, unable to wait to even get me in the bedroom.

"So fucking beautiful, Pixie," he rasped.

He didn't know it, but he'd looked at me like this the first time, too. Afterward, I told myself it was because he was so drunk he was probably seeing whatever he wanted. Now, my heart squeezed to know that he'd always seen me. *That he'd always wanted me this way.*

"Feels like I've dreamt about this moment for too damn long… for my whole damn life." His unsteady breaths tightened his shirt against his chest.

My heart wanted to tear in half.

Instead, I settled for stripping him down as bare as me.

Curling my fingers into the edge of his shirt, I peeled it up over the hot ridges of his torso. And, as though they were slathered in paint and I could mark him, I splayed my hands on the muscles of his chest, feeling them vibrate underneath me with the beating of his heart.

Dragging my fingers on a greedy path lower, I reached the waistband of his jeans. I brushed against the head of his erection in my attempt to undo them and moisture rushed in a hot wave between my thighs. I looked at the long, thick outline of his arousal embedded against the front of his pants.

For me.

Because of me.

A second later, I found my wrists imprisoned and held to my sides.

"Shit, Tay," he whispered, and I gaped at the effect I had on him.

The tensing and tremors of his torso as he fought for restraint in even breaths.

His eyes snapped open and drowned me in a desperate blue sea.

I didn't know why I doubted myself. Every time he saw me, he was like this—on the brink of losing his sanity if he didn't touch me, if he didn't claim me in some way.

He stepped toward me like a predator, ignoring my small

yelp as he gripped the fleshy curves of my butt and hoisted me up against him. My cry was swallowed by his mouth as he kissed me hard, my legs clamping around his waist for security as he carried me back to the bedroom.

It was only a few steps, but in temptation-tainted-time, it felt like eons. And when I sensed him stop in front of the bed, I was moaning against him, frustrated beyond all measure that the swell of my stomach prevented me from grinding my hips harder against him.

"Patience, Tay," he rasped softly against my mouth as he laid me down on the bed, making no move to leave the space between my thighs. "Just let me love you."

My eyes jerked to his. His gaze was consuming and under it, I couldn't breathe.

He looked like a man not about to have sex for sex's sake, not for desire's sake, but for forever. He looked like a man who wasn't just going to make love to me, he was going to mark my soul, stamp it with his name, and never let it go.

Like the reverse of Adam's rib being taken to make Eve.

Ash was going to take something from me, something that would make us one.

I had a feeling that something was going to be whatever was left of my heart that I hadn't already given.

In another world, another Taylor would've been ashamed the way I wanted him—the way my body responded in desperation to his.

My mind called out, searching for the old Taylor and her rules to come charging in. But here... with him... the old Taylor couldn't come to the phone; *she was gone*.

There was a moment of stillness, the moment that always comes when that word is spoken the first time. So heavy, so full of *everything*, it drags time to a stop to make sure it's given deference.

His lips gently touched mine, a kiss that was meant to seal in his words, before he trailed down my neck in search of other parts of me desperate for his mouth.

My heart raced as he fulfilled his promise, his teeth marking a trail down my throat and onto my chest, heading for my breasts that rose and fell unsteadily along with my breath.

I gasped and arched off the bed when one hand closed over the weight, kneading and rolling it possessively in his grasp as though he weighed and measured each change in my body between last time and this.

His hands on my sensitive and swollen breasts were big and hot and rough, and I couldn't stop the way my body trembled and whimpered for more.

"I love your tits like this," he murmured, kissing along the side of the other swell. "So needy, so responsive. Fuck, I know I could make you come just from touching them."

I gasped as my hips jerked up, bumping my belly against his solid stomach.

It hurt. The needing him hurt with how much it filled me. With how much it burrowed out from my cells as though in hibernation all these years.

"Careful, sweetheart."

My breath stitched when his mouth detoured from its path to kiss the top of my stomach while his hands continued to drive my breasts insane.

But then it returned to close over my nipple, and as the pleasure made breathing altogether hard, he brought his jean-clad knee up between my thighs and gave my sex something to rub on.

I lost a little of my sense of time and my sense of control, my other senses stealing from them to work overtime. One hand curled into the sheets alongside me, trying to find some tether to make sure my body didn't completely break from gravity, the other held onto the back of his head, making sure his mouth didn't let go of me.

He feasted on me like he'd never been given food in his entire life. Each pull of his lips, every nip of his teeth, sending hot, demanding sparks of need right down to my center. He licked and sucked and devoured my breasts until they were varying shades of pink and red—a masterpiece made from his mouth.

"You're soaking, Tay, and *fuck*, it's driving me insane."

My sense of comprehension was delayed, taking a second to realize that all this time I'd been grinding against his leg had shoved my panties to the side, so my core was rocking directly against the rough denim. And there was a distinct dark, wet spot to mark my presence—and evidence my need.

My eyes fluttered as his hand slid down along my stomach toward where I needed him most.

But then he stopped, I almost lost it. *I'd never come so close to cursing in my whole life as I did in that moment.*

I let out a soft, ragged noise, my eyes burning with unshed tears as I looked at him staring down at my stomach. Invariably, this moment came every time he touched me. Like the miracle inside my body deserved a moment to be worshipped, too. But this time, it was almost too much for me not to tell him as he slowly bent and gave an open-mouthed kiss just above my belly button.

It was almost too much, seeing the way he looked at me, touched me, like the baby was his.

He looked at me like the baby was his.

It was that moment that almost made my heart burst because it was then I knew with my whole heart, it didn't matter that the baby actually *was* his, in Ash's eyes, it was his baby no matter who its genes were from.

"Mine," he whispered, holding my tear-filled gaze as he stood.

The possession in his voice soothed the deepest part inside of me—a part that's always been his. Waiting. Questioning. *Wanting.* But now, with all the self-righteous shields and crippling commandments stripped away, I was left bare with nothing but the most basic foundation of faith, *to love and be loved,* brought to the surface.

I want to love him.

I want to be loved by him.

My lip quivered, my own voice about to betray me when he reached for the waist of his jeans and my mouth went dry. Instantly, the primal demand of my orgasm began to knit together, tight and tighter as I watched him strip away the rest of his clothes.

My thighs rubbed together seeing the way his jaw clenched when he pulled his jeans down over his erection. Long and impossibly thick, it bobbed free from its confines, the prominent vein pulsing urgently all the way to its purple tip.

I licked my lips. I wanted to taste him. I loved having him in my mouth when he lost control. It made me feel so powerful, so desirable. *I loved how he made me feel that way.*

Ash bit off a curse. "Not tonight, sweetheart," he warned huskily, his grin saying he knew where my thoughts had gone. "I won't survive your pretty little mouth tonight, Tay."

Growling, he tugged my scrap of soaked underwear from me. My legs parted instinctively for him as he climbed back on the bed. I saw the moment his best laid plans ended up with a detour as his shoulders caved and his head dropped between my thighs.

"Ash!"

I jerked against his mouth as it clamped over my sex. Covering... devouring me. His tongue moved angrily through my slick core, greedily lapping and sucking in the spots he knew by now would drive me insane.

"Please, Ash... *Please...*" I choked out the words, knowing what I wanted, hearing myself say what I wanted, but not being able to get the words out.

"I love tasting you like this," he growled as his tongue savagely speared against my clit. "You're like my own personal forbidden fruit, Pixie, and fuck if I wouldn't fall from grace every single day if it meant I got to spend it tasting you."

I shuddered and bucked against him.

My knee worked under his chest and pushed up. His lust-glazed eyes pinned me, demanding to know why I'd pulled him away.

"Please," I panted breathlessly. "I want... I need you inside me."

He slid up my body, pushing my hair back from my face.

"You sure, sweetheart?" he asked, his voice pulled tight.

I was too needy and he was too nice. My teeth clamped down onto his lower lip and I pulled it hard into my mouth. Ash let out a hiss and I felt his arousal jerk against my leg.

"Anything for you."

And the sweetest, most intoxicating truth was that he didn't just mean that in bed.

He pushed up from me. I wanted to feel him against me, inside me, but I knew my belly made that impossible right now. Firm hands gripped my thighs and spread them wide as he stared down.

"Tell me what you want, Tay," he rasped as he began to slide his hard length against my core, coating himself with my wetness, before wedging just his tip against the entrance to my core.

"I-I want you," I whimpered out as he rubbed over the one spot that threatened to make me explode.

"Tell me more," he demanded harshly. "Tell me what your body wants you to say... what your body wants..."

I moaned, hesitant to say the words until he stopped moving, cutting off the path to my release.

My gaze locked with his. "I want… your cock." I shuddered. The word felt thick and foreign and full of promise on my tongue as I set it free into the space between us. I'd never be able to describe how he made my body feel when he lost his composure and whispered naughty things against my skin. For days, the truth wasn't the only thing that had been desperate to escape my lips. I hadn't grown up with these words. I hadn't said them. I'd tried not to hear them. And now, I craved them. They burned to come off my tongue for him.

For him, they didn't feel shameful. For him, they felt essential. For me, they felt powerful.

I didn't know how to explain it. Tonight. His touch. Our desire. My freedom. All I knew was that it was truer than anything I'd ever felt.

Ash threw his head back with a strangled grunt and I saw the tip of his cock begin to glisten.

Just like when looking at my body—in whatever state it was in—made him grow impossibly hard, watching what I could do with just my voice empowered me.

"Please, Ash," I moaned, rubbing myself along his length until I felt him slip just inside me once more, taunting me with his tip. "I need to feel you inside my pussy."

"*Fuck*," he swore as his hips jerked back and he slammed inside me.

Oh, God.

I cried out at the invasion. Pleasure and pain ripped through me as my sex desperately tried to make room for something so large. Stretched and burning, my body reverberated from the shock of having him inside me again, of being opened like this for only the second time.

"*Fuck, fuck, fuck,*" he cursed and pulled all the way out.

My body reeled just as harshly as I tried to gasp in air—unsure which hasty motion was worse. My sex clenched, knowing it had gotten what it wanted only to have it ripped away. Like a chair pulled out from underneath you, I tried to find my balance as my body continued to fall.

"*Shit.* I'm sorry, Tay," he rasped painfully as he bent over my face. His hand cupped my cheek. "Are you okay? I wasn't thinking... I needed to be inside you... I fucking lost it. Please tell me you're okay. Please tell me I didn't hurt the baby."

I whimpered because I didn't know whether to cry or laugh or smack him.

"Look at me," I demanded, watching as his eyes fell and his brow scrunched. "The baby is fine. I, however, am not fine." Tortured horror marred his features just as I continued, "I'm not fine because I told you I needed you. I've needed you for weeks, Ash. You've been gentle and generous, but I don't think you understand how much I need you inside me right now. You want me to tell you?" With each word, my confidence and my desire grew. "I'm telling you that I've dreamt of your cock filling me, finally. I'm telling you I want you buried so deep inside me I feel you against my stomach. So, no, I'm not fine because I'm not getting what I want."

His response was in his eyes as he moved back and pushed two fingers inside me, curling right into that spot that had my pussy squeezing on the edge of release in a second.

I was sore and throbbing from his brief and violent entrance, but the soreness made the pleasure he now followed it with even sweeter.

The air around us seemed to disappear, like we'd finally gone off the deep end into something we were never coming back from. And then I felt him, the blunt head of his cock where his fingers had just been, pushing back inside.

"You feel so good, baby," he growled. "So tight and fucking hot."

The resistance was impossible, my muscles clamped tight against another intrusion. But then his fingers found my clit and began rubbing over the swollen nub, and all the fractured pieces of my orgasm began to pull back together and re-form itself toward a whole.

Ash looked like a man strangled—like a man dangling on the tips of his toes, trying to stop the noose around his neck from doing its job. He was teetering, balancing on determined restraint as he filled me inch by swollen inch.

His hands on my knees tightened as he sunk completely inside me, bumping against my womb. I shivered for a long second, absorbing the feel of him buried inside me once more, heat rolling through my body in waves as the burning length of him pulses violently against my inner muscles, stretching and tugging on him even as he tried to remain still.

I see you, Ash. My words from that night echoed in the cavern of my chest.

I hadn't known all of what I'd meant until this moment. Like being in this town had peeled back the layers of guilt, unshackled me from my upbringing, to let me finally see the truth.

The truth was what would make me free.

And the truth was I'd always seen him.

It had always been Ash for me.

'Ashes to ashes.' I'd heard the phrase a million times, but it was mine now.

Ash to Ash, I would always be his.

And then he began to slide in and out, pulling moans from my chest like incoherent prayers. His hands gripped my knees, widening them so he could fill me completely with each thrust as he picked up his demanding pace. Like a caged lion, it was both controlled yet wild at the same time.

I felt the damp fabric of the sheets in my hands from where they'd gripped them so tightly as my body began to coil tighter. I knew I was moaning his name. I knew I was panting and writhing up to meet each thrust. But all I heard was the slap of his hips against mine each time he shoved all the way inside me, rubbing against the neediest part of me.

I tried to focus on him, to watch as he stared down at where his cock disappeared inside my body, but each stab of pleasure made more and more of that vision go black.

"I dreamt of this too, you know," he growled angrily, his voice losing its composure as his hips began to buck involuntarily into me. "For months, I've dreamt of fucking you."

I cried out as his fingers began to work magic on my clit. The drag of their rough pads over my nerves made me feel like I was on the verge of either the most beautiful desire or the most exquisite death.

Now, I couldn't see anything. I couldn't feel the sheets or the bed or even the air that entered my lungs. I only felt him— on me, inside me. And I heard nothing but his voice, like it was the only thing that could lead me through the darkness to the light my body desperately craved.

"*Fuck, Taylor,*" he grunted as his thrusts lost all semblance of control.

Every muscle on his carved chest pulled tight like a rubber band on the brink of snapping as he lifted and angled me, my body nothing but a small toy compared to how big and strong his arms and hands were.

I knew nothing except the way he slammed into me now as his fingers rubbed on my clit. His other hand slid down to pin my hip to the mattress, no longer allowing me to do anything except take all of him. I knew nothing except that this was both the end of something and the beginning of another.

"Look at me," he croaked in a way that was both a demand and a plea.

My eyes trembled as they rose to his and my teeth sunk into my lower lip, giving my body some semblance of sharp pain to cling to as the pleasure became overwhelming.

And when I couldn't take it any longer, I looked at him, lost in his adoring and ravenous gaze, and breathed, "I see you, Ash."

His gaze swallowed mine in a whirlpool of need as he pulled roughly on my clit and I shattered, screaming his name.

My orgasm felt like nothing short of holy as it flooded me with wave after hot wave of shuddering release. My legs tensed and every muscle felt like it curled and clamped over on itself as my climax gave my body a new heartbeat to pulse with.

It felt like my body was broken and then reformed just for him.

Ash groaned, his hips releasing into me with rough thrusts. My pussy squeezed, grabbing and pushing all around him, urging him on. In the distance, I heard Ash's animalistic roar just before his warmth flooded inside me.

His.

Only his.

The only thing I could think as he continued to push into me until the pulsing of his cock finally slowed.

If I thought I remembered the first time, I thought wrong.

They say that you forget the pain of childbirth otherwise you'd never do it again. As the particles of my body floated back down, putting me back together like an image coming back into focus, I thought the same must go for this. Because, if you could remember this pleasure so perfectly, you'd never do anything else.

"You okay, Pixie?" It sounded like his orgasm had broken him, too.

"Am I still in one piece?" I asked softly.

The gravelly rumble of his laugh sent shivers down my limp and lifeless spine. The remains of my orgasm still lolling over my arms and legs in heavy waves.

"One perfect," he paused as he slid out of me, "piece."

My eyes squeezed shut for a moment, my body registering his loss.

"Don't move, gorgeous."

Like I even could.

I felt like I was floating. My body and my mind. Every so often the clouds would clear and I would remember the promise I made to myself to tell him or I would feel the way he cleaned me with a warm cloth. Time passed in moments in reality stuck between spans of feeling.

The drugged feeling of complete release interrupted by the moment he helped me to my feet to get ready for bed. The warmth of pure happiness punctuated by the way he pulled me into his arms when we made it back underneath the covers. The bone-deep comfort of safety when he bent and pressed his lips to my forehead.

"I dreamt of you, Tay," he whispered against my hair as his hand ran up and down my arm. "So many nights, I dreamt of *this* night—of making you mine. And my God, if I hadn't woken up, I would have sworn the dreams were so real that they must have been memories."

My heart stopped.

I couldn't move. I couldn't breathe.

They were memories.

"Until tonight." His fingers tugged my chin up so I couldn't hide. "Now I know that no dream would compare the this," he murmured. "I know that even Heaven couldn't compare to you."

He pressed his lips to mine, silencing any and all further thought.

Chapter Twenty-One

ASH

It had taken me a long time to be able to wake up in the morning and look forward to the day ahead of me. *A long fucking time.*

For so long, I'd lived like there was no tomorrow because there'd been no tomorrow for me. But the day after I'd signed the papers—the deed for the restaurant and house—marked the real beginning of a future. Of waking up with a purpose other than to crawl out of the endless black hole I'd fallen into.

It was a simple thing—*and fuck if I wasn't grateful for the simple things.*

I'd even thought it was monumental. But it turns out it was nothing compared to waking up next to Tay this morning.

Sure, we'd shared a bed for almost two weeks now, but each of those days, I woke feeling like I was in Wonderland—like I never wanted to fucking leave but at the same time, didn't know how long I was going to be able to stay.

This morning changed everything.

This morning I woke up and looked forward to the future—*a full future.* One that I could share with someone. *Or someones.*

I watched her as she slept on my chest, her soft breaths moving the hair that fell in front of her face. It was comfortable torture to feel her body pressed against me, one leg slung over mine, the brush of her tits against my side and the firm bump of her stomach pressed to my hip. I'd been in a constant state of semi-arousal since I woke—and probably while I slept—but I wasn't going to move for the world.

Larry had been right about a name. She was my redemption, but more importantly, she was *mine*.

My eyes shot to her face when she moaned slightly, her body gently shifting against me. She was trying to get comfortable, something I knew was going to get more difficult until the baby came.

But when she moaned again, I realized it had nothing to do with pregnancy and everything to do with being uncomfortable in a whole different way.

A groan slid from my mouth when her hips angled against me and I felt the heat and wetness of her pussy rub against my leg.

My girl was having a wet dream.

Instantly, my cock was hard as stone. But I didn't want to wake her—I was too intrigued. Instead, I grit my teeth together as her soft moans appeared with greater frequency as she began to rock against me.

I wasn't going to wake her—but I couldn't do nothing while she used my leg to get off.

Reaching down, I fisted my cock, stroking it in rhythm with her.

Sliding my leg out, I angled it so that she could ride it with more pressure. My hand pumped with more pressure, more speed as I felt how strangled her breathing became. She moaned my name in her sleep and a growl tore from my chest, the thought of her dreaming about me shooting right down to my dick.

And then she froze.

Shit.

Ever so slowly, emerald-encrusted irises blinked open and peered up to mine, heavy and pulsing with unfulfilled desire.

"A-Ash?" she stammered, lust mingling with confusion. "I'm sor—"

My mouth crushed hers. "Don't fucking apologize. Hottest fucking thing I've ever woken up to, sweetheart, so you either finish yourself on my leg, or you climb your sweet ass up onto my dick before I explode," I growled against her mouth.

Her whole body quaked against mine as she pushed up. I rose up and tilted forward to capture one of her nipples, hungry for the pebbled peak as she practically presented it in front of my face. Her path halted, a long moan sliding from her lips as she let me suck hard on her.

Whatever words she had were gone as she whimpered and moaned against my mouth, arching and begging for more. I could never deny her. *I would never want to.*

My hands found their way to her sides, rubbing along her silky warm flesh all the way down to her hip. Her body felt as though it was made of clouds and sunshine: impossibly soft and lush, and burning up inside.

I laved over her for long minutes. Her finger found their way into my hair, burying against my scalp, unsure if she wanted to pull me closer or push me away, knowing what came next.

Until she decided, I stuck to my task, flicking and sucking on her swollen breasts. All the while, I relished the way her body shuddered and tensed underneath me because of how sensitive her tits were and just how crazy my tongue could make her. And I did.

"*Please...*"

An electric thrill shot up my spine. I loved when she pleaded for me.

I loved when she needed me.

I loved it because I knew she didn't have to.

Taylor had the kind of strength that propelled her away from family and friends because it was the right thing to do for her baby even though it might not have been the right thing to do for herself. She had the kind of strength that promised her every kind of success no matter which path she chose in life.

So, when she begged me, it felt like the sun asking for help from a nightlight to illuminate the day. It was never about being necessary—*it was about being needed.*

I let her nipple pop from my mouth as I laid back and captured her hooded gaze. Tightening my hands on her waist, I guided her up to straddle me, wedging my cock against the hot wet heaven between her thighs.

My hands reached for her waist, guiding her until she straddled me.

I swelled against her pussy, the thick tip of my dick turning red as I lingered over the sight of her generous tits, red and flushed, knowing how I was going to make them bounce.

"Sit on my cock," I instructed.

With pink-stained cheeks and panted breaths, I watched her rise up. I hissed as a small fist tortured my dick when she grasped and positioned it at her entrance, coating the tip with her slick heat.

I let out a long, strained curse from the very depths of my chest as she carefully lowered herself on me, as though she could break me. Stars exploded in my vision as her hot little pussy sank down inch by painful inch and swallowed me whole.

"Oh, fuck, Pixie…"

Her small gasp at the end told me I'd just pushed a little bit farther inside of her than I had last night.

With a little pressure from my hands, she began to rise up and down along my cock. I wanted to close my eyes, but I couldn't take them off of her tits bouncing, her swollen stomach, and my dick sliding in and out of her slick pink pussy, making it glisten with her desire.

This didn't just outrank her wet dream as the hottest fucking thing I'd ever seen. *It completely obliterated it.*

When she began to ride me, driven by her need to come, my hands slid one up to her stomach and the other to the breast that my mouth had missed. She was so damn soft and overflowing everywhere I touched, like I'd never be able to get enough of her.

She chanted my name over and over, rising and falling frantically as her pussy squeezed around my dick.

The way she rolled against me, I knew I was hitting that sweet spot along her front wall each time she sank down, her body shuddering on the verge of collapsing under the pleasure.

"Ash, *please*," she cried. She was so close and *fuck*, so was I.

Her pussy tightened around me and my balls seized. I needed her to come or I was going to explode without her.

Keeping one hand on her stomach, I reached between us and rubbed my thumb hard over her swollen clit and then she was screaming my name as she came violently like I'd pushed her very own 'detonate' button.

I watched as her orgasm worked her like a pleasurable puppet-master, seizing each and every taut string, winding her tighter and tighter before releasing and letting her crumble around me.

A shout tore from my chest, not expecting the force with which her body seized around me. It felt like the earth beneath me gave out and my release swallowed me whole. I let out a long groan as my cock pumped hard jets of cum deep inside her. One day, I'd put another baby in her stomach like this.

Just like this, I promised myself.

Tay sagged down against me and I pulled my arms tight around her.

"Good morning," I said with a low, hoarse voice.

Her soft mewl of contentment had my dick twitching, still buried inside her. "I'd say that was more than good."

I chuckled. "I'd say you're right."

Securing her limbs, I sat up and maneuvered to the edge of the bed, keeping myself inside her as I lifted her and carried her into the bathroom.

"Gonna get you in the shower and then I'll make us some breakfast."

She looked up at me with a twinkle in her eyes. "You don't want to shower with me?"

My laugh turned into a groan as I felt her muscles squeeze around me. "I do want to, sweetheart, but that wouldn't be a shower, one, and two, there's not enough room in this one for me to be able to do all the things I want to do to you."

With a sigh of resignation, she let me pull myself from her and slide her legs down to the floor.

"Glad to know I created a monster," I said with a wink and a small tap on her ass as she stepped into the warm stream of water. "Now, let me make us some food before baby Ragnar gets cranky."

I couldn't stop my laugh as her shy smile morphed into half-faked displeasure as I pulled the curtain between us.

"That is not the baby's name!" she yelled over the mist as I walked out to the kitchen laughing and trying to think of another moment in my entire life when I'd been this happy.

TAYLOR

I loved him.

It was the only thought that invaded my mind as I rinsed out my hair, hoping the warm water would wash away my fears. Looking at the small shelf of soaps, I couldn't even remember now if I'd conditioned my hair or just shampooed.

Deciding that I really didn't care, I turned the water off and reached for the towel Ash had left for me.

A moan accompanied my first step out of the shower. My body was sore. Not the normal sore from growing another human but a delicious sore. Like it had felt something beyond its limits and was now recovering.

I stopped, looking at the towel hook and tempted to leave mine on it.

No, Taylor. Get your hormones under control.

I finished drying off and tightened the towel around my chest, remembering that I'd read about this stage in *What To Expect When You're Expecting*. Honestly, I didn't know who wanted to keep who in bed more at this point.

I walked out into the kitchen to find Ash standing at the counter, two plates full of waffles that smelled far too good for my own good, staring at something in his hand.

"What's that?"

His head snapped up and clear blue eyes appeared. He held up a blue and gold coin between his fingers. It only took a moment for me to recall the other sobriety tokens he'd had fashioned around a leather-strap bracelet he usually wore.

"Larry gave it to me last night," he rasped. "Six months."

My breath caught and I closed the distance between us, needing to be close to him.

"Why last night?" I couldn't help but ask now that I knew meetings were on Tuesdays, and it was the weekend.

His jaw tightened. "He knew."

Ash held out the coin for me to take. The metal was heavy and warm from his touch. It carried a weight to it that meant it was more than a symbol. It carried a message that, even at six months, there was still a weight to be felt each and every day.

"Knew what?" I said softly.

"That I'm ready for Step Nine."

My eyes widened. "You're going to call Blake?"

I swallowed over the lump in my throat. It was probably better if I didn't hear that conversation in person; I'd need all the tissues in California for that.

"And then Zach and my parents," he told me. "I owe them an explanation."

My chest seized and blood rushed to my head.

Speaking of that... I owed him an explanation.

I'd never felt fear like I did in that moment.

Not when I found out I was pregnant.

Not when I found out my parents were moving back.

We both jumped at the pounding on the front door.

Like a glass of water crashing to the ground, the moment between us shattered, and all the courage I'd built up sprayed out to where I had no idea how I'd ever salvage it all.

With a low growl, Ash stalked to the door and cracked it for a split second to see who it was. There was a low rumble of voices before he opened it wider and Eli walked inside.

"Eli—hi," I said with a strangled voice, feeling my cheeks begin to burn as my arms awkwardly wrapped around my chest.

His eyes widened at my distinct lack of clothing. Normally, a towel would cover most of me, given my size, but because of the delightful belly I was now sporting, the material rode up high in the front. And by high, I mean a slight breeze would've shown Eli *way* more than he came here for.

Ash immediately pivoted himself between me and Eli.

"Hey, Pixie," he said quietly over his shoulder—the nickname always sent chills down my spine. "Eli's my friend and all, but really would rather not have to rip his eyes out for starin' at you like that."

I bit back a laugh at the subtle warning to his friend.

"I'll be right back," I mumbled and darted back into the bedroom, wondering why Eli had just shown up unannounced.

Flustered, I rummaged through my clothes that now hung in the small closet, quickly pulling out a tee and loose, comfortable overalls to throw on.

"Hey."

I jumped at Ash's voice.

"Hey, I was just about to come out," I said, pulling the last strap over my shoulder. His face didn't look the same as a few minutes ago; it was no longer happy and relaxed, there was a cloud of concern and frustration darkening his features. Whatever Eli had come to talk to him about wasn't good. "What's wrong?"

The muscle in his jaw tightened. "I have to go with Eli. Something is going on at Roasters."

"What?" Shock rippled through me as I stepped toward him. "What happened? Is everyone okay?"

"Yeah." He pinched the bridge of his nose. "Nothing like that. Just looks like someone broke in overnight and ransacked the place."

My hands cupped over my mouth, barely muffling my gasp. "Is Larry... Does Larry..."

"Eli told him this morning. Had it out with him to stay home, afraid what might happen if Larry saw the mess."

"So, it was bad..." I surmised, and when Ash didn't try to reassure me it wasn't, I knew I was right.

My hand pressed over my racing heart. Larry might be a

tough nut on the outside, but that coffeehouse was his home—*it was his family*. Eli was right to keep him away.

"Who found it?"

"Eve went to open at five and the door was unlocked."

"Oh, no... Eve." I swallowed; my mind felt like it was spinning in place, like an out-of-control top about to fall. "I'm coming with you—"

"No," he cut me off sharply. "I don't know who did this or what the hell is going on. I want you and the baby safe."

"Ash," I breathed incredulously. "I'll be safe if I'm with you. How is that less safe than me staying here? Alone?"

Turmoil shadowed his face and I could see he recognized I had a point.

"I'm not staying here," I said firmly, grabbing a sweater, about to storm past him. "I'm coming even if I have to walk there myself."

His hand shot out and caught my arm before I could walk by. "Christ, woman, I'd say there is such a thing as pregnancy brain, but Lord knows you're just as goddamn stubborn even when you aren't knocked-up."

"I assume you meant that as a compliment." I folded my arms on top of my stomach.

He grunted.

"Thank you," I said with a tart smile, rising up on my tiptoes to kiss him.

What was supposed to be a quick peck turned into something deeply possessive—something that had me swaying by the time he pulled back and the room came back into focus.

"You're mine, you know that, right?" he rasped softly, his thumb brushing over her cheek. "Both of you."

I swore there must be a Staples' 'Easy' button for my tears hidden somewhere on me that only Ash knew how to find.

"Ash…" I blubbered as his gorgeous golden face turned watery in front of me.

"I'll never let anything happen to you, Tay," he rasped. "No matter what you insist on trying to do."

"Y-yeah."

"Good." His hand reached for mine. "Alright, let's go see what the hell happened at Roasters."

I could only nod, unable to find any words left that could possibly be right. There was a sudden ache in my chest and I realized that my body wasn't the only thing that had felt beyond its limits.

I loved him.

I loved who he was. I loved who he wanted to be.

I loved that what he did for himself also did something to help others.

I loved the way he cared for me.

I loved the way he touched me.

I loved the way he claimed me.

Tears streamed down my cheeks. And I really, *really* loved the way that he saw this baby as his even when he didn't know just how true it was.

I was going to go with him. I was going to be there for him, for my friends, as they sorted out this mess, and then I was going to sit him down and tell him the truth. And I didn't care if aliens invaded or if this state fell into the sea, Ash Tyler was going to learn my baby belonged to him. *Right along with my heart.*

Chapter Twenty-Two

Taylor

Lord, give me strength.

The floor crunched underneath our feet like coarse, dry sand. Only, it wasn't sand. It was devastating debris.

Like layers of an onion, we stepped on levels of shards of glass, plaster, and drywall mingled with the shattered ceramic of plates and mugs, the crumbs of trampled pastries, picture frames, and photographs; and the deeper we got, the more tears spilled from the corners of my eyes.

"You sure you're okay?" Ash asked for the third time in just as many steps, his own voice laden with shock and anger.

I stood tall and nodded even though my insides felt like they were being twisted in knots.

It felt as though we walked over the wreckage of an entire world—*an entire community and history*—in a single spot. Years of Carmel Cove, decades of the Ocean family, a century of this town that made me feel at home... all laid to waste.

"Taylor." The crunch and splintering should have warned me, but I didn't even see Eve coming until her arms wrapped around me and pulled me close.

I gave Ash a small nod, letting him know it was okay to release my hand so I could hug Eve back.

"I can't... believe this..." I murmured in abject horror.

Somewhere between Ash telling me that Roasters had

been ransacked and us arriving, I'd begun to think of it as a robbery—a busted open door, a few broken cups, the register open and the little money inside gone.

Even when we bypassed the police tape and the crowd outside, it didn't change my expectations.

But this was no robbery.

Or if it was, the thief hadn't been sure what he was looking for and decided to destroy everything until he found it.

Tables and chairs were everywhere. Mugs and dishes broken on the floor. Coffee grounds all over the countertops, the floor. It just seemed wrong—to have the rich, welcoming aroma of coffee lingering in a space that had been ripped to shreds.

Even pieces of the walls were torn apart.

What could they have possibly been looking for?

When Eve pulled back, wiping her tear-streaked face with no purpose except to make room for more rivulets, I saw Ash and Eli standing in a group with three bigger guys, who were speaking and pointing at a few spots in the room.

"That's Dex and Ace Covington from Covington Security," Eve murmured to me.

I nodded, having heard the names before, but now finally able to put them to faces—serious, scary faces. *Handsome, but still frighteningly fierce.*

As though he felt my eyes clinging to his back and the way my heart felt like it was failing me, Ash trampled over the sea of debris and put his arm around my waist, pulling me against him as a sob broke free.

Devastating wasn't the right word for what this was.

Roasters was like the heartbeat of the town—and someone had wanted to destroy it. In some ways, it felt worse than desecrating a church.

In some ways, this was pure sacrilege.

He held me for long minutes as people moved around us

until I was able to breathe with any semblance of steadiness again. And when I finally pulled back, his fingers handcuffed mine and threw away the key.

It took only a short time for me to realize, it wasn't just for me that our hands stay tied together; it was for him, too.

There were also two policemen inside who wandered around like they were trying to look like they were doing something even though they appeared just as lost as I was. A few more seconds showed the only thing they really accomplished was making it difficult for Ash's private security friends to find some real answers.

"Dex, this is Taylor. Taylor, Dex Covington."

The large, lean man with slick dark hair was stark comparison to the other man, Ace, Dex's brother according to Eve, who'd been conversing with them earlier.

Dex looked like a world-class businessman—*or a world-class spy*. His brother, on the other hand, who'd disappeared into the back with Eve, looked like a Viking. Blonde hair, half-shaved, the rest long and pulled back... He looked like the real Ragnar.

"Taylor," Dex greeted me with a voice that was just as sophisticated and then focused his attention on Ash and lowered his voice. "This wasn't a robbery," he informed us.

Ash's fingers tightened in mine. "What?"

Even though Ash might be uncertain, this man wasn't. "They're going to write it up as a B and E and robbery but look at it... this wasn't just a robbery. They didn't just grab the money and go..." Dex shook his head in disgust. "They were looking for something. Eli's still trying to figure out if they found it, but the rest of this" –he motioned around us—"it was a message."

"Blackman..."

I looked up to Ash in confusion, never having heard the name before. His expression indicated that he'd tell me later.

A loud, screaming hiss caught everyone's attention and pulled it to Eve, standing at the espresso machine.

She stared at it for a second, her fingers trailing over its various knobs and handles, before she turned to us and said, "It's okay… Pavi's okay."

I got to her just as she burst into another round of tears.

It was a miracle.

And of all people, I didn't take that determination lightly, but there was no better explanation for why the espresso machine that belonged to Larry's great-grandparents, that had sat here for almost five generations, remained unharmed.

"The police said we can start to clean up." Ash put his hand on my shoulder. "Do you want me to take you home first?"

I shook my head forcefully. "I'm not leaving."

Something flickered in his eyes. Something deeper than all the shock and sadness. Something pure and only for me. *Something like love.*

And so, we began to work in a daze of disbelief, the situation becoming all the more real with each broken piece of this place we cleaned up.

Eve and I had waded through the mess, sorting through what was salvageable and what wasn't, and realizing one more small blessing in that none of the photos which had been hanging on the wall were harmed; their frames hadn't been so lucky, but those could be easily replaced.

Until a full inventory was done, Dex couldn't be sure what the intruders had been looking for, and that was going to take some time, given the amount of destruction.

At some point, Josie stopped in and brought us lunch because none of us had thought about stopping to eat. Even Baby Ragnar was too sad to complain.

The group of us worked through lunch, worked through

the afternoon, worked while we ate burritos Addison dropped off and worked until even the sun called it a day.

We worked because it couldn't be left like that. We worked because Eli had left for most of the afternoon, charged with making sure Larry was okay and keeping him away for now; the sight would have broken him.

There was still so much to be done... so much to be repaired. But Ash saw me fading even before I realized. Storming to the back with that possessive, no-nonsense face, he carefully pulled the box of undamaged mugs from my surprised hands and set it on the stove in the back, lifted me in his arms and gave Eve a curt 'It's time to go home' before carrying me out to the car.

I should have argued, but I had no energy to. As soon as we stepped out of the building, reality set in that I'd been on my feet all day and only eaten and drank a quarter of what I should have. And even at that, it was nothing compared to the exhaustion I felt. Every time I thought about Larry seeing what had happened...

I was barely in the car before my eyes drifted shut in utter exhaustion.

"We're home, sweetheart," Ash's murmur accompanied his arms worming underneath me to pick me up out of the front seat of his truck.

I hadn't even realized I'd dozed off, that's how exhausted I was.

"I can walk," I muttered even as I curled in deeper into his chest.

It had been a long day. And not just in time, but in emotion.

Minutes blurred as we stripped out of our dust-covered clothes and shoveled down leftovers sitting in bed.

We didn't talk about it—about what happened. Exhausted and overwhelmed with emotion, there was nothing to say. And when he finally pulled me into his arms once more, my shoulders sagged against him and I felt the tears begin to well again.

"Hey." Ash pulled me against his chest, tugging the covers up over us. "It's alright, sweetheart."

"I j-just keep thinking a-about Larry—" A choked sob cut me off.

"I know, Tay. I know. But he'll be okay. This will all be okay." He dropped small kisses all over my hair and face, finally settling on my lips for one of those soul-soothing kisses—the kind that make the world crumbling around you seem unimportant. "I promise you, sweetheart, it will all be okay. If there's one thing Larry… and the rest of this town… knows how to do, it's how to take something that looks completely unrecoverable and turn it around."

I shuddered, feeling the comfort from his words.

I felt so full—full of emotions that twisted and turned inside of me begging for release. I knew I loved him before today. I knew I loved him before yesterday. I knew that a part of me had loved him even when he was broken. It was the part that had gone for him, that had taken care of him, and that had given him a piece of me because I thought it could save him even if it meant condemning myself.

But today was the last straw.

Over and over I'd watched how life threw things at me that I never could've planned for. Trials. Triumphs. Today, I realized that the strongest emotion I'd felt in the middle of all this tragedy was love. Because in the midst of utter destruction, it's the only thing worth fighting through it for.

And I couldn't go to sleep without letting him know that I'd fight through anything with him… for him.

My tongue thickened and my chest swelled. Thoughts of Roasters fizzling out from my mind.

It wasn't the right time. I was beyond tired. *Deliriously tired.* We'd just spent a whole day in shock and recovery, and the end wasn't in sight. I didn't know if my legs existed anymore because I couldn't feel them or really see them below my belly. And Ash was lying with his head tipped back against the wall, eyes shut as though maybe today was all just a bad dream.

It was definitely not the right time.

But is there ever a right time?

Or is it just that *anytime* is the right time for something like this?

"Ash," I said softly, tipping my head up to his and waiting for his brilliant blues to peel back open. "I love you."

They were just words and the world all wrapped up in one. And for the first time all day, I finally felt peace.

I felt his chest shake underneath me. His eyes glinted like the hottest blue flame as the planes of his face hardened as he, too, tried not to be swallowed whole by his emotions. I could feel the electricity in the air between us, in our breaths.

It had always been there.

And I had just given it a name.

"I love you, Taylor," he said with a voice so hoarse and heavy with sincerity as he pulled my lips to his. "I love you so damn much."

There was no question if I meant it. Or if he did. Too tired for wonders or worries, the only thing that was left had to be the truth.

I came here, to him, with a million questions and searching for answers but the truth was when love is involved, there is no question.

There was only him.

"W-What are you doing?" My breathy gasp hitched in my chest as small bursts of fire flared along my skin where his lips touched.

"Making up for all the years I should have been kissing you," Ash growled as he pulled one of my nipples into his mouth.

How was I supposed to argue with that?

"S-Shouldn't we be going to Roasters?" My small moan protested my own suggestion.

The scent of coffee still lingered in the air around us from all the grounds that we'd had to clean up yesterday.

I arched off the bed as his tongue swirled around the hard peak, knowing it had a direct line straight to the center of my sex that was feeling decidedly too empty.

I groaned. Roasters wasn't even at the top of the list.

I'd told Ash I love him.

I told him I loved him, but I still hadn't told him about the baby.

"Ash," my quaking voice forced out.

Teeth closed down on my nipple and I shot off the bed as pleasure rocketed through me.

And just because I looked like a whale at the moment, didn't mean I was pulling off any *Free Willy* moves. Or at least with any semblance of grace.

"Sweetheart, stop asking questions while I'm trying to make love to you," he instructed against the sensitive skin of my breast before returning to his torture.

I let a loud moan of compliance slip from my lips. It was early; there was still time for this.

Closing my eyes, I felt him. His hard body wedged between my thighs. His mouth and hands covering every inch of my body. I was burning up—like telling him that I loved him was only half of the pact. I needed to feel him. I needed to burn the confession into his body with mine.

Hot, open-mouthed kisses trailed down the center of my chest, over my stomach, and landed squarely on my sex.

There was definitely still time for this.

My fingers claw their way into his silken disheveled hair, holding his tongue hostage against my clit as I moaned his name.

"Ash… please…"

I rose higher and higher, thrashing underneath him as my release just eluded me.

Then his mouth was gone as he slid up over me, replaced with the blunt head of his cock.

There was a split second where I wondered if he remembered what happened last night. *What if he didn't? What if he didn't mean it?*

"Know why you're so wet for me, sweetheart?" he rasped into my ear, holding himself steady even as my hips brushed the slick entrance to my pussy against him. "*Because you love me.*"

My breath lodged in my chest, my gaze hostage to his as he pushed inside me. *Inside my soul.* Hard, consuming, undeniable.

"And I love you, Taylor."

He did remember.

"Ash…" I sighed his name as he pushed up, careful of my stomach, so that he could shove that last inch all the way inside me.

Filled.

Every part of me was filled with him.

My sex. My stomach. My heart.

Ash grunted as his thrusts became less controlled. The subtle sheen of sweat glistened over the taut muscles of his chest. My hands dug into the sheets. *I wanted more.* I wanted to lick him and kiss him everywhere like he'd done to me. I wanted him harder and deeper inside me. I wanted to never let him go.

"I need..." I whimpered not even knowing anymore.

"Me," he growled fiercely as he slammed his cock inside me, knocking against the spot that set off fireworks deep inside my stomach.

I forgot about breathing as the waves of my orgasm began to crest.

"That's it, Pixie," he bit out as his hips drove into me. "Come for me."

He said it like I had any other choice.

My climax ripped my body apart as I screamed his name. Hot and cold, light and dark, pleasure and pain, I felt it all. Vaguely I heard his shout as his cock pulsed inside me, coating my insides with hot desire.

He pulled me to him as our bodies shuddered to recover, those same three words repeating from our lips unencumbered, unabashed, like they were no longer just the feelings we felt, but the air that we breathed.

Ash

I thought love would be one of those things you realize in the middle of some grand fucking gesture. On a beautiful island, in front of the sunset, with all the stars just waiting to shine above you.

Love wasn't any of that shit.

Love is like any other addiction. It starts with one taste. One night. One kiss. And then it grows until it's so much a part of you, you don't know if you can exist without it anymore.

I could exist without it. But that's all it would be—*existing*.

And I didn't want to just exist.

I wanted to live.

And when we walked into Roasters yesterday, all of a sudden it was like watching my heart move outside of my body as Taylor worked to clean up the chaos. There was no pristine scene from a postcard. There was only destruction surrounding her. There was no sunset or ocean waves. There was only the heavy aroma of coffee, the crunch of shattered ceramic, and an audience of police. But none of that mattered because I only saw her.

The light that shined in the darkness.

That was when I realized she was always there.

Even in the darkest parts of my recovery, she'd always been there, in my dreams, tempting me to be better. When I couldn't see the path in front of me, I followed her footsteps. I worked toward my dreams with one goal in mind, being the kind of man that Taylor Hastings could love.

It was an addiction.

It just so happens that this kind of addiction cured instead of killed.

"I don't think I can move," she murmured, her soft form moving against my chest.

I groaned. I didn't want her to either, but I had to go.

"You don't have to, sweetheart, but I have to get back to Roasters to meet Eli."

I didn't miss her wince as she pushed herself up to look at me and insist, "I'm coming with you."

"Taylor," I threaded my fingers into her hair, holding her forehead against mine. "You were on your feet for a straight twelve hours yesterday. You're not coming today."

"But Ash—"

"No," I cut her off with a kiss. "I'm meeting Eli and Dex. Please, sweetheart, I know you want to help. You literally make my heart want to fucking explode the way you are so compassionate and generous. But I can't… I can't let you come today. And not just because I know your body is wiped but because of the baby."

Her eyes fell. There wouldn't be much fight in her because she knew I was right. She was exhausted and while pushing herself to the brink one day was survivable, it would be tempting fate to do it again.

"Please, Tay. It will all be there tomorrow for you and Eve to work on." Her shoulders slumped with a sigh. "And you know how Larry would feel if you went and something happened to you or the baby."

"I know," she said softly. "I just want to make it better."

"Me too, sweetheart. Me too. But these kinds of things don't get fixed overnight. Not the right way at least. So, today we re-group, alright?"

When she remained silent, I sighed and added, "Plus, thanks to your wonderful calendar you made for me, I remembered the kitchen equipment is being delivered today. So, someone needs to be here to sign for it."

Her eyes perked up like I knew they would.

Luckily for me, signing a piece of paper was less taxing—both physically and emotionally—than cleaning and sorting through what still looked like a blast radius of a bomb inside the coffee shop.

I made short work of breakfast while Tay showered and dressed. I was supposed to be in town in five minutes but that wasn't happening. I hadn't planned on this morning. Actually, I hadn't planned on last night. I hadn't planned on her being the one to bring up love. And with that tying us together, there was no way I was leaving this house without being inside her at the same damn second as I told her I loved her.

My dick twitched again at the thought. There was just something so fucking hot about being buried balls-deep in my woman and telling her that I loved her, something so fucking possessive about knowing I owned her body and heart at the same time.

"What is all this?" she asked with a smile, seeing what I'd put out.

"Blended acai bowl. Blueberries, bananas, strawberries. Something to refuel with."

"I think the baby likes to refuel with bacon…" she murmured.

"I think the baby hasn't tried my acai." I winked at her.

She pulled out one of the chairs at the table and sat down slowly, wincing with soreness.

I shouldn't have, but I smirked when her eyes met mine. That tenderness was because of me. *Because she was mine.*

Watching the way her cheeks blushed was probably one of my top five most favorite sights in the entire fucking world.

"Hey, hey, hey." I quickly cupped her face, seeing the tears that collected in the corners of her eyes. "No crying, you hear? That's another of the doctor's orders for today. No crying and no stressing. All of that can resume tomorrow. I'm gonna go take care of some stuff with Eli and then when I come back, we can talk all about this—all about the baby, and the future," I promised.

Love changed everything.

Love meant there was no going back. Not for us. Not for her.

Carmel was never meant to be a permanent place for her, and now we were going to have to change that, or figure something else out. Even if it meant I was the one who had to leave…

"And then I'm going to make love to you… and fuck you… until you're so mindless that you agree to name the baby Ragnar."

Relief shot through me when she laughed. I couldn't leave if she was crying. *I wouldn't.*

"Love you, Tay," I said with a low voice, gently kissing her lips.

"I love you, too."

Chapter Twenty-Three

Taylor

"Hey, Blake. It's me. Taylor. Sorry I haven't called lately," I apologized into her voicemail, hugging my knees into my chest. "I have two things to tell you and I should probably wait to tell you and not your voicemail, but I can't. The first is that I'm in love with Ash. For some reason, I don't think this is going to come as too much of a surprise to you, but I had to tell you. And I have to tell you he loves me, too."

I drew a deep breath.

Love changed everything even though in some ways it changed nothing.

When I came to Carmel, I thought I had everything figured out. Or, at least, I was figuring it out. And then life threw me another curveball when Ash was not what I expected—and everything I still wanted.

I questioned everything. Things I thought were my weaknesses... maybe they're my strengths. The things I'd been told were the most important... maybe they just weren't.

"I wish I was calling just to tell you how completely and utterly happy I am but that's only part of it." I swallowed over the lump in my throat. "The other part is that I haven't told him yet... I haven't told him the baby is his."

I tried to swallow down my nerves. It was like trying to

take a handful of pills with the smallest sip of water; it felt like everything was stuck and clogged in my throat and air was struggling to get by.

"I was selfish, B. Our whole lives I feel like I've just watched Ash make decisions, putting loyalty above everything. How many times did we tell him he was *loyal to a fault?*" I reminisced. "I know you've done more than watch it; I know you've lived through his loyalty. And I couldn't be only one more loyalty to him. After coming here, I realized that the only thing worse than losing him would be for him to stay with me because I was one more mistake he needed to fix."

Grabbing a few tissues, I quickly wiped them over my face.

Stupid, stupid hormones.

"Our baby isn't a mistake," I blubbered. "*I'm not a mistake.*"

I was not a mistake to be corrected.

"So, I'm calling because someone needs to know I didn't tell him because I selfishly wanted him to choose love over loyalty. And in doing so, I'm afraid I might lose both." I let out a deep exhale as the words rushed from my chest. "I just... needed to tell you. I needed to confess to someone. And now, I need to tell him."

I pulled my cell down from my ear, staring at Blake's name on the screen for one more second before I ended the call, my fingers trembling with nerves.

All day, I'd kept my emotions at bay. I'd checked in on the restaurant. The painters were working this week and next to coat the walls with the color Ash had asked me to pick out. I'd gone with a pale, calm blue. Even walking around inside it for just a few minutes earlier had taken the edge off my nerves. Sometimes, it was the simplest things that could calm me.

Ash called around lunch to say that Eli had reluctantly

brought Larry down; the police needed his statement as the business owner and confirmation that nothing was missing—a difficult feat considering how much of a heartbreaking mess everything still was.

I'd asked how Larry had taken it and, with restrained details and a voice that could only be described as tremulous, Ash confessed that Larry hadn't taken it well at all. No matter how they reassured him the place would be good as new as soon as the investigation was closed, the elderly man couldn't seem to get past the destruction right in front of him.

Apparently, Eli had stopped the police interrogation halfway through to take an unstable Larry back home to cool off. They'd have to resume their questions another day. A few hours later, Eli had returned, shaken up from dealing with Larry, to check on everyone before heading out to Covington to see if Dex had learned anything new. My heart broke a little further for the man who'd done so much for everyone—a man who was so good—and who was now subjected to such evil.

As the day dragged later, my anxiety grew worse. I focused for a little reading *What to Expect* on my phone, but soon that wasn't enough. Turning on my laptop, I pulled up another recorded service, closing my eyes and clinging to my faith that the Lord would see me through this.

By the time it was finished, the sun had dipped below the horizon and a slow shower of rain tapped against the roof. When Ash's text came through that he was leaving in a few and would be home soon, my nerves balled in my throat and that was when I called Blake.

Setting my phone down, I padded over to the fridge to grab a seltzer water from inside and jumped when the front door opened.

Goodness, he got here fast.

"Hey, Tay." The soothing rumble of his voice slid over me.

A voice that had admitted to loving me, I reminded myself in an attempt to stay calm.

Just shutting the door, I half-turned when his arms came around me, his face nuzzled in my neck as his lips began a trail of butterfly kisses over my racing pulse.

"Hey," I said breathlessly as he buried his lips in my hair.

"I missed you." Another kiss behind my ear.

The soothing rumble of his voice slid over me. *A voice that had admitted to loving me,* I reminded myself in an attempt to stay calm. I sagged against him, soaking in his warm strength even when he was weary.

"I missed you, too," I said as he kissed the top of my head.

"How's baby Ragnar?" His warm palms rubbed over my stomach.

Yours. He's yours.

I felt like a snow cloud hanging low in the sky, pregnant with the weight of everything it was about to let go of.

I let out a quick, breathy laugh and I winced with another contraction. "Good."

"And how are you?" His eyes bored protectively into mine.

It was the way he asked, like he wasn't just talking about my body. He wanted to know how my heart… how my soul was. He wanted to know so that he could heal whatever was hurting.

"I'm fine." I swallowed over the lump in my throat. "Just some contractions."

He'd re-read the Braxton-Hicks section of our book several times, not believing me when I insisted this was normal.

I sucked in a breath when the cool metal of the fridge hit my back and then choked on the air as his body pressed flush against my front.

My whole body went into overdrive, like he'd turn on a shower of fire and thrown me into the stream. I felt the hard length of him pressing back against my stomach as our breaths mingled in the lust-laden air.

"Want to kiss you, Tay, because I've been dreaming of your lips all day, but 'okay' isn't good enough," he ground out. "What's weighing on you, Pixie? Because it looks like the weight of the world. Tell me what's going on and let me hold some of it."

Tears pricked in my eyes. Even now, drained and beleaguered, he was only thinking of me—only trying to heal whatever was hurting.

I squeezed my eyes shut. *Focus.*

"I need to talk to you about the baby," I began, my tone as unyielding as a bulldozer.

"Of course." He tucked my hair back behind my ears and cupped my face, searching for the answer I'd held caged and buried for too long.

I slid to the side and out of his arms. I wasn't going to do this on my feet. I was going to be sitting and stable. I had to keep the calm before the storm. *Just in case.*

He followed me to the couch. "You know I'm kidding, right? I don't think we should actually call the baby Ragnar..."

My hand shot to my mouth as I choked on a laugh that was dangerously close to a sob. "T-that's not it..." I stammered. "But I appreciate you clearing that up." A small smile flitted across my face as he sat and reached for my hands, not giving me a choice to not be touching him.

"Is this about us?" He drove his hand through his hair nervously, and I could only stop and stare at the intense worry on his face. "Because, fuck, Tay, when I said I loved you, I meant it. I meant all of you. And I meant the baby, too. I don't care who he came from, he... or she... belongs to me. I want it all, Tay. I want it all with you."

Love made my heart swell and fear made it beat

frantically, the combination making me feel as though my chest was about to explode.

"And I know there's a lot, and I've read all about nesting. I know we have a lot to buy and that this place isn't nearly prepared let alone baby-proofed yet, but it will be. I promise," he swore vigilantly. "I'll have this place remodeled before the baby comes—or we can buy a new place if you want—"

"Ash!" I put both my hands up, indicating for him to stop.

I loved him even more for this—for his unabashed eagerness to do anything and everything I needed. And though he wasn't wrong about what he said, it wasn't what I needed.

"It's not about nesting," I choked out, cupping a hand over my mouth.

I hated the tears. Officially. I hated the tears. I hated the hormones. I hated how I cried for no good and every good reason. I was strong. I was put together. I always had a plan for everything. Everything except falling in love.

He pulled my hands to his chest, tugging me practically onto his lap. "I swear to God, Taylor, the second I opened the door to you, I opened up my goddamn heart, and it's been yours ever since."

Frantically, I shook my head.

I needed him to stop. Every word was making it so much worse—so much harder for me to do this—tacking on higher and higher all the things that were at stake.

"No, please, Ash. Stop." I pried my fingers from his and wrapped my arms in front of me. *It was all too much.* "*Please.*"

My desperation granted me his silence. So, I drew one last unsteady breath before my voice became the driving force, sending me straight into the storm.

"It's about the baby's father," I began.

Uncertainty and possessiveness emerged on his face. Maybe it was how shaken I was… maybe it was all the not-knowing over the past twenty-four hours... but I didn't expect him to ask. For months now, he'd never pushed me, never pressured me to tell him who or what had brought me to my current state. Not once.

Until now.

"Do you remember the night you found out about Blake and Zach?" I asked. "You went to the bar. You drank a lot. They called the hotel, and I came for you..."

I watched as vague flickers of memory, like frayed strings on a sweater, floated in front of him as he tried to put the pieces back together.

"I picked you up and took you back to your hotel room."

His gaze widened as each fact led him close to a destination some part of him knew was coming yet was so far off from being believable, he couldn't quite see it.

My next words turned into a small yelp when someone pounded angrily on the front door.

The noise broke the moment—broke the truth—*broke everything.*

ASH

"What the—" I broke off, my mouth thinning as I stared at Tay, seeing how she looked like she was about to dive head-first off of a cliff only to be yanked back at the very last second by whoever the fucker was on the other side of the door.

I was tempted to ignore it. From the look on her face, she was scared. No—fucking petrified to tell me about the baby's dad. Like I'd be mad at her. I couldn't imagine a scenario where that would be the case. Now, if the fucker had *done* something to her or was threatening her now... I didn't care what I had to do or who I had to hire. I'd take care of him because *I take care of what's mine.*

But as far as remembering… I only barely recalled the night—only the fringes of it before alcohol claimed the rest.

I remembered the bar. I hadn't remembered she'd been the one to pick me up until she said so. Then faint images of her arm around my waist in a parking lot, her hand taking another vodka bottle from my fingers.

Flickers of soft lips against mine. Warm skin pressing against me.

I grunted. The memories were too foggy—when I drank, everything was too foggy to look like anything more than a dream.

"Coming!" I shouted as whoever was pounding was even harder the second time around.

I hadn't even heard a car in the drive, I thought as I stood. Whoever the fuck was intruding on my night with my woman better have something important to say about what happened at Roasters. It was the only goddamn scenario that made this okay.

Yanking the door open, all my annoyance dropped in shock to see Eli on the other side.

Was it possible to stare at someone you know and feel like you don't even fucking recognize them?

"Eli?" I rasped, taking stock of his shadowed, hollow expression before my eyes drifted farther down to his rumpled, stained shirt and hands that matched.

He looked like he'd been used as a stunt double in a fight scene—and he'd been the unlucky asshole to lose the fight.

What the fuck was all over him?

Was that…

And when his gaze met mine, I realized that the blood on his hands wasn't nearly as frightening as the hopeless desolation in his eyes.

"Eli?" I rasped. "What the hell happened?" I stepped back

for him to come inside, but he remained frozen. Like a messenger, not a friend, he stayed rooted outside my door. "What the hell is going on?"

"It's Larry…" His voice was a grim thread of sound reaped from the very bottom of his chest.

Hurricanes brought less destruction than the emotions raging inside of me. I felt the blood pumping behind my eyes as everything in my vision turned into shadows of red and black.

"He's gone."

No.

"Gone. Larry's gone."

No.

I shook my head.

No fucking no.

"What?" Taylor's choked gasp uttered from behind me, clutching her stomach.

My hands went to my face, pushing my temples, pinching the bridge of my nose, pushing against my eyes that were squeezed shut. I pushed and prodded because this wasn't real. I pushed and prodded because any second I was going to wake up and realize that this was a giant fucking nightmare.

Of all people, of all times, how could I have forgotten that real monsters don't exist under your bed and neither do real nightmares exist in your sleep.

"What the fuck do you mean he's gone?" Sometimes, there are questions you ask because you don't want to know the answer—*because you don't want to believe the answer you already know to be true.*

I could see the tears on his face now as he said numbly, "Larry's dead."

I shook my head. Side to side. Over and over.

This wasn't real.

It couldn't be.

And when I looked at Eli again, it was with rage-colored lenses.

"Why the *fuck* do you have blood on your hands?" I yelled as I fought for answers—as I fought to understand.

I stalked out for him like he was in some way responsible—for what, I still didn't know. Reaching for his shirt, I yelled, "What the hell did you do, Eli?"

I heard Taylor's shocked gasp from behind me as I grabbed my *friend* and yanked him close.

"Stay back," I clipped harshly at her, vibrating with anger and pain.

I could only handle one fucking thing at a time. No, that was a lie. I wasn't handling this. I didn't know how to fucking handle this.

"I-I tried to save him," Eli rasped. Up close I could see right through him. I could see that the desolation only masked the guilt-ridden emptiness of his eyes. "I went... I went to talk to him... Opened up the garage and he was there. Sitting against the wall."

His eyes closed, more tears coating his cheeks.

"The gun was there. It smelled like smoke and copper. I moved his head. Blood... Blood was everywhere." Eli didn't even push back, instead sagging against my grip as though my hand around his neck was the only thing holding him up. "He killed himself... Larry shot himself..."

The adrenaline followed by the searing pain ripped through every muscle of my heart.

I didn't know if Eli was repeating himself or I was just hearing him over and over again.

He shot himself.

I dropped my hold on him like he was a leper. Like his news was a disease I could avoid believing if I just let him go.

"No." I shook my head. "No fucking no. Something happened. It had to be Blackman. Or Rich. He wouldn't—"

"It's not their fault," he said, devoid of any emotion while mine suffocated me. "It's mine. I tried... I tried to save him..." He spoke, but he wasn't talking to me. He was reliving everything that he'd described. Devoid of tone and probably his own fucking soul because that's how I felt. "I told him about his medication..."

I couldn't listen to what he said, all I heard was '*I failed.*'

With each word, it felt like everything I'd done... everything that I'd become... since moving here was gone. Just like that. All the tethers that grounded me, that gave me a foundation, a solid place to start over from—*they were all fucking gone.*

With one goddamn bullet to the head.

As though he was coming out of a daze, Eli looked at me as though he could ignore the way something in the world had changed tonight. Like he had no choice if he wanted to survive.

"Dex and the police are there. I left after giving my statement and came here. I need to go tell—"

"Go." A voice that wasn't my own spoke, my head jerked to signal him to leave.

"Are you—"

"Get the fuck out," I growled, feeling like in losing one person, I'd lost everything.

I threw the door shut behind me, unsure if Eli was still out there and not caring that the force of it probably would have crumbled my shack to the fucking ground had it been any other day—had enough not been taken from me already. My thumbs pinched the bridge of my nose as my forearms rested on the door for a second. Then, the pounding began. I slammed my fist into the door over and over again until I heard the wood begin to splinter and began to feel blood trickle down my arm.

"Ash!" Taylor's scream and her hands pulling on my other arm made me realized she must have been trying to get my attention for a long time.

Numbly, I stood there. I could feel her hands digging into my scalp, pulling my forehead to her. I could feel her body pressed against me. I could see the tears that scarred her cheeks. I had every sensation, but they didn't seem like they belonged to me. It felt like I was living in the third person. Distant. Disconnected. *Drowning.*

"He can't be gone," I heard myself say. "He can't…"

And then I was gone.

Out the door.

Into the rain and darkness.

Anything to deprive my senses of the pain they couldn't bear.

Chapter Twenty-Four

Ash

For the first time in six months, I felt drunk. Moments blurred until I was on my knees at the edge of my restaurant's deck. The cold rain smacked reality against my skin—that even God wept with me. The water could wash the blood from my hands, but not the hole from my heart.

Taylor's voice was distant and indistinct even though she was close.

My head fell, my shoulders and chest shaking like I held an earthquake inside me—*one I wished would send me into the sea.*

Why?

The word played over and over. In my head. Out of my lips. A curse. A plea. A prayer. I yelled it—roared it—into the tempest outside. And I didn't care if it was God or the Devil who replied, but *someone* had to know the answer.

I screamed until the storm and the sea were blocked from my view. Taylor stepped in front of me, her stomach in my face.

New life blocking out recent death.

I grabbed her waist, blood and tears staining her shirt as I yanked her to me, pressing my face against her firm stomach even though it shook with sobs against my cheek.

This couldn't be fucking happening.

I meant to push her away. I was breaking, and even I didn't want to see it.

But as soon as I held her, I couldn't let go.

She was like a lighthouse in the storm. *She always had been.* She couldn't save me. But she could stand there, bright and shining on the shore, reminding me that there was safe harbor out there if I could just hold on long enough.

Tilting my head up, I searched for her eyes, barely feeling the rain on my face. I searched for something to tell me this was anything but what it was.

"I don't understand, Taylor," I said thickly.

Her body trembled against my hands as she knelt in front of me. Even with tears spilling along her cheeks and her hair matting to her face, she was so beautiful. Too beautiful for such tragedy.

"I'm so sorry, Ash." Her voice broke, but it was her lip that wouldn't stop quivering that captured my attention.

"I don't understand why. I don't understand how this is real. How this happened. Nothing makes sense." My incoherent mutterings streamed out. I stared at her like her beauty could make this better. *Because angels could do that, right?* "Nothing makes sense… *I don't make sense.*"

Not anymore.

It was the first day of recovery all over again. There I was, empty-handed save for the guilt I carried for the horrible things I'd done, lost in the very pit of my despair, with no idea who I was anymore.

But this time, there was no Larry waiting in the shadows, holding out his hand to help me back up.

Even kneeling on the edge of my dream, the hard wood that we'd just laid down not even two weeks ago digging painfully, it all felt worthless now. A fruitless attempt.

Foolish.

"Where would I be without him?" I asked with a low, hollow voice. "I don't make sense anymore."

Desolation rained harder than the storm above us and crashed louder than the waves below.

This was loss in its cruelest, most real form.

No warning. No reason. And every imaginable hurt.

"Don't, Ash. Don't say that. Please," she begged as her tiny hands cupped my face.

"Why?" Cold seeped out from my bones. "Why should I make sense? Why should I care?"

If sadness was the gasoline, anger was the match, lighting everything in my path into burning, careless rage.

My lip curled in disgust. "He shot himself. Why? Because his fucking shop got robbed? Is that really all it takes? What was the point of any of this?" I waved an arm back at the empty structure that was so close to being something worthwhile. "Of helping anyone? How could you sit there and work to convince people that there is always something worth fucking saving and not even follow your own goddamn advice?"

"Ash, please…" One hand shot up to cover her mouth as I made her cry even harder.

"Please what, Taylor?" I snarled, lashing on the very last person who deserved it but the only one who would stand there and take it because she was a warrior. And she would fight for me even when I didn't deserve it. "Please don't say the truth? Please don't point out the obvious that if Larry wasn't worth saving, there's no way in hell that I am? I hate to break it to you, sweetheart, but I'm not worth lov—"

Soft, salty lips pressed against mine. Like a break in the line that sent the train of my thoughts derailing off its destructive course, she kissed me, and the world stopped.

Actually, we just stopped.

Because, sometimes, the world has to go on without you for a little bit until it's time to catch up. It's not about being left behind, it's about staying back until you're ready to move forward.

"I love you," she whispered into the kiss over and over again.

I struggled to believe her at first. *How could I?* But words mixed with tears and desperation and desire made some sort of salve that promised that I would survive this.

That I would survive this with her.

"I don't know what I need," I rasped against the sweet haven of her mouth, the salt of our tears making the kiss even more potent.

She pulled me tighter. "You need someone to lean on," she told me. "Lean on me, Ash. Love me..."

"I don't fucking deserve you."

Her fists bundled into my shirt around my neck. Rain and tears drenched her face, and she was still so beautiful. It only made me hurt even more.

"That's a lie," she returned, fighting my rage with a burningly beautiful brand of her own.

"Then you deserve better, how's that?" I spat. "That's not a lie."

Her mouth slanted over mine roughly and sloppily. I grunted when her teeth bit down on my lip with enough force to make me hope she drew blood.

"You don't get to tell me what I do and don't deserve." Her small fists shook against my chest, my wet shirt slapping against my skin, as she swore, "I know what I deserve. I deserve to love the man I love."

I felt like I was sinking; the man I was pulling me beneath the surface while the man I wanted to be tried to keep me afloat, and I was trying to dislodge one without losing the other.

With a voice both beleaguered and taut with anger, I confessed, "I'm drowning."

She pulled back just enough so that her gaze could find

mine. Her lashes clogged with thick raindrops as she spoke almost out of reflex, "I see you."

Her words sliced through my armor of anger with a deadly parry.

"I see you, Ashton Tyler, and you are a good man."

I see you.

Something burned inside my head, something distant yet familiar when I heard her say those words. It hurt to think about, but everything fucking hurt to think about now.

Larry was gone.

Breaths heaved out of me as though I'd run a marathon—as though they could run my body away from my heart's grief.

He was fucking gone.

But all I could see was that Taylor was still here. Her bright green eyes shining through the dark and rain.

She was still here, and I needed her.

With a desperate growl, I tore into her mouth, needing to lose myself in her love.

I needed to push it. Twist it. *Stretch it…* I needed to feel its limits against me so I knew it wasn't going anywhere.

She was sweet and salty as my tongue stroked her, luring it into my mouth where I could bite down on the tip and swallow her gasp. I wanted pain and pleasure because that's what was ripping me apart inside.

I should have cared about the cold and the rain. I should have cared about it all.

But all I could care about was taking her. All I could care about was burying myself so deep inside her warmth that she'd never be able to let me go.

And she urged me on, needing that comfort, too.

No, her mouth pushed back against mine with equal fervor if not more. She kissed me like she'd willingly drink down my sorrows and my pain—she'd bear it all to make me okay again.

Our mouths ravaged each other until the storm around us felt like mist to cool us off.

"Don't leave me," I pleaded against her swollen lips. The warm fog of our breaths pierced by the falling rain.

"I won't."

She shuddered as I pulled the wet, clinging fabric of her shirt from her skin and up over her head, dropping it onto the deck with a heavy plop. My mouth was back on hers as I flicked open the clasp to her bra, adding that to the pile of barriers that I could no longer stand.

"Cold?" I asked, my hands finding her pebbled nipples straining and waiting for me.

"Hot," she moaned and arched into my hands.

With a growl, I dove forward, viciously sucking one smooth peak into my mouth while my fingers pinched the other. She writhed against me, her hips surging up against my leg like she'd caught fire, gasping my name as she begged for more.

My need for her pulsed through my body and thundered through my veins, the force echoing in the sky around us.

Rain followed the trails of licks and bites I left over her swollen, heavy tits. *God, she was perfect.* I devoured them with my mouth while moving over her, growling as goosebumps coated her damp skin as her back came to lay on the deck.

My dick pushed against my jeans, angry and desperate to be buried inside her as I peeled her sweats and underwear from her legs, growling my appreciation. She looked like a wet nymph that just jumped out of the fucking ocean to seduce me.

Pushing her knees apart, I bent between them and flattened my tongue against her wet sex.

Mine.

I owned her pussy, sweeping my tongue over her until her hips thrashed against my face and her fingers clawed at my hair. I couldn't stop myself. I hurt so bad, all I wanted to hear was that I still made her feel good.

"Ash," she called breathlessly.

Leaving her spread wide, I yanked off my shirt, watching her twitch every time a raindrop landed on her clit.

"Touch yourself," I demanded, knowing it would push her.

I needed her so goddamn bad I couldn't think or breathe. A better man would find the words to ask her for forever. A better man would find the words to tell her just how much she meant and how much he needed her comfort in this moment.

I wasn't a better man.

I was a broken man.

And the only thing I could do was show her and whisper desperate dirty promises because eloquence eluded me. I had nothing left to give but raw, ragged emotion. Nothing but love in its most basic and crude form.

The kind that needs to possess… to claim. The kind that needs to push as much as it needs to pull to see if she'd stay.

I needed to love her… I needed to love her, so I knew I wouldn't lose her.

Taylor

My heart raced inside my chest. Adrenaline and desire threatening to rip me into pieces.

I noticed the rain, but I didn't feel it, not from the moment I launched out the door after him until now. I felt nothing except what I felt for him.

Bone-crushing sadness and soul-searing desire.

Just like that first night, I'd do anything to take away the look in his eyes. At first glance, what appeared to be betrayal, but deeper than that was the hurt. It was a hurt so profound I wouldn't be surprised if blood began to mix with tears as they fell from his eyes.

Whatever he needed, I would give. I refused to give up. I refused to let him shoulder this alone. He could lean on me and no matter how hard, I wouldn't let go.

My heart broke a thousand times as his head pressed into my stomach and grief overtook him. Silent tears poured down my face to hear him plead and then rage for answers. I withstood it all even though my own sadness made my knees shake underneath the weight.

The truth was I didn't have words either.

When you lose someone... when you realize that you'll never see them or speak to them or hold them again... it brings out something primal in you—an unquenchable need for physical connection, hand-held proof that at least one person can't be taken from you in that moment.

And that's why I poured everything into that kiss.

I needed to support him in a way that was beyond words, because sometimes, *words are not enough*.

I didn't think twice as my hand climbed over my stomach down toward my sex. I didn't think twice to do something that I'd never done to myself before. And I couldn't tear my eyes from his, the storm around us just a shower compared to the desire raging in his eyes.

I heard my own strangled gasp as my fingers found my clit, swollen and hot with need. Bursts of pleasure bloomed over me, heightened by the way he rubbed the thick ridge of his arousal.

When my legs drifted wider, giving my hand more room to move as it was slightly hindered by my stomach, he began to slowly undo the waist of his jeans.

My body tensed and vibrated against my fingers as they rubbed furiously over my sex. My moans were lost though when a hoarse groan erupted from his chest. Everything around me was lost except the way the noise set off a quake down his body as he pulled himself free of his jeans.

Even the rain that dripped into my mouth was like sand as one of his hands tugged once... twice... down his angry pulsing cock. My fingers began to move sloppily over my core as my desire drenched them.

His erection bobbed when he let go to grip my hips and yank them up onto his lap.

"Don't fucking stop," he growled at me when my fingers stopped moving in surprise. "I want to watch you while I fuck you, Tay. And then I want to come all over you."

The earth shifted underneath me as desire made me delirious.

I forced my fingers to rub again, gasping for breath just as he slammed his cock all the way inside me, my back sliding against the deck with the force of his thrust.

Stars exploded now behind my eyes.

"You feel that, Taylor?" he rasped, nudging his tip against my womb.

A moan spilled from my lips as my body squeezed around him in response. It was a miracle I still kept my fingers moving.

"That's my cock inside of you. From the first goddamn time you took me in your perfect little body, you've been mine. You hear me?"

I arched up with a garbled nod. *He had no idea how true that was.* He had no idea how far back that first time was. But it didn't matter—a decade or day ago, from the moment I gave him my body, I knew my heart went along with it; I never expected to get it back.

I reached for his gaze, need making my vision turn like a ship on stormy seas.

"I'm not leaving you, Ash," I murmured. "I'm still here. I love you."

I said it because I felt it. It just so happened that it was also what he needed to hear.

With a feral growl, he slid out and thrust completely back inside me. I screamed his name, the bump against that spot deep inside my magnifying the touch of my fingers on my clit.

This time wasn't gentle. He shoved into my body with a fierceness that hurt and healed at the same time. His lack of control making my body arch for more as it convulsed around his hard, brutal length.

"*Mine*. Every part of you. Forever," he promised as his hands clamped down on my hips and he drove mercilessly into me.

The way he took my body took me to a place where not even thoughts existed.

"That's it, Tay. Come for me."

"Ash," I sobbed his name as my body finally broke.

Sadness, fear, tension… everything scattered to the ground as my body dissolved in desire.

"Fuck, Tay," I heard him grunt through the rain and roaring in my ears, followed by the warm rush of his release deep inside me, gushing against my womb.

"I love you, Ash," I said minutes later when I finally felt the rain.

He bent down, placing an open-mouthed kiss on top of my stomach and murmured, "I love you, too, Tay."

Reality was brought back to us drop by drop like the rain from the heavens. It was laid on us in slow, steady layers that allowed our bodies to move with the sadness instead of recoil from it.

With my legs around his waist, he carried me back to the house, leaving our clothes for another day.

The first chill I felt all night was when he slid the sheet up over us and wrapped his arms around me.

"I don't understand, Tay," he said softly. "Why would he do this?"

More than anything in my entire life, I wished I had the reason. I wished I had the answer that would make it okay.

But sometimes, there is no answer.

"No matter what Larry showed the world, no matter what he did for everyone else, sometimes it's impossible to know the battles we fight inside ourselves," I said with a voice that was weighted but at least it was steady.

"Just don't know how to process something I don't understand." I heard the tears in his eyes just as surely as I felt mine down my cheeks. "I don't know how to forgive something I don't understand."

"Sometimes, it's not our place to understand, just to be understanding." I pressed my lips over his heart. "Sometimes, the only way to forgive is to be okay with not knowing."

There was energy in the air, like the kind from the storm outside but stronger. It sparked with grief and disbelief. It tingled with fear and confusion. And it weighed with love—love lost and love found.

And for me, it whispered in my ear, long after all our tears had stopped, long after Ash finally began to breathe deeply, sleep overtaking sadness. It whispered that I still hadn't given him everything.

And the man in front of me—the man who Ash had become, one who wasn't perfect but who was still worthy of praise—*he deserved everything.*

Chapter Twenty-Five

ASH

"I see you, Ashton Tyler, and you are a good man."

I shot up from bed with a gasp, the memory strangling me with its nostalgic noose.

My heart had been ripped open by the news of Larry's death. Shredded into a million pieces by the violence of emotional extremes, and in the process, spilled out pieces of my consciousness that had been previously inaccessible.

"Ash?" My sudden movement had woken her, but I couldn't turn. I couldn't breathe.

All I could do was remember...

Like a lightning bolt, memories flashed in my mind like an old videotape, one that had been damaged so the scenes and the sounds stuttered and skipped, but there was enough of the film to watch most of the story.

'Why does no one see me? Why does no one see me as I drown?' I saw myself saying that night on tour.

And Taylor, looking at me with those same passionate and compassionate eyes had replied, 'I see you.'

She'd always seen me. Even at my weakest.

Like a string of twinkle lights, moments of that night lit up in a bright string of truth.

She'd saved me. *And then she'd cared for me.*

I'd confessed to always wanting her. *And she'd been unable to deny the same attraction.*

I'd begged her to stay. *And she'd begged me to take her.*
I'd been the one to take her virginity. *Six months ago.*

Slowly, I turned to the woman sitting up in my bed, staring at me with concern as her hand rested on her stomach.

The woman pregnant with my child.

My gaze dragged up to her eyes in disbelief and confusion and betrayal.

First, Larry. Now, Taylor.

"You remember..." She choked the words out, her chest caving in from the release of pressure.

The tension between us pulled tight like a rubber band stretched to its limit, and whether it broke or snapped back, whichever came next was going to hurt.

"We slept together that night," I stated with a deceptively low and steady voice. *The calm before the storm.* "We slept together six months ago, and that makes that baby—"

"Yours."

TAYLOR

I inhaled slowly as a searing cramp ripped through my stomach and reminded myself, 'the Lord has not given me the spirit of fear, but of peace, love, and a sound mind.'

I'd been to confession a thousand times, but I'd never felt like this. This felt like the most important confession in my whole life. One that came with no guarantee that a certain number of 'Our Fathers' and 'Hail Marys' would absolve.

"You're the father, Ash," I confessed in full.

When the words released, I sucked in air like I'd been underwater for too long and could now finally breathe. But the relief of breathing was miniscule compared to the pain I felt as he pulled away.

I pressed on, needing to explain, knowing he deserved it. "A-All those months ago on tour, after you found out about Blake and Zach being together, I picked you up at a bar because the bartender called me. I brought you back to your hotel room. Y-You were going to continue drinking through the minibar. You were angry, but that wasn't so hard to see through. You were hurt—hurting. And when you asked me to stay with you, it was as though your words had come from my own heart. So, I kissed you. I just"—a sob lodged in my throat—"you were broken, and I guess, I was broken, too. Lonely and locked up. Wanting things that I thought I shouldn't. And I couldn't do it anymore. I wanted you. I wanted to love you. So, I let myself."

The darkness from his eyes grew like a thundercloud over all his hard features and I realized I wasn't telling him anything he didn't already know. The trauma of losing Larry had jarred free the memories his addiction had locked up tight.

It was ironic that his first strike would be his body *removing* itself from my proximity. I fought to suppress the shiver at the immediate loss of warmth and the inundation of dread into my cells. I jerked forward as another cramp pulled at my stomach, the stress of my emotions making them feel a thousand times worse.

"I'm sorry," I pleaded weakly, pulling my own hands to my chest because it now felt like they were trespassing on his body. "I wanted to tell you—"

"That's why you came here?" he demanded. "Not because of what you thought I could do to help you, but because of what I'd done?"

My heart felt like it was a giant bass drum, thumping, vibrating in my chest with enough force to make me shake.

"Y-yes," I admitted. "You'd disappeared. And it didn't seem quite right, but you didn't tell anyone anything. And... And I needed to tell you in person. But then..."

"But then what?" His prompt was just as hard as the blue stones of his eyes. "Why keep it from me? After everything? Why…" His eyes narrowed. "I confessed everything to you. I told everything to you, and you kept this from me?"

"I was afraid," I blurted out, the goosebumps covering my skin made the soft bedsheets feel coarse and rough against it. "I was afraid that you'd want me out of responsibility. T-That you'd offer to be with me, to be a family, because you felt like you had to. Because your loyalty is your greatest strength and weakness. And that's not what I came here for. I didn't come to force you to do something. I came to tell you because you had a right to know and make your own decision, *whatever* it was."

"So, what? You wanted to make sure I might still want to fuck you after the baby is born before telling me that it was mine? I told you I loved you, Taylor. And even that was months delayed from the moment I *knew* I loved you. I knew I loved you the second that everything I'd been working for glowed brighter knowing that you were and would be a part of it. Telling you that I loved you was like walking out into a thunderstorm and saying that there's a chance of rain. Was that not enough? Was that not enough to deserve the truth?"

If I'd thought the anger in his tone was heartbreaking, I'd take it any day over the pain I heard now.

"Y-yes!" My voice trembled as I reached for him, only causing him to pull back and break my heart a little further. "It was, Ash. It was. I just… I have no reason… no good reason. I could take a lot of things—you not wanting me, you not wanting to be a part of the baby's life, my Church's judgment, my family's judgment… but I couldn't take you only by obligation. I was selfish. I wanted you for myself. Not me, the woman carrying your child. Not me, the woman in need that would be one more good deed to buy your own forgiveness. I wanted you to love just me… *Taylor*… the woman who loves you."

For the first time in my life, the rhythmic sound of the ocean crashing outside the house—the only sound in this silence—wasn't calming at all. It was a reminder of how just one wave could take you under.

"I did, Tay... I did love just you," he finally said with a soft strained voice. "And I loved Larry. And you both—*fuck*." He swore, spearing a hand through his hair before he yanked on clothes faster than I could process what was happening. "I have to go."

My hand cupped my mouth, forcing myself to swallow my sob. He couldn't go now. "But what... what about... what are we—"

"I need to go, Taylor. I need to think." The anger... the pain... they were nothing compared to the distance I heard in his voice—a distance that was mirrored when he walked out of the room.

"Ash, please." I scrambled out of the bed, my body making it cumbersome for me to move quick enough to catch him.

By the time I got a shirt on and made it to the front door, his truck was disappearing up the driveway.

"I love you," I murmured into the wind, hoping the breeze would carry it to the part of his heart that knew it was the truth and praying it wouldn't be left to fall like the rest of the dust he'd left behind.

Chapter Twenty-Six

Taylor

I stumbled back inside in a daze, the pain of watching him walk away only interrupted by the intermittent cramps that tore through my stomach.

It made my skin burn, my muscles ache. It made organs falter and my bones sore. I was left in the unknowing. I was left not understanding what was happening or what was going to happen.

And suddenly my words from the night before seemed just as insufficient to me as they probably had felt for Ash.

Sometimes, it's not our place to understand but to be understanding.

The dwindling rational me knew it was more than okay for him to need time to process. The rest of me wanted answers now. I'd been wrapped in a blanket of comfort and security and love for weeks and now it was ripped from me and I was desperate to know if I'd ever get it back or if I'd need to figure out how to survive in the cold.

It hurt. *It really, really hurt.*

I paused, seeing my phone on the kitchen counter, and knew it was pointless to try and call him.

Pointless and disrespectful.

Ash had been ripped open by Larry's death, and my confession had poured salt in the wound.

As much as I wanted to be there for him, to hold him, to help him... I'd also been the one to hurt him. What else could I do except respect his wishes at this time?

There would be a time to finish this conversation, but there was no point to forcing it now.

I drifted back into the bedroom, took one look at the bed—the one we'd shared, the one where he'd told me he loved me—and turned right back around. Instead of crying, it felt like my tears fell backward and filled up my lungs instead, making it harder and harder to breathe when everywhere I looked, all I saw were the memories of how I'd fallen in love with Ash in these rooms, and how I'd hurt him.

Pushing through the door back outside, I folded my arms over my chest, trying to keep all my broken pieces from spilling out as I walked toward the restaurant and the cliffs. I needed distance from the house, and my body needed to walk.

The pain in my back had become tremendous, and my contractions not only worsened but refused to relax. The constant brutal burn in my stomach and my heart turned my breaths harsh and arduous.

I struggled to focus on anything except how much it hurt.

My bare feet halted at the edge of the restaurant's deck, the serenity of the ocean and cliffs unaltered in the face of my suffering. I caught sight of our clothes from last night, still in discarded piles on the grass just next to the edge of the wood.

I should bring them inside.

Just as the thought occurred to me, I cried out, struck with a pain so sudden and so severe it took me to my knees.

My eyes squeezed shut as I struggled to breathe through it, one hand rubbing over my stomach, the other stabilizing on the wood surface as I bent forward to try and ease the pain.

It wasn't just my heart breaking that made everything painful. It was the baby.

Something was wrong.

I needed to get back to the house and call Ash.

Forcing my eyes open, I focused on my fingers against the wood of the deck and then, the ones on my stomach. With a groan, I pushed myself up to kneel straight and my head protested the movement, everything swimming in front of my eyes.

"*Please, God,*" I pleaded, feeling faint, but it didn't stop the blood from rushing from my head.

The last thing I saw was the small dark pool of blood on the wood where I'd bent over. Blood that had come from me.

From our baby.

"*Ash...*" His name was a feeble prayer on my lips as the world tipped to the side and I fell off the cliff of consciousness into a sea of black.

ASH

Stones sprayed behind my truck as I pulled out of the drive and tested the limited of the aging engine as I headed for town. Driving away from the house… from Taylor… felt like I'd been detoured the wrong way down a one-way street.

Larry was gone.

Tay was having my baby.

Mine.

Actually fucking mine.

I dug my phone from my pocket and dialed Eve's number.

"Hello?" Her water-logged voice answered, and I knew Eli must've already told her about Larry.

"Eve, can you do me a favor?" I grated into the line.

"A-Ash? Did you hear about—"

"Please," I cut her off. "I know, but I need you to go to my house and check on Tay."

Her grief choked. "Taylor? Is she okay?"

My throat constricted. *I didn't know.* "Please," I begged. "Can you just go see her now?"

I couldn't be there. Not now. Not as the fragile foundation I built here began to flitter away like paper in the wind. But I also couldn't let her be there alone.

"O-Of course. Are you—"

"Thank you," I said because I wasn't okay, and then I hung up with a bitter laugh, letting the hot tears I felt shame me even further.

I wasn't okay, and I still couldn't believe it.

I'd fucked the one woman who I'd fantasized about my entire life... and I didn't even remember it.

What. A. Fucking. Asshole.

I slammed my hand against the steering wheel.

Of all the things I'd done while intoxicated—including almost ruining my sister's life—this... well, if it didn't take the cake, it certainly came close.

I slept with Taylor.

One time.

Her fucking first time and I'd taken that from her. While drunk.

I got her pregnant and then left for the other side of the country.

When I looked up and noticed the road in front of me, I realized I was veering off down Larry's drive, not even bothering with a blinker.

Why was I here? I wondered as I pulled by the police barriers and caution tape, ignoring the looks I got from the cops.

My hands gripped the wheel, all of my demons joining forces for one last attack. My forehead dropped onto my knuckles and I cursed myself up and down.

My gaze whipped up. I knew why I was here. *I wanted*

answers. Answers from the man who'd always had them. Why he'd left. And why, by leaving, he'd let me remember.

Then, I was out of the truck and storming toward Larry's front door, my feet crunching over the overgrown weeds coming through the path as I ducked under the tape. The house looked like it belonged to a man who'd died years ago instead of hours; the thought made my stomach turn.

It was wrong to come here angry—to come here needing one more thing from a dead man—but I didn't know where else to turn.

What if this was it? The last mistake. The one I couldn't come back from.

The one that was one too many.

"Sir, this is a crime scene—"

A dagger to the eye would have had more finesse than the look I shot the cop with as his hand came up, just barely stopping in time before it smacked into my chest.

"I'm family," I ground out. It was more truth than lie and I didn't care what anyone had to say about it.

"He's good, Dan." Eli appeared in the doorway, his face drawn and ashen.

The officer moved to the side, giving me a nod.

With a low growl, I stepped around him and into Larry's house. I coughed to mask the choked sounds that tried to escape my chest. It was the most painful kind of déjà vu. I had just been here. In this hall. At that table. Looking out those windows.

And Larry had, too.

"You shouldn't have come," Eli stated, looking even less pleased to see me.

"I had to." Just like I had to apologize at some point for choking him on my doorstep last night, but not now.

I pushed by my grieving friend into the house.

Like I hit a wall, I paused and felt the pressure well in my chest, my eyes burn with tears I refused to shed.

Larry's presence was stifling. Everywhere. Everything.

"Why are you here, Ash?" Eli asked, following me. "What's going on?"

My fist tightened at my side.

Walking through the kitchen toward the door to the garage, I prepared myself for gruesome; goodbyes aren't supposed to be pretty anyway. Goodbyes hurt. They hurt like a motherfucker.

"I need answers." I reached for the doorknob and pulled.

It still had the same squeak as when I'd been staying here. Every morning, I'd wake up on Larry's couch, sick and desperate for a drink, to hear Larry leaving for Roasters. He'd turn and look at me, ask if I wanted to help at the coffee shop, and then leave when I didn't respond.

Until one day, I did respond.

I responded because I didn't feel like I was dying. I responded because the giant hole inside of me that I'd filled with booze was finally empty and dry and I realized there were so many better things to fill it with—like giving back to the man who I'd never be able to repay.

My hands gripped the doorframe as I stepped into the garage. It was the same coppery-sweet scent that had been all over Eli last night. His truck was parked on the far side, in front of an old chest of tools that had lost more pieces than it held.

And all along the wall to my left, the concrete was decorated with the distinct maroon stain of blood.

"*Fuck.*"

Touring with the band and with Blake, I'd seen a ton of abstract art. Smears and splatters of color that were supposed to mean something—evoke something other than the feeling that some five-year-old had gotten lucky with his finger paints.

It looked like one of those paintings. Only it wasn't abstract or art, it was real and death.

"They took the body last night," Eli said hollowly as my eyes trailed along the blood that ran down the wall and onto the concrete floor, pooling around the drain.

I turned and dry-heaved into the small trash can near the door.

"*Jesus*, Ash." A strong grip on my shoulder whipped me around; it was attached to Eli. "Are you alright?"

"No." The word came out more of a threat than an answer. "No, I'm not fucking alright."

Anger poured through my veins, the familiar beast straining against his leash.

"He's gone. And I'm not better." I knocked his hand off my shoulder and spun to face him. "I need to know why he left. I need to know what the fuck he saw in me because I don't see it. I need to know why I was worth saving, but he wasn't."

I advanced on him, but he stood still, my face leveling inches from his.

"You want to tell me?" I demanded. "You want to tell me why when he left, all I got was the memory of what an asshole I was? Huh? *Why is that all he left me with?*" My voice rose with each word until I was shouting in his face. "After everything I've done, why is he the one that's gone?"

I pushed against Eli's chest as though he were responsible, and he stood there like a wall, taking whatever I threw at him, which only made my anger at myself worse because I couldn't control it.

"After everything I've done, how could he just fucking give up?" I roared. "*How*?" I used both hands to push him away. "After what I did to her, how the *fuck* could Taylor still want to love a man like me?"

Eli balked at the last and I realized the spew of my

self-loathing had finally made it down to the very pit of my heartbreak.

"I should've been the one to die in this house in my drunken-fucking-stupor," I spat with a low, despairing voice, and declared, "I'm getting a drink."

One drink. Just one.

Just to drown me a little faster.

I was lost, and I was going to be a father.

What kind of role model would I be? I thought bitterly, the claws of my former monster scraping against its cage, begging to be let out just for one drink—just one to take the pain away.

I felt the parts of me trying to fight it—the parts that had grown and strengthened here in Carmel, in my sobriety—but maybe they weren't strong enough. *Maybe I wasn't strong enough.* If Larry wasn't, who the hell did I think I was?

I felt the hand on the back of my collar before Eli whipped me around and my back slammed against the wall.

"Are you fucking kidding me?" Anger finally bubbled to his surface.

Instinctively, I began to struggle against his hold.

"You come here—*to his home*—and say shit like that?" he demanded, shaking me. "After everything he gave to help you fight your addiction, you fucking throw it back in his face—*on his goddamn grave?*"

"*He's the one who shot himself!*" I yelled back, shoving against his chest "He's the one who threw everything he ever did for me back in my fucking face!"

And then my knees hit the ground as I doubled over and began to wheeze; Eli's punch to my stomach knocking the wind from my lungs. With choking and straining gasps, they began to refill with the sanity it seemed I'd lost for a moment.

Lifting my head, I stared at the bloodstain on the wall as I coughed and sputtered.

"I'm sorry." The words were frayed, just like my emotions. I felt like a failure—*like I'd failed him.*

And Taylor.

And I'd lashed out because it felt as though my heart was being ripped apart at the seams.

Rising, my jaw clenched as I met Eli's unrelenting stare. His fists were still tight at his sides, prepared for my retaliation.

Dragging a hand through my hair, I finally took a deep breath and rasped, "Guess we're even now."

There was hardly a flicker in his eyes of acknowledgment. He'd punched me back from the edge and he stood vibrating with his own anger and grief, but still prepared to do it again if necessary.

"Did you come here for Larry or did you come because of Taylor?" he demanded.

I planted my hands on my hips. "Don't know."

"Why shouldn't she love you?"

Fuck.

I glared at him. "Because I'm an asshole. And I shouldn't have come. I shouldn't have bothered you here... now... It's not the time for this," I told him. "What's between Taylor and I can wait."

"Really? It can wait?" he sneered, folding his arms across his chest and taking a step toward me. "Because last I checked, Larry was dead."

I recoiled like he'd struck me again. *The truth packed a punch.*

"Larry is dead, Ash. You... Me... We can hate that fact with everything we've got but it won't change it; Larry has all the goddamn time in the world. But Taylor? She's still fucking here. There won't be endless amounts of time for you to fix whatever the hell is so important you had to come rail at a dead man for answers. A dead man who would be pissed as hell to hear your horseshit excuse."

"It's not a fucking excuse," I growled, my anger bristling again. "I'm trying to deal. I'm trying to fucking process that he's gone, and Taylor's baby is mine. And let me tell you, it feels like it's a little too fucking much—too many goddamn mistakes at the moment."

"Yours?" he croaked in disbelief.

My head jerked with a nod, the truth erupting from my lips. "On tour, when I found out about my sister and Zach, I got drunk. Which is saying a lot for an alcoholic, I know. She brought me home from the bar and we slept together." I let out a harsh laugh. "And I didn't remember any of it. Not until last night."

His body became less tense. "So, what's the problem? I mean, you basically claimed the kid as yours before this…"

I shook my head. "She didn't tell me, Eli. Why would she not tell me? What have I done to make her think she couldn't give me the truth?"

In my head, I heard her answers like a track on repeat. Too bad everything was blurred together right now with loss and betrayal. First, Larry. Then Taylor.

He let out a heavy sigh. "Don't know, man. All I know is that the only time you fear the truth is when the truth means you have something to lose. Just look at Larry… what would make him think he had nothing to live for? That he had no one who cared enough to get through this with him?" He broke off and I had a feeling he was answering some of those questions for himself. "She's not him. But you get my point. The worst fears are irrational because even reason gives them no solace."

"What if she didn't tell me because I'm just not good enough to know?" I wondered, kicking at the stones by my feet.

Irrational.

She'd loved every moment that I talked about taking care of her and the baby. I couldn't twist the look in her eyes to be anything else.

"And what if Larry didn't tell us because he thought he didn't matter to us?" Eli shook his head and pointed a finger at me. "I call bullshit, Ash. Bull-fucking-shit. You're a good man. We've all made mistakes, but I didn't need five minutes with Taylor to know she doesn't judge you for what you did, to know she believes—like I do, like Larry did—that your mistakes are far from defining you. So, I'm not gonna stand here and let you be a fucking idiot and lose someone else who loves you."

I dragged my stare to his. Both of us, friends before, now brothers in this tragedy. We'd pull it together. We'd do what we had to do. But it wouldn't be the same.

"She didn't keep this from you to punish you, Ash," he stated. "She loves you."

All of the wind whooshed from my chest, taking the last traces of my self-loathing with it.

Yeah, I'd made a mistake. But no, I wasn't that man anymore. And *that* was what mattered: *the man I was now.*

"I'm an idiot," I agreed, clarity smacking me in the face.

I couldn't fault her for questioning who the father of her child had disappeared to become. And I couldn't fault her for fearing the depth of my loyalty when I found out.

Because the plain fucking truth was that it went pretty goddamn deep.

If I had opened the door that day to hear her baby was mine, the line between care and responsibility would've blurred in my own mind, and the one between loyalty and love would've forever remained murky.

And she deserved a helluva lot better than murky.

"I don't know about that," he said with a strained laugh. "But I know Larry would be fuckin' pissed if he saw you here, knowing you walked away—knowing you chose to punish yourself instead of fixing everything with her."

"Yeah, he would," I admitted roughly, his words spilling through the ripped seams of my heart. "He knew she was the one. From the second that sneaky bastard gave her the address to my house, full-well knowing I wasn't alone that morning. He knew."

"Sometimes, it's easier to look out and see what everyone else needs while being blind to your own suffering," he replied, hollowly.

I wished there was something I could do… something to say. I knew if I didn't have Taylor—if she wasn't on my mind and in my heart—this battle would be a lot harder. But Eli, he was alone. No family that I knew of; Larry had been the closest thing… and now he was gone. And just like that, Eli was left to handle everything.

"Can't believe he's gone. Doesn't seem real."

Life wasn't fucking fair, forcing him to pick up all the pieces when the hollowness in his eyes said he didn't even have the strength to pick himself back up.

"It will." His face shadowed and his eyes ducked. "And it'll hurt like a bitch."

"Thank you." I reached out and gripped his shoulder, his focus returning to me. "If there's anything you need… anything I can do."

His jaw tensed but he only jerked his head in a short nod.

"I'm good. Have to get Dex to track down Laurel, but we have it under control." Grief was shoved back down underneath his stoic control. "Just… go take care of Taylor. That's what I need," he muttered, reaching and pulling me in for a hug. "He'd never forgive me if I didn't remind you what was important right now."

Loss was important. But so was love.

Loss was a season, sinking in slow like fall before turning colder and bleak like winter. But winter comes to an end, and in that loss, something new would grow. Not better, just different, but still good.

Love, though, love was like the sun. You had to fight for it when it finally shone in your life because if you weren't careful, if you lost it, it would leave your whole world dark.

Chapter
Twenty-Seven

Taylor

"Taylor!" Eve screamed as she saw me, running over and locking her arms underneath mine to hold me up. "Oh my God, Taylor. Wake up!"

I blinked, feeling my body being lifted up against hers.

I must've passed out.

I doubled over, almost taking Eve with me, as the pain struck again, and remembered what caused it.

"Something's wrong," I grunted, bright red pain searing around my abdomen like a belt of fire.

"Oh my God." She slung my arm around her shoulder. "I'm taking you to the hospital."

Putting one of my arms over her shoulders, I leaned on her as we staggered over to her car. Thank God, she was here. Between the moans of pain, I thanked God that she'd come outside to find me.

My hands shook as I tried to get the seatbelt in place, sagging in relief at the click before I turned against the seat and curled up into a giant ball of pain.

"Hang on, Tay. Just hang on." She reached for my hand as she peeled up the drive, stones kicking up angrily against the car.

In between the moments where I was consumed with the pain, I heard her first on the phone with the hospital and then, another minute later, cursing Ash as she hung up the phone.

"Dammit, Ash. Pick up your goddamn phone," she huffed as she squeezed my hand. "It's going to be okay, Tay. I'll get ahold of him."

"Told him… about the baby…" My head rubbed against the seat. "Doesn't want… to see… me."

"Bullshit," she told me, speeding around cars that were slowing us down. "I don't know what happened, but he called me to ask if I would come check on you. He may not know what he thinks about whatever you talked about—but he sure-as-shit knows how he feels about you. And that look I told you he had before? Yeah, it hasn't changed."

I cried out as another burst of pain wracked me, leaving me gasping and crying.

By the time we reached the hospital, Eve was crying, too, as she scrambled out of the driver seat screaming for help.

It felt like I was in a movie—or a scene from *General Hospital*—as they lifted me onto a gurney and rushed me through the emergency room, all the white and painfully bright lights blurring. It would have felt so much cooler if I could have felt anything but the mind-numbing pain.

I didn't feel the needles that poked into my arm even though I normally would be queasy and faint at the sight. I stared blankly at the nurses and techs who were moving and feeling and attaching things to all sorts of places on my body. And when I closed my eyes and finally gave in, there was no doctor or Ash in sight.

Ash

I jogged back through the musk of mourning pervading Larry's house until the cool outside breeze blew against me, taking with it the fear my lungs had been filtering from my heart.

I wasn't the same man I was months ago.

Larry had played a big role in that and words weren't enough to be able to describe just how much he'd come to mean. But, in the end, I was responsible for my change. *For my choices.*

Larry might have been the match, but I was the fuel—my need to be better is what burned the imperfections from me.

Alcohol hid the monsters inside me that I couldn't face; Taylor healed them.

Months ago, I was broken.

Today, it was still a struggle to see the light.

But it was there. Bright. Burning. True.

Only by breaking can we heal stronger.

And I couldn't get back to Tay fast enough.

My truck roared to life and I threw it into gear just as I heard vibrating coming from the passenger seat. I remembered tossing my phone over there when I left the house. I almost didn't reach for it. Couldn't be more important than what I was about to do now. But after the third buzz, I couldn't stop myself.

Eve?

"Hello?"

"Ash! Oh, thank God," she bawled and hiccupped into the phone.

"Eve, what's wrong? What's going on?" And then the fucking earth fell out from underneath me. "Where's Taylor?"

"A-Ash, we're at the hospital. T-Taylor collapsed. I went out to check on her like you said and she was just lying there… o-on the deck. There was blood." She coughed and sputtered. "I don't know what's wrong. I-I tried to call you… They took her to do tests and they won't let me back, they won't tell me what's going on, they won't let me see her—" She broke off and sobbed.

"Eve, where are you? Carmel General?" I cut her off, my brain going into overdrive.

"Yeah," she whimpered, trying to breathe steadily. "I'm coming."

I didn't know how I made it to the hospital or how many laws I broke along the way. And the whole way, I wept. I wept and prayed to God—begged him—to let her and our baby be okay.

"Taylor Hastings, where is she?" I demanded as I ran up to the desk.

I wasn't huge like the Madison brothers, so I knew it had to be the look on my face that made her move frantically to give me the room number.

I took the stairs because the elevator felt like too much of a risk.

White walls. White doors. They blurred as I ran past them. No matter how bright they were, all I saw was dark.

Rounding the corner, I saw Eve, red-faced and curled up in a ball.

"Ash!" she exclaimed, rising to hug me, her body shaking against mine.

I didn't want to be cruel, but I wanted to throw her off of me. *I needed to see Taylor.*

"Where is she?" I rasped.

My heart was living outside of my chest, and if I didn't see it and make sure it was okay… if it wasn't okay… I didn't know what would happen to me.

"I haven't seen her since they took her back. T-There was a nice nurse who told me she'd come back a-and talk to me as soon as she knew what was going on."

"What happened?" I gripped her shoulders and forced her back. "Tell me exactly what happened."

"I-I went outside to find her because she wasn't in the house," she stammered, pausing to wipe her nose with a tissue.

"And she was just lying on the back deck of the restaurant. At first, I thought she—" Eve broke off and shook her head, unable to even say the words. "W-When I got to her, she woke up a little, saying something wasn't right but in a lot of pain. When I got her up, I saw the blood and knew I had to get her to the hospital. So, I got her to the car and brought her to the hospital. I tried to call you…" Her gaze, framed by red and swollen eyelids, rose up to mine. "She was in so much pain, Ash. I'm so scared. I'm so scared for the baby…"

"Miss Williams?"

We both turned to face a wide-eyed nurse.

"I'm… sorry. And you are?"

"Where's Taylor? Is she okay?" I rounded on the woman, hating to make her think I was a pushy asshole, but I just couldn't give a shit right now.

She had kind eyes and a bubbly countenance given her job, but as soon as I stepped forward, a potential threat to her patient, her spine turned to stone.

"I'm sorry, sir. I'm afraid I can't tell you anything unless you are a relative. If that is going to be a problem, I will have to call security," she said firmly.

Later, I could be grateful that my woman had someone else so protective to look after her.

"No need," I ground out. "I'm the baby's father."

Her eyes widened and the 'o' her mouth formed was there for just a split second before a cloud of sympathy covered her features that made walking back through the doors feel like I was walking into limbo, the space between life and death, the world of not-knowing.

Chapter
Twenty-Eight

Taylor

My eyes opened lazily like a Sunday morning.

There shouldn't be an alarm beeping on Sunday. But there was.

Only it wasn't an alarm.

I blinked again, blinded not so much by the white as by the blandness of the room. It seemed to lack anything to make you feel comfortable even though it being here could save your life.

It took only a few more seconds for everything to come rushing back to me.

My hands that now had tethers snaking out of them to various machines, immediately reached for my stomach, needing to feel my baby. I felt my left fingers on the mountain in front of me, but my right hand was heavy—*solid*—like it'd been turned to stone.

Was something wrong? Did something happen to my arm?

Feeling like I was looking through a fog, I turned my head to see the anchor holding my arm to the bed was Ash, holding it to him as he lay slumped over the bed.

This wasn't real.

My chest heaved as tears collected in my gaze.

Something bad had happened and I hadn't made it—it was the only explanation for this. *For him.*

My small sob echoed the beep of the machine and he

stirred, the quick shudder of not realizing that he'd fallen asleep followed by the jerk of his head up to look at me.

"Ash?" I croaked, not quite ready to believe it.

"Oh, thank God, Tay." His shoulders heaved as his head bent; his hands clasped around mine and he froze for a second, like he truly was thanking God before his eyes sucked me back in and he was pressing soft kisses all along my hand and fingers. "I was so scared, sweetheart. So fucking scared."

"What happened? Is the baby—" I couldn't even finish as I choked on the simplest of words.

What if I had made it but the baby hadn't?

"Hey, hey… she's okay. Baby is just perfect, sweetheart." He reached up and quickly swiped away the tears that had leaked down my cheeks pre-emptively.

I blinked at him; I couldn't reply until his words sunk in. Really, truly sunk in.

And when they reached the most vulnerable part of my heart, the part that was split in two with love for our baby and Ash, that I let out a small cry.

"It's okay, sweetheart. I got you. She's okay… you're okay…" Ash climbed on the hospital bed next to me. Wrapping one arm around me, he laid his other hand on top of mine that held my stomach; together, we held our baby.

Minutes later, I looked up at him through the puddles in my eyes and asked, "It's a she?"

I hadn't found out up until now, which was strange for me because I always needed to know all the details; it was why Blake hired me to be her press manager and life organizer. But not once in this journey had I felt compelled to know. Maybe I was waiting for this moment—the one where I could find out the sex knowing Ash was there with me—not just because he loved me, but because he knew he was half responsible for this baby too—by choice and by genes.

"Yeah," he said with a crooked smile and half a laugh. "It's our girl."

My heart burst.

For years, I'd watched Blake walk out onto that stage, cheered and loved by tens of thousands of fans. Every once in a while, I imagined what it must feel like to have everything.

Now, I knew.

I cried again, but this time the tears were warm with happiness.

"Taylor," he rasped into my hair. "Look at me."

He waited for my head to tip back before he spoke again, his voice thick with emotion and his face ragged from exhaustion.

"I'm sorry, Pixie," he spoke as he brushed damp, matted hair back from my face. "I'm so damn sorry, sweetheart, for pushing you away. I didn't mean…" He paused as his jaw tightened with remorse, "Fact is, beautiful, you came here looking for shelter and to give me the truth. At first, I… I told myself to be the hero, the one to make up for the asshole who got you pregnant and didn't want anything to do with the baby. And it turned out, that asshole was me."

"I'm s-sorry," I murmured hurriedly, afraid that if I didn't get it out, this would all end and he would disappear again. "I'm sorry I didn't tell you. I thought I was strong coming here. I didn't care what anyone else had to say, because I loved the life I was growing so much. I thought I was strong until you opened the door… until you took care of me… and then I realized there was a weakness inside of me—a weakness for you. *For loving you.* A-And the strangest part was it didn't feel weak at all with you… but without—" I broke off to gulp in air. "Without you… it felt like it could consume me."

Ash nodded as his large, warm hand cupped my cheek before sliding back into my hair, gently rubbing along my scalp as my pulse began to calm from my outburst. I just knew, right then, that it was going to be okay. No matter what he said next, I felt that he was planning on holding me like this for the rest of our lives.

"If I've learned anything during my recovery, it's that the biggest villain and the strongest hero don't live in the world, they live inside us," he told me, his voice colored with emotion. "I can't promise you perfect, Tay, because perfect isn't real; although I'm pretty damn sure you're as close to it as someone can get."

"Ash…"

Shivers held a parade up and down my spine, cheering and waving his compliments from my brain down to my body and back again.

"There will always be good and bad, strong and weak inside me. But I've never wanted to be strong… I've never wanted to be the hero more than I have for you… for our baby."

My lower lip shook violently, just like my heart.

"Ash," I choked out his name, my arms, and their various cord attachments, twining around his neck as I pulled his face to me. "I love you. I love you so much. I'm sorry for being afraid."

"Taylor," he growled as his forehead pressed to mine. "I love you. First… *always*… I love you. I love you and I'm not leaving you. Second, you are the strongest woman I know. And kindest. And generous. And most beautiful fucking nymph I've ever seen. But sweetheart, I've learned what 'loyal to a fault' means. I've done the fault. Hell, I've gone so fucking far past the fault that it looks like a damn crack in the road compared to the canyon I created."

My watery laugh matched his.

"I love you, Taylor. Not because you're beautiful. Not because I took your virginity. And not because you're having my baby. *I. Love. You.* Because you've always been mine."

All my life, I'd heard the phrase 'peace beyond all understanding' resonate through sermon after sermon, lesson after lesson, but until this moment, when I lost myself in his ocean eyes, I'd never fully understood; in him, I found peace and love beyond anything I'd ever dreamt, let alone came here expecting to find.

"Tonight… tomorrow… the rest of my life, Tay, I'm going to be the man you need me to be."

I drew a wavering breath.

"You already are that man, Ash," I whispered thickly. "And I love you."

"I love you, too," he said with a low, hoarse voice before his lips crushed mine.

It didn't matter where we were or who was watching, he made sure this kiss would erase any last doubt I could ever dream up that he was letting me go. I sighed into him as he pulled me close, his tongue sweeping inside my mouth, promising and possessive as he wiped away any trace of every thought other than him.

"And I love our baby." His chest rumbled against my sensitive breasts as he spoke. "I love our baby girl."

I knew peace and now, I knew heaven.

"Knock, knock," a calming voice said softly as our moment was opened to the public.

I looked over from Ash's face, heat flooding my cheeks to see a familiar face on the nurse who entered first followed by the man who must be the doctor. Ash calmly sat up, pulling my hand in his while I adjusted the sheets, trying my hardest not to appear embarrassed.

I hadn't even asked, I realized.

As soon as I knew our baby was okay, I hadn't even asked what had happened or if there was anything wrong with me. *I hadn't cared.* I had our baby and I had him, what else could I need?

As they walked up to the bed, I realized what else I could want… a life to live with them. More babies.

What if something was seriously wrong with me?

"Miss Hastings," the doctor spoke with a voice that sounded like my priest from back home, calm with the certainty of the news he was about to deliver. "I'm glad to see you're awake and feeling better. I'm Dr. Snyder. I've been overseeing your care for the past day."

"Hello," I said with a weak smile.

"First, as I'm sure your husband has shared with you." My face flushed deeper at the way he referred to Ash. Ash, on the other hand, squeezed my hand tighter as if to say 'not soon enough' when he heard the doctor's words. "I want to assure you that everything with your baby is fine. We've been monitoring her this whole time and she is healthy and kicking and doing just perfect given the situation."

The lightness in my chest began to disappear.

"You were admitted with a variety of symptoms and we're fairly confident that you've suffered a partial placental abruption."

What?

My mind flipped through the stack of notecards in my head of all the things that could possibly go wrong—all the things I'd learned from everything I read. But I didn't make it to this one fast enough before he explained.

"Placental abruption is when the placenta separates from the lining of your uterus," he said calmly and slowly so I could process. "It's very rare and only occurs in about one percent of all pregnancies. There are certain risk factors, however, I think the most likely cause of yours is just an abnormality in your uterus."

"What… what does it mean? Did it harm the baby?" I asked even though he said the baby was okay because what he'd just said sounded terrible.

"Because yours was only a partial separation and all your

tests have come back normal, I don't think the separation had much, if any, effect on her." I think my sigh of relief could have been heard all the way in Hawaii. "However, this can be a very serious condition since the placenta is what supplies all the nutrients to your baby," he continued seriously. "If it had been a complete separation, we would have had to deliver her immediately. Since your case was only partial, we're going to monitor you for another day before sending you home tomorrow with instructions to take it very easy for the remainder of your pregnancy."

I swallowed hard and nodded.

"Gwen will give you both information about the condition and signs and symptoms to be aware of and you should come to the hospital immediately if they occur. But," he paused and offered us both a kind, hopeful smile, "I have a feeling that you and the baby are going to make it just fine."

I nodded. "Thank you."

Ash stood and murmured something to Dr. Snyder before shaking his hand.

As he exited, the nurse, Gwen, came bouncing into the room. It was hard not to feel even just the little bit better at the cheer she seemed to bring with her.

"How are you feeling today, Miss Hastings?" she asked, walking around to the other side of the bed to adjust the pillow behind my back.

"Tired. Sore."

"Well, you went through a lot yesterday and with all the testing and then the bleeding—"

"Bleeding?" My eyes shot up, and then I remembered the blood I'd glimpsed on the deck.

She placed a calming hand on my arm. "Not a lot. And it stopped on its own which is a very good sign. You were a little out of it because of the medications we had you on. Placental abruption is truly difficult to diagnose until after you give birth, so we had to partially sedate you in order to run a full complement of tests to rule out some other possible causes of your abdominal pain. Right after we finished with the physical exam, you started bleeding, so we were concerned. But like I said, it stopped on its own just over an hour later and all the tests came back normal for the baby."

"Oh, I see," I said softly, trying to peel back the layers of my blurred memory.

"He wouldn't leave the room, you know." She looked at the monitors by the bed while she spoke, clearly trying to be less obvious that she was talking about Ash. "I went out to talk to your friend, Eve, about what was going on and he'd just gotten here. I put on a brave face, don't let him tell you otherwise, but there was no chance that I or anyone else in this hospital was keeping him from you even if we wanted to. He would have taken on the world and more to get to you."

She spoke with a soft, wistful tone, the kind you hear when people talk about fairy tales as though they only exist in movies or for others.

"Everything okay?" We both turned to Ash as he reached for my hand again and brought it to his mouth.

"Yes, she's doing great," Gwen said with a smile. "Everything still looks good, so you'll just be here a little longer to be sure, and then you'll get to go home."

"You're sure that's okay?" he asked cautiously, glancing down to me. "What do we need to know? What do I need to look for?"

I couldn't stop looking at him. I could ask the questions, but when he did it… when I saw the way he stared at me, held me, I just knew that he was being strong for me so that I could be strong for our baby.

"You're just going to want to take it easy for the remainder of your pregnancy. No heavy lifting. No overexertion. But you're not on bed rest. Most normal activities for this stage of your pregnancy are fine," she told us, giving me a quick glance when she mentioned *normal activities* so I'd know she meant intimate ones.

"As Dr. Snyder said, we believe it was only a partial disruption, so you may deliver a little earlier than your due date. However, since the baby is still getting all the oxygen and nutrients she needs, you may not. The most obvious things to look out for are the same kinds of pains you felt yesterday along with any signs of bleeding. In those cases, either contact your doctor or come straight to the hospital."

We both nodded.

"I think that you are in very good hands, Miss Hastings," she finished gently, looking longingly between the two of us. "But I'll give you my card as well if you have any questions."

"Thank you," I murmured as she reached into her pocket and handed Ash a business card.

"I'll be back in in a little while to check on you."

As soon as she left, Ash made his way back to my side to hold me again.

"It's gonna be okay, Pixie. It's all gonna be okay."

He wasn't the doctor or the nurse. He had no qualifications, aside from just hearing what they said, to make such a bold claim. But hearing the reassurance from his lips made all the difference. Like because he said it, it would be true.

I sagged against him, my hand on my stomach and his hand over mine, and it felt like coming home. Warm. Safe. *Loved.*

"I loved you before, Tay. Before the baby. I love you because you saved me—not from my wrongs but from myself. I would have spent the rest of my life living to make up for the past instead of making peace with it, instead of living to make more from the future. I love you because you remind me of the best in me when it's easier to focus on the worst."

"I love you, Ash," I whispered, wanting to say more but too exhausted to form the words.

I wanted to know so many things. About the shop. About Larry. But for now, knowing this contentment was enough to let my heart finally rest.

Chapter Twenty-Nine

ASH

"Don't even think about it," I growled, jogging around the truck to finish opening the door for her.

"Ash, I'm fine," Tay insisted. "I'm pretty sure getting out of a car is considered a relatively mild normal activity."

I grunted, not giving a shit. We'd just left the hospital. She had to be out of her mind if she thought I was going to take any chances.

I stood in front of the door, blocking her descent.

"Ash, what—" She broke off with a small squeal as I wedge my arm underneath her knees and around her back. "You can't carry me! I'm pregnant!"

I laughed. "I hadn't noticed," I teased as I shoved the door shut and walked us to the house.

Even pregnant, she weighed only about a pixie and a half.

"I hope you know you can't carry me everywhere for the remainder of the pregnancy," she stated as I reached for the doorknob.

I met her gaze with an easy smirk. "Is that a dare?"

Her response was cut off when the door opened and a resounding '*Welcome Home*' echoed through the room.

It wasn't anything huge, but Eve, Eli, and the Madison brothers had wanted to be here when she got back.

I never would've asked—not with Larry's death leaving

the community in the kind of utter devastation one finds in Category 5 hurricane-ravaged lands—but it seemed like everyone, including us, clung to any happiness that crossed our paths in the wake of the tragedy; it was the only way we'd ever get through it.

Taylor's wide eyes and round mouth as she looked at me did things to my body that I really shouldn't have been thinking about at that moment. So, with a tight jaw, I shoved away my desire to worship her and promptly placed her on the couch, dropping a kiss on her head just as Eve swarmed in to gush over her friend with Mick not too far behind.

I walked away to the tune of baby names being discussed.

Brushing by Miles, who stayed back from the crowd, I thanked him for stopping by. I couldn't help but notice how he made no move to get closer though his attention never wavered to me or even to Eli; it remained trained on the two women. For a second, I thought his intense focus was on Taylor and my blood heated, but then I realized it wasn't Taylor he was looking at; it was Eve.

With a soft laugh to myself, I shook my head and headed for Eli.

We hadn't had a chance to talk since Larry's house—which wasn't exactly talking. And the past two days at the hospital, Tay had been my only focus, though Larry wasn't far from my mind.

"How are you holding up?" I asked, almost immediately regretting the question.

Eli looked alright on the outside; *he looked like the outside was all he had left.*

Hollow eyes ducked from mine as he nodded to the door. Glancing over my shoulder, I made sure Taylor was still securely sitting on the couch before stepping back outside with him. I needed to know about Larry and what was going on, but I didn't want Taylor to hear it, too. Not now.

He cleared his throat. "They're ruling it a suicide."

I nodded. "And Dex is sure…"

"Yeah."

There wasn't much doubt left in my mind that Larry had killed himself, but with what just happened at Roasters, I wasn't willing to put it past Blackman to fucking frame Larry for his own death.

"He'd stopped taking his medication," my friend went on, staring out toward the cliff as though he was confessing to me, rather than telling me the details I needed to know.

"Medication for what?" I'd heard him that night when he'd come to the house. But I couldn't think—couldn't process anything except that Larry was gone.

"Mood stabilizers for depression. Doc Shelly put him on them after Laurel left. And he was doing this shit for years. On and off again."

"Why? Why stop taking your fucking medication?" I said roughly, my heart still raw—still bleeding from the loss.

"Because he was raised in a different time. A time when you didn't talk about things like depression, let alone take something for it." He paused and then continued in a rough, hoarse impression of Larry. "'*I went to war, boy. I don't need no damn medication to help me.*'"

Yeah, that sounded like Larry.

A tear slipped from my eye. *Fucking stubborn old man.*

"Instead, you just manned up and did what you had to do… because they didn't know that the thoughts could kill you," Eli finished heavily.

"Then why take them in the first place?"

"Because they made him feel better," he said with a sharp

edge of irony. "They made him feel better to the point where he'd decide he never needed them in the first place since he felt fine."

I still didn't understand. *You have medication, you take it.*

Sometimes, it's not our place to understand, just to be understanding.

I stared out toward the horizon next to him, letting the cool salt air carry the reality down into the most vulnerable part of my soul.

I'd only known Larry for a handful of months. Months—days even—are more than enough to see the goodness in a person, but the darkness they battle is harder to uncover. Everyone hides their shadows, embarrassed of the monsters that hide inside us all.

It was hard to accept that the man who'd helped me find mine, bring them out into the light, give them a name, and overcome them, would be the same man who lost the battle to his own.

"You're sure it wasn't... You're fucking sure?"

"It's my fault," he replied, and I flinched at the vehemence in his tone.

My eyes jerked to Eli. His temple pulsed with the way blood pumped to the muscles clenched along his face.

"What are you talking about?"

"I had a feeling he wasn't taking them with how he's been acting lately. He was angry and upset and I yelled at him, Ash. He was talking about selling Roasters... giving up everything... after the robbery and I couldn't take it. I yelled at him to take the damn meds so that he wouldn't be a giant pain in the ass, so that we could move forward with fixing this, so that he could be what we needed him to be," he said hollowly and if murder could be convicted on confessions alone, it was clear Eli would've taken full responsibility for this in a heartbeat. "I was too frustrated. Too angry that he'd so easily want to give up everything when I should have known it was the depression talking, when I should have been more patient."

"Eli, this isn't your fault," I said with a confidence that I had no business having.

Was it anyone's fault? Was it even Larry's fault? I had no fucking clue.

All I knew was that someone who'd meant a lot, who'd done a lot, was gone and we were all figuring out how to cope with it.

"Guess we'll never know," he replied.

I almost wished Taylor were hearing this because she'd know the right thing to say. She'd know how to make it okay. I shuddered with the sudden violent urge to hold her and tell her how much I loved her.

"He didn't do this to punish you, Eli," I told him, repeating the words he'd spoken to me the other day. "He loved you. He didn't do this to punish anyone."

Eli didn't respond. He stood as still as a petrified tree for so long, I wondered if he was growing roots made of remorse into the ground at his feet.

Ever so slowly, he turned to me, his eyes sharp with sorrow. "Do you believe that?"

I drew a long breath. I didn't know how to explain the actions of a hurting man, especially when I couldn't claim to understand them myself.

But I could tell him what I chose to believe.

"When we talked the other day, I said when Larry died, all it did was remind me—literally—of the man I was and the mistakes I'd made." I swallowed over the thick bittersweet ball of love and grief lodged in my throat. "I was wrong."

His eyebrows rose.

"When he died, those memories didn't come back to

punish me for who I was, they came to show the man I was meant to be—the man Larry wanted me to be." I bit off a curse and wiped a tear away. "A good man. A good husband." I looked over my shoulder, knowing that day was going to come as soon as I could make it happen. "And a good father," I said the last with a thready voice.

"I lost Larry that night, but he didn't go without leaving me something to hold onto forever."

There were many things Larry gave that would stay with me forever, but Taylor and our baby girl? They were the most important of them all.

Eli's mouth thinned, a range of emotions flashing over his face. Grief and longing, but it was the hint of jealousy that surprised me.

But just as quickly as it surprised me, it was gone again.

"I'm happy for you," he told me, a strained smile struggling on his face as he pulled me in for a hug. "Guess all we can do is focus on the good things, right?"

I patted him on the back, uttering as I pulled back, "Start where you are..."

"Use what you have," he returned in kind.

Do what you can went unsaid between us as we turned back to the house.

"What do you need from me? Is there anything that I can do?" I asked with a firm tone, hoping at least focusing on the immediate future would help pull us all through something so hard to see past.

"I've told everyone here... Josie. Eve's siblings. Went up to Rock Beach the day after I saw you and broke the news to Jules and her parents."

"Did you find Larry's other granddaughter, Laurel?"

His head ducked. "Dex found her; she's been working for Ralph Lauren in Frisco." He sighed. "I just had to find someone else to tell her. Laurel... doesn't know me. I think it would be better for her to find out from someone she knows, given her past—and *not* her aunt."

I nodded, remembering that Laurel's parents—Larry's son and daughter-in-law—had died in a tragic boating accident. *And now this.*

"Let me rephrase, I found someone to tell her, I'm just waiting to hear back from the woman so I can let them run the announcements in the paper, though I doubt Laurel gets or wants any news having to do with Carmel Cove after what she's been through." He stopped at the door. "Funeral will be this weekend."

"You coming back in?"

He shook his head. "I should get going. Still trying to sort out everything with his will and the funeral arrangements. Plus, I'm still trying to figure out the motive behind the break-in."

My jaw tightened. Though everything he said was one-hundred-percent true, I had a feeling he just couldn't keep up the façade of being okay for any longer.

"If you need anything—*anything*." I gripped his shoulder. "My door is always open."

I watched him nod and head back to his truck, wishing there was something more I could do. But sometimes, offering to help bear the burden was all that could be done.

Unlike Taylor, I hadn't grown up going to church every Sunday. I believed in God, but I wasn't religious. Even after starting at the AA meetings, I hadn't made it to church on Sundays, but I had begun to pray.

In the hospital, I prayed for Taylor.

Now, I prayed Eli, that somehow—some way—he'd be able to make peace with what happened.

And, as I walked back inside, I prayed I'd never again doubt the man Larry knew I could be.

Chapter Thirty

Taylor

My fingers rubbed circles around the crest of my stomach as I stood on the lip of wood between the bedroom and living space. I was in one of Ash's shirts which just happened to be the perfect size for a pregnant woman like me and a super soft pair of sweatpants he'd bought me to try and bribe me to stay in bed.

I'd left the hospital two days ago and he still acted as though I'd been put on bed rest.

I should've felt settled—being back home, knowing our baby girl was okay, but I wasn't quite there; the cabin didn't look quite the same. The weight of my confession had hung over me for so long, the rest of my worries and plans about the future seemed to fall by the wayside in comparison.

The trip to the hospital made my future reality come barreling in like a SWAT team of worries through the windows of my mind.

We had nothing for the baby.

I *knew* a lot. I'd read too much not to have a Ph.D. in pregnancy by now. But when it came to physical things—*like a crib*—or, you know, a room for the baby, or... *anything*.

"Tay?" Ash came through the door, worry immediately scarring his face as he scanned over me.

He'd been out at the restaurant dealing with the last

round of inspections. The stress of them had weighed on him, on top of my small trip to the hospital, and on top of Larry's funeral this weekend. Because of the manner of his death, Larry had been cremated, and the service held off for a few days until Dex could track down Larry's long-gone granddaughter, Laurel, and tell her what happened.

The word on Ocean Avenue was that she was due to arrive in town tomorrow.

But because of all of it, I'd waited to mention all the things that had plagued my mind and my sleep.

Though I'd made substantial progress on filling up my Amazon cart with the essentials.

"Are you alright? Are you having pain again?"

He rushed over to me, pulling out his phone ready to call the hospital. I reached out and stopped him.

"I'm fine—I mean, I feel fine," I assured him, reaching up on my tiptoes to press a kiss to his lips. "Did everything go okay?"

His shoulders sagged, his forehead dropping to mine as a smile tugged at his lips.

"Passed."

I let out a small cry of happy relief and wrapped my arms around his neck, hugging him as tight as I could.

"I'm so happy for you," I murmured, relaxing in his embrace.

"Me, too, Pixie. Me, too." He took a deep breath against my neck. "Now, tell me what's on your mind."

"How'd you know?"

"It's about as obvious as your stomach," he quipped.

I sighed. "I just… Coming back from the hospital… it hit me how not prepared I am. *Me.* Not prepared at all for this baby."

"*We,*" he corrected with emphasis.

My heart swelled amid my anxiety. "Well, if you want to be in that boat with me," I teased softly.

"I want to be anywhere so long as it's with you." He dropped a kiss on my nose and continued, "Alright. So, tell me what you need."

"We still have two months before she's here. That's plenty of time to get a crib and diapers and all—"

"No."

"No... it's not?"

"Not that." He held his arm out. "Taylor, this place isn't ready for a baby. There's no room. Plus, the whole structure is just..." He trailed off in dismay. "No, it's not right."

I didn't completely disagree with him, but he made it seem much more drastic than it was.

"I think it will be okay..."

Ash's hands fell away from me as he ambled through the room, examining... calculating.

And then, before I could stop him, he brought his phone up to his face—but he wasn't calling the hospital.

"Hey, man. Got a minute?"

"Ash..." I mumbled, unsure what for and too softly for him to hear me.

"I know you got a lot on your plate right now with Roasters and Larry," he began regretfully, and I realized he must be talking to Eli. "But I was just talking with Taylor about the baby... and we've got to do something with my place. It barely fits us."

There was a pause while he listened to Eli reply.

"Really? Are you sure? That would be awesome." My head turned. "We still have a few months, but I'd like to see what we can get done in that time."

I bit my lip, padding quietly into the kitchen to grab a cup of water.

Ash nodded, his eyes meeting mine as he ended the call. "Thanks, Eli. I really appreciate it."

"You didn't have to do that."

He came over and kissed my forehead. *Always my protector... and my lover.*

"I did," he told me. "And I always will."

My body flushed and I shifted uncomfortably as that heat pooled between my legs, making my panties damp and my core instantly ache.

It had become clear that hormones didn't stop for life... or death... or hospital visits. And Ash... he was more than attentive and caring, making sure that I *really* didn't have to do anything over the past two days, but aside from that, he hadn't done more than kiss me. *And I really needed him to do more than kiss me.*

But it was more than the hormones... We'd lost Larry. And since the hospital... I lost count of how many times I'd prayed, thanking God that our little girl was okay, while knowing just how serious and life-threatening things could have been. Life could be so uncertain. But love... I'd never felt more sure of anything than I did of this.

Unfortunately, the one thing that *would have* guaranteed that I remained in bed for extended periods of time was the only thing that Ash avoided like the plague.

I knew it was hard for him. *I felt it.* Still, he stuck to soft touches and tender kisses, never letting them get within range where his desire would overcome his restraint.

At first, I was touched, thinking how loving and sweet it was.

But that sensation faded rather quickly when I began to ache to have him inside me.

I wanted that intimacy. I wanted that fullness. *That pleasure.* Mostly, I wanted him to make love to me now that he knew the truth.

Rubbing my thighs together, I asked, "What did he say?"

"He thinks he has some plans he did for the previous owners of this property."

"Really?" I pressed, already losing focus on the question I'd asked as his shirt stretched and pulled against his biceps, the sinewed muscle tensing and releasing as he unloaded the dishwasher.

"They wanted to turn this into a guesthouse," he informed me. "So, some remodeling and adding on. I'm hoping he can find them so we can take a look this week. We don't have to do all of it now, but at least get some of the current space re-done before the baby comes."

Even just talking about it, I found my worry begin to dissipate, knowing I wasn't alone.

Knowing Ash was in this with me. For me.

And for our baby.

I came out of my thoughts when those strong arms wrapped around me, pulling me tight against my very protective and very hard man. *And the temperature of my blood rose to boiling.*

"Alright, Pixie," he rasped, his chin bumping against my head as he spoke. "What else do we need?"

I groaned. "Do you maybe want to shower first?"

He laughed. "The list that long then?" He pulled back. "Or do I just smell bad?"

I shrugged with a sheepish smile. "Maybe."

His head fell back, and I playfully swatted him when he feigned disgruntlement. Meanwhile, excitement brimmed in his eyes.

"Alright, let me rinse off real quick."

It had been a debate up until that moment—whether or not I wanted to try my luck at seducing my overly protective baby daddy who had staunchly decided it was too dangerous with my condition.

Just like everything else that involved getting out of bed.

No matter how many times I'd checked with the nurse, Gwen, that *all* normal activity was okay for the baby.

But when his hand swatted my butt as he sent me a jaw-dropping wink—the kind that would melt more panties than #TeamJacob's shirt-stripping scene in *New Moon*—there was no more debate.

Nope, definitely not, I told myself, following him and staring as he stripped off his shirt, revealing cut and corded back muscles and his perfectly sculpted behind.

When he glanced over his shoulder just before entering the bathroom, I gulped down my water, feigning innocence and fleeing his gaze so he wouldn't know just how turned on I was.

Because *if he knew, he'd beg me not to do what I was about to do out of fear.* And I needed to do this.

For both of us.

With a confidence in myself and my body I hadn't thought I lacked nor expected to find here, I discarded my comfy clothes in a tell-tale trail leading into the bathroom.

Inside, the mirror was almost completely steamed up. The thick, warm air was clogged with moisture like I was with desire. Heavy. Aching. *Needing.*

I pulled back the curtain to his truncated curse.

"Taylor!" He wiped the soap from his face just as I stepped fluidly inside the shower. "What the…"

I reveled in the way his voice died off like a shooting star—plummeting into nothing in a split-second.

My nipples, now a deeper red, tightened painfully under his stare that was doused with desire as he drank in my enlarged breasts.

For my own pleasure, I licked over my lips, watching how his cock began to thicken where it hung heavily at the base of the V in his hips. Lust turning the stiff length a greedy reddish-purple.

"Taylor…" he rasped, half in warning, half in wanting.

"I need you," I told him bluntly as I stepped closer to him, sacrificing the view of his erection due to my stomach in order to be closer to him.

Large palms reached out and stayed me on the sides of my stomach.

Ash fought with himself and the war projected on the perfect lines of his face.

"But Tay... I don't want..."

"You won't hurt me," I assured him, placing my hands over his own. "I promise."

And then, with a new boldness I'd found in myself, I held his gaze and slid his palms up over my swollen breasts.

His nostrils flared.

He was slowly and savagely losing the last bits of his control, and it was the most beautiful thing I'd ever seen.

I felt the subtle tense of his fingers and even just the small flex sent a shudder rocketing down my body, pooling into fire between my thighs.

"Ash, please..."

A low groan reverberated from his chest as his thumbs brushed over my nipples.

My knees almost gave out, knowing I'd succeeded.

"Think you might be the only addiction I'll never be able to resist." Both hands plucked and pulled on my sensitive nipples and I cried out in pleasure.

Ash wasn't the only one with an addiction.

The needing. The craving.

The constant thoughts of him when we were apart.

But I wasn't ashamed of my addiction.

Because you should never be able to get enough of the very best things in life. There should always be more... always be too much. It was what kept us longing for the future.

"Was I gentle?" he rasped as his knuckles brushed back and forth over my nipples.

"W-What?"

"That night." His jaw ticked. "Was I gentle?"

My eyes shot wide. It almost felt like he was asking me what sex had been like with another man.

Was it good?

Was he better than me?

Did you come?

Except the other man was himself.

"At times," I gulped. I wouldn't lie. That night was like sticking a needle into a balloon of desire that had been building for a lifetime: it could only release so gently.

"Did I tell you how beautiful your tits are?" He stared at them as he spoke. "Did I tell you how many fantasies I've had about them?"

"No," I confessed, watching his face fall again. "But the way you touched and kissed them… it was heaven."

Sharp blue eyes sliced to mine, melting me with the hottest blue flame.

"Tell me."

My cheeks burned, regretting my added statement.

Closing my eyes, I went back to that night, the memories bobbing like buoys in front of me, hard to grasp onto when his hands were still toying with my breasts.

"Y-You kneaded and squeezed them." I bit my cheek, feeling him do the same. "You made them so achy before you even touched my nipples."

He plumped my flesh, his fingers avoiding the very tips as he asked, "And what happened when I did that?"

"I thought I was going to die… or maybe I had died." I drew a shaky breath. "But I still wanted more."

"You wanted my mouth," he declared, and I nodded. "And did I suck on them?"

My eyes squeezed tighter.

"You laid me back on the bed." My pulse raced. "You were so tense climbing over me, I wanted to touch you, but I thought I might break you."

Ash shuddered under where my hands held onto his arms.

"You kissed over them until I thought I was going to lose my mind."

"And then?"

"And then it seemed like you gave in." I sucked in a breath. "And I realized I was going to die a lot more times that night when you first sucked on my nipple. I'd never felt so… much… and still needed more."

I gasped loudly and my hand shot out to brace against the tile wall as Ash dipped his head and suckled one of the taut peaks into his mouth.

"Like this?"

I choked out a yes as my other hand speared through his hair, locking him against me.

I whimpered as his tongue danced viciously over my flesh. It made my body so sensitive that even the water spray felt like tiny, teasing foreplay against my skin.

Even though he'd given in, I still felt his control. He let his body take… *but carefully*.

With his hands and mouth, he worshipped my breasts, telling me how perfect they were and how hard they made him. He told me all the things he felt like had lacked from my first time.

I wanted to tell him there was nothing lacking about our night together, except that he didn't remember it, but I couldn't find the words.

I took my first full breath in several minutes when his hand slid up around my nape and his mouth rose to claim mine, stealing away the oxygen I'd just reclaimed.

He devoured me and I arched against him, feeling the

blunt head of his arousal poking against my stomach, hotter than the shower.

With harsh pants, his hands planted possessively on my waist. "Turn."

It took two tries to swallow over the lump of need in my throat as I complied, facing the side wall of the shower.

"Hands against the tile."

They were already on their way there... *I didn't trust my own feet when it came to keeping me steady while he touched me.*

His fingers skimmed down the length of my spine, dragging all my nerve endings with them. But his touch fell away when he crested over the curve on my ass.

I shifted my feet slightly wider, knowing I was bared for him. Open. Wet. Waiting.

"So beautiful, Pixie," he murmured, though he still wasn't touching me. "And what about here?"

He dipped one finger along my seam.

"Was I gentle with you here?"

"I... you..." I shoveled air into my lungs but it didn't seem to make a difference. All I could think about was the softest brush of his fingertip against my most sensitive skin. "You used your fingers, but not for long."

He growled in displeasure.

I dragged air through my lips, bracing myself for the feel of his fingers once more.

"*Ash!*" I gasped when I felt the warm slice of his tongue along my slit.

"And what about my mouth?" he demanded as my heart hammered harder. "Did I savor your pretty pink pussy with my tongue, Pixie?"

My tongue felt like a thousand pounds and all I could do was shake my head back and forth.

He hadn't.

"Then I was a stupid, stupid man."

I opened my mouth to disagree but only a wordless gasp escaped, my eyes shooting wide as his mouth closed over me.

Spots flared in front of my eyes as I looked between my feet to see him kneeling, his hands sliding to grip into my thighs. My eyelids drifted shut as he explored and traced every inch of my sex, driving me insane with need.

"All mine," he growled, delving his tongue between my folds again and spearing against my clit until I saw stars.

Small moans rolled off my lips in waves, rushing down my skin along with the rivulets of water. It felt like a million caresses, touching every inch of me as they went.

"Ash," I choked out his name, my chest caving as my orgasm turned my body into a black hole of desire, sucking in every sensation without mercy.

His lips closed over my clit and I exploded.

Gasping in deep breaths, my only goal was to remain upright as his mouth ate up the rush of my release.

He rose from behind me, his hands securely gliding up my sides to hold me steady. With subtle encouragement, he tipped me farther forward.

My teeth sunk into my lip, knowing he always managed to fit so deep inside me positioned like this. My core, still pulsing from my climax clenched harder at the thought.

"*Fuck, Tay,*" he groaned, and I felt his head slide against my entrance, gently probing.

Everything about him screamed torturous restraint. It had been days since we'd had sex—days since he found out the baby was his and days since the hospital scare.

I could see it in his gaze each time it fell on me that he was desperate to claim me—to mark me once more, through it all, as his.

"And how about this?" He pushed just the tip into me. "Was I gentle with this? Was I gentle when I finally shoved my cock into your perfect cunt?"

He wanted to stay still—to wait for my answer—but he couldn't. The warm suction of my body slowly inching him deeper inside me.

"Y-You were." I angled my hips to encourage him. "Until I begged you for more."

A low, rich sound escaped with his exhale. One of pleasure. One of need.

"I want to tell you I remember the first time," he bit out. "I want to so fucking bad." Regret laced the strain in his voice. "But it feels like every time is that time. Every time I'm inside you obliterates the last, and when I'm not here," he paused, shoving himself deeper inside me for emphasis, "I crave you like I've never been in you before."

"Ash…" I whimpered. I tried to push back against him, my sex squeezing violently, but his hands held me firmly.

"Gentle this time," he told me as he rocked his hips all the way forward.

I sagged against his arms, feeling him bottom out inside me, his thick length pressing against that tender spot which would have me convulsing as soon as he began to move.

He groaned. His palm splayed on my back while the other secured my hip.

"Swear to God, Tay, your pussy feels like it goes to heaven every time."

My mouth dropped open soundlessly as he pulled out and thrust back in. Slow and steady. Long and deep.

He was careful. Because of the baby. Because of our first time. And I thought being careful would make the pleasure less, but it only made me squirm and shake more.

The slap of his hips against my butt was accentuated

by the water, our slick flesh gliding against each other as he claimed every inch of my body and my heart.

Hot tears spilled from my eyes, it felt so good. Him inside me. Finally knowing the baby was his.

Still gentle, his thrusts picked up their pace, rubbing against all the tender needy spots inside me. His hand slipped around to my front, skating down over my stomach to reached between my legs.

"*Ash!*" He plucked my clit and stars shimmered in my vision, another orgasm tugging me closer to its precipice.

He grunted and his control began to wither at my plea.

"I see you, Pixie," he growled, the length of him growing and thickening inside me. "I've got you."

The tender encouragement to let go spiraled me to the edge. The size of him stretching me was the kind of fullness I craved. My eyes jammed shut as the glide of him against my muscles created a symphony of pleasure inside me.

I whimpered as my body began to share, my release claiming me with the slow strength of a tsunami. And when his fingers rolled over my clit, the crash of the wave began, drowning me in the most intense orgasm I'd ever had.

My mouth opened, but neither a cry exited nor air entered. I was paralyzed by the unrelenting waves that seized through my body. The very peak of pleasure seemed to extend on and on with no break in sight, like the center of a piece of caramel as the ends were pulled apart, desperately clinging together until the very last moment. And then I broke, dragging in air as though I'd been held underwater for minutes on end.

My cries came in small pants as the pleasure spread like cracking glass through all my cells, making them weak and shaking.

I felt Ash's fingers tighten on me and I felt the last few

frenzied, rough thrusts as he shoved himself possessively inside me before pinning himself tightly against my womb.

His ragged shout echoed in the small space as the heat of his release flooded me in heavy, pumping waves.

I was still shaking when he slid out of me, helping my weakened limbs upright and pulling me into his arms—and into the stream of water.

"This is Heaven," I murmured and squeezed him tighter, feeling the baby begin to kick as though she agreed.

He pulled back to tip my face up and kiss the tip of my nose. "I don't think so, Pixie." My head was still slightly dazed with pleasure, but I still managed a small frown as I drowned in his blue stare.

He continued huskily, "Last I checked, God only sends saviors to Earth."

Heat suffused into my cheeks as I fought back tears. "I love you."

"I love you, too, Tay." His lips pressed tenderly on mine. "I'll take care of us, I promise."

"I know."

Maybe it wasn't Heaven, but happily-ever-afters certainly came close.

Chapter Thirty-One

Taylor

It's an odd feeling to see how the world continues to turn after a life is lost.

The wind blew my hair across my face as I directed the delivery men where to put the last of the patio furniture Ash had ordered.

The last thing Ash needed right now was to lose track of his dream because of grief.

And it was the last thing Larry would want, too.

"You know where he wants these, ma'am?" the leader of the three moving giants asked when I approached.

Nodding, I instructed them where to put the table and chairs, along with the outdoor heaters.

"Excuse me, does someone live here?" the bald mover asked, peering in from the door to the deck.

My brow scrunched. "No. I mean, not in this building. There's a house on the property. Why?"

He held up his hand, pale pink lace pinched between his fingers.

"Well, just looks like someone lost a pair of underwear..." He trailed off and my face blazed red.

Ash had gone out and retrieved our discarded clothes from that night after we got back from the hospital, but he must have missed a piece.

"I-Interesting," I stammered as I reached out and plucked the fabric from his fingers. "Let me... I'll just take these and, umm, look into it... thank you."

With my back turned to him, I could pretend like I didn't hear his chuckle as he went back inside with the other two guys to finish unloading.

Looking at the wad of underwear, I thought back to that night—only a few days ago, but it felt like lightyears had passed. Then again, someone had died—someone who meant something to someone I loved.

Watching Ash's pain and knowing that there was nothing I could do to make it better—nothing except love him through it—was a kind of agony I never thought could be so debilitating.

The moist, salty air washed down deep into my lungs as I watched the cloudy, calm surface of the ocean out to the horizon.

I felt the hurt in Ash's heart just as surely as I felt my own beating in my chest. But I breathed in deep again knowing that at some point, just like the sea, his storm would calm, his grief would run out of rain, because even the darkest of nights break for day.

And weeks... months... years into the future, it would be easier to look back and see what has grown from the healing waters that was once nothing but a trail of tears.

"Taylor?"

My head tilted to see Ash appearing behind Brett.

"Hey, man," he stuck out his hand to the local delivery guy. "Thanks for your help. Sorry about that... I just had to take care of a few things in town."

"Don't worry about it," Brett replied.

"I think we got everything squared away," I said cheerfully.

"Yeah, no worries." He shook Ash's hand with a smile. "Everything should be there. If you have any trouble or any problems, just give us a call."

When he left, I turned to Ash and asked, "Are you okay?"

I searched his gaze for anything I could do to make this easier.

His head turned to the side even as his hands reached for my waist.

His body shook against my fingers with the force of his sigh. "Don't know how Eli is holding it together. If I'd been the one to find him... to see him... I can't even—"

"Tell me how you feel. Whatever it is, Ash." I reached up and cupped his cheek. "However bad it is..."

"Feels hollow, walking in places where he should be. His house... we were just there... he was just there... at dinner, talking to us, eating with us. It's like walking into a hospital and finding no doctors. Or walking into a church and feeling like God is no longer there. Like something you never thought could be separated from a place is actually gone."

My throat constricted. "He may not be there anymore," I told him thickly, placing a hand on his chest over his heart. "But he'll always be here."

Ash's gaze grew sheltered as he rested his forehead on mine for a second before bringing my palm up to his lips and kissing the center.

"I just wish he would have said something. I never lied to him. Not once since I met him. Not about the things I'd done, not about all the times I'd searched his house for any kind of alcohol to drink. Not even the times I thought about having just one sip. I asked him for help so many times... Why couldn't he just ask the same from me?"

I drew a shuddered breath.

"Sometimes, those of us who are the strongest for others

are the ones that are the weakest when it comes to fighting for ourselves."

He tightened his hold and then turned us back to the house.

"Eli gave me those plans for us to look at while I was in town," he told me. "I set them inside."

Grief was like a rainstorm. Sometimes, you were stranded out in the deluge, feeling every cold, wet drop on your skin. Other times, you found yourself sheltered by a person or a situation where it became less noticeable, though it didn't stop the rain from falling.

There were moments when we were soaked with the loss, and there were others where pockets of happiness and a future to look forward to sheltered us from the hurt.

"Oh, good." I smiled up at him.

ASH

"I'll let Eli know these additions are good then," I said as Taylor shoved one more forkful of mac and cheese in her mouth with a sheepish smile.

The old blueprints for my small shack included enlarging the bedroom and adding a master bathroom, an overhaul of the kitchen to allow for more space, an addition off the living room for a second bedroom, and a wide front porch.

I'd told Taylor if she didn't like it, then we'd buy another house, but she insisted she didn't.

"*I don't want another place. I want this place. The one you offered me to stay in. The one you took care of me and our baby in. The one where you gave me your truths. And the one you loved me in.*"

"There's no—"

"It'll be done before the baby comes, I promise," I cut her off.

She was afraid it was a lot to be added to our plates, along with Eli and the Madison brothers who would be doing the work. She was right. But we also needed a lot right now in order to not fall stagnant in our sorrow.

"Does Eli need anything else for tomorrow?" she asked.

They managed to get ahold of his granddaughter, Laurel, thankfully. The whole town felt like it was in this strange grief-laden limbo, waiting for his funeral to finally say goodbye. I wasn't convinced that it would change much but I had hope.

"He still says no."

I'd asked a thousand times what I could do to help. And every time, Eli responded that I needed to take care of my girls and let him take care of this. *How the hell was I supposed to argue with that?*

There was one thing, though, I knew I needed to do before the funeral. It was one of those things that felt impossible until a switch flips and suddenly, what you need to do is so simple it's hard to believe why it was so difficult in the first place.

"You sure you're okay?"

Tay lovingly rolled her eyes and nodded to me. "Yes."

"Tomorrow's going to be hard," I told her. "So fucking hard."

"I know," she agreed softly. "I didn't get a chance to tell you in the hospital, Ash, but you saved me, too. You showed me in so many ways that no matter how strong we can be, love always makes us stronger together."

I walked over and kissed the top of her head.

"I'm here, Ash," she murmured. "Whatever you need. I'm here."

Whatever it was that tomorrow brought, we'd face it together; we'd get through it together.

Together, we'd be stronger.

Clearing my throat, I declared the one last thing I needed to do before tomorrow, "I'm going to go outside and call Blake."

I knew I wouldn't be able to walk into the funeral and face Larry one last time without speaking to my sister first—*without finally forgiving myself.*

Tay squeezed my hand. "I love you."

"Love you, too."

Salty ocean air greeted me as I stepped outside and walked down the path to the restaurant, searching for Blake's number in my phone.

Maybe that's why I picked this place, I thought as I came to the clearing. Saltwater—so simple and incredibly healing. Maybe that's why I'd risked everything to buy this place. So I'd never forget that it's the simple things in life that heal—good friends, purpose, and perfect love.

"Ash?" my sister's voice answered the phone, resonating with the shock that she felt.

"Hey, Blake," I said hoarsely. It felt good to hear her voice after all this time.

"What's... what's going on? Is Taylor okay?" she demanded.

Taylor had called her when we'd returned from the hospital to tell her what happened. Naturally, my sister was almost as worried for her best friend as I was.

"Yes, she's fine. Home. Resting."

Blake paused. "Sorry. I'm just... I wasn't expecting you to call is all. But I'm glad. So glad."

"I called because I needed to tell you I'm sorry, B." My sigh was heavy as the wind carried it from me, heavy with the weight I should have let go long ago.

"Ash," she breathed my name incredulously. "I already

forgave you. *We* already forgave you. You didn't… you didn't have to go—"

"No, sis, I did… I did. And as much as I'm apologizing for that, I'm apologizing because I lied to you." I'd dreaded this conversation for so long but now, each word only brought relief. "When I came to the house that day and we talked, I lied to you by not telling you the whole truth. The truth is that I had a problem with alcohol. I had a problem and I thought because I was outwardly functioning it wasn't actually a problem. And then I found out about you and Zach and I reacted not like I should have, no matter how shocked or hurt or upset I was. The alcohol… it's not an excuse, but it is part of the reason."

There was silence on the other end of the line, and I knew Blake was trying to process. Like finding out Larry was depressed, some people are so good at hiding their monsters it's hard to see them even when they come out into the light.

"I want you to know that I'm sorry for what my addiction almost cost you. I'm sorry for the pain it did cause you and I'm sorry for the distance and distrust it put between us," I said tightly, trying not to choke up as the heaviness lifting off my soul felt like the water pulling back from the shore.

"And I'm sorry that I had to leave. The band, that life… it put me too close to things that needed to be removed in order for me to get better. I want you to know I didn't leave because of you or because of you and Zach. I left because of me—because I needed to fix myself."

I heard her unsteady breath and I knew she was crying and trying not to let me hear. "Oh, Ash… a-are you okay? I mean did you…"

"I'm sober," I interjected, knowing that's what she was trying to discreetly ask. "I've been sober for months now. Hell, B, I've been more than sober. I've been healing… and happy."

"Yeah?"

"I met good people out here, Blay. Really good people." I wiped a tear from my cheek. I couldn't talk about Larry yet. It was too soon. "I got sober and then I bought a restaurant."

"Wha—What? A restaurant? Seriously?" she stammered.

"Yeah." I laughed. "I bought this building—well, you could hardly call it that when I bought it, but it's right on the ocean. I'll send you a photo. I've been fixing it up and it's ready to open in like two weeks."

"That's… that's amazing, Ash. I just… I'm sorry—" She broke off and began to cry. And fuck me if I didn't hope that Zach was somewhere nearby to hold her. "I'm just so happy… so relieved. I've been… so… worried," she bit out between sobs and I found myself pinching the bridge of my nose so that I wouldn't break down too.

"Don't cry, Blay," I begged. "It's good. I'm good… I'm recovering…. And Taylor… she and I… the baby…"

How did I even begin to explain how I felt about Tay? *About being a father?*

"I know," my sister said softly. "I know exactly how you feel."

I stared out to the horizon, the sun just beginning to dip toward the edge of the sea and bathe it in red.

"Kinda crazy, sis," I said hoarsely, "how love manages to find you…"

"And save you."

I turned back to the direction of the house, already worrying if Taylor was okay even though she'd roll her eyes again at me if she knew. Later, I'd show her—*carefully*—just what I thought of that eye roll.

"I'm sorry I didn't tell you until now. I just… guess I felt like I needed to have something to show, something to prove I'm not the person who hurt you anymore."

"But you know I've already forgiven you?" she asked bluntly.

"Yeah..." I agreed with a sigh. "But it was never your forgiveness I was worried about; it was my own."

"And have you forgiven yourself?"

The hardest thing I'd ever done wasn't accepting that I had a problem with alcohol; it wasn't leaving my family and friends; it wasn't forcing myself to stay dry until the cravings stopped; and it wasn't even admitting to Taylor or to my sister just how far I'd fallen and asking their forgiveness. No, the hardest thing I'd ever done was forgive myself.

When you screw up so badly, the hardest thing you'll ever do is look yourself in the mirror and say, 'I forgive you. You did a bad thing, but you are not a bad person. It's time to move on.'

But eventually, something or someone comes along that makes you realize that you've repented enough, *you've done enough,* and the time you waste pulling yourself down is only time that could have been spent bettering yourself or someone else.

"Yeah," I confessed with more relief than I thought possible. "I have."

"Good." I could hear her watery smile through the line. "That's good."

There was another beat of silence between us, one that was filled with the breeze and the waves below. I was finally free. Not of my addiction. Not of the road ahead and whatever new trials it would bring. I was free from the past that held me from every step forward, from finally healing, and it felt like the first time I'd stood on the edge of this cliff, knowing that this property would be mine.

Inspiring. Hopeful. Full of promise.

"So... can we come visit you? Can we come see your business?"

I smiled, hearing just how excited she was to support my dream the way that I'd supported hers over the years.

"About that…" I trailed off and looked back at everything I'd been working toward. "How does two weeks sound for the opening?"

She laughed and immediately agreed.

I walked back toward the house as our conversation turned toward lighter topics, finally filling in the gaps that the months disconnected had caused.

Chapter Thirty-Two

ASH

One Week Later...

"Eli?" I shouted as I pushed open the door to Roasters. The place wasn't back open yet. Not even close. With Larry's death, everything was put on hold. It was strange... haunting... to step onto the floor that still crunched with dirt and debris from the mess that had been made.

The tables and chairs—the ones that had been salvageable—had been moved to the back. Barely a third of the pictures still hung on the wall, the rest still sitting in their broken frames on the counter.

But it was the emptiness. No Larry. No customers. No family. That was what really made the place feel more desolate than the rest of the mess that needed to be cleaned. There hadn't been a day before two weeks ago that I hadn't walked into this place when there wasn't people in it, sharing love and a cup of coffee.

Larry was gone and his funeral created fractures through Carmel—fractures everyone was looking to Roasters to pull back together. But instead, it just sat. In a desolate purgatory.

With a long sigh, I put my hand on the counter and pulled away dust.

Soft footsteps from the back drew my attention as Eve

walked in wearing sweats and a Roasters tee that she'd designed and made for customers to buy.

"Hey, Ash. Eli's not here," she said with a weary smile. "He was supposed to come meet Dex, but something came up with Laurel."

The prodigal.

She'd been at the funeral. Strawberry hair and tortured eyes. I'd given her my condolences, feeling even worse at the blank stare that had greeted them. There were some that knew her from *before*, like Diane, and Josie, and the Covingtons—and obviously her aunt and uncle. But for most of us, she'd been a name and a photo, a sad story that ate away at Larry until there was nothing left. Now, she was back—she was real. And the rest of us wondered what was to become of Roasters because of it.

"You holding up okay?"

She nodded, about to say something when the door opened behind me and Dex and Miles walked in. Like she was a living alarm, Eve's face turned bright red when she greeted them.

"Ash," Dex shook my hand. "Wasn't expecting you here."

"I was on my way to the jeweler. Figured I'd stop in and see if Eli was around. I haven't heard much from him since the funeral."

"Little Laurel's been keeping him busy," Miles said with a half grin, his eyes purposely avoiding Eve.

"He's not here?" Dex asked.

"He told me to meet you," Eve interjected. "Something with Laurel came up."

"Shit," Dex swore.

"What's going on? You find out something?" With Taylor in the hospital, I wouldn't be surprised if Eli told everyone to keep me out of the loop for the time being.

"We have more information, but I wouldn't say we found

out anything," he said with a low voice. "Eli said someone from Blackman approached Laurel a few days after the funeral offering to buy Roasters. I guess Larry left it to her in the event of his death."

"He didn't leave it to his daughter?" I asked. Not that Jackie Vandelsen would touch this place with a giant twenty-four-carat pole, but she was still his daughter.

Dex shook his head. "It all went to Laurel. And, to be honest, she seems like a nice girl, but I don't know that she wants much more to do with this than her aunt does."

It was hard to imagine this town without Roasters.

Impossible, really.

I cleared my throat, not ready to think about that right now. "So, what are you thinking?"

Dex looked on edge, like his mind was working through a million scenarios, a million possibilities, but he was forced to wait until someone else made the next move.

"We know they approached Larry to sell. When he wouldn't, they tore this place to pieces looking for something that they presumably didn't find because now that he's gone, they're trying to convince Laurel that this place isn't much—isn't worth the effort."

"Motherfuckers." Red rage burned me from the inside out. "What is she going to do?"

"He said she told them she needed to think about it. Said she seems lost—torn between wanting to go back to the city and feeling beholden to her grandfather and the family business. He's trying to convince her not to sell. Hard to do when the only thing that ties her to this place is tragedy."

First, her parents. Now, her grandfather. I didn't want to understand why her decision would be hard, but I did. I wouldn't want anything to do with a place that held so much loss either.

"Truthfully, I'm more concerned with what happens if he succeeds. They trashed this place when Larry refused, I'm afraid to think about what they might do next if Laurel turns them down, too."

There was a heavy silence that punctuated his concern.

"We're working on it," Dex continued, slapping me on the back. "Don't worry about it now, man. Take care of your girl. Take care of your restaurant. Let me do my job and we'll get these fuckers."

Biting back a curse, I checked my watch. I was supposed to be at the jewelers ten minutes ago and Taylor thought I'd just run into town to pick up something quick from Mick for the opening.

"Alright. Just… let me know if you need anything. Please," I said tightly.

I knew my priority would always be Taylor and the baby, but if I could do anything to help catch the fuckers that were trying to ruin Larry's legacy, I'd do it. *After everything that man had done for me.*

"Don't tell Taylor you saw me." I turned to Eve and instructed. When her eyes widened, I added, "Please," with a wink.

TAYLOR

'Love and forgiveness are two threads of the same twine. Just as you love without qualifications, so should you forgive. Just as love is given without asking, so should forgiveness be given. The twine that binds them is that of selflessness, and it is what lightens the heart from the expectations that weigh it down.'

I hit pause on the sermon I'd been listening to when Ash walked through the door, the evening sun glinting off his wind-tossed hair and casting shadows over all the hard planes my finger itched to touch.

"Everything okay?" he charged, raising a lightly accusing but perfectly sculpted eyebrow.

Instantly, I felt the familiar ache between my thighs.

I'd yet to read anything like it, but I wondered if a *person* could be considered a legitimate pregnancy craving… *because Ash certainly felt like mine.*

I met his gaze with a sad smile. "I talked to my mom today," I told him.

After we came home from the hospital, telling my parents about the baby was one more preparation I'd needed to address.

My parents who would be disappointed in me, who might not forgive me…

My parents who I would forgive if their judgment was greater than their love and compassion.

He swore under his breath and came to sit by me. "Are you okay? Why didn't you wait for me? Did she—"

"Ash." I placed a hand on his chest, biting back a smile as my man's increasingly protective switch flipped and he was ready to fight the world to defend my honor.

"Sorry," he grumbled, though we both knew he wouldn't stop his responses like this—*and I didn't want him to.* "How did it go?"

"Probably as you would expect, at first," I confessed.

"*Did you learn nothing all this time? Did the way you were raised make no difference before you decided to act like a wh—*" My mother broke off with a horrified gasp. "*The Bible says—*"

"*To forgive and not judge,*" *I finished for her,* having to wonder if she really knew what the Bible said at all. "Maybe when you finally learn that, along with what love means, you'll want a place in your daughter's and granddaughter's lives."

"Oh, Pixie," he rasped. "I'm so sorry."

"It's a hard thing for her to process." I reached up and cupped his face.

"Seems pretty damn easy to me," he growled, protectively.

"We all have our own demons." I met his eyes. "Judging hers won't change anything."

He grabbed my wrist and pulled my palm up to his mouth, kissing the center. "You're too good, Tay."

I shivered.

"I'm not," I promised him. "I just try to do better." Pausing, I added, "It's all we can do."

People were complicated. They didn't always fit inside even the best-intentioned rules. But all we could do was *better*.

"I love you."

I closed my computer so I could re-arrange my cumbersome self to lean forward and kiss him.

"She knows I'm happy and loved, and that's what's important," I told him. "I never needed her forgiveness, only to tell her the truth."

He kissed me again before standing and heading to the fridge.

"Did everything go okay in town?" I asked, wanting to move on from things—*from people*—I couldn't change. "You were gone for a while."

"Ran into Dex." His shoulders sagged. "Talked about Roasters."

It had only been a week since the funeral and there were some moments when it seemed like life was moving normally, and then there were others where the loss of Larry, the uncertainty of Roasters' future, and the weight of finishing the restaurant weighed on both of us to where we just held each other and cried.

"What did he say?" I sat up against the cushions on the couch.

"It belongs to Laurel and Blackman is trying to convince her to sell."

My heart sank. "Oh no. Is she going to?"

He shook his head solemnly. "Not sure. Hope Eli can convince her not to."

"That must be hard though, coming back to inherit something this way," I murmured, imagining how heavy that decision must be for the small redhead that seemed to stand alone at the funeral. Like Joan of Arc, she looked like she was facing a battle that no one but her could understand—*and that no one but her could win.* "Maybe I could try talking to her if she's going to be in town for a little."

Ash walked over to me and bent down for a kiss that I was more than willing to give.

"I don't know how such a big heart fits into such a small body," he murmured as love swelled in my lungs. "But Roasters isn't for you or us to worry about right now."

My chest deflated with a heavy sigh. He was right. As much as I wanted to help, we both had so much on our plate right now that all I could do was pray for her… for the whole town… that everything would work out the way it needed to.

"So, how far ahead did you get?"

"Not very far," I admitted. "I was distracted looking up names."

"So, I guess Ragnar is still off the table?" he teased with a wink, his jeans molding to his butt as he walked over to the fridge making it hard for me to deny him much.

Except Ragnar. I was still aware enough to deny him that.

"Yes. Definitely, yes." I laughed and it made me have to pee.

"Well, I guess we'll have to survive one more night with our baby and our business lacking a name," he said with a playful sigh as I waddled to the bathroom.

"I know you picked your name," I yelled, leaving the bathroom door open. "For the restaurant."

There was a pause before he replied. "How do you know?"

I waited until I was back out into the kitchen before I replied, "Because you seem calmer."

"Oh?" He looked over his shoulder at me, arching an eyebrow as I rubbed my stomach.

"I know Larry always said that giving a name to the problem allows you to finally face it. Not that the restaurant is a problem, but I think it having a name finally makes it real, finally means your dream is coming true. And *that* is why you seem calmer."

His eyes roamed my body like he was stripping me down like my words had done to him. My heart rate instantly picked up the pace and my lower back ache was forgotten for a different lower ache.

"I might have picked my name," he said huskily.

"Are you going to tell me?"

"Can't. It's not time yet," he said as he sautéed the chicken for dinner, enjoying being secretive—and I let him because I knew how much the restaurant meant. "But soon I'll give you my name."

My heart jumped. I knew he was talking about the business—*of course he was*. But I couldn't help but imagine that he was talking about something else.

I was afraid of this moment. From the second that I'd stepped off the plane, I was afraid of the thought of Ash proposing because he felt obligated to the baby. I didn't want to be an obligation and I dreaded it so much that I kept the truth about our baby from him. But now, I wasn't afraid anymore. If it happened… whenever it happened… I knew loyalty would be a shadow compared to the bright light of love that was the reason behind it.

"Cold?"

I looked up to see him in front of me, realizing that my arms were crossed over me like I'd gotten a chill.

"Maybe," I stuttered, thinking my goosebumps were more from the idea of him proposing than any change in temperature, but marriage was the last thing I wanted to bring up right now. I had everything I wanted—a ring wouldn't change that.

And then his lips crushed mine, stealing the breath and any last wonderings from my mind. He didn't need to give me his name for my body to know that with every lick of his tongue and every bite from his teeth, with every touch on my body, he made me his.

"What about dinner?" I asked breathlessly, as he picked me up and carried me into the bedroom.

"It'll keep warm," he growled. "While I keep you warm."

I moaned as my back hit the bed.

I really liked when he kept me warm.

Chapter Thirty-Three

ASH

Two weeks later…

"Hey." My head tipped back as Taylor came up behind me, putting one hand on my shoulder as concern clouded her perfect features. "You okay?"

I nodded tightly, looking back out at the water.

Time had felt like a car revving at a stoplight but not in gear ever since the funeral—no matter how much fuel I dumped into it, I didn't feel like I was moving forward even though I was. Somehow, the restaurant came together like the final few pieces of a puzzle—no problems, no delays. I liked to think it was Larry's lookin' out.

"Are you sure?" She reached for me. "We don't have to do this…"

"I'm good, Tay," I murmured, pulling her under my arm and dropping a kiss on her forehead. "And we do. We definitely do."

I might have felt like everything was at a standstill, but I knew today would change that.

It was opening day. The moment I'd been waiting for, for months—a moment that I'd imagined completely differently than the one that was about to transpire. Months ago, Taylor wasn't in the image. Or our baby girl. Or my parents. Or Blake and Zach. There were so many people who loved me who were here today, on top of the Carmel crew, that I never imagined; I savored my chest feeling like it was about to explode with love.

Larry was the only one missing.

But the more I was around my friends, my family, the people who loved him like I did, the more I realized that he wasn't really missing at all.

It was an hour before opening. I'd asked my brand-new staff, along with the Roaster's crew, Eli, the Covingtons, my fellow AA members, Addy, Zeke, and the women from Blooms, Josie, Mick and Miles, and then my family to come early for a small grand opening celebration before we opened for our very first lunch.

There were two reasons, the first being that I needed to finally tell these people just where the hell they were working.

Yeah, I'd waited until opening day to reveal the damn name.

Surprisingly, a restaurant with no name only added to the hype surrounding the opening. Everyone was desperate to find out what I decided on.

Truth was, I decided two weeks ago, the day of the funeral when I said goodbye to the man who changed my life.

I had the signs and menus and everything printed up and rushed, but no one was allowed to see because even though I knew what it had to be, I wasn't ready to say it out loud quite yet.

"Alright, let's do this," I said, snagging her hand in mine as we walked back up toward the restaurant and the small crowd of people gathered out front, waiting for me to come make a speech and cut the damn ribbon that my girl had insisted on.

My gaze strayed to her serene expression. She was incredible. I refused to let her do *any* of the work to help us set up, but that didn't stop her from being out here every day with me and the guys, directing and organizing everything when my brain was too foggy to think straight. I'd never be able to tell her just how much it meant—how much she meant—to me. But later… later, I'd sure as shit try to show her.

When we made it to the front doors, Tay squeezed my hand before stepping off to the side to stand by my sister and Eve. Blake immediately reached for her hand and rubbed her stomach before shooting me a smile. I think for the first time in all my life, I finally let her be happy for me because I was finally happy for myself.

"Thank you, everyone, for coming out today to help me celebrate what is such a huge day for me," I began as their murmuring quieted. "I won't go into the details, but I think it's enough to say that the past six months have changed my life in so many ways, so many ways that I still wake up wondering if it's all been a dream.

"For a long time, I ignored my dreams, I ignored myself, and I lost my way. And then I wound up here, in this crazy small-town and I found myself. I pulled myself back and pushed myself up—and I have so many of you to thank for that. So this… my restaurant… it's my monument to 'never too late.' It's my dedication to redemption. And I hope it's a reminder to everyone in this community, that you, your dreams, they're worth another chance, they're worth fighting for."

My eyes scanned the crowd, trying to ignore the hands that swiped across cheeks, the dabs of tissues, and the slight nods of solidarity so that I could move forward.

"But I wouldn't be standing here today if it wasn't for one man." I let out a small laugh as I tried to hold my shit together. "I think a lot of us wouldn't be standing here, or standing tall, today if it wasn't for one man who… isn't here any longer." I took an unsteady breath. "*Shit…*"

I thought I could do this. I really fucking thought I could.

And then I felt a small hand intertwine with mine and

looked down to see Taylor by my side, her watery eyes and soft smile encouraging me. I squeezed her fingers and took her strength to continue.

"Larry was the voice in the desert—calling me out, calling me to be better—in what felt like the dead of night. He fought my battles with me… for me. He lifted me up from the ashes, because that's all I was when I came here—ashes, not Ash." I felt the first tear make its way down my cheek. "And every time I tried to turn him away, he was louder than my guilt—louder than my shame." I broke off and wiped the back of my hand over my face.

"He never gave up on me," I choked out. "He *never* gave up on me."

Soft cries and murmurs of agreement filtered through the group.

He never gave up on any of us. On anyone who needed it.

Taylor's soft fingers rubbed mine encouragingly and I let out a deep breath, knowing I was losing it.

"It's not the final step you take that's the most important, it's the first. It's the first step that defines us." I didn't bother to wipe the tears now. "And Larry's first step was to always take care of everyone else. So, today… the first step of this business is to keep a piece of that legacy alive."

I bent down and pressed a kiss to Taylor's head, needing to touch her, smell her, breathe her in and know she was still here and that everything was going to be okay.

"He'd kill me if he knew I was taking up time to talk about him like this right now. He'd also kill me for waiting so long to name the damn place," I went on and drew a few watery chuckles from the crowd.

There was so much more I wanted to say, so much more I thought he deserved, but I couldn't.

"I just need to say that this space will always be safe. It will always have a friendly face, an ear to listen, and a spaghetti and meatball dinner every Sunday. This place will always be the most important thing I ever learned from Larry Ocean: made to be here for each other."

I turned, wiping the tears I couldn't stop from falling, tugging Taylor's shaking shoulders against me, and pulled the rope attached to the fabric covering the sign, sending it tumbling to the ground next to me.

"Welcome to Larry's Lookout."

For how much of a fucking mess I turned most of my staff into when I opened the place up earlier, we somehow managed to pull ourselves together and serve far more people than I'd expected.

It was a miracle.

Actually, *she* was my miracle.

I watched Taylor as she sat at the hostess stand and greeted customers when they came in, chatted while they wait, and said goodbye like they were leaving a family dinner instead of a restaurant.

I didn't give a shit about what the papers or the reviews said tomorrow. This was every fucking thing I could have wanted. And with her here, it was more than everything.

"Are you sure you want us here?" I turned as Blake came up beside me.

I pulled her in for a hug.

"Yeah. She'll want you here." I sent her a knowing smile. The last few tables were just finishing up and then there was one more speech that I had to give tonight. One more heartfelt confession. And one more name that I was going to ask to change.

"I'm so happy for you, Ash," she whispered softly. "So happy."

"Thanks, Blay," I said hoarsely as she pulled back and wiped her eyes.

"This place… it's incredible. You did an incredible job."

"You know Taylor helped pick out most of the decor, right?" I teased, knowing that she meant more than just how we'd decorated the place.

She laughed. "Yeah, I know. I was just trying to give you some of the credit."

"Congrats, man." Zach clapped me on the back, joining the two of us at the door to the kitchen. "Food was delicious. But I didn't expect anything less."

"Thanks," I smirked. "And thanks for coming out, both of you. It means a lot."

"In the end, love wins," my sister said, giving Zach the same smile that Taylor gives to me.

The only thing I'd picked out was the sign above the door. And I hadn't really picked it out, I'd asked Mick to make it for me just like the one he'd made for Roasters.

Carved and stained wood above the doorframe read:

Start where you are. Use what you have. Do what you can.

Above the words, a small clear-resin circle held my sobriety chip. The first one. The first one Larry gave me. Because as important as it is to know where you're going, you can't forget where you came from—*you can't forget the first step in a new direction.*

"Go get your girl," Zach said, nodding to where Taylor had just said goodbye to the last family as they left.

I palmed the box that I'd snuck into my back pocket a few minutes ago from where I'd stashed it in the kitchen. Asking Miles to make the sign had also been my excuse to go into town and visit the jeweler. I picked both things up yesterday morning after making sure my girl was thoroughly exhausted.

"Come with me," I whispered into her ear.

The love that shone in her eyes when she looked at me was clearer and purer than the goddamn diamond I was about to give her.

"Where are we going?" she asked with a smile as I led her through the chairs and out onto the deck, twinkling with the lights that she'd suggested.

I pulled her right to the edge of the wood before I turned and kissed her, threading my fingers into her hair. She sagged into me and I gave myself a few seconds to treat myself to the delicious warmth of her mouth. With the rush all day, I hadn't been able to hold her hand since we opened, let alone kiss her and thank her.

"Thank you," I murmured against her soft lips. "You were incredible today. So fucking incredible. I just—fuck."

I kissed her again because I was so damn drained I couldn't even thank her properly.

"Are you okay?" She pulled back and asked breathlessly, her lips slightly swollen and her cheeks tinted pink.

"I'm more than okay, gorgeous," I answered, dropping my forehead to hers.

"You sure? Everything was amazing today, Ash. Really..." she gushed, and I just soaked up her love. "Everyone loved it— the place, the food, everything... Larry would be so proud."

My eyes squeezed shut.

She always knew just what to fucking say to calm my heart.

"You know," I started with a laugh. "He gave me hell about you the night we were at his house. He demanded to know what you were to me. Just like this place. Always with the name."

She stared up at me. "What did you say?"

"I told him you were my redemption. My everything," I rasped, gliding my hands down her arms to grasp her hands as I stepped back.

Of all the lives we could've led, all the choices we could've made, and all the people that surrounded us, she'd found me in what I'd thought was her moment of weakness, when it turned out to be mine.

"Taylor, it took me forever to figure out what the name for this place needed to be…. But you, it only took me a second to realize that the only name I ever wanted to give you was mine," I swore to her.

"Ash…" Her breath caught as her eyes widened, wonder and love glittering like stars in her eyes.

My lips worked their way into a nervous, crooked smile as I dropped down on one knee, reaching in my pocket for the ring box.

"I'm not perfect, sweetheart. You know I'm not. But I love you—and I'm gonna love you—with everything I got, forever. So, Taylor Hastings, will you take my name?" I popped open the box, revealing the simple round-cut diamond that sat in the center, about the same time as she covered her mouth with her hands. "Will you marry me?"

It was a clear night, so the stars littered the sky like discarded diamonds and the moon shone like a spotlight in the dark. Both shimmered off the giant moving mirror that ebbed below the cliff.

It was breathtaking.

It didn't hold a candle to her though—the stars in her eyes or the glow on her face, especially when her head began to frantically shake yes.

"Y-yes," she stammered, letting me take one of her hands so I could slide the ring up her finger, trying my best to hold myself together. "Yes, a million times, yes."

She didn't even look at the ring before she was pulling my face up to hers, her lips tasting salty and sweet against mine as I wrapped her in my arms.

Muted cheers and shouts erupted from inside the

restaurant where my family and our friends had been watching from the windows.

I chuckled when she pulled back and couldn't decide whether she wanted to smile and laugh or smile and cry.

"I love you so much, Taylor."

"I love you, too."

This time, when I kissed her, I felt the soft press of her stomach against mine as our baby girl kicked her approval between us.

EPILOGUE

ASH

Three months later...

"She's perfect," I murmured, lying in the hospital bed next to Tay. We were both staring at the softly breathing baby girl nestled in her arms.

Taylor had been amazing—a warrior really, seeing what she'd gone through to bring our daughter into the world; I was so damn enraptured by the both of them.

And so fucking in love.

"Baby Grace," she cooed softly before angling toward me for a kiss.

Grace Laurelin Tyler.

We'd toyed with a lot of names over the last few weeks—*though none of them Ragnar, unfortunately.* Many variations with ties to Larry or Lawrence.

But one Sunday night, after we'd finished cleaning up from the Lookout's sold-out spaghetti and meatball dinner, Taylor had looked at me and said Grace.

And I couldn't think of a more fitting name for our daughter and the gift she'd given us.

"You ready to go home?"

"More than ready," she confessed with a laugh. "And definitely excited for more of your home-cooked meals."

I chuckled, kissing her head as I slid from the bed.

I'd been smuggling in some of my food for the last two days; hospital food was everything it was cracked up to be.

"Alright, let's get my girls out of here. I think there are some people waiting to see you both."

When we got back to the house, a much different structure after Mick and Miles had completed the additions, we walked into a room full of people—*a room full of love.*

Almost immediately, I lost track of my fiancée and daughter in the swarm of women who rushed to greet her. Eve, Josie, Laurel, and Jules. The women from Blooms. Meanwhile, Eli clapped me on the back with a grin, his eyes on our women as they embraced.

"Congrats, man," he said.

I thanked my friend, no longer seeing any trace of the hollowness in his eyes or the heaviness of his heart.

"You'll be next," I tacked on with a nudge.

"I hope so." He laughed and then reached out to slap Miles on the back. "But I have a feeling this guy might be first."

Miles glared at him. "Hell no."

Even though it was mostly said in jest, there was a thread of steel-like sincerity laced in the words. I'd only gotten pieces of the story that brought the Madison brothers up here from Texas, and I'd seen first-hand how Miles avoided anything that wasn't temporary. But, when I looked at Taylor, I knew that anything was possible and that there were some things stronger than hurt or fear.

It was a solid hour before everyone finally filtered out of the house and Tay and I were alone with our newest addition once more.

"Can we go for a walk?" she turned to me and asked.

Behind her, I could see the sun setting through the windows and the warm rainbow it cast on the horizon.

"Anything for you."

We made our way to the back deck of the Lookout, Grace in one arm and Tay underneath my other, and we stood on the edge of the world.

With my whole world in my arms.

"Do you ever think how incredible things have worked out?" she murmured against my chest.

"I do." I nodded. "And I thank God for it every day."

Her head tilted up to mine.

"Sometimes, I just can't help but think of what would've happened if things hadn't… gone the way they did," she mused.

"I don't think there was any other way, Pixie," I told her softly, losing myself in the warm green of her eyes. "It was always you for me."

She smiled as I touched my lips to hers.

There was no other way for our story to happen.

Because in the end,

Love Wins.

Don't go yet…

Check out the author's note for some personal inspiration for this story, an exclusive scene, and to see what's coming next for the residents of Carmel Cove!

AUTHOR'S NOTE

Dear Reader,
    Welcome to Carmel Cove.
    Open-heartedness. Charity. Perseverance. The foundations of this Pacific-coast town.
    I hope you've enjoyed Ash and Taylor's story. I wanted to take a moment to talk about how special this book is to me and where it's brought us.
    I hadn't planned on writing Ash's story, but when it came to me, it came in full force. And I knew from the very start it had to take place somewhere else—a haven. A place where the broken come to heal amongst family and friends (and friends who become family.) A place to find strength and (*of course*) find love.
    Carmel Cove became that place—not just for the characters but for me.
    Carmel Cove is inspired by a variety of real-life places. Most of its location comes from the town, Carmel-by-the-Sea, along Big Sur in California. But the feel and the people there were inspired by my Italian-immigrant hometown, Roseto, in Northeast Pennsylvania.
    However, this story—and my story—wouldn't be what it is without one man: Larry Ocean.
    Larry is my grandfather.
    Though he never owned a coffee shop, from his love of chocolate to his gruff, no-nonsense personality, to his military service and his (and my grandmother's) magical spaghetti and meatballs, and to the way he looked out for everyone he came in contact with… his character is anything but fictional.
    My grandfather, Larry, committed suicide in 2011.

I was in dental school, coming home from the grocery store with some friends, I walked inside my house and my husband (then-boyfriend) handed me his phone; it was my dad on the line.

My grandfather had shot himself in the garage of his own home.

He'd been given a prescription for anti-depressants however, he'd stopped taking them.

And all it took was one bad day… one weak moment… and he was gone.

There was no warning. There was no reason. All things you may have thought while reading this story—*there was no reason for him to die. There was no indication.*

You're right. There wasn't.

Because in real life, there was no author to leave me hints. There was no one behind the scenes to hold my hand and prepare my heart for the blow it took that day. Real life doesn't leave kind clues before breaking your world.

The most real loss comes with no preparation. It rips your heart from your chest and screams in your face '*Do you still want this? Do you still want this beating, bleeding thing? Because this is the cost. This is the price of love.*'

And you want to say no because it hurts so much. But you can't… because you can't live without it.

And when it's all said and done, you're left with so much love for someone you can't give it to—so much love that has nowhere to go.

So that is how I wrote it—why I wrote it—because it's how I lived it. My love for him is still searching for places to go, and it found somewhere in this story.

My grandfather was from a different generation. Tough to the very last nail. Stubborn. Able to take on the world… until he couldn't.

Mental illness… Suicide… Depression… All big topics anymore and yet so many of those afflicted suffer in silence, determined to be strong for everyone around them. Not wanting to burden those around them—*like Larry*.

And, very simply, I wrote him… I wrote this book… because I missed him.

Because I still miss him.

Because he was never a burden to anyone.

And because there is still love to be found in even the greatest of losses.

So, I brought his memory to this story for myself. For these characters. And for you. Because at some point or another, we've all lost someone who looked out for us—who took us in at the very worst of our mistakes, extended a hand to help us up instead of beating us down, and let us lean on them until we found the strength to stand on our own once more.

And sometimes, it's good to remember good people.

So, here's to good people. #herestolarry

And I'm not ready to stop writing about them yet…

Redemption is the precursor—the prologue, if you will, to my Carmel Cove series. Similar to Redemption, the interconnected standalones in this series will be high on emotion and heavy on the heartstrings—the epitome of small-town romance complete with a dash of suspense.

I hope you've enjoyed your first trip to this healing and heartwarming Pacific hometown, and that you'll return for Laurel and Eli's hard-won happily-ever-after in BEHOLDEN, arriving May 2020.

You can pre-order your copy
books2read.com/ReadBeholden.

To read the prologue
www.drrebeccasharp.com/beholden-prologue

And remember, as Larry would say…
Start where you are.
Use what you have.
Do what you can.

With love,
Rebecca

If you are suffering from depression or thoughts of suicide, please know you are not alone. Please know there is someone waiting to help you, and that there are people in this world who need you.

There is always someone available to talk at the National Suicide Prevention Lifeline: **1-800-273-TALK (8255).**

And my door is always open.

You can email me at author@drrebeccasharp.com.

ACKNOWLEDGMENTS

To my husband—You are forever and always my lobster. I love you.

To my family and friends—I'm so blessed to have all of you in my life.

To BJ—Thank you for always being the best sounding board!

To Jen—Thank you for reading all the various endings I wrote for this book until I could finally sleep at night knowing I got it right. You are such a positive force and a cheerleader that I can't help but believe in myself because you do!

To Najla—Thank you for always thinking outside the box. I was unsure where to go with this cover and you created something so jaw-dropping, I couldn't imagine Ash's book looking any other way.

To Ellie—Thank you for all your hard work as always!

To Stacey—Thank you for creating magic between the covers. You're a wizard!

To all the bloggers who work enthusiastically to help me spread the word about each and every one of my stories. You are amazing. None of this would be possible, be imagined, or be happening without you. None of it…

To my Sharpies—Thank you for being such a supportive place. This book was a big step for me, and I wouldn't have been able to take it without you.

And, as always, to all my readers:
Thank you for asking for Ash's story. I didn't know if I had it in me. But you did. And now, I know I needed to write this for so many reasons. Thank you.

OTHER WORKS BY DR. REBECCA SHARP

Standalones
Reputation
Redemption

The Odyssey Duet
The Fall of Troy
The Judgment of Paris

Carmel Cove Series
Beholden (Spring 2020)

Winter Games Series
Up in the Air
On the Edge
Enjoy the Ride
In Too Deep
Over the Top

The Gentlemen's Guild Series
The Artist's Touch
The Sculptor's Seduction
The Painter's Passion

The Passion & Perseverance Trilogy
(A Pride and Prejudice Retelling)
First Impressions
Second Chances
Third Time is the Charm

Want to #staysharp with everything that's coming?
Join my newsletter!
bit.ly/StaySharpSignUp

About the Author

Hey there!

So, you want to know a little bit about me and my writing? Awesome! Even though I write *a lot*... writing about myself always proves to be difficult. I wonder if my 'About Me' could just consist of memes... that would be fantastic!

Alright, let's give this a go. First and foremost, I should warn you that I have a serious obsession with coffee. If you've already found my Instagram, you know this. Other things I love? Wine. Friends (the real ones and the TV show), laughing so hard I cry, painting, snowboarding, cooking, traveling, reading, and, of course, writing. OH, and Disney movies.

Rebecca Sharp is a pen name. One of these days maybe I'll include my real name at the end of a book or something. Anyway, I'm also a dentist living in PA with my amazing husband who we affectionately refer to as Mr. GQ.

Okay, okay. That's enough about me. Let's move onto my books. I (currently) write contemporary and new adult romances. My first book was published in the Fall of 2016 and I haven't slowed down since. I love strong heroines and bad boys that turn out to be good men. There will always be a happy ending because I just can't stomach anything else. Let's see... Happily Ever Afters? Check. Hot alphas? Check. Feisty heroines? Check.

Oh! And I love hearing from readers! I really, really do. I've been so blessed to make so many friendships through this whole Indie author adventure and I would love to meet you and chat with you! How to go about that? Well, you have a ton of options!

If you just want to be emailed with cover reveals, new releases, etc. sign up for my mailing list on my website here. I also host a giveaway in there every month that is exclusive to subscribers, so be sure to check it out: www.drrebeccasharp.com

If you want to see hilarious coffee memes, wine memes, life memes, interspersed with book teasers and info, Follow me on Instagram here: www.instagram.com/drrebeccasharp

If you want all of that good stuff, but on Facebook, as well as the ability to message me privately, go ahead and follow my Facebook page here: www.facebook.com/drrebeccasharp

If you love my work and want the inside scoop on my books, upcoming releases, secret projects, and exclusive giveaways, join my Sexy Little Sharpies reader group here: www.facebook.com/groups/1539118689482683

And as always, you can follow me on Goodreads (www.goodreads.com/drrebeccasharp) and Amazon (http://amzn.to/2n8ffbK) to stay updated that way with new releases and info.

I'm pretty sure at any of those places you have the option to message me in some way or another so feel free to do it! You can also just email me directly at author@drrebeccasharp.com!

Happy reading, loves!
xx
Rebecca

Made in the USA
Middletown, DE
17 February 2020